IN DUE TIME, DISASTER WILL ARRIVE,
AND DESTINY WILL OVERTAKE THEM.

UNLUCKY

A WESTERN EPIC

BY

BEN WOLF

Published by

SPL⚡CKETY
PUBLISHING GROUP

WWW.SPLICKETY.COM

Unlucky
A Western Epic

Published by
Splickety Publishing Group, Inc.
www.splickety.com

Print ISBN: 978-1-942462-41-5
Ebook ISBN: 978-1-942462-42-2
Copyright © 2020 by Ben Wolf, Inc. All rights reserved.
www.benwolf.com

Cover design by Olivia Pro Design

Available in print and ebook format on amazon.com.
Contact Ben Wolf directly at ben@benwolf.com for signed copies and to schedule author
appearances and speaking events.

Printed in the United States of America.

For Grandpa Gary and Judy,
who gave me a most excellent set of
Time Life Encyclopedias about the Old West.

Those volumes, many of which I read cover-to-cover,
provided the historical setting for this book
and sparked this project to life in my imagination.

CONTENTS

Every society reaches a point of desperation. In that moment, when everything is at stake, one of two things happens: either they fail and are overcome...

...or a warrior arises and saves them.

This warrior is a phenomenon, a master of extraordinary proportions, a god among men. Sometimes the people love him, and sometimes they hate him.

But no matter what they think, he rises to the occasion and saves the day despite impossible odds and every conceivable disadvantage.

Though his body may die and his soul may drift into the great beyond, his name lives on forever... in legend.

Unlucky is one such legend.

"I will take revenge; I will pay them back.
In due time their feet will slip.
Their day of disaster will arrive,
and their destiny will overtake them."
Deuteronomy 32:35, NLT

♠ ♥ CHAPTER 1 ♦ ♣

rizona Territory, 1848
A   Blood oozed from a bullet hole in Tommy Roebuck's chest and saturated the Arizona dust. His single-action revolver, a relic from the War of 1812, rested in his limp right hand, its muzzle digging into the dirt.

All six cartridges remained in its cylinder.

Dalton Phillips moseyed down Main Street and holstered his silver-plated Colt, still hot from the solitary round he'd fired. Its twin sister rested in the holster on Dalton's left side.

He stopped at Tommy's husk. The fool shouldn't have challenged him.

Dalton scanned the town. People gawked at him from storefronts and porches. Ladies gasped and yanked their children closer. Shop-keepers and proprietors pretended to mind their own business but still chanced occasional glances at him. Grizzled trailblazers—men born to face the worst of nature's fury—watched him with subtle terror in their eyes.

Dalton took it all in with a grin. He'd inspired deep, terrible fear with only a single shot.

Same as the last three times.

He bent down and pulled a thick wad of banknotes from the pockets of Tommy's trousers and a fist-sized leather satchel stuffed with gold nuggets from Tommy's belt.

A steel flask poked out the bottom of his coat. Dalton grabbed it, too, and the last few gulps of whiskey burned his throat.

"Hands up, Dalton," said a rough voice behind him.

Dalton tossed the flask onto a patch of dirt caked with Tommy's blood. He smirked. "Well, Marshal. Good afternoon."

He turned and faced the stern, middle-aged man pointing a lazy revolver at him. His black pinstriped trousers matched his vest, and he wore a brass star on his chest.

Marshal John Garmer.

"Here to take me in?" Dalton asked. "Again?"

"You know the law, kid." Marshal Garmer's pistol quivered.

"And *you* know it was self-defense."

"Don't matter. Gotta take you in anyway, least 'til the judge can see you." Marshal Garmer's drawl ran like smooth honey over warm cornbread, a sharp contrast to Dalton's polished New England diction.

A drop of sweat rolled down the side of Marshal Garmer's face, and Dalton smirked again. If Dalton reached for his gun, there'd be two bodies laying in the street, neither of them his. The idea tickled him, but Marshal Garmer didn't deserve to die.

Marshal Garmer swallowed hard and exhaled a long breath, his gun still fixed on Dalton.

Old lawman sure has guts. Dalton shrugged and raised his hands.

With shaky steps, Marshal Garmer closed in. He collected Dalton's guns with his left hand and pressed the barrel of his own revolver in between Dalton's shoulder blades. "Move."

Dalton knew the way by now. Tommy marked his fourth duel since he'd arrived in Spider's Rock two months ago. An average of one every other week—more action than he'd expected. His uncle's letters hadn't exaggerated after all.

At that rate, maybe Marshal Garmer should just keep a cell open for him.

Reverend William McCarroll stormed into Marshal Garmer's office. His brow scrunched as far down as Dalton had ever seen it, but somehow his expression complemented his dark, pastoral garb.

"Afternoon, Marshal," Reverend McCarroll said.

"Don't got time for this right now, Reverend." Marshal Garmer waved his hand and reclined behind his cluttered desk, reading all two pages of *The Spider's Web*, the town's local newspaper. He tapped it with his finger, not even bothering to look up. "Reports of a group of outlaws headin' our way from Mexico. I'm in the midst of preparin' our response in case they show up in town."

Reverend McCarroll looked him up and down. "I can confidently say I've never felt safer."

"Your tax dollars at work, Reverend." Marshal Garmer sucked at his teeth. "Well, not yours specifically, bein' a minister, and all that."

Dalton scoffed, but neither of them paid him any mind.

"I need you to release that boy into my custody."

With a sigh, Marshal Garmer finally met Reverend McCarroll's gaze. "Didn't do much good the last three times I done it."

"I'm his only kin for 2,000 miles."

"I know you're his uncle, but this is the fourth man he's killed—" Marshal Garmer sat upright and set the newspaper down. "—over a *card game*."

"John, I'm asking you as a friend."

Dalton had to admire his uncle's persistence—and his influence. Reverend McCarroll could spur more souls to action than anyone else in Spider's Rock, save for maybe one.

"That's what you said the last three times." Marshal Garmer added, "Bill."

Dalton smirked.

Reverend McCarroll's austere expression lingered. Maybe this time Marshal Garmer would finally stand his ground.

But he didn't.

"Alright, Reverend." He sighed. "But I'm keepin' track of these 'favors,' you hear?"

"'The wicked borroweth, and payeth not again: but the righteous sheweth mercy, and giveth.'" Reverend McCarroll gave the marshal a nod.

"I'm countin' on it," Marshal Garmer said. "An' he better show up for the judge this time, too."

"I'll see to it personally, Marshal."

Marshal Garmer stood and fumbled with his keys. He caught sight of the smug expression on Dalton's face. "Keep smilin', Dalton. One day, your uncle might not be around to save your neck. We'll see if you smile then."

"The day he's not around, I'll *definitely* have something to smile about," Dalton replied.

Marshal Garmer just shook his head and unlocked the cell.

"Thank you, Marshal," Reverend McCarroll said, eyeing Dalton, who walked to his uncle's side and stood there. A silent moment passed, then his uncle smacked the back of Dalton's head.

"Uh—thank you," Dalton added. His uncle turned to leave, but Dalton stopped. "Oh, Marshal?"

"Hm?"

"My Colts, please."

Marshal Garmer met Reverend McCarroll's gaze again. With a long sigh, Marshal Garmer unlocked one of his desk drawers and pulled out Dalton's black leather belt, holsters, bullets, and the Colt sisters. He handed the bundle to Dalton, who strapped it all on.

"Thank you, Marshal." Dalton gave him a big grin. At the door, he added, "You can keep Tommy's money. I can always get more."

The walk from Marshal Garmer's office to the parsonage wasn't far, but it would last long enough for his uncle to get a lecture in. Around them, townspeople milled about, back to their usual routines, as if Tommy Roebuck had never even existed.

"Awful nice of the marshal to give me my guns back, don't you agree?" Dalton tried to get the jump on the conversation. "Be a shame if I had to walk around unarmed in a town as high-strung as—"

Reverend McCarroll turned in the middle of the street and grabbed

Dalton by his shirt with both hands. Dalton got a good look at his bushy eyebrows, stern blue eyes, and stubbly chin.

"Now you listen here," Reverend McCarroll said, his voice fierce and focused. "You *murdered* a man today, the fourth in two months. Your behavior is unacceptable."

Dalton scoffed. "It was a duel. He started it. I can't believe I have to explain this to you. Now let me go."

Reverend McCarroll's grip endured. "You're becoming the town pariah, the type of person decent people despise."

"Maybe I'm not trying to attract 'decent' people." Even as he said it, Dalton noticed some of the townspeople around them staring. He jerked free of his uncle's grasp and brushed out his shirt.

"You're a reflection of *me*." Reverend McCarroll pointed an accusatory finger at him. "These escapades tarnish *my* reputation."

"I don't care about your reputation."

"Oh, I'm well aware of that. You're too selfish to care about anyone but yourself. But if you had *any* common sense, you'd realize that you're turning the town against you."

Dalton rolled his eyes and continued walking toward the church. He nodded and smiled at a pretty, young brunette in a purple dress who couldn't seem to take her eyes off of him.

"Your actions *always* have consequences." Reverend McCarroll's voice chased Dalton's dry footsteps. "Everything you do comes back on you one way or another. Listen—you've got more education and smarts than ninety-five percent of the people in this town, yet you act like you're one of the dumbest."

Dalton stopped, turned back, and glared at him.

"Go ahead, get mad at me, but you know I'm right. You're behaving like a common brigand. An ingrate." Reverend McCarroll approached him. "If you don't stop this rampage, you're gonna get killed."

"No." Dalton scoffed again. "I won't get clipped. I'm too fast for any—"

SLAP.

Dalton recoiled from his uncle's firm backhand, stunned. His left cheek stung.

Had his uncle really just slapped him, had he? Dalton glanced at the brunette in the purple dress. Their eyes met, and she turned away, flustered and embarrassed for him.

Then he saw her look over her shoulder at him.

Reverend McCarroll stood there, stoic, his hands tense and at his sides.

Dalton loved his uncle, but he'd gone too far this time. He couldn't let this stand. He reached for his guns.

But Reverend McCarroll grabbed Dalton's wrists faster than a rattlesnake strike and pinned Dalton's hands to his sides. No reaching the Colt sisters now.

Dalton clenched his teeth. The brunette was still watching, and this whole fiasco had just gone from bad to worse. He growled, "Let go of me."

Reverend McCarroll's grip only tightened. "Go ahead and shoot me, if you can. I know where I'm going when I die. But if you think you can gun down an old, unarmed preacher in the street and dodge the noose, you've got another thing coming."

After a protracted exchange of cold stares, Reverend McCarroll finally let Dalton loose. He stood firm, his iron stare stalwart as ever.

Dalton wanted to turn him to stone with his eyes. Instead, his fingers brushed against the engraved ivory grips on his Colts.

A small part of Dalton wanted to admit that his uncle might be right, but his pride wouldn't allow it. After all, he was just an old, worn-out preacher. He didn't understand. He *couldn't* understand.

The brunette was gone. Where she'd gone, Dalton didn't know. Didn't matter now.

Dalton adjusted his black hat and closed what little distance remained between Reverend McCarroll and him.

Compared to most other men, Dalton was tall, but his uncle matched him eye-to-eye. Reverend McCarroll had broader shoulders, the result of some hard labor in a past life that Dalton knew almost nothing about. His cold blue eyes raged, stark against his worn, tanned face.

Out of everyone he'd ever met, Dalton only feared his uncle.

But perhaps "feared" wasn't the right word—"respected" or "revered" fit better. Reverend McCarroll exuded an unnerving aura that made Dalton uncomfortable.

What's more, his uncle was probably the only person in town unafraid of Dalton. It made sense—he shepherded a town of wolves. With nothing to lose, why should Reverend McCarroll fear one of them more than any other, let alone his own kin?

"How'd you do that?" Dalton couldn't help but ask. "How'd you get so fast?"

Reverend McCarroll eyed him. "I've learned a few things in my time."

Dalton shook his head. "Old buzzard."

"Little twit."

They shared a smile.

"Now get inside, and get cleaned up," Reverend McCarroll motioned toward the church. "You've got to be at the Imperial before sundown. I'll fix you something so you don't starve tonight. I'm sure Marshal Garmer's stale bread and watered-down soup didn't do you any good."

As soon as Dalton walked into the Imperial, Randolph yelled at him.

"You are *late*." Randolph rounded the bar and lumbered over with gorilla steps. His brown eyes burned with hellfire as he shook a thick finger at Dalton's face. "I should throw you out and never let you back in."

Dalton smirked. "Then who's gonna play for you?"

Dalton set his hat on the bar and took a seat on one of the barstools. Around him, royal blue wallpaper and dark Bavarian oak cast a regal ambience throughout the space. Frosted-glass light fixtures and a fancy chandelier made from real Austrian crystal illuminated the Imperial's interior.

"That's the *only* reason I keep you around." Randolph's thick Prussian accent battered the consonants in his words like a blacksmith pounding hot steel. "If you are late again, I will cut your pay in half."

"Then I'll have to win twice as many hands."

"You are here to play the piano, *not* cards."

The craps, faro, roulette, blackjack, and poker tables, also solid oak, were upholstered with a unique pale-blue gaming felt. It made sense that

Randolph would choose it over the classic green—the blue better suited the rest of the Imperial's décor.

A few oak tables and chairs filled the area opposite of the Imperial's gaming half, reserved for private games or as seating for those who just wanted to drink.

Dalton folded his arms. "We agreed I can do as I please on my own time."

"And right now, your time is *my* time." Randolph glowered at him and smoothed his bushy brown-and-gray mustache with his fingertips. He pulled out some banknotes and smacked them into Dalton's hand. "Go to the mercantile. I have ordered a crate of whiskey from New York. Bring it back unopened."

"Sure thing, boss." He gave Randolph a wink.

"Unopened."

"Right."

"*Unopened.*"

"Okay, okay." Dalton held his hands up. "I'll be back in a few minutes."

Back behind his solid oak bar, Randolph continued drying shot glasses. His grizzly demeanor faded into a proud smile as he surveyed his kingdom.

The Imperial Saloon was the product of Randolph's life savings, the sum of forty-five years of hard work and persistence. Even Dalton couldn't help but get caught up in the majesty of the place.

Everything except the floors, at least. They were the only part of Randolph's empire that lacked the prestige that oozed from everywhere else. No matter how diligently Randolph worked, the oak floors never lacked for brown Arizona dust.

Dalton recalled him cursing the dry earth outside his front door and vowing to invent a solvent that would prevent dirt from coming into his saloon ever again. To date, Randolph had created no such solvent.

The other half of the Imperial served as an inn with several rentable rooms above the saloon ceiling. A rear entrance led directly into the inn where Madame DeBuire welcomed inbound guests. If they were alone and male, as most of them were, she offered them feminine companionship for the evening from one of several beautiful young ladies in her employ.

Despite his aversion to her trade, Randolph allowed her to operate in the Imperial because she ensured a consistent flow of rent revenue. If it made Randolph money, he didn't mind looking the other way.

Amid his admiration of the Imperial, Dalton caught a pair of steamy green eyes that had fixed on him. They belonged to Vanessa Clark, one of Madame DeBuire's favorite girls.

One of Dalton's favorites, too.

She stood in the doorway that connected the saloon to the inn and studied Dalton like a ravenous wolf eyeing a chunk of raw meat.

Her fair skin, blonde hair, and rare beauty attracted all sorts of men, which meant no shortage of income for her. Vanessa's seafoam-green corset, its sleeves hanging just off her shoulders, accentuated her luscious shape and flowed into a wide, ruffled dress trimmed with silver fabric.

Dalton returned her gaze with a lusty look of his own. What else did she have to offer—and how much would it cost him?

"*Dalton*," a gruff voice barked.

"Huh?" He looked at Randolph.

"Mercantile. Whiskey. *Unopened.*"

"Right. I'm leaving." Dalton's head swiveled back to Vanessa, and he savored one last glance.

She gave him a wink and a sultry smile. She mouthed the word, "Later."

His heart thrumming in his chest, Dalton gave her a nod, then he walked out the door to fulfill Randolph's mandate.

♠ ♥ CHAPTER 2 ♦ ♣

Gilbert Jacobs ran Warren's Mercantile. A wiry brown-haired man in his thirties, he often spoke of moving even farther west to participate in California's booming gold rush, but everyone knew his adamant wife would neither go with him nor trust him to strike out on his own.

When Dalton walked in, Gilbert and an Indian were squabbling over some coyote pelts. The bell above the door jingled and Gilbert turned his head.

"Afternoon, sir." The tension in Gilbert's face relaxed upon Dalton's entry. "Remind me your name again?"

"Dalton Phillips. I'm here for Randolph Schultz's order. For the Imperial." Dalton's gaze wandered to the Indian's hawk eyes. A warrior by the looks of him, probably Apache. Not as tall as Dalton, but lean and strong.

"Yes, yes. I remember now." Gilbert focused his attention and a fresh dose of ire at the Indian. His voice hardened. "This fella was just leavin', weren't you?"

Without so much as another word, the Indian grabbed his collection of pelts and stormed past Dalton out the door.

Dalton eyed Gilbert. "What was that all about?"

Gilbert shook his head. "He comes in here every now and then, tryin' to peddle his stinkin' desert-dog pelts. I didn't like 'em the first time, and I sure won't like 'em next time, neither."

"The Indian or the stinking desert-dog pelts?"

"Might as well be both." Gilbert gave a mirthless laugh. "Blasted Injuns. Nothin' but bloodthirsty savages. They ambushed my cousin's wagon caravan to Oregon, murdered everyone, and scalped 'em. My blood boils every time I see one."

Dalton's eyebrows rose. "Apaches did that?"

"Dunno which tribe it was, but they're all the same to me. Blood-thirsty savages."

Dalton leaned against the wall. He'd had scant few encounters with the native population thus far, and while he'd heard his fair share of stories about them, he hadn't really formed his own opinion of them yet.

Might've been as dangerous as folks said, but maybe they were just fighting back against the white man, who kept advancing deeper and deeper into the wilds of this country.

Whatever the case, they clearly weren't smart enough to keep their land, or they would've figured out how to do it by now.

"Bloodthirsty savages," Dalton repeated.

"You got it. So watch your back when you're alone at night, 'cause they'll sneak up on ya."

"No one's gonna sneak up on me." Dalton patted the Colt in its holster on his right side.

Gilbert squinted at him. "*Oh*, I know you. You're the Reverend's nephew, ain't you?"

"The one and only."

"You're the one who gunned down poor Tommy Roebuck." Gilbert pointed a bony finger at him.

Dalton unfolded his arms and let his hands rest at his sides. His fingers flirted with the Colt sisters. In cool, measured tones, he replied, "Yeah, that was me."

Gilbert's gaze drifted down to Dalton's guns. "I ain't sayin' you *murdered* him or nothin'—just makin' a statement, that's all. Everyone knows Tommy was a lyin', cheatin' two-timer anyway. Probably had it comin', right?"

Dalton relaxed and folded his arms again. "Wouldn't be dead otherwise."

"I'll drink to that. Speakin' of which…" Gilbert's green eyes lit up, and he reached down. Bottles clinked against each other as he set a wooden case on the cash wrap. Gilbert whispered on the sly, "How's about we sample some o' this here whiskey to celebrate?"

Unopened. Randolph's holler resounded in Dalton's head.

"We'd better not," Dalton replied. "The old Prussian will have my hide if I bring 'em back in any condition other than perfect."

Gilbert nodded. "Payment?"

Dalton produced the banknotes.

"Looks good. Thanks." Gilbert popped the register open with a *ding* and deposited the bundle.

Dalton nodded to him. "You should come by the Imperial tonight for a drink."

"On you?"

"No, but I can swing you one for free. I'm on the ivories all night."

"We'll see if I can sneak in without my wife findin' out. Take care, Dalton."

Saturday nights at the Imperial roared with revelry. Alcohol practically rained from the ceiling, and banknotes, clay poker chips, and even finger-sized wedges of silver and gold hit the card tables.

At the piano, Dalton's wild renditions of Stephen Foster tunes mingled with sensual Mexican-inspired melodies throughout the night, a continuous accompaniment to the carousing all around him.

The only time he felt more alive than playing the piano was right before he drew down on someone. Flourishes and improvisations streamed out of his fingertips with every ounce of artistry flowing through his veins.

Here, at the keys, Dalton could share his true self with the world. Here, if he coughed, the noise from the piano would drown out the sound.

Here, he was free.

Madame DeBuire's girls prowled the saloon looking for the night's bread money, some of them already looking to turn their third or fourth trick. Dalton caught Vanessa's gaze from across the room again, but she turned away.

He kept plunking the piano. Maybe it wasn't "later" enough yet.

Closer to midnight, the crowd had fizzled to a few diehard gamblers and the usual regulars. By then, most of the girls had matched up with the last of their paying customers for the night.

With his time at the piano now complete, Dalton swam through torrents of Randolph's New York whiskey as he gambled the night's earnings at the poker table. He laid down four Jacks and took in a pot worth well over $200, a huge sum compared to the fourteen dollars he'd made between tips and what Randolph owed him.

As Dalton pocketed his cash, he noticed Clyde, one of his opponents, glaring at him from across the table. Through an alcohol-haze, Dalton weighed his options. He'd already had a *lot* to drink. Probably best to defuse the situation if he could.

"Don't worry," Dalton said to him. "You can always win it back."

"If you weren't the Reverend's nephew," Clyde pointed at him. "I'd shoot you dead right now."

"Forget about my uncle. *I'm* the one you need to worry about." Dalton grinned and leaned back in his chair.

The more he considered it, the more confident he became he could beat Clyde, even while drunk. After all, Clyde was drunk, too.

"Didn't you hear about Tommy Roebuck?" Dalton asked. "And David Burke? And Mike O'Connor? And—and—that other fella? Hey Randolph, what was his name?"

"Mark Fountaine," Randolph grumbled from behind the bar.

"Fountaine." Dalton laughed. "His chest was a *Fountaine* after I shot him."

"Yeah, well you'll get yours someday, too," Clyde said. "I know you chea—"

Silver flashed above the table.

Clyde shut up and stared at Dalton's Colts, wide-eyed.

"I cheated, Clyde?" Dalton glowered at him. "I *cheated?*"

It was one thing to suffer a fool moping about because he'd lost some card games, but it was quite another to let an insult go unanswered in these parts. Everything about this dog-eat-dog lifestyle hinged on strength, or at least the appearance of it.

It had taken Dalton two months to establish the kind of reputation he'd wanted in Spider's Rock, the kind of reputation that the bold men of the west were already known for long before he'd venture out here. But he could lose it in an instant—one wrong move, one slight gone unanswered, and he could lose it all.

So now Clyde was staring down the barrels of the Colt sisters.

"I don't *need* to cheat against a dullard like you, Clyde," Dalton said. "I've known horses that played better cards than you. Maybe you ought to recalibrate your opinion of your gambling skills instead of accusing me of grift."

Randolph rounded the bar and stood next to Clyde with his hands halfway up. "Easy Dalton. He's drunk. You're drunk. The hand's over, and Clyde's leaving now."

"What?" Clyde gawked at Randolph. "*He* threatened *me*, and *I* gotta leave?"

"This isn't a conversation," Randolph growled. "You will leave now, or you will not return."

"You." Clyde turned and pointed at Dalton again. He snarled with crooked teeth as he stood. "Your time's comin', Dalton."

"I don't take threats well, Clyde. 'Grievous words stir up anger.'" Dalton replaced one of his pistols and gulped down the last of his whiskey. "But even so, I'd hate to have to put you in a coffin too early. Then I couldn't take any more of your money."

Randolph walked a scowling Clyde over to the door and let him out with an encouragement to return and win it all back tomorrow night.

Seeing an opening in Randolph's defenses, Dalton stumbled over to the bar and groped for an open bottle, but Randolph got there first and slapped his hand away.

Dalton scrunched his eyebrows.

"No more until you pay me for what you already drank," Randolph growled. "And didn't we agree that you weren't going to gamble while you're on the job?"

"You *suggested* that, but I never *agreed* to it." Dalton pulled his winnings from his pocket and flipped through the banknotes.

"From now on, you either play the piano here or you gamble here, not both," Randolph said. "If you don't agree, I'll have to find another—"

Dalton slapped fifty dollars into Randolph's rough right hand. "That's a quarter of my winnings. Should cover my drinks, my inconvenience, and my next drink."

Dalton reached for the whiskey bottle, but Randolph slapped his hand away again. He did, however, pick it up himself, and he poured Dalton a shot.

"Fine," Randolph conceded. "You can gamble on my time as long as I keep getting twenty-five percent. But if you start losing, I'll throw you out like the rest of the drunks. Now finish up and get out."

Dalton downed his last drink and coughed. His lungs burned and his vision blackened, so he clamped his eyes shut until it passed. Fortunately, it had only been a small fit this time.

When he opened his eyes, Dalton saw Vanessa approaching him, a picture of radiance, stark against his world of liquor and rustic grime. Though still clad in her seafoam green corset and dress, she looked even better now than she had that afternoon.

He didn't know her well—not yet, anyway. But he had a feeling that was about to change.

"Well, Mr. Phillips, it appears you're the big winner tonight." Her hand found his shoulders and slowly migrated down his torso.

"Call me Dalton." A chill from her roving hand spiked his nerves. He breathed heavier. "What's your pleasure this evening, my dear?"

"Oh, I can think of one or two things I'd find pleasurable." Vanessa's Virginian accent was more refined and cultured than the abrasive Texas-talk of the region. Her fingers caressed his firm stomach then sank to his round belt buckle. "And maybe one or two things I could do for you, handsome."

The sweat on Dalton's forehead creeped over to his sideburns. For all his bluster about strength ruling life out west, he sure found it hard to stand tall in the presence of such a beauty.

It's just the whiskey, he rationalized. *If I weren't drunk already…*

Just when he thought she would take the exchange further, she withdrew her hand and held it out for him to take.

"Interested?" Temptation burned in her green eyes.

Dalton's heart rate slowed. Despite the booze marinating his brain, his rational mind incited his tongue. "What's it gonna cost me?"

"Not a thing." She winked. "This one's my treat."

Dalton glanced back, but Randolph ignored him. So much the better—Randolph *had* told him to get out, anyway.

Dalton refocused on Vanessa. "Lead the way."

She did.

♠ ♥ CHAPTER 3 ♦ ♣

Morning sunlight crept through the sheer lace curtains. Dalton squinted at first, but as his eyes adjusted, he took inventory of his situation. Royal blue wallpaper and dark oak trim—he was in one of the Imperial's rooms on the second floor.

Vanessa lay next to him in bed, asleep. Her long blonde hair sprawled across her pillow, tousled. White sheets and a blue quilt covered her up to her shoulders.

A headache, a hangover. Just like the last time he'd drunk too much. At least he'd enjoyed last night—from what he could remember, anyway.

Last night. Saturday night. That meant today was—

Dalton cursed under his breath. He slid out of bed and slipped into his clothes. He slapped on his Colts and checked the pocket watch hooked to his black vest, then cursed again. No time for a bath or even a quick wash. Dalton glanced back at Vanessa.

Still asleep. Good.

Dalton winked at the blue-eyed charmer in the mirror, then donned his black hat, snatched his wad of bills, and snuck out the door.

Other than the Imperial Saloon, the church, and the bank, most of the buildings in Spider's Rock were just gray copies of each other, set against the rugged Arizona landscape and pale blue sky. The brim of

Dalton's hat shielded his eyes from the midday sunlight. Was he already too late?

As Dalton approached, the First Church of Spider's Rock seeped parishioners from its grand front entrance. Reverend McCarroll stood outside, shaking hands with people and imparting blessings as they walked out.

Dalton scampered over, his face flushed, guilt rising in his chest. Whether he'd wanted to be at the service or not was moot—he'd promised his uncle when he'd moved there to attend every Sunday morning, and he was a man of his word.

Or at least, he wanted to be. So far, he'd barely made it to half of the services.

Reverend McCarroll noticed him, shot him a scowl, then refocused on his flock with a smile.

"I'm sorry, Uncle Bill," he half-whispered at Reverend McCarroll's side.

Reverend McCarroll thanked a family for coming. They greeted him and Dalton in return, though their expressions soured at their proximity to Dalton.

"You reek of alcohol, smoke, and sweat," Reverend McCarroll uttered without looking at him. "Go clean up, and I'll meet you in the parsonage."

"You're not mad about this morning?"

His uncle made eye contact with him for only the second time that morning and gritted his teeth. Slower, more ominously, he repeated, "I said go clean up, and I'll meet you in the parsonage."

Dalton's jaw tensed, and he nodded.

A half-hour later, an angry, man-sized bird of prey burst through Dalton's door.

Shirtless, Dalton reached for his pistols but stopped when he realized it was just his uncle in his pastoral garb. "Do you ever knock? Barging in's a good way to get shot."

"You can't wear that." Reverend McCarroll pointed to the shirt in Dalton's hands.

"Suddenly the preacher's an authority on fashion? Care to describe the latest trends from Paris?" Dalton scoffed.

"It's too black. Too dark."

"You wear black every day."

"I'm a reverend. I'm supposed to wear black."

"Why does it matter anyway?"

"We're heading to Mr. Warren's house for brunch in ten minutes. You can't be dressed like you just came from a funeral," Reverend McCarroll said.

Dalton smirked. "I *did* just kill Tommy Roebuck."

"Change now." Reverend McCarroll's voice hardened. "And from now on, if you say you're gonna be somewhere, *be there*. If you make a promise, keep it."

"Sorry." Dalton hesitated. "I was up late."

"Doing what?"

"Hunting nocturnal plains buffalo in the Dakotas." When Reverend McCarroll's sour expression didn't change, Dalton said, "I was working."

"Why didn't you come home last night?"

"None of your business."

Reverend McCarroll continued to scowl at him. "One of these days, Dalton, your wild lifestyle's gonna get you into more trouble than you can fathom."

"I'm not worried about it."

THWAP. Reverend McCarroll's hand slapped the top of Dalton's dresser. "Your mother sent you down here so I could keep you *out* of trouble."

"Not her brightest idea. She just wanted to get rid of me." The thought of his mother twisted Dalton's gut. "She didn't care how."

Reverend McCarroll shook his head. "The excessive drinking, the smoking, the gambling and gunslinging and philandering…"

Dalton folded his arms. "What about it?"

"It's detrimental. You're exacerbating your condition. You're killing yourself."

"If I'm gonna die anyway, I might as well enjoy what time I have left," Dalton countered.

"You're throwing away your life."

"It isn't worth anything anyway."

"That's not true, Dalton," Reverend McCarroll started toward Dalton. "You have a purpose. You just haven't found it yet."

Dalton waved him off. "No. My life is over. We both know I'm a dead man just waiting to die."

A long silence lingered between them. It was all Dalton could do to keep from coughing and proving himself right.

"Suit yourself, Dalton. Someday you'll realize the truth. I just hope it's not too late."

"Save the hellfire and brimstone for your congregation, alright?" Now Dalton allowed himself a fit of coughs, and the tang of blood hit his tongue.

He covered his mouth with his bare forearm, and when he pulled it away, he saw flecks of red on his skin. Reverend McCarroll saw them, too.

"Get dressed. We're gonna be late." Reverend McCarroll shook his head. "And no black."

Max Warren, III ruled Spider's Rock like a king.

"He owns the bank, the real estate company, most of the land, the mining company, and more," Reverend McCarroll said.

Spider's Rock amounted to no more than a flea on the Arizona Territory's vast, rugged hide, but it had doubled in size over the last year and seemed poised to do it again. Even so, the walk from the parsonage across town to Mr. Warren's mansion only took about two minutes.

"In fact, the only real estate he doesn't own is the church, which he donated to the town."

"And the Imperial," Dalton added.

Randolph made just about everyone who walked through his doors aware of his sole ownership of the business, the building, *and* the land. If Mr. Warren had even a shadow of a rival, it was Randolph.

"How'd he get all of it?"

"Knows some people back in Washington D.C.," Reverend McCarroll said. "I think one of his relatives is a congressman. And he got lucky, finding all that silver. Some gold, too. Soon as he did, he used that connection in Washington and took possession of the land. You know they want to make Arizona part of the Union, right?"

"Yeah, I heard about it back east. Sounds like a bunch of talk with no real action."

"That's politics in general, if you ask me. But it'll happen eventually." Reverend McCarroll nodded. "Don't expect to see it in my lifetime, but it will happen."

Dalton shook his head. "Too many complications. Mexico may have signed over the land, but that conflict is far from over. And the Indians won't just let us have the land, either."

"Let the government worry about 'em. In the meantime, they're enabling people like Mr. Warren to mine the territory and establish permanent settlements. Ever since they found gold at Sutter's Mill earlier this year, the government's been heading west in a hurry."

Dalton shook his head. "Mr. Warren's just one sliver of a very big American pie."

"Don't underestimate him." Reverend McCarroll eyed Dalton. "Here in Spider's Rock, he *is* the pie."

As if on cue, Dalton caught the scent of a fresh apple pie wafting from the colossal home in front of them. Reverend McCarroll led him up the grand steps between two white marble columns and knocked on the red door.

When a well-dressed Negro man opened the door, Dalton wondered what position the Arizona Territory held on slavery.

Back east, places like Boston and Philadelphia had no slaves of any sort, but many blacks still worked as servants in white households, and even so, they weren't treated much better. Here in Spider's Rock, Dalton had encountered a few free blacks, scarce as they were, but this was the first one he'd encountered in a servile position.

"Good afternoon, Charles. We missed you and your family at church this morning." Reverend McCarroll shook the man's hand and smiled. "Did the Warrens keep you here to prepare our lunch today?"

"Yes, Reverend," Charles replied with a quiet voice and a guarded smile on his face.

"Hosting us for lunch is no reason to keep you from attending church. I will speak with Mr. Warren about it for you."

Charles gave a slight bow. "Thank you, Reverend."

Even as the exchange continued, Dalton wondered whether his uncle's interference would make things better or worse for Charles and his family. He hoped it was the former.

"How is Mary?" Reverend McCarroll asked.

"She's well, thank you."

"Charles, this is my nephew Dalton. Charles is not a slave, but I fear that sometimes the Warrens forget that."

"Pleasure to meet you, sir." Charles extended his hand and nodded.

Dalton shook it. "Likewise."

"Please come in." Charles stepped away from the door and motioned them inside. "You are expected."

The Warren home merged the elegance of a southern plantation mansion, the luxury of a New England estate, and the rustic flare of the gritty southwest. Two grand staircases snaked down opposite walls and filtered into the mansion's immaculate lobby, complete with a marble checkerboard floor and a marvelous chandelier sparkling above them.

Charles showed them into a grand dining hall with burgundy-colored walls where the Warrens awaited.

Max Warren, III looked just as Dalton imagined: slightly taller than average, imposing in demeanor but not physically big, and never smiling nor frowning. Instead, he perpetually expressed something between a smirk and a scowl under his thin silver mustache.

A few articles of gold and silver jewelry adorned his fingers and wrists. He wore a wide-brimmed gray hat that covered his thick silver hair, a gray three-piece suit, and black snakeskin boots polished so well that Dalton could see the bottoms of Warren's gray pants in their reflection. At their approach, he stood and removed his hat.

While Mr. Warren wore his wealth in relative subtlety, Mrs. Warren dripped with it. Her purple silk dress had probably been imported from Europe, and a lustrous gold necklace with a ruby teardrop pendant hung from her neck. Long white gloves, also silk, covered her arms up to mid-bicep.

Her pure blonde hair, neatly gathered behind her head, shined in the sunlight. A few playful curls dangled from the gold clips that held her hair in place. Her pleasant, perfectly white smile set Dalton at ease. She, too, stood when they entered the dining hall.

Reverend McCarroll reached across the table and shook Mr. Warren's hand, then he motioned toward Dalton. "Max, this is my nephew, Dalton Phillips."

Warren grabbed Dalton's hand over the table and delivered a firm gentleman's handshake. When Warren spoke, Dalton recognized the dignified southern drawl of the Carolinas in his deep voice. "A pleasure to meet you, Dalton."

"Likewise, Max." Dalton's response earned him a corrective glance from his uncle.

Warren eyed him with piercing blue eyes, but his expression shifted to a smirk as he introduced Mrs. Warren. "This is my wife, Giselle."

"Your *wife*? I expected you to say she was your daughter." Dalton took her hand and bowed low to kiss it. "It's a pleasure to meet you, Mrs. Warren."

She blushed, which made Dalton smile. "How kind of you, Dalton."

Her light-blue eyes flashed a suggestion that might mean the end of Dalton's life should he ever take her up on the offer. If only she were twenty years younger and unmarried.

"Dalton, allow me to introduce my daughter, Camille." She gestured past him.

A brunette version of Mrs. Warren walked toward him with a smile on her face. Despite her otherwise proper disposition, mischief glinted in her soft, royal blue eyes. Twenty years younger and unmarried—Dalton's wish come to fruition.

♠ ♥ CHAPTER 4 ♦ ♣

Camille Warren wore a light blue dress accented with white and silver trim in the same style as her mother's, only she showed more of her shoulders than Mrs. Warren and wore no gloves. A sapphire pendant that matched her eyes hung from a delicate silver chain around her neck.

Dalton caught himself staring at the pendant and abruptly adjusted his focus back to her eyes. For a moment, the internal system that produced his charm failed, but he accepted Camille's outstretched hand and kissed it, using the time to recover his poise.

"I am *delighted* to make your acquaintance, Miss Warren," Dalton almost whispered. He noticed a hunger flaring in her eyes like he'd seen in her mother's—still a dangerous proposition, perhaps even more than Mrs. Warren's.

"The pleasure, Mr. Phillips, is entirely mine." The way she said it seemed more alluring than cordial.

"Camille," Warren said, his tone firm and almost corrective. He lightened his tone and motioned to a chair he'd pulled out from the table. "Won't you sit next to me, my dear?"

"Of course, Daddy."

Dalton smirked. He could play that game too. He cut off Charles before he could get ahold of Mrs. Warren's chair and pulled it out for her instead. His action drew gawks from both Reverend McCarroll and Warren, but Mrs. Warren practically swooned.

"What a gentleman," she raved. "Pay heed, Maxwell. This handsome young man is showing you up in your own home."

"Have a seat, Dalton." Warren's offer sounded more like a warning.

Dalton took his place opposite of Camille and Mrs. Warren—closer to Camille, of course. To his right sat Warren, a sultan seated in comfort at the head of his table. Reverend McCarroll occupied the opposite end seat across from Warren.

Within moments, Charles and a Negro woman—Dalton presumed she was Charles's wife, Mary—had lunch spread across the polished cherrywood table. The tempestuous aroma of fried chicken, mashed potatoes, and green beans ignited Dalton's latent appetite. Charles poured amber-colored ale into Dalton's glass then moved on to Reverend McCarroll, who declined.

"Charles makes this brew. It's delicious." Warren sloshed it around his glass, and sunlight glinted through the liquid. "Not having any, Reverend?"

Reverend McCarroll tapped his neck. "Gave up drinking when I donned this collar."

"Suit yourself." Warren took a swig.

Dalton did, too. The frothy ale played with his tongue and cooled him from the inside out.

"Sweeter than you expected, isn't it?" Warren asked.

"Yes, it is." Dalton finished the glass in a few more gulps. "That's great. Really refreshing."

"Glad you like it. I'll have Charles refill your glass," Mrs. Warren said.

Dalton noticed Reverend McCarroll eyeing him. "I'd love another glass, but I probably shouldn't have more than that. Too much can turn your stomach sour."

He glanced at Camille and gave her a wink he hoped Warren would miss. This would be an interesting lunch, to say the least.

"It was good to see all of you in church this morning," Reverend McCarroll said.

"Thank you," Warren said. "I hope to attend more often now that my traveling schedule has run dry. Given my consistent attendance, I expect I should be appointed a deacon soon."

Dalton almost choked on his gulp of water, but he recovered. His eyes landed on Warren. This man was even more brazen than Dalton was.

Dalton cleared his throat and dabbed at his mouth with a napkin. "Excuse me."

Reverend McCarroll ignored him and wrung his hands. "Deacons are required to tithe regularly."

"I've done enough of that to last a lifetime. I donated the land, the labor, and the lumber for that church. And more besides."

"We certainly appreciate your patronage, Max. We'd still be meeting in the town hall without you. But that alone won't justify a deaconship."

"Then make me an honorary deacon," Warren said, his voice firm.

Reverend McCarroll's posture straightened. "With all due respect, I won't do that. Tithing is a biblical principle that all church leaders *must* adhere to."

Dalton caught Camille staring at him while the two men tussled. He returned her playful gaze with another wink and she beamed. He looked her up and down, as much as he could take in, given that the table hid half of her from his sight.

Let the old men discuss theology. Dalton was more interested in the subject of biology—Camille in particular.

"Well, we enjoyed the service today, Reverend." Mrs. Warren smiled at Dalton. "Although we certainly missed your nephew's magnificent piano-playing this morning."

"Please pardon my absence, Mrs. Warren," Dalton said. "I had hoped to be there for worship, but I accidentally overslept due to a long night."

"And what made your night so long, Dalton?" Camille's voice played like notes from a soothing Beethoven concerto in his ears.

"I was—" Dalton cleared his throat. If he'd been treading carefully with his uncle on this subject, he'd need to dance across hot coals now. "—working late."

"How lovely that you're already earning a wage so soon after arriving in town, dear." Mrs. Warren beamed at him. "Where do you work?"

"At the Imperial. I play piano every evening and run errands for Randolph."

"The Imperial." Warren scoffed. "A worthless establishment. I never should have sold the property to that Prussian fiend."

"On the contrary, Mr. Warren, the Imperial does incredible business," Dalton said. "Randolph has a keen eye for what his patrons want."

"Including the whores trolling the premises?" Warren said. "The entire operation is a disgrace. As Reverend McCarroll's nephew, you should be ashamed to work in such a dump."

Dalton bristled at Warren's attack. Did he pick on everyone he met? "While my uncle and I don't agree on my choice of employment, I am my own man and enjoy the diverse opportunities that working at the Imperial affords."

"You mean gambling, free alcohol, and loose women?" Warren turned to Reverend McCarroll. "Is *this* what you teach on Sunday mornings?"

"You know full well that I preach against *all* sin, including those transgressions named," Reverend McCarroll growled.

Warren scoffed again. "Perhaps you should put your own household in order before you try imposing your dogma on the rest of Spider's Rock."

Dalton slapped the table with his palm, rattling the fine china and the silver utensils. Camille's eyes widened, but at second glance, Dalton recognized a dash of intrigue in them as well. He might have held his tongue for her sake, but the time for diplomacy had passed.

"Mr. Warren, you have *no* right to question my uncle's dedication to pastoring this miserable little town."

"Dalton," his uncle protested.

"And I'd rather work at the Imperial than for a spoiled, power-hungry weasel like you."

"*Dalton.*"

He ignored his uncle and stole a look at Camille, who diverted her eyes right away. It didn't look like he was currying her favor anymore, but he'd already said what he'd needed to say.

It was one thing to endure his uncle's lecture every time he did something wrong, but it was quite another to listen to Max Warren, III accuse Reverend McCarroll of a lack of trying to whip Dalton into line. Dalton didn't care if Warren had owned the entirety of the Arizona Territory; his words were heinous and unjust, and he deserved the rebuke Dalton gave him.

"This from a reckless thug who murders people in the street." Warren didn't even bother to make eye contact with him.

"That was justified. You don't know *any* of the circumstances, so don't pretend you do." Dalton pointed at him. "And if you don't watch yourself, you might catch my next bullet."

"*Dalton!*" Reverend McCarroll shouted. "Shut up."

"But he's—"

"I said *shut your mouth*. Get up. We're leaving."

Mrs. Warren protested, "Oh, Reverend, don't—"

"Please, Madame. I insist." Reverend McCarroll held out a hand in surrender, or possibly to silence her. "We've embarrassed ourselves enough for one afternoon."

"Let them go, Giselle," Warren said, still seated at his spot, still working through the food on his plate.

Dalton stood up. His uncle was right—he'd done enough damage. He didn't regret any of it, but he recognized it all the same.

He nodded to their hostess. "I apologize for causing a disturbance, ma'am. With the exception of your husband's foul mood, thank you for an otherwise pleasant meal."

Mrs. Warren just looked at him, her mouth open to speak, but no words came out.

He shifted to Camille. "A pleasure meeting you, Miss Warren. Good afternoon."

He didn't bother saying anything else to Mr. Warren. He'd already said everything he had to say.

So Dalton stormed out of the dining room and out the front door with his uncle close behind.

Reverend McCarroll caught up with Dalton on the other side of Main Street, as empty as if it were the dead of night, thanks to Sunday afternoon lunches and dinners. "What in Heaven's name was *that*?"

Dalton just kept walking, his jaw tight.

Reverend McCarroll grabbed his arm and spun him around. "I asked you a question."

Dalton jerked away. "He attacked us. He's an arrogant, impudent—"

"I could say the same of you," Reverend McCarroll cut in.

"But he slandered you. He slandered Randolph and the Imperial and me."

"You played right into his hands. You played the fool at *your* expense, not his."

Dalton wanted to explode. He skinned the Colt from the holster on his right hip and within two seconds flat, he fired all six rounds into a hitching post about fifteen yards away. The bullets splintered the top of the post and sent a nearby chicken coop into a frenzy of feathers.

Still breathing heavy, Dalton holstered the revolver and glared at his uncle.

"Shooting up the town won't change anything. You're only wasting ammunition."

"It makes me feel better."

"It makes you feel like you have control," Reverend McCarroll countered. "But you don't. And *that's* why you're mad."

"You don't know what you're talking about." Dalton coughed hard and turned away. Needles pricked the inside of his lungs. *Not this again.* "I wish you'd just let me live my life. You don't have to dictate my every step."

"I made a promise to your mother."

"Don't care." More coughing. "I'm releasing you from that arrangement."

"It doesn't work that way, and you know it."

Instead of cursing like he wanted to, Dalton found himself coughing and hacking even more. A fit swept over him, and he couldn't stop. He clutched his burning chest.

Amid his coughs, Dalton tasted blood again. He grabbed a handkerchief from his pocket and covered his mouth as he hacked some more. When he pulled it away, bright red spots dotted the white cloth.

Reverend McCarroll sighed. "Your consumption?"

"I'm fine," Dalton lied. Fire raged in his lungs. He finished his coughing spree and pocketed the handkerchief. "Let's just go home."

♠ ♥ CHAPTER 5 ♦ ♣

The Arizona heat fizzled as a red sun set beyond Spider's Rock. Inside the Imperial, the piano sang raucous tunes that matched the saloon's atmosphere. Amber alcohol splashed from bottles to glasses to bodies, and occasionally it skipped the glasses entirely.

Ladies roamed the premises, entertaining both weary, lonely travelers and the regular clientele. Royal families, aces, and numbers vied for space atop poker tables with burning cigars, banknotes, and gold.

As with the night before, another small fortune from a variety of angry players now resided in Dalton's pockets. Randolph got his cut, of course, and that night Dalton took it easy on the whiskey. Good thing, too, because Vanessa was headed right toward him.

At Vanessa's approach, all Dalton could think of was Camille Warren. The way she'd looked. The kindling connection they'd shared, masked by her innocence. As pretty and alluring as Vanessa was, Camille was just a finer woman, high-class and unique.

And if Dalton meant to make any inroads with her, especially in spite of how he'd confronted her father earlier that day, he couldn't play around with Vanessa at the same time. A woman like Vanessa wouldn't mind, but a woman like Camille would—and that alone made enough of a difference to Dalton.

"Hey, stranger," Vanessa said, her voice smooth as velvet. Her luscious flesh glowed under the Imperial's lights. "Where'd you disappear to this morning?"

Dalton swallowed a glass of whiskey and stood up. "Church. Had to be at church to play piano for my uncle's service. It *is* Sunday, you know."

"Church is the *last* place you need to be, Dalton." She rested her hand on his shoulder and ran her fingers down his chest. "And besides, you don't have church tomorrow, do you?"

"No." When Dalton took her hand in his and removed it from his abdomen, Vanessa smiled, her green eyes full of mischief. "But I'm tired tonight, and you need to make some money."

"I've made enough for this evening." Her fingers played with his belt line.

That was yet another crucial difference between Vanessa and Camille: simply put, Vanessa was a whore, and Camille was not. Dalton had no future with Vanessa, but he could see potential for something to develop with Camille on the horizon, if he played his proverbial cards right.

Dalton stepped back. "Madame DeBuire's gonna lash you with that stick of hers if you don't get to work. Then Randolph will hound me for it, too."

"So leave me some coin in the morning," Vanessa leaned close to him, and her sultry words oozed into Dalton's ears. "I know you've got it to spend."

He gently pushed her back and held up his hands to maintain the distance he'd established between them. A pang of regret jabbed at his gut, but it wouldn't keep him from saying what he needed to say. "I'm not interested tonight. Sorry, sweetheart."

She gawked at him, and her tone sharpened. "So if it's free, it's good, but when it's not, you're not interested? Is that it? Well, suit yourself, Dalton Phillips."

Vanessa stormed off, and Dalton didn't say anything or try to stop her. He caught some furtive glances from the lingering patrons in the Imperial, but they all looked away just as quickly.

Apparently, his reputation in the wake of Tommy Roebuck's death was still very much intact.

The jabbing pang in Dalton's gut subsided. He put another coin on Randolph's bar, slammed one last shot of whiskey, then walked into the cool night air.

A half-moon drenched Main Street with silver light. Dalton strolled along the dirt road, at ease for the first time in days. He'd be home in plenty of time, which would make his uncle happier, and he'd spared himself from complicating his relationship with Vanessa.

Perhaps his hopes for Camille were juvenile and unfounded, but at least now he could pursue her, if he so desired, with a clear conscience.

He exhaled a long, deep breath. Amid the whispering wind across the surrounding desert, a high-pitched howl sounded in the distance— probably the coyote equivalent to a sigh.

Something shuffled behind one of the buildings, the one that the Chinese owners of Song's Tailor Shop rented from Warren. It was unmistakable—Dalton had been drinking, but not nearly as much as he usually did.

Maybe that coyote was closer than he'd thought. If it showed itself, he could use it for target practice and sell the pelt to Gilbert at the mercantile.

Then again, maybe not. If Gilbert hadn't wanted the Indian's stinking coyote pelts, he probably wouldn't want Dalton's, either.

Beyond the storefronts, gravel crackled in the pattern of quick, light footsteps.

Maybe it *wasn't* a coyote after all.

Dalton jerked his Colts from their holsters. Sobriety, or at least semi-sobriety, had its advantages. Two clicks later and he'd pulled both hammers back.

Maybe it was Clyde, come to give Dalton the reckoning he'd promised the night before. Dalton doubted Gilbert would have any use for Clyde's pelt either, but at least Dalton would take personal joy in knowing he'd rid the town of yet another urchin.

"Show yourself," Dalton commanded, just loud enough for the person hiding to hear, but not so loud as to awaken anyone sleeping in the surrounding buildings. If it came to a gunfight, though, they'd wake the whole town in no time.

A figure crept from behind Song's Tailor Shop, leading with tan gloved hands extended, followed by a trim form in a tan dress. Soft, curled brown locks bobbled from under her matching wide-brimmed hat.

"Dalton?" a female voice whispered.

"Who are you?" Dalton lowered his guard, but not his pistols.

"It's Camille Warren, from lunch this afternoon. Remember?"

Dalton's lips cracked with a smile. The "horizon" must've been closer than he'd guessed. "How could I forget?"

"Would you mind putting your guns away?" She took a tentative step in his direction. "Please?"

"Oh, yes. Sorry." He slid them back into their holsters but didn't take his hands off of them—not yet. If her father was lurking nearby, Dalton wanted to be ready. He doubted it, but just in case... "What brings you out here so late, Miss Warren?"

"Very private, personal business, Mr. Phillips, so kindly keep your voice low."

"Of course." Dalton savored her. Her casual attire flattered her shape just as much as her ornate dress had from earlier that day. "Does your father know you're out?"

"No, and I'd like to keep it that way."

Dalton stared into her royal blue eyes. They flickered with the same fire he'd seen that afternoon—fire that burned for *him*. "What do you have in mind, Miss Warren?"

She smiled. Her face glowed with silver light, and she pulled in close. "Can we go somewhere more private?"

Her warm body sent cold prickles down his back, and he *loved* it. Dalton took her hand in his, kissing it as he had that afternoon. "I can arrange that. Follow me."

They snuck into the parsonage, stealing past Reverend McCarroll's room with light feet. The old pastor's door was shut, but Dalton could still hear him snoring.

Good.

He led Camille through the darkness to his room at the opposite end of the parsonage and pushed the door open. While he lit a few candles, Camille latched the door behind them.

As soon as Dalton turned around, Camille was there, her hands working the buttons on his shirt. He kicked off his boots and they clattered against his wooden bed frame. He regretted the noise only momentarily as Camille pulled off his shirt and set to work undoing his belt.

Dalton set the leather strap, holsters, and Colts on a dresser next to the bed and slid out of his shirt.

Camille ran her hands over his firm chest and caressed his abdominals with her fingers. She reached for his neck and pulled him down, and they kissed. When his lips dropped down to her neck, her hot breath hit his ear in an impassioned sigh.

Then she pushed him back. "Wait."

Dalton scowled at her—until she started undoing the buttons that ran down the front of her dress. Excitement bubbled in his chest, overflowed into his stomach, and continued to trickle even farther down.

Tonight would be a good night.

♠ ♥ CHAPTER 6 ♦ ♣

*T*hud-thud-thud.

The pair had just hopped into bed when Dalton's door shook with the pounding of a furious fist. Dalton's feet hit the floor, and he yanked his pants back on. He motioned for Camille to stay hidden under the covers, and she gave him a timid nod.

"Dalton," Reverend McCarroll's muffled voice came from behind the door. "Open this door."

Camille had locked the deadbolt—that would buy Dalton some time. Maybe he could convince his uncle to go away.

"Open up," his uncle called again. "Mr. Warren is here. We know Camille is in there."

So much for getting him to leave.

Muttering curses, Dalton slid on his boots then strapped the belt and holsters around his waist. He patted his trousers and felt the wad of banknotes still lodged in his pocket from the night's winnings. How had they found out so soon?

He ogled the big window opposite of the door—his only escape route. Warren's presence undoubtedly meant he'd brought friends, too, ready to skin Dalton alive the instant Warren gave the order.

At least Dalton had two loaded guns with him. They might buy him some time.

"Move aside, Reverend," Warren roared in the hallway. "You open up right now, or I'll kill you myself, Dalton Phillips!"

No chance of that happening. They'd have to break the door down to—

Wood snapped and the deadbolt clanked.

Camille screamed.

The door flared open and four men spilled into the room: Reverend McCarroll, Mr. Warren, and two robust men, probably in their late thirties. The two men held rifles, but Dalton already had the drop on them, so they didn't dare raise their barrels.

"Don't move." Dalton's Colts flickered in the candlelight. "Take one more step, and I'll burn you down."

They all froze. Reverend McCarroll held up his hands. "Take it easy, Dalton. No one means to harm you."

"Speak for yourself, *Reverend*," Warren growled. His eyes flashed from Camille, still bundled under the covers, back to Dalton. "I'm going to rip him apart."

"Not another step." Dalton leveled both pistols at Warren's head. "Tell your men to back out of this room, or I'll split your head open like a melon at an Independence Day party."

Warren growled at his men, "Do *not* leave this room."

Dalton pulled the hammer back on the pistol in his right hand, still aimed at Warren, then he cocked the one in his left and pointed at one of the two henchmen. "Last chance. You know I'll do it. Even in front of Camille, I'll do it."

Warren snapped, "Don't you *dare* say her name, you lecherous—"

"*Enough*," Dalton barked. "Back out now, or get ready for the world's shortest fireworks show."

"He's serious. He doesn't care," Reverend McCarroll said. "He'll do it."

Warren's jaw stiffened and he clenched his fists. His eyes fixed on Dalton, he ordered, "Do as he says."

Dalton shook his head. "Rifles on the floor. Then take your guns out, slowly, and put 'em on the floor."

37

The guns hit the floor.

"Kick 'em all toward me, and put your hands up," he said. "And Mr. Warren, please take the pistol from under your coat and add it to our collection. I'd hate to shoot you on accident if I thought you might be reaching for it. Better to avoid the temptation altogether."

Dalton stole a glance at Reverend McCarroll, who glared at him and shook his head.

Warren tossed his gun next to the others.

"Thank you." He backed toward the window and lowered the hammer on the gun in his left hand and holstered it. "I'll be on my way, now."

"Dalton, don't you *dare* leave," Reverend McCarroll said.

"Sorry, Uncle Bill, but I don't have a choice." He snatched up his shirt and stuffed it into the back of his pants, then put his black hat on. "It's been a pleasure, gentlemen."

"I won't forget this, Dalton," Warren said through clenched teeth.

"I know it." The best Dalton could hope for now was to offer an apology once Warren cooled off.

After all, he hadn't actually done anything with Camille. They'd been interrupted too early to make any real progress. Warren's ire had to stop somewhere.

He turned back to Camille, still covering herself with Dalton's sheets, and showed her his wide white smile. "Miss Warren, it's been a pleasure."

Warren stepped toward him. "I'll tear you limb from—"

"Ah, ah, ah!" Dalton raised his gun higher. "Stay put. I'm leaving."

Warren froze in place.

Dalton opened the window, swinging it out into the warm night air. He glanced back at Camille, gave her a wink, then stepped outside.

Under the moonlight, Dalton scampered from the parsonage into the shadows of the town buildings. He darted from shadow to shadow, gradually making his way toward the Imperial where he could rent a room from Randolph for the night—or possibly longer if Warren's embers continued to burn against him.

It was the only place where he'd be safe. Warren's men would know to look there, but they wouldn't dare violate Randolph's sovereignty... or would they?

38

Whether they would or not, short of fleeing into the desert, it was Dalton's only option.

Behind him, Warren's men scraped around town like bloodhounds chasing a scent, but he had a lead on them. What's more, the building whose shadow now provided him cover was none other than Warren's home.

Located on Main Street, Warren's home served as the halfway point between his uncle's church and the Imperial, which sat on opposite corners of Spider's Rock. Dalton figured that the last place Warren would look was at his own house.

He took a moment to slide his black shirt back on and then buttoned it up. Warren's lackeys still roamed the streets, peered into windows, and ventured into dark areas. Moonlight glinted off the gunmetal of their rifles.

In the distance, Warren hollered at Reverend McCarroll, still inside the parsonage, loud enough to wake the entire town and any Indians within three miles of Spider's Rock. That ruckus would help cover Dalton's approach to the Imperial. He dashed to another shadow, checked around for threats, then dashed to another, and finally into the alley behind the Imperial.

At almost three in the morning, Dalton doubted Randolph would be awake, which boded better for them both anyway. All things considered, Randolph might've handed him over to Warren as a peace offering if he thought he'd profit from it in some way.

Instead, one of Madame DeBuire's ladies always tended the inn overnight, just in case a weary traveler or a late-night patron should wander in. Tonight, Dalton was both.

He went inside and gently shut the door behind him.

"Dalton?"

He whirled around to find a rotund, busty young woman. Still beautiful, but without the edge she'd probably had a few years and a few meals earlier. He thought her name was Delilah, but he couldn't be certain.

She sashayed over to him with a wide grin on her face. "What you doin' here so late? Lookin' for some love?"

"No, De—" He checked himself. Didn't want to get her name wrong. "—Dear. Just need a room. Vanessa free tonight?"

Delilah put her hands on her hips, shifting her excess weight back. "Vanessa's never *free*, Dalton. An' besides, I thought you weren't lookin' for that."

"Oh, I'm not. I owe her some money."

Delilah raised an eyebrow. "Is that a fact?"

"Gambling debt. She lent me some scratch so I could win a big hand. I forgot to settle up with her."

"So you felt obliged to come over in the middle of the night to pay her back?" She leaned even closer and eyed him.

"What can I say? Couldn't rest until my debt was paid."

Delilah smirked. "An' who says chicanery is dead?"

"I think you mean *chivalry*." Dalton scrunched his eyebrows. "And if you don't mind, I'd like to see her if she's not... busy."

Delilah squinted at him.

"Please?" He gave her a dose of charm with his eyes and his best smile.

"Aw... I can't say no to you, Dalton. Not with a face like that," Delilah said. "She's up in room twelve, an' she's alone. Said she wasn't feelin' well at the end of the night an' hit the sack early, 'bout the same time as you left."

"Thanks, Dear." He leaned over and kissed her chipmunk cheek. "You're a doll."

"Aw, you're sweet, Dalton."

He gave her a wink, and she blushed.

After his third knock, Dalton considered giving up, but then Vanessa opened the door a crack.

Her sleepy green eyes took a second to register him, and then they narrowed with anger. "What do *you* want?"

In hushed tones, Dalton replied, "I'm wondering if I could stay the night with you."

She scoffed and shook her head. "No. You had your chance."

"Look, I'm sorry I declined your offer earlier. I just need a place to stay for the night."

"Oh, really? That's all you need me for? A place to stay?"

Dalton couldn't believe his ears. This didn't have to be difficult, but Vanessa might not even give him that option.

"So you'd rather I wanted you for meaningless sex?" Dalton countered. As soon as he said it, he regretted it.

"*Meaningless?*" She pulled her robe tighter. "Is that what you think I'm about? This is my *job*, Dalton, not who I am. I'm a person, same as you. I thought we'd started something special."

Dalton didn't have time for this, nor did he want to work out every iota of their relationship in the hallway at 3am. "Well, you thought wrong. I was drunk, not thinking straight. Now I'm asking you as a—"

"No chance. Forget it. Good night, Dalton." She shut the door in his face.

He sighed, but with over $300 in his pocket from gambling that night, maybe having his own room would be better anyway. Dalton headed back downstairs to have Delilah let him into one.

Alone in his new room, Dalton locked the door and stripped down. He lay in bed, his head on the lumpy pillow, thanks to the Colt sisters lying in wait underneath. Warren probably wouldn't come for him here, but he'd sleep better knowing they were accessible.

If he could fall asleep.

His mind spun with the last few days' events, starting with Tommy Roebuck's death and ending with his escapade with Camille Warren. He had to smile at that one: caught in bed with the daughter of the town's most powerful man, and inside the pastor's parsonage no less. Could it have been any worse?

Dalton chuckled. Then he coughed. Blasted illness. He hacked some more and brought up blood with his mucus—but most of it was blood. A bit spattered on his chin. He nabbed a handkerchief from the little nightstand next to the bed and dabbed himself clean.

Between the illness and the debacles he'd found himself in over the last few days, he felt wrong, somehow. Like something about him wasn't quite right. He felt...

Hollow. A strange emptiness yawned inside of him, and he didn't know why.

Dalton rubbed his stomach. Maybe he needed food. Or maybe he still hadn't adjusted to the abrupt cessation of his interaction with Camille.

Or maybe he needed another gulp of whiskey to put his mind at ease. Too bad he couldn't get into the saloon half of the Imperial.

He lay back and closed his eyes, trying to drown the storm clouds of thoughts swirling in his head. Not long after, his mind finally faded into sleep.

Dalton woke up to pounding on his door and an angry voice hollering threats from the hallway. Still groggy, his cognition sharpened the instant he heard a key rattling in the lock.

He yanked one of his Colts from under the pillow. If Warren wanted to die today, Dalton could arrange that.

He pulled the hammer back on his revolver and aimed at the door.

♠ ♥ CHAPTER 7 ♦ ♣

Instead of Warren, Randolph opened the door and stormed into Dalton's room, but he stopped when he noticed the pistol in Dalton's hands.

"Get out," Randolph said, his voice flat.

Once Dalton verified Randolph was alone, he lowered his Colt and disengaged the hammer. "Come on, Randolph. You don't mean that."

Randolph pointed to the open door. "I mean it. I want you out of here *now*."

"I need a place to stay. And I'm a paying customer."

"I don't care." Randolph stepped toward him. "Max Warren is after you. I'm sure he knows you're here, and if not, he will soon. The last thing I need is Warren's men haunting my property looking for you."

Dalton put up his empty hand. "But if you let me stay, you'll have another advantage over War—"

"Save it, Dalton. I want you out in ten minutes." He turned to leave.

Dalton cursed under his breath. "I'll pay you the normal room rate plus half."

Randolph stopped.

"I'll be a good tenant. I won't wreck your property like these other ingrates." When Randolph still said nothing, Dalton added, "And I'll pay you in advance."

At that, Randolph turned, hand extended. "The normal rate, as you know, is two dollars and twenty-five cents per night. You'll give me five dollars every night *before* you leave the saloon, in addition to twenty-five percent of your take at the poker tables. I'll still pay you two dollars for five hours of playing the piano every night, and you can still keep any tips you make."

Dalton frowned. "How *generous* of you."

"Take it or leave it. I'd toss you to Warren if I thought it would actually get him off my back, but I know not even that would appease him. So for the time being, I don't mind aggravating him further, as long as you keep paying." Randolph pointed a thick finger at Dalton. "But if you miss even one payment, I'll throw you out before you even have time to blink."

"Whatever you say, boss." He reached over and pulled a few banknotes from his trousers.

Most paper money in Spider's Rock came straight from Warren's bank. Even as stable as the bank was, most folks still preferred the federally-minted gold coins from back east, just in case Warren's bank should fail, but Randolph couldn't care less.

Green or gold, it was all good with Dalton as long as he could spend it.

Dalton held a fiver out toward Randolph. "This should cover my room for tonight."

Randolph snatched it and slid the bill into his pocket. "Get dressed. I need you to pick up a few things from the mercantile. I have a list for you in the saloon."

"Alright," Dalton said. "Let me get dressed, and I'll be right down."

Randolph walked out and shut the door behind him, and Dalton breathed a sigh of relief. If he could win a few rounds of poker every night, he'd make enough money to pay for the room and to buy food and supplies. To survive on his own.

He doubted Reverend McCarroll would allow him back in the parsonage after last night. And even if he could go back, Dalton wouldn't.

At twenty-three years old, it was high time he truly started to care for himself, even with the disease wracking his lungs. He didn't need help, didn't need his hawk-eyed uncle watching his every move or lecturing him on his lifestyle every day.

Perhaps now, forced to fend for himself, he'd find a meaning for his life. Or at the very least, he'd be truly free to do what he wanted, when he wanted.

Dalton got out of bed and got dressed with a smile as he mulled over the new range of possibilities that lay before him.

When Dalton reached Warren's Mercantile, he glanced over his shoulder one more time to make sure no one had followed him. Max Warren didn't strike him as the forgiving type, and Dalton didn't want anyone sneaking up on him.

Sure, he could handle himself in a fight, but getting ambushed would make for a different story altogether. Hopefully, the worst consequence that came from crossing the most powerful man in town would be a sore neck from perpetually scanning his surroundings.

Dalton inched the door open and poked his head inside the mercantile with his right hand on his pistol, still holstered. After a quick inventory of the few patrons inside, Dalton stepped in, satisfied that none of Warren's goons were waiting for him. He slunk down an aisle and began collecting the items on Randolph's list, as well as some extra ammunition for his Colts.

Gilbert was reading the latest issue of the local newspaper, the Spider's Web, at his spot behind the counter. How the press managed to get enough material to fill two sides of two large sheets of paper in such a small town, Dalton didn't know.

When he noticed his name and likeness on the front page, Dalton smirked. They'd published the story of poor Tommy's death.

Gilbert looked up. "Howdy, Dalton. Just readin' 'bout you here in the paper."

"Did they get the story right?"

"Sounds like." He flipped to the front page again and set the paper down.

"Good."

"Hey, John and Greg," Gilbert called. "C'mon over here, and meet Dalton."

Two thirty-something men, one lanky and wearing a red shirt, the other short, chubby, and wearing a blue shirt, walked over from the opposite wall. The chubby one introduced himself as John Vernon, the lanky one as Greg.

"Pleasure," Dalton said.

"You wouldn't know it, but these two yahoos are brothers," Gilbert explained. "They don't look nothin' alike, do they? Anyhow, Dalton's the man who put down Tommy Roebuck."

"That was you?" John asked.

Dalton took in the sight of both of them. He agreed with Gilbert. They looked about as related as Dalton might've been to a chimpanzee. "Sure was."

"Well, guess I won't be gettin' that half-dollar he owes me, will I?" Greg lamented.

"'Less he's got access to God's treasury, I think not," Gilbert said.

"Here you go." Dalton pulled a half-dollar coin from his pocket and dropped it into Greg's palm. "Took a few banknotes off him after he went down. Sorry for the inconvenience."

"Well, thank you, Dalton. Not necessary, but much appreciated." Greg pocketed the coin. "Guess we can afford that new rifle today after all, huh John?"

"Got that right. And we'll have money leftover to buy Dalton a peppermint stick."

"That's kind of you, but—"

"No, no. We insist. After such an act of decency, you deserve a little treat. On top of that, you took out Tommy Roebuck, a favor for which the whole town should be lickin' your boots."

"Well, I appreciate it, John."

"Now what's this I hear 'bout you and Mr. Warren's daughter last night?" Gilbert asked.

Dalton smirked, shook his head. "Now *that's* a good story."

He recounted the tale of meeting her at lunch, how she'd approached him outside the Imperial, and then ended with him jumping out of his own window to escape Warren and his men.

When their laughter finally calmed, John piped up. "So Dalton, tell me—how's she look with nothin' on? I've always wondered that."

Gilbert nodded, and Greg looked like he might start drooling.

Dalton's eyebrows went up. With Camille's reputation already at stake, Dalton saw no reason to further entertain three half-witted towns-folk with such illicit details at her expense. Telling his side of things was one thing, but a lady's honor was something else entirely. "Um… well, I don't think it's very polite to—"

The chimes at the mercantile door jingled, and the same Indian warrior from the other day walked in with a stack of pelts draped over his shoulder. He headed straight to the counter and spread them out for Gilbert to see.

The Indian stood almost Dalton's height, wearing buckskin trousers and bare-chested from the waist up. His face, his strong arms, and his lean, toned torso were all cast in a regal shade of dark bronze.

Dalton expected to see tattoos or war paint, but saw neither. Long black hair flowed over his shoulders except for an occasional thin braid decorated with beads and leather.

The rifle slung over the Indian's shoulder reminded Dalton of Tommy's old pistol leftover from the war of 1812. He guessed the Indi-an's gun came from a similar vintage. The black sidearm holstered on his hip looked newer, probably made around the same time as Dalton's Colts, though not nearly as nice in quality.

"What do *you* want?" Gilbert folded his arms and didn't move from his place behind the counter.

"Trade," the Indian said. "These good hides."

Gilbert wrinkled his nose. "That's the same trash you brought in the other day, isn't it?"

The Indian shook his head. "Good hides. Not trash."

"Didn't I tell you not to come back? I don't want your stinkin' dog pelts."

The Indian shook his head. "They no stink. Good hides. Not all dog. Some rabbit, wildcat, wild pig leather. Very good."

"I don't care." Gilbert rounded the counter, but not to examine the pelts. "Now you get out of here before I *throw* you out."

The Indian shook his head again. "No, we trade. Good hides."

"Didn't you hear the man?" Dalton heard himself say. "He said *get out.*"

The Indian stared at him for a moment, then gestured to the pelts. "No, this a good trade."

Dalton didn't know why he spat in the Indian's face, but he did it anyway. Perhaps he wanted to reinforce his newfound popularity with the halfwits, or maybe it was to assert the white man's dominance over Indians on the whole. Maybe he didn't have a reason.

What did it matter anyway? The Indian was only an Indian, a soulless savage.

But if that were true, why did Dalton feel the chasm inside his soul widening?

The Indian's muscles tightened. Instead of wiping off his face, he reached for his sidearm.

♠ ♥ CHAPTER 8 ♦ ♣

Dalton's Colts ratcheted up to the Indian's chin and turned him to stone. The Indian's revolver hadn't even made it out of his holster.

"What are you thinking?" Dalton asked in a calm, confident voice. All traces of his guilt had vanished in the threat of real danger. He leaned close to the Indian's face. "You wanna die? Is that it?"

The Indian slowly shook his head, but his brown hawk eyes burned with wrath.

"I'd blow your head off right here if we weren't inside this shop. The only thing keeping you from meeting your Maker is the blood in your body. I don't want poor Gilbert to have to clean your brains off the floor."

The Indian didn't move. His nose also resembled a hawk's, turned down slightly, and he had a statue's chiseled cheekbones. Not bad-looking, overall. The women in his tribe probably all wanted him.

But in the end, he was still a savage. Lawless, godless, and stupid.

"Boys," Dalton said. "Grab him."

The Indian reeled back, but when the hammers on Dalton's pistols clicked back, he stopped.

"Don't move," Dalton warned. "I *will* shoot you if I have to."

John and Greg grabbed the Indian by his arms and held him tight.

A tinge of guilt filtered back into Dalton's gut, but he washed it away with fervor. He was building his reputation yet again by keeping the town free of outside influences. Maybe this could be his new purpose—preventing undesirables from making their way into Spider's Rock.

If so, it would begin here with a definitive message for this Indian to take back to his heathen tribe.

"Here's a little reminder not to come back in here." Dalton holstered his pistols and threw a hard punch into the Indian's gut. The Indian keeled over and wheezed. "Alright, toss him out. Gilbert, make sure he gets his stinking pelts too."

The brothers hauled the Indian to the door then literally heaved him out of the shop and onto the dry dirt street. The pelts soon followed, and the Indian gathered them up with disdain on his tan face. He recovered his footing and his pelts, glared at Dalton, then stormed away without looking back again.

"Well, he ain't comin' back." John hiked his pants up an inch.

"Got that right," Gilbert said.

John patted Dalton on the shoulder. "Way to show those Injuns who's boss 'round here."

"Thanks." Dalton watched the Indian mount a nearby white stallion with brown patches.

As the Indian galloped away, Dalton's stomach tinged with guilt, but he smothered it like he had before. He'd done the right thing. After all, if one of them saw fit to come to town, more of them might get the nerve to do the same. Then it would be that much harder to clean them out.

Dalton turned to Gilbert. "He won't bother you anymore."

The window through which Dalton had crawled to escape Warren and his thugs was still open, so he entered his old room at the parsonage that way. He had hoped to avoid his uncle, but as he began collecting some of his personal items, Reverend McCarroll's hulking frame appeared in the doorway as if he'd been waiting there all along.

At the sight of him, Dalton sighed.

"Good to see you too." Reverend McCarroll leaned against the door-frame with his arms folded.

He would expect an apology, and after two months out here and everything that had transpired, Dalton had decided to just give it to him right at the beginning from now on.

"Uncle Bill, I'm sorry about last night, but—"

"Save it for the manure pile. We both know you're only sorry you got caught."

Dalton shrugged. "Can't argue with that. I'm living at the Imperial until I find something more permanent. I'm just collecting my things, and then I'll be out of your way, out of your life. Oh, and I won't be back to church to play on Sunday mornings for you either."

Reverend McCarroll shook his head. "You're making a mistake, Dalton. I don't want you to leave."

"It's not your choice anymore." Dalton coughed.

Reverend McCarroll raised an eyebrow and folded his arms. "And who's gonna look after you when you're sick?"

Dalton coughed again. "I'll survive. And besides, if I need help, I can have one of the girls at the saloon fetch some."

"I don't like this. You're not ready for this kind of responsibility."

"*That's* why I'm leaving. You keep trying to dictate my every move. I might as well be your prisoner. I'm done with it."

Reverend McCarroll hesitated, and gave a small nod. "I'm sorry, Dalton. I'm not trying to lord over you. I'm just concerned for your wellbeing, for your soul."

Dalton raised his eyebrow. Why the kind tone? Was his uncle genuinely concerned?

It didn't matter. It was too late. If he'd really cared, his uncle would've treated him differently.

Dalton didn't need him. All he needed was his freedom, his Colts, and his right hand for shooting them. He could handle himself.

Dalton shoved his few belongings into a sack and slung it over his shoulder. "You had your chance. I'm on my own now, and that's the way I want it. Now are you gonna move aside and let me out, or do I have to climb out the window again?"

Reverend McCarroll sighed but stepped aside, and Dalton brushed past him.

Monday nights at the Imperial never got as busy or as exciting as on the weekends. Dalton played some tunes and some poker, and he consumed extra whiskey to pass the time and drown his boredom. He'd just about decided to turn in for the night when the saloon doors swung open and smacked against the inside wall.

Everyone in the Imperial turned toward the newcomers, a pack of five grubby bandits: two Mexicans, two whites, and one Negro. They stayed close together and headed for the bar with one of the Mexicans in the lead.

"Tequila?" he asked.

Randolph scowled at them but nodded and pulled out a glass. He filled it with golden liquid from a bottle with a green label.

The Mexican snatched the bottle from Randolph's hand and took a huge swig. As Randolph began to protest, the Mexican dropped a gold nugget half the size of a man's fist on the bar. It disappeared into Randolph's hand as quickly as it had appeared, and Randolph's protests ceased.

As if on cue, Randolph took out another bottle of the same stuff and set it on top of the bar. The other four men swarmed over, and they gulped down shot after shot of the booze amid a loud conversation, a rough mixture of Spanish and English.

Dalton didn't like it. He'd never seen these five men before, and something about them felt... off. Dalton usually considered himself to be a good judge of character, and none of these men would've ranked as people he'd want to associate with.

He continued plunking notes on the piano with his right hand, but he reached for one of his Colts with his left. His fingers tapped the ivory grip, then they retracted. It was still in its holster in case he needed it. Part of him hoped he wouldn't need to draw his guns, but another part of him—a hungry, ravenous part—hoped he would.

As Dalton resumed his piano playing, Vanessa walked in through the door connecting to the inn side of the Imperial, decked out in a red dress trimmed with black lace. A red-and-black bow in her curly blonde hair topped off the ensemble.

She headed straight for the five men, a sheep walking into the middle of a pack of wolves at play, and she engaged them in some small talk. The Mexican who'd led the others inside seemed especially interested.

"What's your name, handsome?" Vanessa asked him.

Dalton coughed to keep from scoffing. Maybe she'd said it because she knew Dalton was sitting there and she was still mad about their exchange the night before, but in no lifetime could the Mexican pass as "handsome," not by anyone's measuring stick.

In fact, someone might've *beaten* the Mexican with that measuring stick. It would explain why he was so ugly.

"Alejandro Zamora," the Mexican replied. "But everyone calls me '*el Diablo*.'"

His companions laughed, but Zamora didn't.

"And what does that mean?" Vanessa asked.

"'The Devil.'" Zamora grinned.

"How'd you get such a *ferocious* name?" She caressed his arm with her fingers.

"I killed some people," he said.

His buddies let out more raucous laughter, but Zamora's hard, stoic face told Dalton that he wasn't just boasting.

Vanessa's eyebrows went up. "My, my. For what reason, may I ask?"

"They had something I wanted. They didn't give it to me, so I killed them and took it anyway." Zamora took another swig from his bottle. "That's what I do. I take what I want."

His arm curled around Vanessa, and his hand migrated to her hips. He gave her buttocks a firm squeeze. She jumped, and Zamora laughed.

"How very nice." Vanessa's face reddened. Maybe she'd finally realized what she'd gotten herself into. "Well, it's been a *pleasure*, gentlemen, but I must be going."

When she tried to escape Zamora's grasp, he pulled her close again. "Why so soon? You haven't even told us your name, right?"

She recoiled again, her hands pushing on his chest. "I don't think it matters anymore. You boys have a good night."

Zamora clamped down on her wrist and pulled her back. "Your name?"

Dalton saw her swallow hard, even from across the room.

Well, she could handle herself. She'd made that perfectly clear last night.

"Vanessa. Vanessa Clark."

"Vanessa. It's a beautiful name, right?" Zamora's fingers played with her curls. "You remember what I said about those people I killed? I *take* what I want."

His hand drifted down her neck, toward her chest.

SLAP.

It resounded throughout the Imperial like a gunshot. Vanessa's eyes widened as if she couldn't be sure she'd just done what she'd done.

Zamora reeled back from her slap and released her... at first. Then, his reddened face twisted into an even uglier visage of rage, and he snatched her arm again as she tried to get away.

He returned the slap with one of his own, a blow that would've knocked a grown man off his feet. Vanessa dropped to the floor, stunned.

Red fire seized the corners of Dalton's vision. He arched his eyebrows, and his eyes flared wide open. His entire world centered on one man. His fingers abandoned the piano keys mid-song and he stormed toward Zamora, his fists harder than Randolph's oak bar.

♠ ♥ CHAPTER 9 ♦ ♣

"*P uta*." Zamora stood over Vanessa with a twisted snarl on his face, so focused on her that he didn't see Dalton's first punch coming. Dalton landed two more blows to his face and another to his gut before Zamora's men grabbed him from behind.

Dalton wrenched his body, faced the bar, and pushed off of it with his feet. The three of them crashed into an empty table and chairs, and the bandits lost their grip on him.

Dalton sprang up, grabbed one of the chairs, and slammed it down on the nearest bandit so hard that it splintered upon impact. He followed with a ferocious kick to the other, and then something crashed into the back of his head.

Pieces of glass and splashes of tequila showered over him. Pain ripped through his head, and he struggled to stay conscious. The strong odor of the alcohol kept him awake, but only barely.

He whirled around, his vision now an erratic dance, and threw a punch at the first target he saw—the other Mexican, a stocky man with a face almost as ugly as Zamora's. The Mexican took the blow on his jaw, and the small of his back hit the bar's edge as he teetered backward.

In the corner of his eye, Dalton saw Vanessa scampering away. She took cover behind a table near the far end of the bar. Good.

A knife flashed in the other white man's hand. He slashed, but Dalton blocked the man's wrist with his forearm then delivered a stunning uppercut to the man's chin.

Something clunked behind him. Instinct threw his elbow back, and it jammed into the fat Mexican's face, who promptly slumped to the floor.

Dalton couldn't believe his luck. He was taking on five men at once —and he was winning. Now he just had to make sure they stayed down.

But as Dalton swiveled back, Zamora's enraged, bloody face filled his view. He swung something at Dalton's head, and then everything went black.

The howl of a coyote woke Dalton.

His eyes burned with sand, and he felt the coarse stuff under his fingers and in his hair. Everything was still dark, except for millions of little white dots flickering in his vision, and one large white blur off to his right. It registered in his mind as the clear night sky.

Where am I?

A dull pain throbbed in his head. His limbs ached. His face was sore. Zamora's men had probably beaten him to a pulp. It sure felt that way. And then…

Had they just dumped him in the desert?

A dark form blotted out the moon. Dalton's vision focused, and he recognized Zamora standing over him. His buddies stood just behind him, two on each side, four specters haunting the cool Arizona desert.

"Welcome back, amigo," Zamora said.

A silver pistol gleamed in his hand.

Dalton reached for his Colt, but his right hand found only an empty holster. His left hand groped for the other but also found nothing. He cursed under his breath.

Why hadn't he just blown Zamora away in the first place? He'd done worse for less. Tommy Roebuck had only cheated at a card game. Zamora deserved death ten times over for hitting Vanessa.

Too late now.

Zamora waved Dalton's Colt in his right hand then tapped the holster on his left hip, which held the other. "Looking for something?"

"I don't suppose you'd consider giving one of those back so I could shoot you and your friends, would you?" When he spoke, Dalton's jaw hurt, too.

Zamora laughed, along with his friends. "No, amigo. But if you like, I'd be happy to give you back some of your bullets."

"Won't do me much good without the gun," Dalton said.

"I'm counting on it." Zamora smiled a jagged, yellow smile. He raised Dalton's pistol, cocked the hammer, and fired. The crack echoed off nearby mesas and rock formations.

Instinct raised Dalton's right arm to shield his face. A red-hot poker seared through his skin and burned the flesh in his forearm from the inside out. He yelped, and warm blood trickled from the fresh bullet hole.

Another gunshot sounded, and the sensation in Dalton's arm plunged into his stomach. He clutched his gut, and gasped, then curled into the fetal position. Hot sticky liquid oozed from the wound.

Oh, God… I'm gonna die out here.

"Leave him for the coyotes," Zamora said.

When Dalton finally summoned the strength to look back at Zamora, all he saw was a plume of fire from the pistol.

A sharp pain knifed through his head—then nothing.

♠ ♥ CHAPTER 10 ♦ ♣

Dalton's eyes cracked open. The Arizona desert had been submerged underwater. He breathed the liquid but somehow didn't drown.

Pain flared in his gut, his head, and his arm. A coyote howled, not far away. Something fell off his leg when he moved and skittered away.

Above, the blurred stars and moon faded to darkness again, and the sounds went with them.

A desert sunrise. Pink sky, tinted with red and orange clouds. Blue mountains shrouded in powdery mist. A dog licked Dalton's forehead.

When Dalton moaned, the coyote bounded away, followed by two other mutts, their tails wagging behind them.

The sun, a white ball of light hovering just over the mountains, fizzled away as Dalton's eyes pinched shut again.

Whispers. Giggles. Blinding light. Had he somehow made it to Heaven?

If so, why did everything still hurt so bad? Were the angels laughing at him?

Dalton squinted, thwarted by the white circle burning his eyes. He turned his throbbing head to the side and blinked to clear his blurred vision.

A brown-faced cherub looked down at him.

It figured that the angels in Heaven would look like Indians. Now they'd never let him in, especially after his confrontation at the mercantile. The cherub's brown eyes flashed with lightning, and then he vanished.

Dalton's eyelids weighed as much as a horse. They pulled shut and blocked out the luminescence above. Pain and darkness consumed him again.

The same fire still flared in the sky when Dalton next opened his eyes, but this time, a shadow blocked it out. Dalton's body convulsed, and he could feel fresh blood seeping from his wounds.

The shadow moved closer, a demon come to drag Dalton's miserable soul to Hell.

He turned away. He wanted to scream, to beg for mercy, but fear seized his throat.

More demons stood around him. Brown skin, feathers, leather. Guns, bows, arrows, moccasins. Indian demons bent on avenging themselves upon him for his many sins.

When he looked back, Dalton's gaze locked on the central demon's sharp eyes—two dark orbs, full of fury yet twisted with delight. He recognized the demon's hawk-like nose, solid jaw and cheekbones, and his long black hair, some of it braided.

Not a demon—the Indian from the mercantile.

Dalton moaned. This was it. This was the end.

The Indian slowly pulled a scalping knife from a sheath on his belt. A conniving smile cracked his bronze face.

Cool water trickled from a wet cloth on Dalton's forehead down to his neck. Gentle fingers caressed his face, then worked off his soiled clothes.

When Dalton opened his eyes, the bronze angel attending him smiled and blushed. She had long, shiny black hair and soft features. Her eyes, dark as a raven, exuded comfort.

To Dalton's dismay, she vanished through a portal of light, replaced by two larger forms.

One of them had long, silver hair and a wrinkled face like worn leather. His attire resembled that of a jester from a Shakespearean play Dalton had seen back east, only with an Indian flair.

The other man towered over him and wore two feathers in his black hair. A necklace made of curled talons from some animal hung around his neck.

They mumbled nonsense as Dalton struggled to stay conscious, but he finally succumbed to the darkness that encroached in his vision.

Light tore Dalton from his dreams of the angel tending to him. His eyes opened to a familiar blur like he was underwater. He blinked hard several times, and the excess tears squeezed out of his eyes.

"Good morning," rumbled a deep voice.

Dalton lifted his head, which he realized was bandaged, and saw the man with the two eagle feathers in his hair and the gaudy talon necklace. Age lines and wrinkles marred his otherwise handsome face, and he had dark hawk eyes like the Indian from the mercantile. Same hooked nose, too. He sat on a straw mat across the room from Dalton.

But they weren't in a room—it looked more like the inside of a beast, or maybe an oddly shaped tree. The remnants of a fire smoldered near Dalton's bare feet, and thin lines of smoke drifted up and out the beast's mouth directly overhead.

"You are inside a wickiup. We make them out of tall grass and yucca plant stalks. Sufficient to keep the sun out during the day and to keep most of the heat from the fire inside at night." The old Indian spoke the English words with a heavy accent.

"Where am I?" Dalton asked. "I mean aside from inside a... a..."

"A wickiup," the old man said again. "You are closer to the Mexican border than you are to that town you came from, Spider's Rock."

"How do you know where I came from?"

"I found a slip of paper in your pocket from Warren's Mercantile in Spider's Rock."

Dalton rubbed his eyes with his left hand—his good hand—and blinked a few times. It still hurt to move, so he didn't do much more of it. "You're an Indian?"

Dumb question. Of course he was.

"We are *Dine*, 'the people,' but the white man knows us as Apache." The old man touched his forehead with his hand. "Excuse me. Where are my manners? I am Beduiat, Chief of the Chihenne band of the Chiricahua Apache."

Dalton couldn't fathom how he'd survived his encounter with Zamora and his men. They'd shot him three times, including once in his head. He should be buzzard fodder by now. "How...?"

"You must rest," Chief Beduiat said. "You have many questions, but you have not fully recovered from your wounds. I estimate it will be quite some time before you are well enough to move around. For now, please go to sleep. We will bring you food and water in a few hours."

Dalton couldn't refuse. His body and mind agreed, and his will complied. He laid his head back again, still focused on Chief Beduiat. All he could say was, "Thank you."

The last thing he saw was Chief Beduiat nodding, a trace of a smile on his tan face, then Dalton closed his eyes once more.

Late that night, Dalton awakened to a rustling sound. The fire in the wickiup burned with small flames, just enough to keep his feet warm, and the blankets draped over him handled the rest.

Those flames illuminated the form of a tall man standing in the entrance. Dalton recognized his shape first, then his face.

The Indian from the mercantile.

He glared at Dalton with piercing hawk eyes, alive with the reflection of the fire, but when Dalton made eye contact with him, the Indian slipped back into the night.

More than a week passed before Dalton could stand again, and even then, the dull pain in his gut sprouted long porcupine needles when he moved. All the while, the Apaches tended to him, brought him food and water, and cleaned and dressed his wounds.

Within another week, his right arm had healed, but his hand still functioned poorly. When he tried to make a fist, his hand wouldn't close all the way, and a sharp pinch flared inside his forearm.

The next week, he noticed no measurable progress in his hand's functionality, even as the wounds in his stomach and on his head healed to scars.

Dalton had only a basic understanding of human anatomy—his expertise didn't extend much further than killing men and entertaining women—so he didn't know exactly what was going on with his hand.

Perhaps the bullet had severed tendons in his forearm that connected to his hand? Or maybe a bone was broken somewhere deep inside that prevented his hand from functioning properly?

All he knew for sure was that it didn't work, and if it didn't work, he probably couldn't play the piano anymore, and he certainly couldn't hold a gun.

The thought of his right hand—his dominant hand—being rendered useless for the rest of his life made him ache more than the bullet in his gut. He could still shoot with his left hand, but not nearly as well. He certainly couldn't count on defending himself with his left hand in a showdown.

What did that mean for his future? Did he have any future left after what had happened to him?

The more he thought about it, the more it depressed his mood. Dalton couldn't do anything about it now except to try to rest and heal, so he shifted the focus of his thoughts to something more pleasant.

To her.

He'd seen the angel several more times since he'd been recovering.

He'd learned she was Chief Beduiat's daughter, named Nizhoni. It came as no surprise to Dalton that her name literally meant "beautiful," but in the Navajo language, not Apache.

"The Navajo are our neighbors to the north, our brothers," Chief Beduiat had said.

Dalton didn't need an explanation. Her name could have been Chinese for all he cared. He recalled Shakespeare, Juliet's line, *"What's in a name? That which we call a rose by any other name would smell as sweet."*

And Nizhoni was indeed a rose. A desert rose—splendor amid the desolate wasteland of the Arizona territory.

Every time Dalton laid eyes on her, his heart began to beat a little faster, and the pain in his stomach sweetened to excitement. Whenever their eyes locked, she would blush and fight off a smile.

The Indian from the mercantile had appeared several times as well, mostly with Chief Beduiat. The Chief introduced him as his son, also named Beduiat, then added that most white men called him Victorio, a name which he'd proudly embraced as his own.

Dalton couldn't blame Victorio for his hateful glares. In light of the mercantile incident, Dalton was just glad to be alive. Victorio could have killed him at any point over the last few weeks, but, inexplicably, he'd let Dalton live.

The fact that Dalton still lived only seemed to sour Victorio's mood ever more. Most of the time, Victorio looked ready to kill him anyway, but some unseen reservation stayed his hands.

Today, Dalton's first steps awakened the porcupine in his gut again, but in recent days, he'd felt strength beginning to return to his body. Coupled with anxiousness at being all but bedridden for the last few weeks, Dalton was eager to get moving again.

As Dalton stood to stretch his legs, Chief Beduiat walked into the wickiup, followed by Victorio, who wore the same cold expression as always.

"Good morning, Dalton."

"Morning, Chief Beduiat." He fixed his gaze on Victorio and hoped he could convey his sincerest remorse through his eyes. "Victorio."

He got no response but the same icy stare.

"How do you feel today?" Chief Beduiat asked.

"Better." Dalton managed a small smile. "My arm feels almost healed. My gut still hurts, but only when I twist or bend, and the cut on my head has healed."

"You have a big scar there."

"I bet I do." Dalton touched it with his fingers. It ran from just above his right eyebrow on a diagonal line toward his hairline, but it tapered off before then. "That bandit must've been drunk. He stole my own guns and used 'em against me. I know exactly how accurate they are."

Chief Beduiat smiled. "*Usen* has shown you favor."

"*Usen?*" Dalton asked.

"You would call him 'God.' He is the Giver of Life. The Source of all power."

Dalton sighed. Even out here, lost somewhere in the desert, he couldn't escape talk of God. "And here I thought it was just dumb luck."

Chief Beduiat squinted at Dalton. "Instead of delivering a fatal blow, the bandit shot you in the arm when you held it up to shield your head. Dumb luck?"

Dalton had already explained what had happened to Beduiat in a previous conversation. He nodded. "Absolutely."

"He shot you in the stomach, but the shot was not fatal. Still dumb luck?"

"Yeah," Dalton said.

"Then he shot you in the head, but because he was drunk, the bullet only grazed you. Dumb luck?"

"Yes." Dalton's voice didn't sound nearly as firm as it had just a moment earlier.

"And I suppose it was dumb luck that you survived a long, cold night in the vast desert, were found by Apache children, and lasted long enough until they brought back warriors who took you to our camp.

"Dumb luck that you survived the move, the stomach injury, the loss of blood, and the recovery. Dumb luck that none of your wounds became infected, even after we removed the bullets. Dumb luck that you are even here at all." Chief Beduiat tilted his head slightly. "Yes?"

Dalton kept silent. He began to wonder if Chief Beduiat and his uncle were sharing notes for their lectures.

"That is enough 'dumb luck' for every prospector, gambler, and gunfighter within 200 miles, Dalton." Chief Beduiat's cunning smile widened. "You are the luckiest man I know."

Dalton clenched his teeth. Chief Beduiat had a point, but Dalton wouldn't give in quite so soon. "I find it easier to believe than divine intervention."

"We choose to believe what we want, do we not?"

"It goes both ways, Chief," Dalton said.

Chief Beduiat's countenance leveled out, but his smile remained, albeit smaller, simpler. "I agree completely."

Something about Chief Beduiat's expression made Dalton regret his tone.

"Now Dalton, I understand you've asked for a revolver," Chief Beduiat continued. "May I ask for what purpose?"

"I'd like to try to fire it with my right hand," Dalton said. "I have to know if I'll be able to shoot again, or if I can even grip it with my right hand. It was... it was something I was good at before... all of this. I need to know what I've lost and if I can ever get it back."

"Very well. But know that even though a warrior is less without his weapon, he is still a warrior all the same." Chief Beduiat looked Dalton over. "The gun will not be loaded. Fair enough?"

That part didn't make any difference to Dalton. He wasn't about to use it on his Apache saviors, and he had no desire to use it on himself, either, but if it made Chief Beduiat feel better, then it was fine. "Sure."

Chief Beduiat nodded to Victorio, who removed his old black pistol from its holster, emptied the cartridges into his other hand, and then gave it to Dalton. That old familiar loathing continued to smolder in his dark eyes.

Dalton strapped on his belt and holsters with difficulty—the fingers on his right hand refused to perform as they should. Not a good sign. He slid the pistol into the holster on the right side and faced away from Chief Beduiat and Victorio.

In his mind, Dalton visualized himself stripping the gun from the holster, his thumb pulling back the hammer, pointing it at a target, and then squeezing the trigger while it was still at his hip, all in one swift motion.

The gun barrel would plume with heat and spew a bullet into the target, dead center. Then the gun would slip back into his holster just as quickly as he'd drawn it. The whole exchange, something he'd practiced for more than a decade, long before he ever came out west, would take no more than two seconds.

Dalton's eyes opened. He reached for the gun, his arm remembering the motion. His elbow bent, he angled his wrist and—nothing. Not even the click of the empty gun. His fingers had failed to grasp the weapon's handle.

Instead, raw pain stretched from the tips of his fingers to his elbow, and a pinching sensation wracked his tendons. Dalton gripped his right hand with his left and winced, drawing a sharp breath of air through his gritted teeth.

He couldn't do it. His greatest strength—his speed and accuracy at the quick draw—was gone. Destroyed by a bullet from his own gun.

Maybe forever.

Dalton cursed his stupidity. He should've known better than to pick a fight with five men.

"I... can't do it," he said, his voice just above a whisper. "My hand can't grip it."

"I am sorry, Dalton," Chief Beduiat said.

Dalton noticed a faint smirk on Victorio's face. It ignited his sorrow to anger. He refused to appear any weaker than he had to in front of Victorio.

He reached across with his left hand and switched the gun to the holster on his left side. He took a deep breath and steadied himself.

Then Dalton performed a sloppy draw with his left hand, a second slower and probably nowhere near as accurate as his right hand would've been.

"It's not pretty, but I suppose I could eventually learn to be as good with my left." Dalton added, "Maybe."

"I had hoped you would abhor violence after such an experience," Chief Beduiat said.

"Violence for its own sake is one thing, but self-defense is quite another."

"I understand. Victorio has told me exactly how dangerous your town can be."

Dalton froze. His gaze bounced between Chief Beduiat and Victorio as he waited for a lecture. Lord knew he certainly deserved it for once.

It never came.

"I am glad your health is improving. If you can, please join us for dinner this evening in my wickiup. It is large enough to accommodate at least one extra person, if not an extra family."

Dalton nodded. "Thank you, Chief Beduiat. I'm looking forward to it." He realized he was still holding Victorio's pistol. He extended the gun toward him. "Almost forgot. Here."

"Keep it." Victorio's jaw tensed. "I'll get a new one soon enough."

Victorio's first words to him since the incident at the mercantile sounded exactly as Dalton imagined they would: saturated with hurt, anger, and vengeance.

"Thank you," Dalton said. He meant "I'm sorry," but Victorio didn't seem to get the message. Or he was deliberately ignoring Dalton's attempts at humility.

Or Dalton was avoiding having to give him an actual apology.

Still, as Chief Beduiat and Victorio walked out of the wickiup, Dalton realized he'd been dead wrong about the Indians. They weren't mindless savages after all.

That night after dinner, Dalton woke up to Nizhoni, the Chief's daughter, changing his bandages. As always, when his eyes found hers, she blushed and broke eye contact.

Dalton peeked over her shoulder, wary of her father, but more wary of Victorio. Seeing no one, he spoke to her.

"Nizhoni?" He hoped he was pronouncing her name correctly. He thought it sounded like how Chief Beduiat had said it.

She looked at him, her eyes wide, and she blushed again.

"You're beautiful." Dalton wondered if she understood English as well as the rest of her family seemed to. When her expression didn't change, he decided she must not. "I think I'm in love with you."

He got nothing but a blank stare, though her cheeks stayed red. He wished he spoke Apache.

Oh, well. If he spoke his mind and she didn't understand it, perhaps that was for the best, but it wouldn't keep him from trying.

"One look at you, and the rest of the world fades away," Dalton said. "Flowers spring up in your footsteps, and the sunlight follows you as you walk. Every time our eyes meet, you send fire shooting through my veins."

Nizhoni showed no sign of comprehending his words.

Dalton smiled. How could he not? Slowly, he reached out to her with his good hand.

She recoiled at first, then she went still. Her face flushed, and fear flickered in her eyes.

"It's okay." Dalton pulled his hand back a bit, then he extended it again, palm-up. "I won't hurt you."

She eyed him but this time didn't move as he reached for her anew.

He stroked her soft bronze cheek, his fingertips as light as feathers. The sensation of it sparked an unbridled joy and happiness in Dalton's chest, the likes of which he'd never felt before. He had found a language they both spoke, both understood.

Nizhoni closed her eyes, and the tension in her face dissipated. She leaned into Dalton's caress and cupped the back of his hand with her own. Her mouth opened, and she exhaled a delicate sigh.

"*Nizhoni*," a deep voice thundered.

Dalton's hand snapped back to his side. Nizhoni whirled around, her black hair pinwheeling behind her.

Victorio stood in the wickiup's entrance.

68

Victorio's jaw hardened, and the muscles in his arms tightened as he clenched his fists.

A blacksmith hammered inside Dalton's chest at the sight of the primal rage ignited in Victorio's eyes. He swallowed the lump in his throat. Had he finally pushed too far?

Nizhoni abandoned her bandages, stood up, and left, her head down. Victorio let her pass, never once removing his gaze from Dalton.

They stared at each other for an eternity, neither of them moving or speaking. Then Victorio receded into the darkness.

Dalton sat in the wickiup alone again, thankful that his pounding heart meant he was still alive.

Within another two weeks, Dalton began to move around the camp on his own. He'd interacted with more of the tribe than just Chief Beduiat's family and even started picking up some of the Apache language.

A kindhearted old man took it upon himself to teach Dalton how to build his own wickiup, a skill Chief Beduiat said was essential to the Apaches' survival in extreme desert heat.

Dalton's first attempt fell down at the slightest Arizona breeze, but after a few more lessons, a lot of frustration, and having learned a few Apache words—some of them curses—he got one to stand up. Sure, the wickiup looked awkward and leaned to one side, but he'd done it.

The old Apache patted his shoulder and smiled.

The next day, Chief Beduiat put Dalton to work. The Apache women had long-since dug irrigation ditches to support the growth of corn, a staple in the tribe's diet, and they seemed pleased to have a strong young man to help with some of the more labor-intensive farming.

The pain in his stomach had dulled to almost nothing, but every now and then it would pinch, usually whenever he moved the wrong way, but it didn't stop him from doing his fair share of work. Given that they'd saved his life, he owed them that much, at least.

Early in his recovery, he'd been anxious to return to Spider's Rock. Upon experiencing the kindness from the Apaches, he'd begun to rethink that idea entirely. Their life was simpler in most ways yet surprisingly more fulfilling. The longer he'd stayed, the fewer reasons he could conjure to leave.

The whole day, Dalton kept scanning the camp for Nizhoni, but he couldn't find her anywhere. Then, as the hot sun finally sank toward the horizon, Dalton finally saw her preparing some deer meat that the warriors—led by Victorio—had brought back from the day's hunt.

He savored her form, especially how her buckskin skirt hugged her strong thighs. Matching moccasin boots stretched up to her knees so that only a bit of the rich bronze skin on her legs showed.

Dalton's heart thumped, and he realized the sweat on his forehead wasn't just from the dry desert heat anymore. He took a deep breath and, after she wouldn't make eye contact with him, continued working until the sun went down.

As more time went by, Dalton performed any task that Chief Beduiat asked of him. He'd not only given Dalton his life back but also allowed him to stay with them as a long-term guest.

And when Dalton expressed his desire to remain with them rather than going back to Spider's Rock, Chief Beduiat honored his request and instated him as a full member of the tribe.

Dalton owed him for that and so much more, and he always would.

At the close of every day, Dalton set out to a secluded spot at the base of a nearby mountain. He'd found a path that overlooked the valley where the Apaches had camped and followed it until a large boulder blocked the path.

There, Dalton set up his targets—anything from old tin cans to sun-bleached deer skulls leftover from the warriors' hunts—and took aim with Victorio's old revolver in his left hand.

Dalton never wanted for ammunition. Chief Beduiat made sure Victorio or another warrior traded for it at least once a week. Dalton couldn't ever bring himself to go on his own.

He didn't want anything to do with Spider's Rock anymore. If he could help it, he'd never go back. It was as dead to him as he was dead to it, and to all the people there.

Dalton sometimes practiced for hours at a time, never shooting fewer than fifty rounds a day. After a few weeks, he could draw the pistol with his left hand almost as fast as he'd done with his right, and after several more weeks, he'd grown nearly as accurate.

One day, Chief Beduiat came with him on the mountain path, and Dalton showed him the progress he'd made. The pistol jumped from the holster into his left hand and then roared with six quick shots. Four empty tin cans and an old iron mug went flying, and a dried deer skull shattered.

"Very impressive, Dalton," Chief Beduiat said.

"Thank you, Chief."

"I think you are ready."

Dalton looked at him. "Ready for what?"

Chief Beduiat smiled. "Ready to hunt with the warriors."

Dalton's eyebrows rose. That seemed like a good way for him to "accidentally" get killed.

"You have learned enough of our language to get by on a daily basis, you are well enough to ride a horse, and, without question, you are capable of firing a gun."

It didn't sit right with Dalton, but whether that was just his nerves or an actual, legitimate fear, he couldn't say.

He could, however, envision a number of ways Victorio could kill him and make it look like an accident, and his fellow warriors would doubtless cover for him. If they knew what Dalton had done to Victorio back at the mercantile in Spider's Rock, they might even help him do it.

Dalton hesitated. "I don't know…"

"Tomorrow you will go with Victorio and the other warriors." Chief Beduiat put his hand on Dalton's shoulder. "May you have a good hunt."

The last time Dalton had hunted, his other uncle, Roy, had taken him into a dense, wooded forest a day's ride north of New York City. That was nearly ten years ago, and all he'd seen were squirrels. All day long, they'd chattered away, and as an adolescent boy with a vivid imagination, he'd assumed they were constantly warning the deer to stay away.

So when Dalton managed to bring down a young stag in the Arizona desert with only two shots from Victorio's old pistol, he had to smile.

Bagging the deer, however, was the only part of the hunt he found pleasant. Every time he made eye contact with Victorio, Dalton got nothing but the same vengeful stare he'd grown accustomed to over the last several months.

As dusk began to settle across the desert, Victorio ordered the rest of warriors to gallop ahead, leaving Victorio and Dalton alone, riding side-by-side. The idea of it worried Dalton at first, but perhaps this was his opportunity to make amends.

"Victorio," he said. "I'm sorry about how I treated you back in the mercantile."

Victorio said nothing. He just continued riding, his gaze fixed on the horizon and the warriors who'd just ventured out of sight.

That didn't bode well for Dalton. He wondered if he should say more. Instead, he waited as they continued to ride along at a steady, gentle canter.

Finally, Dalton couldn't take it anymore. He leaned forward and peered at him. "Did you hear what I said? I said—"

Victorio's hand lashed out and dragged Dalton off his horse. The two men tumbled to the ground as the horses trotted away but stopped a few yards ahead.

Before Dalton realized it, Victorio sat on top of his chest, his fists full of Dalton's shirt, fire raging in his eyes. He spoke to Dalton in Apache.

"The only reason you still live is because my father *ordered* me not to kill you." Victorio's muscles tensed. Black hair cascaded over his shoulders and reached toward Dalton like tendrils yearning to choke the life from him.

Dalton didn't know how to respond, so he just repeated, "I'm sorry."

Hot breath from Victorio's nostrils blasted Dalton's face, followed by warm, gooey saliva.

Dalton clenched his eyes shut and wiped the stuff from his nose with his good hand. "I deserved that, and more."

"Like I said, I would kill you if not for my father." Victorio leaned even closer to Dalton and whispered in clear English, "And if you do not stay away from Nizhoni, I will kill you *anyway*."

Victorio's dark eyebrows lowered even farther. He pushed off of Dalton and headed for the horses. Rather than waiting for Dalton, Victorio mounted up, took the reins of Dalton's horse, and galloped away with it in tow, leaving Dalton alone in the desert.

Dalton pushed up to his feet and frowned. He'd deserved all of this, too. He wiped the rest of Victorio's spit from his face and brushed the desert dust off of his clothes.

"Well," he said aloud, "at least he didn't kill me."

Then he set out back toward the tribe on foot.

Despite Victorio's warnings, Dalton couldn't help but fall in love with Nizhoni. Their first touch haunted him every day, and it had kindled a need inside his heart that only she could meet.

Over the time he'd spent there, Nizhoni had demonstrated her interest as well, albeit in small, subtle ways. Oftentimes Dalton wondered if he wasn't just misinterpreting her behavior, but the sheer consistency of it had convinced him.

And there was no denying what he felt—what they both felt—in the moment they'd shared in the wickiup before Victorio had caught them.

He caught her staring at him almost every day. Her telltale blushing whenever he spoke to her or came within her vicinity was another indication of her feelings.

But most of all, the look in her dark eyes whenever their gazes met—there was no hiding it, and there was no faking what Dalton saw, either. She wanted him too, and he decided it was time to talk to Chief Beduiat.

"Thank you for seeing me." Dalton avoided eye contact with Chief Beduiat at first.

They sat inside Chief Beduiat's wickiup, alone with only the fire crackling before them. "Of course, Dalton. What is troubling you?"

Dalton hesitated. "I—I need to ask you something."

Chief Beduiat remained silent.

"I'd like to ask for your permission, your blessing, to—"

Victorio's hateful face filled Dalton's mind, and he second-guessed the wisdom of his request. But a competing image of Nizhoni's beauty quickly washed it away and gave him the courage to continue.

"—to court Nizhoni," Dalton finished.

Chief Beduiat drew in a long breath and let it out through his nose. He lowered his head, just breathing. When he finally looked up, Dalton was certain he'd say "no."

"I feared this might happen," he said. "My daughter is beautiful, the jewel of my eye. The last reminder I have of her mother, my wife. She is everything to me, Dalton. I must tell you that there is no man in this world, not one with whom I would entrust such a treasure."

Dalton's heart dropped to his knees. Disappointment stabbed his stomach worse than Zamora's bullet. If he couldn't be with her, then what did any of this matter?

"But I know that someday I must give her up," Chief Beduiat continued. "There are many warriors in this camp who are worthy of her. Why should I grant you a chance over them?"

Hope flooded Dalton's body. But what answer could he possibly give? He struggled. He tried not to show it as he formulated his answer. "I love her. I need her. She makes me want to be better than I am. When

I'm around her, I don't want to go back to all the drinking, all the carousing, all the killing that I've done. She's the only thing in my life worth living for."

Chief Beduiat raised an eyebrow. A grin teased his lips. After a moment of reflection, he said, "You may court her under the supervision of the tribe. You are not to touch her until you are married. *Dine* are a people of fidelity, and so shall my daughter be."

Dalton nodded, and his heart thumped with new life. "Anything you say."

"And if you do marry her, you must promise that you will never take her from her people, even upon her death. You cannot take her back to the white man's culture. You must stay here and live among us for the rest of your lives."

Dalton hadn't expected that condition, but he didn't find it unreasonable. After all, he had no life to return to anyway. "Agreed."

"And finally, you must care for her. You must meet her needs. You must protect her."

"I will." Dalton looked into Chief Beduiat's warm, dark eyes. "With my own life."

Chief Beduiat studied him. "Then you may court Nizhoni... if she agrees."

♠ ♥ CHAPTER 12 ♦ ♣

Dalton and Nizhoni sat at his spot on the mountain while Chief Beduiat's brother, his brother's wife, and Lozen, Nizhoni's younger sister, kept busy off in the distance. Dalton's command of the Apache language continued to improve every day, but he quickly learned that where Nizhoni was concerned, it didn't matter after all.

"You *know* English?" he asked.

She nodded, a tentative smile on her face. "I know enough."

"Enough to what?" Dalton eyed her. "Enough to understand what I said that night we were alone in the wickiup?"

Nizhoni's smile stretched wider, and she blushed. "Yes."

"You could have fooled me. You've got the best poker face I've ever seen."

"Poker face?" she asked.

"It means you're good at hiding your thoughts. You didn't give away your secret." Dalton rethought his assessment. "Then again, you did blush every time I tried to talk to you, and I could see in your eyes how you felt."

As expected, Nizhoni blushed again. "But why is it called 'poker face?'"

"You... never played poker?" Dalton asked.

She shook her head.

"Blackjack?"

She shook her head again.

"Cards? You ever played cards? *Any* card games?"

"I do not know what this is."

Dalton scoffed. "Well, I'll to have to teach you sometime."

"I would like that," she said.

Dalton gazed into her deep brown eyes. He wanted to take her hand in his, to feel her soft skin touching his own, but he dared not violate Chief Beduiat's conditions for the courtship. He yearned to touch her face again as he had back in the wickiup that one night. It felt like an eternity ago.

His entire life, Dalton had been free to approach women as he pleased. Oftentimes his relationships would progress from initial introductions to intense physical interaction within a matter of days, if not hours or even minutes.

He'd grown accustomed to immediate gratification rather than persevering through the traditional mediums of courtship and engagement. Following Chief Beduiat's conditions would stretch his patience, his resolve, and his dedication.

On the positive side, courting Nizhoni could mean he'd finally found someone worth staying with forever, unlike all the other women he'd been with. He'd gladly trade his old lifestyle of one-night stands and short-term flings for lasting love and, hopefully, true happiness.

"So when I said you were beautiful—you understood that?"

"Yes." Nizhoni blushed again. "That poetry you recited, was it yours or someone else's?"

"Made it up on the spot. Did you like it?"

"Yes. It was wonderful."

Dalton smiled. "Good. I'll come up with some more for you. Can you read English, too?"

She titled her head to one side and smiled. "Some. I am still learning."

"Then I'll write you some practice material. Who's teaching you to read?"

"My father."

"How did he learn?"

"I do not know. You would have to ask him."

Dalton rubbed his chin. He'd never encountered an Indian of any stripe who spoke English as well as Chief Beduiat. "Hmm. I think I will."

"How is your hand?"

Dalton held up his right arm. "Still hurts when I try to grip anything, and I can't properly hold a gun. I'm starting to lose hope it'll ever heal completely."

To her credit, Nizhoni said nothing. She just gave Dalton a sympathetic smile.

Dalton gazed across the valley, taking in the warm Arizona scene. The sun had started to sink into the horizon, casting all the colors of fire onto the few wispy clouds that floated in the sky.

"It's getting late," Nizhoni said, her English crisp and articulate. "Perhaps we should go back for dinner?"

Dalton nodded. "Yes, let's go."

Two days later, Dalton took Nizhoni for a walk. Dalton wished he could take her hand in his as they walked. Even that small bit of affection would've satisfied him, but he didn't risk even that—especially not with their entourage in tow.

Once again, Lozen, her aunt, and her uncle followed, but this time Victorio joined them. He brought up the rear, alone and sulking.

"He does not like you pursuing me," Nizhoni said.

"Your brother?" Dalton scoffed. "I think it's more accurate to say he doesn't like *me*."

"He is a protector. Ever since our mother died, he has watched over Lozen and me. He will grow to like you someday, even to love you as a brother."

That was about as likely as Dalton sprouting wings and flying away. "I doubt it."

"Why?"

When he looked into Nizhoni's innocent brown eyes, familiar guilt seeped into Dalton's heart.

"I—I insulted him once. More than an insult, really," he explained. "It was back in Spider's Rock at the mercantile. Your brother came in to trade some pelts, and I helped to… humiliate him, beat him, and throw him out of the shop. He's hated me ever since, even though I've apologized and tried to make amends."

Nizhoni frowned and looked away.

Had Dalton ruined everything by telling her? He'd finally revealed his true nature to her, the kind of man he really was. Coupled with his sickness, which Nizhoni already knew about from caring for him for so long when he'd been shot, it might've proven too much for her to bear.

He braced himself for rejection as they walked in silence.

Finally, she said, "You have done wrong, but you have tried to make it right. If Victorio will not forgive you, then it is his problem, not yours."

Wise like her father, Dalton mused. But even if it was true, it didn't change anything in the here and now.

"I wish that made a difference to him. He *loathes* me. And now that we're—"

"Dalton." She stopped walking and stared into Dalton's eyes. "It is Victorio's decision to hate you. It is my decision to love you. You must choose which of us your thoughts will dwell on."

Dalton's eyebrows went up, but he considered her words. She had a point. Ultimately, worrying over Victorio wouldn't get him anywhere, and Victorio could've killed him dozens of times by now, so why continue to focus on it? "I want to dwell on you."

She smiled. "That is what I want too."

Dalton's relationship with Nizhoni blossomed over the next few months. He shared the full extent of his past with her, and she chose to accept him as he was. Though she'd also entrusted him with secrets of her own, nothing she said compared to Dalton's wild lifestyle.

Most of her admissions surrounded her reaction to her mother's death. Nizhoni confessed that she still wept for her mother, usually late at night. Other times Nizhoni thought she'd heard her mother's voice drifting on the wind, but then it would vanish just as fast.

Dalton wished he could empathize with her, but his own mother was still alive and estranged from him. As for his worthless father—well, Dalton had never really known him. He just knew he'd been a politician of some sort, and that alone had dissuaded Dalton from ever considering a life of politics, even though he'd often been told he had the aptitude for it.

When Nizhoni spoke of her mother, Dalton wanted nothing more than to wrap his arms around her and comfort her, but didn't dare violate his promise to Chief Beduiat.

That test continued to stretch him, but he'd learned to show affection in other ways, particularly by giving gifts and words rather than through physical contact. Since he'd begun courting Nizhoni, Dalton had written almost thirty poems either about her or for her. She'd become his muse, and what a muse she was—he never once lacked inspiration.

Dalton longed for a piano. He'd never been much of a composer, but he thought he might try it if he had access to one. Plus, he wanted to see if his right hand could perform the complex melodies it used to. While he still couldn't grasp anything, he'd regained some use of the fingers on his right hand.

Sometimes, when he found time alone, he'd drum his fingers on a rock or on the ground, playing through songs he'd memorized long ago as the music played in his head. His hand still hurt with dull pain, almost as if he'd pulled a muscle, but his fingers did as he commanded— he *could* perform the motions. Dalton believed he could play again, should he ever have the chance.

Yet despite his fingers' improvement, Dalton still couldn't hold a gun with his right hand. They refused to work in tandem, and every time he tried, the gun drooped in his weak palm. His fingers couldn't squeeze the handle or the trigger.

However, thanks to months of diligent practice, his left hand could snap his gun out of the holster faster than a rattlesnake strike. Better still, he nailed his target every time—always a kill shot. Even so, he still had a long way to go before his left hand could reach the same level of mastery that his right had achieved—if ever.

Dalton found it strange that the longer he stayed with the Apaches, the less he felt the need to perfect his quick draw. In his old life, he'd trained his right hand to sling bullets to ransom himself from death's grasp for just a little longer.

It was a necessary element to the mythos he'd been building around himself. If he was faster and more deadly accurate than anyone else, his legend would precede him wherever he went and with whoever he encountered.

But none of that mattered anymore. He had nothing to prove to the Apache, and fancy shooting skills weren't very impressive in the first place. Now, out here in the desert, the only things that might kill him either slithered, skittered, or were named Victorio.

For the most part, Dalton avoided Victorio, but Victorio's eyes weighed on Dalton wherever he went, especially when he spent time with Nizhoni. Dalton tried to focus on her, but ignoring her brother's hawk eyes seemed impossible at times.

Yet Nizhoni's encouragement lingered in Dalton's memory: perhaps one day Victorio could forgive him, and they could be brothers.

And if not… well, as Nizhoni had said, that was up to Victorio.

One day, as Dalton worked the ground alongside the tribe's women, a dark-skinned warrior wearing only a loincloth approached on horseback. One hand guided the horse he rode, and the other held the reins of a black-and-white mare. Dalton recognized him as Ahiga, one of the tribe's finest warriors and horsemen.

"Come." He smirked and handed Dalton the reins.

"Where are we going?" Dalton asked in Apache.

Ahiga laughed, then he gave Dalton a small nod. "You will see. Do not be afraid."

Dalton hesitated at first, but he mounted the mare and followed Ahiga away from the camp. After a few hours of a medium gallop through the yellow-orange desert, they approached a greenish-brown valley near a drying lake. Wild horses grazed along the water.

Ahiga turned to Dalton and the smirk on his face stretched into a smile. "Pick one."

Dalton raised an eyebrow. "What do you mean?"

Ahiga laughed as he had before they'd left the tribe. "I mean, *pick one.*"

Dalton still didn't understand, but he scanned the herd nonetheless. From Dalton's vantage point a hundred yards above them, the horses resembled a colorful assortment of children's toys until one of them reared up on its hind legs. The afternoon sunlight shined on his black coat, highlighting his strong muscles and powerful form.

"That one." Dalton pointed.

Ahiga threw his head back and bellowed with laughter so loud that it surprised Dalton. "Very well. Catch him, and he's yours. Once you break him, give him to Chief Beduiat. Perhaps then he will allow you to marry his daughter."

"Wait... what?" Now both of Dalton's eyebrows rose. "I have to catch him and give him to Chief Beduiat?"

"If you want to marry Nizhoni, yes. Such a gift is customary. And you have chosen a truly worthy animal. I have been trying to catch him for almost a year now, but he is faster than any horse I have ever seen." Ahiga grinned with a spark of mischief in his dark eyes. "As you say when gambling, 'good luck.'"

Ahiga laughed again, loud enough that Dalton worried it might spook the horses down below. Even so, Dalton couldn't help but crack a smile of his own.

He refocused his attention back to the rare beast below. "Should be a breeze."

The "breeze" was more like a maelstrom.

Dalton's first attempt failed miserably. His mare charged down the hill at full speed and almost threw him from the saddle in the process. He'd never been much of a rider, but he somehow managed to stay in the saddle and line the mare up with the stallion, which broke into a run along with the other horses at the waterline.

The pursuit barely lasted two minutes, with Dalton nearly catching up to the stallion once. When Dalton and his mare drew within twenty feet, the stallion jerked forward, ridiculously fast, leaving a trail of dusty air in his wake.

Within another minute, the stallion disappeared beyond the horizon, leaving Dalton and his struggling mare much too far behind to ever catch up.

When Dalton returned, Ahiga laughed and laughed. In his old life, Dalton might've picked a fight with him over it, but he'd already decided that he liked Ahiga.

"Well, I ruined that one." Dalton shook his head and rubbed his saddle-sore thighs. Oh, what he wouldn't give for a hot bath and a massage from one of Madame DeBuire's girls right about now…

No, he couldn't think that way anymore. Nizhoni was his focus now, not anyone else. He needed to leave those other thoughts behind, along with his old life.

When Ahiga's laughs finally subsided, he said, "Do not worry, my friend. He will be back tomorrow. This is the only water source for miles, and this is his domain. You will have a second chance."

The next day, Ahiga led Dalton out to the valley for a second try. This time, Dalton managed to catch the stallion by surprise. The mare rounded the sharp corner of a rock structure and spooked the entire herd, and she brought Dalton within arm's reach of the stallion.

He threw out a lasso to ensnare the horse's nose or neck, just as Ahiga had shown him the night before, but Dalton made a far better left-handed shooter than lassoer, and he missed. By the time he got his rope back, the stallion had sped off again. And again, Dalton returned to Ahiga, who guffawed and hooted, all while encouraging Dalton to try again the next day.

And then the next day. And the next, and the next, and the next, and many more days after that.

Nearly a fortnight later, Dalton's failures threatened to discourage him from trying. Perhaps he should've just picked a different horse.

But he also wasn't the type to just give up. He needed to break the horse, not be broken by it. He also reminded himself that success would secure his marriage to Nizhoni, and it fueled him with determination.

Dalton decided to employ a new method this time. After his last several attempts, he realized that no matter what he did, he'd never manage to catch the horse with speed. His mare just couldn't run fast enough—no horse in the Apache camp could, especially not while carrying a rider.

Catching the horse by surprise offered a better chance, but training to work the lasso properly might take weeks, even months. For all his persistence, patience wasn't one of Dalton's stronger virtues. Weeks or months to learn a new skill just would not do. He'd already waited long enough to be with Nizhoni.

So Dalton decided to try something different. He left the mare behind with Ahiga, who laughed again and insisted that Dalton would be back for her soon.

"We'll see."

Ahiga laughed. "Yes, my friend, we will."

Dalton crept down to the valley and approached the same corner where he'd burst forth with the mare on the second day, this time wielding the rope and a halter. He rounded the corner with slow, tentative steps toward the herd's outer fringe. They seemed to ignore him at first, but as he stepped closer, the horses stirred... but they didn't gallop away.

The stallion grazed near the stream, and the herd seemed to part as Dalton approached. Whenever he made eye contact with any of the horses, they grew skittish and galloped a few strides away from him.

Dalton took quick breaths in and out. Perspiration dotted his forehead. A voice inside him called for whiskey, rationalizing that under no circumstances should he try to do this sober, but he blocked the idea outright. He didn't need alcohol anymore.

There was no longer any empty space inside of him that needed to be filled. He had no more apathy to drown.

Instead, he had a horse to catch.

The stallion turned his large head toward Dalton, and they locked eyes, but only for an instant. Dalton's heartbeat thundered, and he quickly shifted his focus to the horse's sinewy hind legs instead.

But it was already too late. The stallion trotted away and stopped about fifty feet from where he'd been standing.

Dalton swore. Maybe this idea was as stupid as it seemed.

Still, he'd committed to it. He was already there.

He approached again, still taking his time, now also avoiding eye contact. It didn't make a difference—no longer among the herd, the stallion trotted away again as soon as Dalton came within twenty feet. Dalton swore again.

This give-and-take, punctuated with profanity and curses from Dalton, happened three more times before the stallion finally allowed Dalton to close within ten feet.

As soon as he did, Dalton's lungs filled with burning gravel, and he coughed.

The stallion trotted away again, this time much farther.

Dalton threw his rope on the ground and slung curses at the stallion, at the sky, and at God for cursing him with consumption in the first place. Part of him just wanted to take out his pistol and shoot the damned horse.

After a series of breaths, Dalton started toward the stallion again. On Dalton's first step, the horse trotted a few more steps away. Dalton clenched his teeth but pressed forward.

This time, the horse didn't move away. Instead, he began grazing on a new patch of green grass near the stream.

Now within reach, Dalton stretched his trembling right hand toward the stallion's head. He hadn't given much consideration to how he'd secure the horse now that he'd gotten to it, especially with one hand not functioning properly, but he was here. He'd figure it out. He had to.

The stallion pulled back and looked square at Dalton, who again averted his gaze. That much, at least, Dalton knew to do.

Dalton took a step back and lowered his hand. Hot breath pushed out the stallion's nostrils in long, furious flows, and the drum in Dalton's chest beat faster. What if it kicked him?

When the stallion finally resumed his grazing, Dalton reached out again, even slower than before. His fingers made contact with the rough hair on the stallion's neck.

The stallion looked at him again, and Dalton froze. It sniffed at his chest then brought his nose up to Dalton's face, still sniffing.

The stallion's breath reeked of grass and vegetation. His moist nose—whether from a recent drink or equine slime, Dalton didn't know—tickled Dalton's neck, and he recoiled. He expected the stallion to gallop away again, but it didn't.

It surprised him that the horse had stayed put. Maybe that was a good sign.

Dalton put out his right hand, palm up. The stallion sniffed at it then went back to grazing. Definitely a good sign. Dalton reached out, stroked the stallion's neck, and spoke to it with his deep voice.

"Good boy. Nice and easy."

Dalton may not even need the rope after all. He unslung the halter from his shoulder and held it low. Maybe that way it wouldn't scare the stallion away.

Dalton stroked the horse's nose with his right hand—he'd need his left to do the brunt of the work in getting the halter on the stallion.

The stallion raised his head again.

"Good boy. Just here to bring you back with me." More to himself than the horse, he added, "Take it slow."

Dalton slowly lifted the halter. When the stallion recoiled, Dalton waited a beat, then he let it smell his hand again. Once the stallion calmed down, Dalton reached a second time.

♠ ♥ CHAPTER 13 ♦ ♣

W hen Dalton rode up on the stallion, Ahiga laughed so hard that
he fell off his horse.

"I do not believe it!" he cried between guffaws.

"Told you I wouldn't need the mare." Dalton smirked.

"You are a madman!" Ahiga's laughter proved infectious, and he laughed, too.

Once they finally regained their composure, Dalton asked, "So what do we do now?"

When Chief Beduiat finally granted him permission to marry Nizhoni, Dalton couldn't stop smiling…

Until he saw Victorio.

Upon Victorio's return from the day's hunt, the laughing Ahiga had told him the good news. Victorio's calm visage shifted to the same livid expression he'd worn back at Warren's Mercantile.

Dalton knew that look all too well. He'd seen it across poker tables. He'd seen it from down the street under the scorching Arizona sun. He'd seen it in Tommy Roebuck's eyes after he'd lost everything to Dalton in that last hand at the Imperial.

Hatred like that didn't just go away. Tommy's had lingered until Dalton's bullet burrowed its way into his heart and spilled it with his blood. No matter what, Dalton couldn't ever let his quarrel with Victorio reach that point.

A rush of guilt filled Dalton, both for his treatment of Victorio and, to his surprise, for gunning down Tommy. Had his old life of alcohol and apathy really erased any remorse over Tommy's death until this moment?

Dalton clenched his teeth. Tommy hadn't deserved to lose his life. Dalton had goaded him into the confrontation. And then he'd shot Tommy dead, and Dalton had laughed about it, just like Ahiga had laughed at him for the past three days.

When Victorio finally diverted his icy gaze, Dalton felt no relief. He had to do something, and he had to do it before he married Nizhoni.

The next morning, Dalton set out with the hunters again. After nearly a full day of roaming the desert, he'd only bagged one cottontail rabbit, and a skinny one at that. He was just about to shoot an even smaller one when it darted away, spooked by the sound of approaching horse hooves.

Dalton and Ahiga had split up for the day, spaced about a half-mile apart on opposite sides of a ridge, to cover more ground. Why would he come back over? Perhaps he'd landed something too big to carry on his own and needed Dalton's help.

A horse and rider crested the horizon, silhouetted against the blazing summer sunset, but it wasn't Ahiga. The rider's lean, muscular form didn't match Ahiga's stocky, pudgier shape.

Victorio.

He guided his horse down the hill and dismounted only twenty feet away. As Dalton dismounted his mare he eyed Victorio's hands and double-checked them for weapons—not that it meant anything. Victorio wouldn't need weapons to kill Dalton if he wanted to.

"How did you fare today?" Dalton asked.

Victorio said nothing. He just stormed closer.

Dalton noticed the familiar burning in Victorio's eyes. This couldn't be anything good. "Did you get anything?"

Victorio stopped three feet from Dalton. In English, he said, "I told you to stay away from Nizhoni."

Dalton realized the lump in his throat and swallowed hard. "I, uh—I was hoping to talk with you about that."

A rocky cliff couldn't have outdone Victorio's stern visage.

"I wanted to apologize again for what happened back at the mercantile," Dalton said. "It's been eating at me ever since, and I wish I had never treated you so poorly, especially now that—"

"Now that you are pledged to my sister? Now that you realize we are not just dumb savages?" Victorio tapped the scalping knife that hung in a sheath on his belt. "Now that we are alone in the desert and you don't have any of your friends here to help you?"

"Yes. All of that." Dalton swallowed hard. Was he fast enough to draw on Victorio if it came to it? Could he get a shot off before Victorio's knife dug into his throat, or his chest, or his gut? He decided he'd rather not find out. "I've tried to make amends with you several times, but you just won't listen to me."

"I told you to stay away from Nizhoni," Victorio repeated, his voice low and threatening.

"I'm sorry, but I love her. That isn't going to change."

Silver flickered in Victorio's hand, then to Dalton's neck.

Instinct sent Dalton's right hand to his holster, but he found no gun there. He cursed. Even after practicing to master his left hand for so many months, his body had defaulted to his dominant hand. His primal defenses hadn't remembered that he was a necessity lefty now.

Cold iron pressed against Dalton's throat. He sucked in a quick breath, trying to decide if he should resist or not. If he did, it would just get him killed. Victorio had all the advantages.

He stared into Victorio's hawk eyes—cold and angry, but troubled too. Conflicted. Hatred burned the brightest, but Dalton also saw apprehension and distress smoldering in the background.

If Victorio took his revenge, he'd have to answer to Chief Beduiat and Nizhoni. Even so, the slightest provocation now might encourage Victorio to ignore his reservations, so Dalton kept his mouth shut.

The knife at Dalton's throat quivered. Sweat rolled down the side of his head and trickled to his jaw. Beads of sweat clung to Victorio's forehead as well.

The two men stood there, both trembling in anticipation, their eyes locked.

"There is nothing you can do to earn my forgiveness. *Nothing.* We are enemies forever." Victorio pulled the knife from Dalton's throat. "No matter what."

He left Dalton standing there, stunned, and walked back to his horse. As quickly as he'd appeared, Victorio vanished beyond the horizon.

Dalton exhaled a deep breath and wiped the perspiration from his brow. He was no pushover, but Victorio was absolutely menacing—even more imposing than Dalton's uncle.

He stood in the same spot and just breathed, inhaling and exhaling relief, until a set of horse hooves clopped along the ground behind him.

"What are you doing off your horse?" Ahiga asked in Apache. "Did you shoot something?"

Dalton looked up at him. How much had he seen? "Just stretching out. My legs were getting sore."

"Was that Victorio riding away?"

"Yeah."

"What was he doing here?"

Dalton glanced back to the horizon. "He wanted to talk with me."

"About what?"

"About—life."

Ahiga laughed.

Weeks later, Dalton's wedding day arrived. After much help from Ahiga and even Chief Beduiat himself, he'd learned to make his own wedding garment: a long white tunic with two crimson stripes across the bottom.

He'd made one for Ahiga too, in part to thank him for his help, but also because he'd chosen Ahiga as his best man. Neither of them fit exactly as they should. Dalton would've blamed his defunct right hand, but in reality, he was just terrible at sewing.

Even so, he now wore that very garment along with a pair of buckskin pants and his trusty black boots. He'd considered wearing his gun to the ceremony, just in case Victorio decided to finish what he'd started in the desert weeks earlier, but decided against it.

Dalton's heart hummed. He'd faced men in the street and gunned them down without so much as a tremor in his chest. He'd bluffed card sharks out of hundreds, perhaps thousands of dollars throughout the course of his life. He'd even braved the edge of Victorio's knife, helpless to save himself.

Yet none of those experiences wracked his nerves like this very moment, standing in his wickiup and waiting for Ahiga to bring him out to the ceremony.

He'd been drunk during most of those gunfights and card games. Dalton had often relied on alcohol to take the edge off of his dour emotions, but when it came to fear, whiskey made him immune.

Dalton yearned for a drink now, but he didn't need it. He could manage. After all, he'd been sober when he decided to ask Nizhoni to marry him. He'd better be sober when he actually married her.

Ahiga popped into the wickiup. As usual, a big smile stretched across his face. "It's time."

Dalton sucked in a deep breath and followed Ahiga.

Together, they approached the temporary altar outside Chief Beduiat's massive wickiup and sat down. Ahiga had happily agreed to take the place of Dalton's family and sat to Dalton's right.

Even so, a part of Dalton wished he'd made time to contact his uncle to try get him out to the wedding, but he just couldn't bring himself to do it. In so many ways, his uncle represented the life he'd left behind, and he'd decided that to move forward, it all had to stay behind him, including his uncle.

When Nizhoni emerged from her father's wickiup, Dalton's attention snapped back to reality, back to the most important day of his life. She gave Dalton a furtive smile, then she sat down next to him.

Like Dalton, she wore a long white garment with two crimson

stripes at the bottom. The dress's sleeves ended just above her elbows, and her bronze skin seemed to glow in the setting evening sun.

Long strands of white fabric hung from the sleeves like drooping vines, and beaded necklaces in many earthy colors hung from her neck, including some that matched her earrings. She held a small bowl of mushy white cornmeal in her hands.

Victorio emerged from Chief Beduiat's wickiup, clad in buckskin, his hawk eyes boring into Dalton's forehead—better his gaze doing it than his knife or a bullet from his revolver.

He took his seat on Nizhoni's left.

Finally, Chief Beduiat walked out of the wickiup. Silence gripped the landscape as if even nature itself revered his presence. He wore buckskin as well, but an elaborate headdress tipped with eagle feathers and decorated with silver and turquoise distinguished him from everyone else.

Dalton peeked over at Nizhoni, then looked past her at the group of relatives sitting around her, including Victorio, her younger sister Lozen, and several aunts and uncles. Chief Beduiat had explained to Dalton that an Apache wedding was just as much an assimilation of both the bride and groom into their new families as it was a union of two people.

In many ways, Dalton already felt as though he'd been welcomed into their family—his interactions with Victorio notwithstanding. After today, though, it would become official.

Chief Beduiat raised his arms in the air and asked Usen's blessing upon the couple, then he nodded to Nizhoni. She dug a glob of cornmeal from the bowl with her hand and separated it into two parts, one for Dalton and one for her.

Together, they ate the mush. It tasted sweet, yet gritty, which Dalton thought was a good metaphor for marriage in general.

Ahiga produced two silver rings, both inlaid with brilliant turquoise stones. He handed them to Dalton, who gave his friend a blank stare.

"A little taste of your home tradition." He displayed his huge smile. "You can thank Chief Beduiat for these."

Chief Beduiat returned Dalton's gaze with a faint smile and nodded.

Dalton took the rings, gave his to Nizhoni, and kept hers.

For the first time since the night he'd caressed her face, Dalton touched Nizhoni. He took her hand into his and slid the silver band onto her ring finger.

"With this ring, I thee wed," he said to her in English, his voice barely louder than a whisper.

Her eyes flashed with delight, and her cheeks rounded as she smiled. She took his hand in hers and mimicked his actions and words. "With this ring, I thee wed."

Dalton wanted nothing more than to take her into his arms and hold her tight, to kiss her. He didn't want to suppress his ravenous hunger any longer.

He glanced at Chief Beduiat, whose smile grew wider. When he nodded, Dalton did exactly what he wanted to do.

He swept Nizhoni into his arms, held her tight, and kissed her.

The wedding celebration continued late into the evening with dancing, music, and food. Just as Dalton started growing anxious to leave with Nizhoni, Chief Beduiat approached him with a wooden box, shiny with lacquer.

"This is for you, my son," he said.

Dalton bit his tongue to quell his rising emotions. He'd never known his father, and his mother had all but disowned him, but over the last several months, he'd been blessed with an entire family. He cleared his throat to help regain his composure. "What is it?"

"Open it and see." Chief Beduiat held it out for Dalton.

The light of the campfire danced across the box's smooth surface. Dalton lifted the brass clasp and pulled the lid open, exposing a layer of fine red velvet.

And beneath that velvet flap lay two glistening revolvers, silver plated and replete with intricate engraving on their ivory grips. Dalton removed one of the guns with his left hand and examined it with the conviction of an art connoisseur studying a masterpiece.

He looked at Chief Beduiat. "These are unlike anything I've ever seen. Who made them?"

"There is a firm in Massachusetts. A man named Wesson made these for you."

"What kind of rounds do they fire?"

"They are .38 caliber rimfire cartridges."

Rimfire cartridges? Dalton had only heard of them. Some people claimed they were far superior to traditional integrated paper cartridges, but critics supported the old style because rimfire shooters had to remove spent metal cartridges before reloading.

"But I don't have any—"

Chief held up another box, this one not lacquered, but made of rough, thin wood. He opened it, revealing ten even rows of six brass cartridges inside. "I have ten more boxes for you as you need them. In the meantime, learn to shoot these."

"I don't believe it. This must have cost a *fortune.*"

Chief Beduiat smiled. "I am glad you like them."

Dalton laid the revolver back in the box's velvet cutout next to its twin, and he remembered his old guns, the Colt sisters. Memories of losing them to Zamora, the pain of getting shot, and losing most of the function in his right hand resurfaced in his mind.

He cast them aside. Today was a happy day, one that ought to be devoid of painful memories.

"Why'd you get two of them?" he asked. "I can't even hold a gun with my right hand anymore, much less shoot one."

"I still believe that will change someday. *Usen* will show you favor. I feel it." Chief Beduiat rested a big hand on Dalton's right shoulder. "Besides, they were made as a set. It did not seem right to separate them."

Dalton stared into Chief Beduiat's dark eyes. "How can I ever repay you for all you've given me?"

Chief Beduiat matched his gaze, showing his faint smile again. "I do not expect you to."

Dalton fought back the tears stinging the corners of his eyes. "Thank you."

"Perhaps there is one way," Chief Beduiat tilted his head. "You are now bound to my daughter in the covenant of marriage. See to it that you honor it, and honor her, always."

Dalton nodded. "I will. Always and forever."

"I believe you." Chief Beduiat patted Dalton's shoulder with his heavy hand. "Now go. It is time for you to be with your bride. Ahiga will take you."

Ahiga left them alone with their shared horse at a grand wickiup on the side of a mountain about two miles from the Apache camp. He'd explained that the tribe had prepared the place in advance for the newly-weds, then he'd sped back toward the camp on horseback.

Dalton helped Nizhoni down from the horse, and to her delight, he carried her inside the wickiup. Nizhoni didn't weigh much, and Dalton had grown strong again from working with the tribe over the last several months, so he scanned the dwelling before setting her down.

A small fire in the middle illuminated its large interior. Clay jars lined one of the walls, full of food, he presumed. Buckskins stretched across the ground to form a makeshift floor, and on top of those buckskins lay more animal skins shaped into a sleeping area.

Festooned from floor to ceiling with desert flowers of all kinds, the wickiup's interior smelled wonderful, like swimming in a river of nectar.

"Dalton?"

He looked at Nizhoni. "Yes?"

"You can put me down now."

He did, but held her hand as they took in their honeymoon quarters together. "This is amazing."

"Yes, it is."

Dalton gazed into her eyes and savored the touch of her hand in his. "I love you, Nizhoni."

Nizhoni's shyness evaporated. Instead, she gave Dalton a hearty smile. "I love you too, Dalton."

They spent the rest of the night in each other's arms and drank deeply of their love.

One glorious month later, Dalton and Nizhoni began the short ride back to the tribe, sharing their horse. They'd finally run out of food, and while Dalton had suggested they ought to just stay and that he could hunt wild game for them, Nizhoni had insisted it was time to return to the tribe.

As they rode along, they passed a contingent of white men wearing blue army uniforms. United States soldiers. They galloped in the opposite direction, away from the tribe.

Their colonel, a man with silver hair and a thick gray mustache, led the soldiers away. While most of the soldiers took a good long look at him and Nizhoni as they passed, the colonel had only given him one steel-eyed look, and then he'd refocused his attention forward.

Dalton had encountered confident men before—even shot a few of them—but the colonel had something else entirely in his eyes... something darker and more ferocious than anything Dalton had ever seen. Almost as if he lacked a soul, or if the one he had was as black as a clear desert night.

When they finally arrived back at the camp, they received a warm greeting lined with concern. Dalton read it on the Apaches' faces, and he heard it in Chief Beduiat's voice as he welcomed them back. Even Victorio looked angrier than usual, if that was possible.

"What did they want?" Dalton asked.

"They said—" Chief Beduiat exhaled a deep breath through his nose, and his eyebrows arched down. "—we have to leave the valley. They said we must move, or we will be removed."

♠ ♥ CHAPTER 14 ♦ ♣

"What?" Dalton gawked at Chief Beduiat. "Why?"

"They said the United States Government has mandated our removal from these lands," Chief Beduiat replied. "We have three weeks to leave, and then the soldiers will come back in greater numbers to claim the land. *Our* land."

Dalton cursed. "They can't take your land from you."

"They seem to think they can." Victorio glared at Dalton. "White man always thinks he can take what he wants."

"Be silent, Victorio," Chief Beduiat said.

Victorio grunted. "I refuse to be silent. We cannot give in to them, father."

"We will not discuss this now, my son. Gather the warriors. We will meet in one hour." Chief Beduiat looked at Dalton. "I hope you will join us."

Dalton nodded. "Of course."

"Good. I must see to other tasks in the meantime."

With that, Chief Beduiat and Victorio walked away, leaving Dalton and Nizhoni standing there, hand-in-hand. Dalton's gaze found hers, and he saw she bore the same concern in her eyes as her father had.

"Don't worry." He squeezed her hand. "Everything will be alright."

BEN WOLF

She wrapped her arms around his torso and buried her face in his chest.

What would have been a raucous, uncontrollable meeting in Dalton's world played out as a calm yet tense gathering of Apache men. Each man was allowed to voice his thoughts, and the vast majority agreed that staying was necessary, even if it meant they had to fight.

When Dalton stood to speak, Victorio grumbled, but Chief Beduiat silenced him with a wave of his hand. By that point, Dalton's Apache was good, but he didn't want to risk any confusion, so he spoke English, and Chief Beduiat translated for him instead.

"I know I'm new here, but perhaps that's not a bad thing. Perhaps God let me end up with you for exactly this reason." Dalton paused, unsure if he believed that last part or not. "You showed me kindness when I was on the brink of death, so please allow me to do the same for you now, because death is *exactly* what you'll face should you decide to stay.

"Those soldiers are trained to kill. They have better weapons, greater numbers, and no honor when it comes to fighting Indians. If you don't leave, they *will* kill you, and they'll enjoy every moment of it. They'll taint the sand with your blood, and with your wives' and children's blood, too. They won't stop until you're either gone from this land or until you're all dead."

Dalton scanned the sea of brown faces and dark eyes. "I've had less than a year to learn your culture, but I spent my first twenty-three years growing up as a white man. I know the world I came from. It's a place full of violence and death. We take what we want, by force if necessary.

"We took our sovereignty from England. Then we took the land out east from other Indian tribes. Now they're coming to take yours, and they won't stop until they have every last inch of this continent in their possession, from New England to California.

"The United States Government is too powerful. Even if you *do* defeat these soldiers, more will come, and then more after that. If you cross them, they'll hunt you down to the very last man and wipe you off the face of the earth.

"They don't even consider you to be human beings. You're nothing but savages to them, no better than dirty, stupid wild animals." Dalton hated having to phrase it that way, but it was absolutely true. That's how his fellow white people viewed Indians. "You *cannot* win. Please… leave before it's too late."

Once he concluded, Dalton sat down and listened to the sound of the campfire crackling.

After a moment, Chief Beduiat stood to his feet and addressed the men in Apache. He looked at Dalton. "My brothers, Dalton is right about many things, but we must stay. We must fight for our land. Dalton was right when he said the white man will keep coming no matter what.

"But if we move once, the white man will return to make us move again. And again. And again. If we do not resist him now, we will become the white man's slaves, just like the black man. No, we must stay and fight."

Dalton scanned the group. Most nodded, and some even smiled. He just shook his head, not at their ignorance but rather at the injustice of the whole situation. The government had no right to move *anyone* from their land, Indian or not. If only other whites could see them as he did, then—

"Victorio will lead us in battle. If the white man wants to fight, then we will give him a *fight* the likes of which he has never seen," Chief Beduiat said, his voice strong and confident. "We have three weeks to prepare. When they arrive, we will be ready."

The Apache men roared their approval, with Victorio's voice louder than all the others. If anything good could come out of this, it might be that this battle could provide the outlet Victorio needed for all his pent-up aggression.

Even so, the thought of these people—his family and his tribe—going into battle for their very way of life sickened him. It was so profoundly unfair. Why would God allow these good people to endure such a tribulation?

"Dalton." Chief Beduiat's large hand weighed on Dalton's shoulder.

In English, he said, "We need your help. Will you teach my warriors how to shoot more accurately?"

He stared into Chief Beduiat's dark eyes, and the sick sensation in his stomach dwindled. If he could focus on what had to be done, maybe he wouldn't feel so wretched about the situation anymore. "Yes. I'll do whatever I can. Is there any chance we can ally ourselves with other tribes? We're gonna need all the help we can get."

"You are correct. I will contact Geronimo, a *Chiricahua* brother, to see if he will join us. Perhaps if we can rally the support of our neighbors, we can defeat the soldiers."

"It's a long shot no matter what. But if you can't leave, I'll do whatever I can to help."

"Thank you, my son." Chief Beduiat faced the men and exhaled a long, quiet breath. "To war."

The warriors erupted.

Nizhoni approached Dalton after the meeting and latched onto his arm. Together, they headed back toward Dalton's wickiup.

"You cannot let my father take us to war," she said. "We Apache are strong, but we cannot win."

"I told him that." Dalton shook his head. "I told all of them that, but they're determined to stay and fight. I guess I can't blame them."

"We are full of pride. Among the other tribes, we are the most respected, the most feared. Once, we could defeat all of our enemies, but over the years, the white man's sickness has killed many of our number. Now the white man is much stronger. We cannot defeat him. He is too numerous, too powerful."

"I know," Dalton said. "Believe me, I know. But your father intends to stay. I can't change his mind, and I certainly can't change your brother's."

She stopped him mid-stride. "Then run away with me."

"What?"

"Run away with me. We cannot win. We will all be destroyed if we stay." Nizhoni's countenance shifted from desperation to one of hope.

"But I love you. I don't want to see you die. We can live off the land together, just you and me."

"We can't—"

"Yes, we can. We can leave this place, make a new life somewhere else. We can avoid the bloodshed on the horizon."

She was right. They could avoid it. They could just pack up and leave, perhaps go back to the mountain and live there. Chief Beduiat had provided him with more than enough bullets to—

No. He couldn't go. He'd promised Chief Beduiat that he would never take Nizhoni away from her home or her people. He'd promised to help Chief Beduiat in any way that he could. In order to leave, Dalton would have to break all his promises to the man he now regarded as his father.

Chief Beduiat had saved his life. Dalton couldn't betray him now, not when he needed Dalton most. Doing so would be worse than spitting in Victorio's face a hundred times.

"I can't go," Dalton said. "I made promises to your father that I can't break. I need to stay. The tribe needs me."

Her voice low and cryptic, Nizhoni insisted, "The tribe is dead, with or without you."

Dalton gritted his teeth. He feared she was right, but it didn't change anything for him. He'd determined to fulfill his promises to Chief Beduiat no matter what. It was a matter of honor. "Your father saved my life. I owe it to him to stay. I'm sorry."

Nizhoni's eyes filled with tears. She turned away from him and walked ahead to the wickiup. As he watched her go, Dalton wondered if he'd made the right choice.

Footsteps rustled behind him. He turned and saw Victorio crossing to his wickiup.

Victorio gave Dalton another icy glare.

It occurred to him that if Victorio hadn't kept *his* promises, Dalton would be dead by now. That was enough to reinforce Dalton's decision.

I have to stay. I'm a man of my word. I'm staying.

Two-and-a-half weeks later, Ahiga thundered into camp on his horse early in the morning. "They're coming! They're coming!"

Dalton sprung to his feet, slipped on his clothes, and strapped on his new guns. Now more than ever, he wished his right hand would just do what he needed it to do.

They'd planned for this eventuality. Dalton had rightly suggested the soldiers would show up early to ensure the Apaches were either gone or getting ready to leave. His guess had come to fruition, but the tribe had already made preparations in case of something like this.

As Dalton finished dressing, he looked down at Nizhoni. "Pack up. They're early. You've got to get out of here now."

He stepped toward the wickiup's exit, but she called his name, and he stopped and turned back.

She stood up, walked over to him, and enclosed him in her arms. "Be careful."

They shared a long kiss. Dalton didn't want to leave her, but right now, he had no choice. "I will. You too."

Nizhoni nodded.

As Dalton approached, the first words he could discern from an out-of-breath, gasping Ahiga were, "We're outnumbered five-to-one."

At the sound of that, Dalton couldn't find his next breath, either. Was their situation really that dire?

Chief Beduiat, Victorio, and a group of warriors had gathered outside of Chief Beduiat's wickiup, and Dalton joined them.

"Those devils came early." Victorio glared at Dalton. "I knew we couldn't trust the white man."

"Our plan does not change," Chief Beduiat said. "We need only to hold them off until Geronimo and his warriors arrive this afternoon, and then the numbers will be in our favor."

"Hold them off?" Victorio said. "Father, they will wash over us like a flood."

"Then we must break their strength, just as rocks break waves on the riverbed," Chief Beduiat countered. "We will use the land. We know it. It will slow their advance. We will hide behind rocks and strike like rattlesnakes. We will blend in with the grass and ambush them like wolves. And when we can no longer do that, we will stampede over them like wild horses."

For all of Chief Beduiat's confidence, Dalton could tell his hubris was a veil for the truth—they faced an overwhelming foe. Defeat was almost a foregone conclusion. Just surviving the battle would take all the luck, divine intervention, and fortitude they could muster.

And winning the battle… that was nothing more than a dream being chased away by the break of dawn.

But now all the men were looking at him, as if they expected him to impart some wisdom to them about their enemy's strategy. The truth was, Dalton didn't know what would happen. He hadn't studied much by the way of military tactics or procedures back east.

They probably hoped he could provide some insight simply because he looked like the soldiers did. The irony of the situation didn't escape his grasp; all white people were the same to them—excluding himself, of course—so he would therefore have deep, hidden knowledge of their plans as a result.

He couldn't blame them. It was a line of thinking likely more rooted in desperation with a dash of hope than in anything malicious.

Well, with Victorio it *was* probably malicious.

But that wasn't the point. They were looking for something—anything—that Dalton could add to the conversation that might help.

The warriors stayed silent until Dalton finally spoke up. "The way I see it, Chief Beduiat is right about using the land to our advantage. They'll plow right over us if we risk a head-on attack. Ahiga said we're outnumbered five-to-one. That means that if each of us manages to kill at least five men, we can level the odds… and maybe even win."

Dalton almost believed it himself.

"Victorio and Dalton will lead us," Chief Beduiat said.

Victorio's dark eyes widened. "Father—"

"That is my decision. We must be united, or we will be destroyed." He turned to Ahiga. "You must prepare the women and children to flee to safety. Go now."

Ahiga nodded amid heavy breaths then bolted away.

"Dalton and Victorio, go now. May *Usen* grant us victory."

Within an hour, the warriors were in place, and a swarm of navy blue uniforms had just broken the horizon line.

Dalton had led one third of the warriors, about forty of them in total, up into a natural rocky fortress of sorts. There, he and the Apaches could use large red boulders and occasional trees for cover while they fired on the approaching soldiers.

Victorio and another third of the warriors hid in the tall, semi-arid grass below, ready to ambush the soldiers. Chief Beduiat and the last forty Apaches waited to the southeast, all on horseback, ready to swoop in and flank the soldiers when the time was right.

As the soldiers drew nearer, Dalton studied their faces, their mannerisms. They embodied the same savagery he'd attributed to the Apaches not even a year earlier. They looked even more bloodthirsty than Victorio at his angriest.

The whites closed in, about two hundred on horses and three hundred on foot. Once they moved within range, Dalton reminded them to aim especially for the officers and told them to open fire after he took the first shot.

He snatched a nearby rifle, an old muzzle-loader, and took aim at an approaching sergeant on a brown horse less than fifty yards away. Dalton held the gun like a lefty—his right hand still refused to pull the trigger. Maybe it never would again.

He centered the sight on the sergeant. If there were ever a time for God to show up, it was now.

Dalton squeezed the trigger. The rifle cracked, and a soldier ten yards behind the sergeant and to his left dropped to the dirt. Dalton had either twitched, or the rifle's sites were off.

Or he should've practiced more as a left-handed rifleman.

Gunshots split the desert air around Dalton, but fewer soldiers dropped than he would have liked. The Apaches would have just enough time to reload and fire again before the soldiers overtook them.

The soldiers shifted their advance and accelerated their approach, heading straight toward the rocky area where Dalton and his men had taken cover. The soldiers returned fire immediately, and bullets smacked and ricocheted off the rocks around them.

The Apaches had an elevated position, but that small advantage wouldn't last for much longer. The soldiers would reach them soon, and then the fighting would change entirely.

Once he finished loading his next round, Dalton took aim at the sergeant again. Left-handed or not, this time Dalton would put him down.

Dalton exhaled a breath. He lined up the shot and fired, and the rifle kicked into his shoulder.

The sergeant clutched his chest, his body contorted, and he toppled over, taking his horse to the ground with him. Dalton smirked.

More bullets chipped the boulders around him. Too close, like the approaching soldiers. Time to signal Victorio. He turned to his left and scanned for Ahiga. Usually jovial, he had hardened into a stoic stone pillar. "Ahiga!"

Ahiga arched his body from behind a short rock structure and looked at Dalton.

"Signal Victorio!"

Ahiga nodded, then he threw his head back and let out a howl that pierced through the gunfire.

Dalton faced the soldiers now wading through the tall grass, some as close as thirty feet away. Dark forms rose from the gray-brown grass like phantoms in a graveyard, both in front of the soldiers and among them.

Victorio and his warriors opened fire, and several soldiers fell, followed by dozens more in physical combat. Dalton saw Victorio personally cut down three soldiers before he disappeared into a patch of tall grass.

A sizable portion of the soldiers caught in the tall grass went down, but more continued to advance. Shouts and screams joined the sounds of battle.

The sounds of death.

Dalton drew one of his new revolvers and took aim at an approaching horseman with his left hand. He squeezed the trigger.

The gun spat fire and smoke, and the soldier fell off the back of his horse. Dalton lined up five more shots, each one taking out another soldier. Three of his shots saved his fellow warriors from imminent death.

But the soldiers kept coming.

Dalton shouted another order to Ahiga. This time Ahiga only made eye contact, then he darted off to signal Chief Beduiat and the warriors on horseback. But even with the added strength of cavalry, Dalton knew they simply couldn't withstand the encroaching army.

Within two minutes, Chief Beduiat's horsemen flanked the soldiers and shredded their formation. Victorio's warriors sought out and eliminated a few stragglers who'd been separated from their compatriots while Dalton and his warriors continued to lay down suppressing fire.

Somewhere in the distant, an earth-shaking boom tore trough the sky. But by the time Dalton realized what it was, it was already too late.

Then the first cannonball hit.

♠ ♥ CHAPTER 15 ♦ ♣

A solid ball of lead struck the ground beyond the clashing armies. It ricocheted off the Arizona dirt and it ripped through Chief Beduiat's horsemen and Victorio's warriors until it finally smacked into a rock face behind some of Dalton's men. Red boulders rained down on them and buried at least one warrior, and several others sustained injuries.

"Pull back!" Dalton yelled in English, then in Apache. "Pull back!"

Chief Beduiat turned to face him, then nodded. The time to attack was done. They had to retreat, had to get out of the meat grinder on the battlefield below.

Chief Beduiat's black stallion, the one Dalton had given him, reared on its hind legs and then darted away as Chief Beduiat hollered for his men to retreat. Victorio requisitioned the horse of a dead soldier and began to organize his warriors.

Dalton holstered his empty pistol and drew his other one from the opposite hip. He fired two quick rounds into a soldier who'd emerged from nowhere and taken aim at Victorio.

The soldier dropped flat on his face, but Victorio just met Dalton with another cold stare. But this was no time to worry about settling scores.

Chief Beduiat rounded the ridge and approached Dalton. His stallion slowed to an abrupt halt. "We cannot weather this kind of attack. We must retreat."

Dalton nodded as he began to reload his pistols. "I agree."

"I have ordered Ahiga and some other warriors to accompany the women and children south on their retreat. We must fight to give them time to escape."

"You should go with them."

Chief Beduiat shook his head. "My place is here with my warriors."

Arguing wouldn't get Dalton anywhere. "Alright. What do you want me to do?"

The boom of cannon-fire snapped through the hot, hissing desert air. Another cannonball blundered its way through the fleeing Apaches and smacked into another rock formation with a loud *crack*, this time farther away from Dalton's position, but he shielded his head with his arms anyway.

Chief Beduiat said, "My warriors will lead them north, away from the women and children. Victorio's men will circle around behind you to flank them from inside the pass once they begin to follow us. You must assist Victorio, then follow after Victorio and his men."

"Alright. We'll do what we can."

Chief Beduiat nodded. He started to say something else, but he didn't. Instead he looked at the battlefield, paused, and then rode off.

With his pistols reloaded, Dalton worked on his muzzle-loader as the next wave of soldiers closed in on their position. Once he got it reloaded too, he raised it and pointed it at the soldiers.

The seeming randomness of his decisions in battle made him wonder. He could take aim at any of the soldiers coming toward them, yet his bullet could only kill one, or maybe two if he got lucky. And for the soldier whom he would shoot, it would be the most unlucky and final day of his life.

Ultimately, all that mattered was doing whatever he could to hold the soldiers off, so he picked a target and fired his rifle. Meanwhile, Victorio's warriors flanked the soldiers who'd followed Chief Beduiat in the pass.

Dalton got a glimpse of their situation. The combined force of Chief

Beduiat's horsemen, Victorio's warriors, and Dalton's men amounted to about fifty or sixty fighters, a number far less than half of the remaining soldiers.

The sight sickened Dalton to his core. They'd lost nearly half of the men in the tribe in just a matter of minutes. Dalton had probably known many of them well, but he didn't have time to take an accounting of who'd survived thus far and who hadn't.

At least fifteen warriors still guarded the women and children, a good number as long as the soldiers didn't figure out where they were.

Cannons thundered in the distance yet again. Their shots shattered rock formations and bounced off the turf like erratic black devils, but most of the cannonballs landed too far behind the Apaches.

The fighting in the pass, however, was a different story.

Chief Beduiat and his men fired back at the approaching soldiers while Victorio's men hurled large rocks and spears or fired guns or loosed arrows down on them from above.

Some descended the steep grade to engage the soldiers in combat face-to-face, but what the Apaches lacked in numbers they could not make up in tactical prowess. The soldiers exercised more discipline and fought as a unit rather than as rogue berserkers like the Apaches.

They fired synchronized volleys of gunfire—while one line fired, the other reloaded. Then they advanced. Soon the fifty to sixty Apaches had dwindled to forty. Then thirty. Then twenty-five.

Then Chief Beduiat got hit.

"No!" Dalton saw it happen and immediately hurtled down into the pass. When he reached Chief Beduiat, who'd fallen from his stallion, he quickly hefted him back up onto his saddle with Victorio's help.

As he did so, Dalton noticed his hands were smeared with blood. Chief Beduiat's blood.

"Get him out of here!" Victorio yelled. He pointed his rifle at an approaching soldier, one-handed, and fired. The man's head erupted in red, and he dropped onto what little remained of his face. "Go now!"

Dalton mounted the stallion as well, his right arm around Chief Beduiat and the reins in his left hand. They pulled out of the pass and behind a ridge where Dalton found a flat plot of dry earth. He helped Chief Beduiat off the stallion and laid him on the ground with care.

Chief Beduiat moaned. Dalton ripped open his bloody shirt and cringed when he saw that the bullet had pierced the left side of Chief Beduiat's chest.

Tears welled up in Dalton's eyes, but he bit his tongue and garnered the fortitude to look Chief Beduiat in the eye. "You're gonna be alright, Chief."

Chief Beduiat's lips curled into a soft smile. "No, my son. I will not."

Hoofbeats plodded behind them, and Victorio rode up on a brown horse with white patches.

"Father!" He dismounted and ran over to the two of them. "Father?"

"You are Chief now, my son." Chief Beduiat took Victorio's hand into his own. "You must lead our people to safety."

Victorio's expression steeled. "Father, our warriors are scattered, but if we can regroup then we can continue to fight the soldi—"

"No," Chief Beduiat said. "Dalton must go after the women and children. You must gather what remains of our warriors and follow after Dalton and those escaping."

"But father, Geronimo and his men will arrive in only a few hours, and then we—"

"No, my son. We do not have a few hours. Our people will be totally destroyed if you continue this fight. We must survive. My time is done. Now you must lead our people." He turned to Dalton and winced. "Dalton, you must go. Take my horse. You must make sure our people escape."

"I can't want to leave you." Dalton clenched his teeth. "You've done so much for me."

"You must go *now*. You promised to protect Nizhoni. Go and do so, with my love. I have one final command for Victorio, and it is for his ears alone. Go and protect your wife, Dalton." Chief Beduiat's voice sounded weak, but his eyes remained firm and resolute.

He nodded. "Thank you, Chief Beduiat. I won't forget you."

Dalton leaped onto the stallion and galloped south, knowing he'd just seen Chief Beduiat for the last time. As tears streaked down his cheeks, he realized he was without a father once again.

When Dalton reached Ahiga and the other warriors, the soldiers still had not discovered their location. Lucky, so far.

Dalton sidled up next to Ahiga. "We have to get these people out of here. Give me five of your warriors, and we'll hold them off to give you more time to escape."

Ahiga shook his head. "No. You go back. Protect your wife. She needs you. I will stay with the warriors."

Dalton had hoped for such an offer. "Are you sure?"

Ahiga bellowed his classic laugh, a welcome respite from the carnage catching up to them. "Yes, I am sure. Why else would I have said it?"

Dalton smirked. "You stay alive, got it? Victorio is rounding up his warriors near the pass and will come to help you, but Geronimo won't get here in time to help us."

Ahiga smiled and laughed again. "Then let us hope Victorio gets here soon."

"He will. He's determined to—"

"You need to go." Ahiga's happy face hardened, and his eyes focused on something behind Dalton. "Now."

Dalton turned back. At least a hundred of them, most of them on horseback, approached fast. "Yeah, I think you're right."

He rode toward the group of Apaches as Ahiga hollered the names of five warriors to help him hold off the soldiers. Dalton found Nizhoni atop a horse with her twelve-year-old sister Lozen.

When Nizhoni saw him, she smiled, but her eyes reflected distress. "What's going on?"

"Start riding," he replied. "Make sure the people follow you. I'll catch up once I have the rest of the warriors placed at the rear of the group."

To her credit, she didn't ask about her father or her brother. She just nodded and said, "Be careful."

"I will." Dalton watched her ride off, followed by dozens of women and children on foot and a few on horseback. The remaining eleven warriors rode up to him on their horses. He pointed to seven of them and said in Apache, "You stay behind the people. Form a line to protect them. The rest of you, come with me."

Dalton led them to the front of the group and rode next to Nizhoni.

Behind them, sounds of gunfire crackled. He glanced back once. "Come on. We need to pick up the pace."

As they rounded a bend, Dalton's heart stopped. A platoon of navy blue uniforms awaited them, their guns ready. There had to be at least thirty men lined up.

Before Dalton could even speak, the soldiers opened fire. His stallion reared up on his hind legs again and nearly threw Dalton off.

He shouted to Nizhoni, "East! Head east now!"

She nodded and turned her horse, and the people followed her lead.

Dalton ripped the pistol from his holster and fired three quick shots at the platoon. His first round struck the dirt in front of them. Shooting on horseback was difficult enough under normal circumstances, and in an all-out battle it was even worse.

Nevertheless, his second and third shots struck two soldiers. His fellow warriors fired their rifles, then switched to their bows and arrows, all while advancing toward the soldiers.

"No!" Dalton yelled in Apache. "Come back! We need to retreat!"

It was too late. The soldiers fired in unison with each other and cut down three of the four warriors.

The fourth rode directly at the platoon, brandishing a club made from a buffalo's jawbone. He made it to the platoon before the soldiers could finish reloading, but they brought down his horse with their bayonets.

The warrior launched off of his felled horse, recovered his footing, and thrashed his club in big, powerful swings. He took out at least five of them before the others finally brought him down, but more importantly, he'd bought Dalton, Nizhoni, and the escaping Apaches precious time.

"Nizhoni, keep them going," Dalton shouted. "I'm heading back to get more warriors to support at the front."

She nodded and kept riding with Lozen clutched tightly to her chest.

Dalton wove his stallion through the Apache people until he reached the warriors. He ordered half of them to help cover the front of the line. When Dalton turned back, his heart plummeted into his stomach.

Another line of soldiers was approaching them from the east.

Nizhoni was leading the people that direction.

Dalton's stallion couldn't gallop fast enough—he seemed to move at half-speed.

The soldiers from the east opened fire on the people.

On Nizhoni.

"No!" Dalton cried.

Then Nizhoni's horse went down.

CHAPTER 16

Lozen and Nizhoni spilled onto a patch of tall grass. A clatter of bullets struck several Apache on foot, and they dropped, either wounded or dead, accompanied by desperate shrieks and wails.

"*No!*" Dalton kicked the sides of his stallion. When he reached them, Dalton's heart skipped a beat—both Nizhoni and Lozen were alive and uninjured. He dismounted and held Nizhoni close. "Are you alright?"

She nodded and pulled Lozen toward her. "We're fine."

Dalton looked around. "I have to get you another horse."

A group of soldiers on horseback galloped toward the Apaches, their swords drawn. Dalton skinned his revolver and gunned down two of them, which freed up two horses among the scattering Apaches, whom the rest of the soldiers pursued.

"Take those and go." Dalton mounted his stallion. "I need to help the warriors save the rest. I'll meet up with you at our spot on the mountain. Go!"

Nizhoni nodded and pulled Lozen with her toward the horses. Dalton gunned down another soldier riding toward them, then he scanned the area around them as he reloaded his revolver. They would make it out of the ruckus. They had to.

As Dalton urged his stallion back into the fray, a soldier to his right took aim on an Apache woman. Dalton crossed his left hand over, lined up the shot with his revolver, and fired. The soldier crumpled to the earth, and the woman got away.

At the rear of the group, only two of the seven warriors Dalton had left as guards remained. Several yards away, Ahiga and two more warriors rode toward the fracas with fury etched on their faces.

Dalton squeezed off a pair of quick rounds into a nearby soldier and urged his stallion closer to Ahiga. Over the ongoing battle, he shouted, "Have you seen Victorio and the other warriors yet?"

Ahiga shook his head. "No. Have you?"

"No." Victorio should've arrived by now. Had something happened to him?

The air crackled with gunfire, and the warrior to Ahiga's left cried out and then dropped from his horse, clutching his neck.

"We have to move." Ahiga pulled the reins on his horse to redirect it. "I will stay back and cover the rear."

"No, come with me to the front. Help me cut a path for the people to follow."

Ahiga hesitated.

A bullet buzzed past Dalton's head. He jerked away out of reflex, uninjured.

"We gotta go *now*, Ahiga!"

Ahiga nodded. "I will follow you."

"We'll cut through them and meet on the other side of that elevated rock formation behind the soldiers. If we can get through, we can bring the people there as well."

Together, they knifed through the fleeing Apaches until they reached the front of the group—and the approaching soldiers. Dalton caught sight of Nizhoni riding away from the soldiers in the distance, still far enough from harm.

Dalton and Ahiga blasted through a clump of soldiers. When their ammo ran out, they resorted to using their buffalo jawbone clubs. Dalton had never made one of his own—he just used the one already strapped to the stallion's saddle. It must have been Chief Beduiat's.

With all of his rage over Chief Beduiat's death, Dalton swung it at a nearby soldier's head and struck it with a hard *crack*. The man withered, his face a mask of blood.

Several more brutal swings and some fancy horsemanship helped Dalton avoid the soldiers' bayonets and gunfire, and he managed to carve a small hole in their defenses that the Apaches trailing him could use to escape.

Still ahead of Ahiga, Dalton rounded the big rock formation out of the soldiers' line of sight and reloaded his revolver, ready to go back and fight off more of them to give the Apaches time to escape. The clopping of hooves soon followed as Ahiga rode into view.

He was clutching the left side of his chest with his right hand, wet with crimson blood, and he gawked at Dalton with hurt, desperate eyes.

♠ ♥ CHAPTER 17 ♦ ♣

"Ahiga?" Dalton reached for him as he slumped over. They slid off their horses together and dropped to the ground. Dalton swore. "Ahiga!"

No response. No movement.

"Ahiga?!"

Nothing. No familiar laughter, no toothy smile stretching across Ahiga's face.

Only silence.

Only death.

Dalton ground his teeth and screamed a string of profanity.

Ahiga's left arm lay motionless in the dirt, extended out, his forefinger pointing. Dalton followed the line from Ahiga's arm.

From his elevated position above the skirmish, Dalton saw a group of cavalry soldiers chasing after two lone people on horseback across a flat expanse of desert dirt and scattered patches of arid grass. He recognized them immediately.

Nizhoni and Lozen.

Dalton left Ahiga in the dirt, mounted Chief Beduiat's stallion, and tore back into the violence below. Gunshots zipped past him, but Dalton ignored soldiers and Apaches alike.

Only one thing mattered now.

He headed straight for Nizhoni and the soldiers chasing her.

Chief Beduiat's stallion powered over the turf, a black bolt of lightning kicking up a burning cloud of dust in its wake. Within minutes, he'd caught up to the back end of the five soldiers pursuing Nizhoni and Lozen.

Dalton raised his pistol, pulled the hammer back with his thumb, and—

A gunshot echoed across the flatland. In the distance, Lozen's horse dropped, and she tumbled off. Nizhoni tugged the reins on her horse, darted over to her sister, and positioned the animal so it would shield them both from any more shots.

The soldiers would catch up to them now. Dalton took aim at one of them, fired, and the bullet dug into the man's back. He fell from his horse and rolled past Dalton's stallion. None of the other soldiers even bothered to turn around.

When Dalton took down a second soldier, one of them turned his head back for a look. He got it next.

He'd been in the lead, so when he dropped off his horse, the other two soldiers turned back for a look. Dalton dispatched them just as quickly. He stole a glance over his shoulder then galloped over to Nizhoni and Lozen.

"Is she alright?" Dalton asked as he dismounted.

"She is scraped up, and she hit her head, but she will be fine," Nizhoni replied.

"They are coming," Lozen said in Apache, her eyes distant.

"What?" Dalton asked.

"More soldiers. From behind you."

Dalton turned back to see a band of soldiers headed their direction from the battle, then he refocused at Lozen. With Nizhoni's horse shielding them from the approaching soldiers, there was no way Lozen could have seen or known those soldiers were coming. "How did you know that?"

Lozen just looked at him.

It didn't matter now. Dalton turned to Nizhoni. "You need to go. I'll hold them off."

"What about the tribe? Victorio? My father?" she asked.

He hadn't even told her about Chief Beduiat yet. Dalton shook his head. "We can't win. We're too divided, too outnumbered. We just have to get away. Go. I'll buy you some time."

"Dalton—"

"Go. Please." He gestured toward a rock formation, desperate to get her out of this mess. "I'll meet up with you beyond that ridge. Take Lozen, and go."

Nizhoni hesitated, but she nodded. "Come back to me."

"I will." Dalton led her to Chief Beduiat's stallion. "Your father's horse is the fastest. Take him and go."

He helped Nizhoni up first, then Lozen, and he slapped the stallion's rear end. It shot forward and blazed across the flatland toward the ridge.

Dalton stalked over to the two dead soldiers nearest him and picked up their rifles. They were newer models than the old musket he'd been firing earlier, but they still only had one shot each.

He slung one on his shoulder and took aim with the other, then fired. The gun kicked and spewed brimstone, and one of the soldiers running toward him dropped onto his face.

Dalton tossed the rifle aside, unslung the other one, and fired it into the crowd of approaching soldiers. Another one went down.

He stole a quick count—seven soldiers remained, none of them on horseback. Dalton pulled his revolver, cocked the hammer, and fired its last round. He immediately began to reload it.

His bullet must've struck one of the soldiers in his ankle, and he fell with a yelp. The other six soldiers took aim at Dalton with their rifles and fired, but he dropped low and took cover behind a rock. None of their shots managed to hit him.

"Charge!" one of the soldiers yelled. "Bayonets!"

Dalton swore. They were several yards away, but he still might not have time. He fumbled with the last bullet, cursing his malfunctioning right hand, the bullet itself, and the man who'd receive it on the back end.

The bullet finally went in, and Dalton popped the cylinder back into place, pulled back the hammer, and stood to his feet. He took quick aim at the closest soldier and squeezed the trigger.

The soldier went down. Now only about thirty feet away, the other five still charged him, their bayonets raised.

Dalton exhaled a calm breath. He had to do this right, or they'd overrun him. He reacted with clean alacrity as he cocked the hammer with the flesh of his right palm, then fired. The hammer clicked again, the off-beat amid the chorus of bullets blasting from his revolver.

One by one the soldiers went down. When only two remained, one of them hesitated, but the other kept coming. Dalton put a bullet square in the approaching soldier's chest, then took aim at the soldier who had stopped.

The soldier gasped. He was just a kid, maybe as young as sixteen, and already a soldier. Already a murderer.

Dalton could kill a murderer.

He pulled the hammer back.

The boy soldier dropped his gun and put up his hands.

Dalton swallowed. Could he kill an *unarmed* murderer?

Nizhoni. He needed to get back to her more than anything else.

He spun on his heels and headed for a brown horse grazing behind him—one of the horses from the soldiers he'd killed earlier. With one last look at the stationary soldier, Dalton mounted the horse and headed for the ridge.

In the distance, a group of Apaches who'd escaped the fracas now huddled around Nizhoni, now on her feet instead of on horseback, tending to Lozen. Chief Beduiat's stallion, and a few other Apaches on horses stood around her. The tightness in Dalton's stomach eased, but he didn't slow his pace.

Then someone in the group screamed and pointed to the west. Heads turned, people cried out, and they began to scatter. Dalton's muscles tensed. He kicked the sides of his horse and urged it forward even faster.

Apaches already mounted on horses galloped in every direction except to the west. Most of them headed north. Nizhoni tried to help Lozen onto the stallion, but it reared up on its hind legs. As if dazed, Lozen slid off the side, then quickly tried to get back on.

Dalton cursed again. Why had they even gotten off the horse in the first place?

As Dalton charged toward them, Nizhoni got Lozen on the stallion, but she couldn't mount it with her. Instead, she slapped the stallion's rear end. He shot off with Lozen on his back, leaving Nizhoni alone.

Dalton kicked the horse harder, but it was already running at its top speed.

I can reach her. I can save her from—

Nizhoni turned. A group of soldiers on horseback approached her from the west, now visible to Dalton as they surrounded her.

A silver-haired officer with a bushy gray beard, a light-gray, wide-brimmed hat, and a colonel's rank on his shoulders led them until they nearly surrounded her. Even from a distance, there was no mistaking the man—he was the colonel from the other day—the man with eyes like steel.

Dalton was still too far away.

Nizhoni did not move, except to raise her hands in surrender.

The colonel pulled out his revolver and shot her anyway.

CHAPTER 18

Dalton couldn't even breathe, much less cry out. He pulled on his reins, astounded, and his horse slowed to a stop about a half-mile away as his Desert Rose wilted to the earth.

The colonel dismounted, walked over to Nizhoni, and stared down at her. A dozen more soldiers emerged on his left side from behind the ridge.

He bent over and took Nizhoni's left hand in his. When the colonel pulled the silver ring from her left hand and slipped it onto his little finger, something in Dalton snapped.

He kicked his horse, and the beast lurched forward. He was going to kill that man, even if it meant he would die in the process.

But before Dalton could get there, the colonel mounted his horse and rode to the north, possibly in pursuit of some of the fleeing Apaches. His soldiers followed, completely ignoring Dalton's approach.

By the time Dalton reached Nizhoni, the soldiers had already galloped a good distance away. Upon seeing Nizhoni lying in the dirt, he couldn't bring himself to go after them—he had to check Nizhoni. Maybe the bullet had only skimmed her. Maybe the shot wasn't fatal.

Maybe it was.

"Nizhoni!" Dalton leaped from the horse and dashed to her. His stomach twisted with tension at the sight of her bloodstained shirt. He skidded to a halt at her side and cradled her in his arms. "My God—Nizhoni, are you alright?"

She smiled at him. In a quiet voice, she said, "I am now."

Dalton bit his tongue and stared up at the sky, blinking away tears, then he looked back at her. He could see her reddened hand resting over a spot in the middle of her chest, but he still asked, "Where'd it hit you?"

She weakly lifted her hand, exposing a black, bloody hole in her chest.

Dalton shuddered. *God, no. Not this. Anything but this.*

He bit his lip as tears streamed from his eyes and ran down his cheeks. "Stay with me, Nizhoni. You're the only thing in my life worth living for. I need you."

She slowly shook her head. "No, Dalton. I no longer have a choice."

Dalton bowed his head to hide his quivering bottom lip, but his whole body shook anyway. This was his worst nightmare come true. She'd become his everything. His joy. His peace. His salvation from everything he'd left behind.

Dalton couldn't lose her… not now. Not ever.

He whispered, "You can't—"

"I can. I will."

"No…" Dalton whimpered. "Nizhoni… You have to make it. I can't live without you."

"You can. You will."

"*No.*" Dalton pounded the dirt with his fist. "If you die, my life is over. It will have no meaning, no purpose."

"You are wrong, Dalton." Nizhoni reached up with her bloody hand and gently cupped his face. He leaned into it, desperate for this moment to never end. "*Usen*—God is not done with you yet. Do not give up. Do not give in to anger or hatred." She trembled and inhaled a weak, shaky breath. "Do not… waste your life."

Dalton had nothing to say. There was no time. He just sniveled and held her close. Through his tears, he managed to say, "I love you, Nizhoni. I have since the moment I first saw you."

She rasped. "I love you, too. Now, Dalton—kiss me ."

Dalton's heart dropped into his churning stomach, and he wept.

"Dalton." She touched his cheek again. "Kiss me. Before it's too late."

He marshaled the last of his fortitude, every ounce of his will and being, and he leaned toward her. He touched his lips to hers, feeling their fleeting warmth on his own. Her body rose to meet his as it had on their wedding day. Dalton pulled her tight against him, and they shared one last embrace.

When they finally released each other, Nizhoni touched his cheek with her fingers again and smiled. Her gaze locked on Dalton, then drifted past him up into the sky, her eyes now empty, lifeless.

She was gone.

Dalton shattered. He buried his face in her shoulder and wailed.

She was gone. Everything he loved in this world was gone.

He cursed God. Cursed the world. Cursed everyone in it. Cursed his own life.

The sound of horse hooves plodding the ground grew louder, but Dalton didn't care. They could gun him down right now, and he'd count it as a mercy. They could inflict no pain that could compare to that which already ravaged him. Dying was a welcome alternative to living without the one he loved.

"Nizhoni?" a deep voice said from behind him.

Dalton recognized the voice, and he turned. Victorio.

He dismounted and hurried over, but he stopped short when he saw Nizhoni's limp, bloodstained body in Dalton's arms.

"Is she—" he began.

Dalton gave a slight nod. Tears still streamed from his eyes.

"How?" Victorio asked, his voice shaky.

"The colonel. She was unarmed, but the bastard shot her anyway." Dalton's sadness boiled into anger. Nizhoni had spoken of God before she died. How could God let this happen? If He was supposed to love people, then why had He taken Nizhoni away?

Victorio stayed silent and still. He simply bowed his head, a stoic statue with tears rolling down his chiseled cheeks.

Dalton pressed his face into Nizhoni's shoulder again and cursed God between his sobs. Had God brought him from the brink of death only to make him suffer even further?

It wasn't fair. It just wasn't fair.

Gunshots sounded in the distance. The soldiers must have found some of the Apaches who'd scattered. Dalton raised his head and looked toward the sound.

Rage—no, absolute, unbridled *hatred*—blossomed in his heart like a black flower, fueled by his pain. Nizhoni was right about one thing: he needed to stay alive. He needed to live so he could avenge her.

He would *kill* that colonel. Dalton would put a bullet between his eyes, even if it was the last thing he ever did. Swear to God.

Dalton laid Nizhoni flat on her back and closed her eyelids with his fingers. As he stood to his feet, his pants and shirt, sticky with her blood, clung to him. He rolled up his sleeves, removed one of his revolvers from its holster, and replaced the spent cartridges with new ones.

"What are you doing?" Victorio raised his head.

"What does it look like I'm doing?" Dalton didn't even bother to look back.

"You cannot go after him," Victorio said. "They will shoot you dead before you even get close."

"No." Dalton shook his head. "Not after this. Nothing would stop me."

Victorio strode forward and positioned himself in Dalton's line of sight. His lean, bloodstained body tensed, and his usual scowl resurfaced on his face. "I do not care how well you can shoot or how angry you are. You will not succeed. You will only die."

Dalton pushed past Victorio and headed for the dark-brown horse he'd been riding. "Then I can't lose. I'd rather be dead than live without her."

Victorio cut him off again and held his hand up. "Dying as a *fool* will bring you no honor, and it will not bring her any either. It will not honor your love for her at all."

"I'll be the judge of that." Dalton brushed past him.

"Dalton—" Victorio grabbed his right arm.

Dalton locked eyes with his brother-in-law. His adversary. His fellow tribe warrior.

With a low, ominous tone, Dalton warned, "Let go of me, Victorio."

He didn't. "You are being a stupid white man. Your death will accomplish *nothing*."

"I said *let go* of me, Victorio."

"You cannot go."

"Like hell I can't." Dalton yanked his arm from Victorio's grasp. "He killed my wife. Your sister. I'm gonna kill him, and you're *not* going to stop me. Now *let go of me*."

"No. Not until—"

Dalton swung his fist at Victorio's head, but Victorio blocked his obvious left hook and delivered a stunning uppercut that knocked Dalton on his back.

He glared up at Victorio, the brunt of his rage now focused on him. Yet another injustice doled out by an unjust God. Not only had the three people Dalton loved most perished on the same day but God had also left Dalton alone with the person who hated him the most.

It just wasn't fair. Would Dalton be denied his vengeance? His hatred? They were all he had left, and now he couldn't even have those.

A teardrop streaked down Dalton's cheek, then another. Victorio's blow hurt, but it couldn't begin to compare to the destruction in his soul.

Victorio extended a hand to Dalton. "Get up. We must find Geronimo and his men before the white—before the soldiers find us."

Dalton gave him another glare, one that he knew projected more grief than fury. He didn't want to go along with Victorio. He would've been content to never see Victorio again, to forget any of this had happened, to sanitize it from his memory forever.

But he knew he'd never forget. No matter what he did, he could never leave this life behind him. And before he did anything else, there was one thing he had to do.

So Dalton grabbed Victorio's wrist and stood up to his feet. "We're not leaving without burying Nizhoni."

Victorio hesitated, but he nodded. "Very well. I will help you. But then we must go."

They buried Nizhoni in a shallow grave near the rock formation where she died. Dalton etched her name into a nearby boulder with one of the soldiers' bayonets and said his last goodbye to her. When he finished, Dalton stood up, wiped the last of his tears from his cheeks, and walked over to Victorio.

The sounds of battle had finally ceased. Dalton heard no approaching hoof beats or even distant gunfire. Everyone's fates were sealed. It was over.

"Come," Victorio said. "We must find Geronimo. We will join with him and continue our fight. We will be victorious against the white man."

Dalton shook his head. "You can't win, Victorio. They're too strong."

"No," Victorio shook his head. "We can win. We will ally ourselves with other Apache tribes. Not just the *Chiricahua*, but the *Mescalero, Jicarilla, Lipan*—"

"The more people you organize, the larger the force they'll send against you. You can't win, not in a million years."

"The Apache will be restored to our land, to our way," Victorio said, his eyes alive with fire. "They cannot take what is ours."

Dalton swore. Was Victorio really so blind? "Yes, they can, Victorio. They just did."

Victorio narrowed his hawk eyes, and his muscles tensed again.

"Look around," Dalton continued. "The soldiers didn't just kill your warriors. They killed the women and children, too. They don't even think you're human, remember? You might as well be animals to them."

"We are *not* animals."

"I know that, but *they* don't. They'll hunt you down until they kill every last one of you. Either you give them what you have and save your lives or they'll kill you and take it anyway." Dalton swallowed and fought back his tears anew. "And if you need proof, look around. Your father and Nizhoni are gone."

"No. I refuse to accept defeat so quickly. I am the chief now. I will lead our people to victory over the white man."

Dalton let out a sad laugh and shook his head.

"You laugh at me?" Victorio asked with an edge to his voice.

"No, Victorio. Not at you. Just at something you said. You said you were chief—"

"I *am* the chief. You heard my father say it before he…" Victorio's voice trailed off.

"Think about it, Victorio. What are you the chief of? Whom do you lead?" Dalton looked at him and motioned to the arid land all around them and the bodies lying in the distance. "Your people are scattered, mostly dead. Your warriors are all but gone. So whom do you lead?"

Victorio's face hardened, and he glared at Dalton with the same loathing as when they'd first met—and every day since. It was a look Dalton no longer feared.

"You can be as mad at me as you like, Victorio," Dalton said. "But you know I'm right. You're a great Apache Chief of nothing but a broken heart."

Nothing changed in Victorio's face. It didn't matter. He'd never liked Dalton anyway, and Dalton had never liked him. No reason to stick around.

"I'm leaving." Dalton stared at Victorio. "There's nothing for me here anymore."

"Where will you go?" Victorio finally asked.

Dalton stared at the silver-and-turquoise wedding band on his ring finger and sighed. He didn't want to do it, but what better choice did he have? "I have only one place *to* go. Back to Spider's Rock."

Victorio gave him a solemn nod. "I must still meet with Geronimo. Goodbye, Dalton."

"Goodbye, Victorio. Don't get yourself killed." Dalton stared at him for a moment, then he turned and began the long walk north, into the past he'd left behind.

Gray buildings loomed on the dusky horizon like gravestones marking the dead Arizona dust. Even now, almost a full year since the Apaches found him in the desert, Dalton could remember every inch of Spider's Rock.

He knew the dark alleys he'd used to escape Max Warren, III and his goons after the Camille incident. He knew Main Street, where he'd gunned down three of his four victims within two months after he'd first arrived in town.

Dalton knew Warren's house, the Imperial, the Chinese tailor shop near the outskirts, the mercantile, and the bank. He knew his uncle's church and parsonage—and he refused to go back there if he could help it.

But Dalton didn't know anything about the new growth that Spider's Rock had experienced since he'd been gone. The number of buildings had tripled, probably all owned or partially owned by Warren. New houses, new businesses, and even a new saloon-and-inn combination called the Continental filled some of the once-empty arid earth.

Randolph probably wasn't too thrilled about the appearance of the Continental in town—assuming Warren hadn't found some way to have him murdered in the last year.

From across town Dalton could hear the raucous sounds of carousing, shouting, fast-paced music, and gambling. As he got closer, Dalton realized it was all coming from the Continental. Perhaps he should stop there, see what he might be missing.

He glanced over at the Imperial. Its lights blazed, but no sound emanated from within its walls, and very little moved within its windows.

No, Dalton would stop there first. He had some words for Randolph.

And maybe a bullet.

♠ ♥ CHAPTER 19 ♦ ♣

"Welcome to the Imperial." A saucy young redhead, a new addition to Randolph's "staff" since last year, sauntered over to Dalton. She teased the fabric of his shirt with her forefinger. "Can I get ya somethin', stranger? Drink? Smoke? Some… company?"

"No, thank you," Dalton said, his voice level, but firm. The thought of even looking at another woman in that way turned Dalton's stomach, and it took everything he had to maintain his composure.

"Gonna be another slow night," the redhead mumbled and then clomped away.

Dalton took in the Imperial. Still colored royal blue and contrasted with dark-brown Bavarian oak trim. Still clean and pristine. The only difference now was how brightly the solid oak floors under Dalton's feet shined.

Had Randolph finally invented a solvent that repelled the harsh Arizona desert tracked in by his patrons? Or did the Imperial so lack for business that he actually managed to keep the floors clean?

Dalton didn't know, but the man who did stood behind the big oak bar, drying out a shot glass. He also didn't know what, exactly, he had in store for Randolph yet. His reaction to Dalton would determine his fate.

Randolph looked exactly the same as Dalton had left him: gruff,

UNLUCKY

grizzled, and grunting. He still wore his bushy mustache, its corners manicured and waxed to perfection. When Randolph growled for no apparent reason, Dalton had to smirk, but it was out of disdain, not mirth.

After all, Randolph could've intervened the night Zamora and his men dragged Dalton away to kill him. Instead, he'd done nothing except to let it happen.

The row of open barstools called to Dalton, so he plopped down on one only a few feet from where Randolph stood. He pulled out a leather billfold he'd taken from one of the dead soldiers. It only had two federal dollars inside, but it was better than nothing.

He tossed the two dollars in Randolph's direction and they floated to a halt on the bar under his nose. "What'll that get me?"

Randolph set down the shot glass in his hand and looked at Dalton. "What do you want?"

He removed the black wide-brimmed hat he'd taken from a dead soldier and set it on the bar, then nodded at the old upright piano in the corner. "I'd like to hear some music."

"No music here, Mister." Randolph hadn't lost his thick Prussian accent or his gruff demeanor. "Not for a long time. What else do you want?"

Dalton returned Randolph's cold stare, amazed that he showed no indication of recognizing him. He'd changed over the last year for certain —perhaps a bit scruffier and not clean-shaven like usual, but for the most part, he looked the same.

He stood, walked over to the piano, and sat down on the bench. Could he still play? Even if he could, would he remember any of the music he'd memorized?

He looked at his right hand, palm up, and squeezed his fingers toward his palm. Dalton still couldn't make a solid fist, still couldn't grip anything, and ancient pain pinched in his wrist whenever he tried.

But could his fingers still navigate and press the keys?

Only one way to find out.

Dalton placed his hands on the ivories and pushed them down to play a chord, the first of Beethoven's piano sonata number eight, *Pathétique*, the second movement in A-flat Major. The chord warbled and

131

gnawed at his ears—the piano probably hadn't been tuned since he'd left, but it wasn't going to deter him from trying to play.

His right hand played the corresponding melody, and to his surprise, he didn't miss a single note. He played the entire movement from memory, a little better than five minutes of music, and finished the song with the grace and reverence it deserved.

He sighed, flexed his right hand, and then let his hands rest at his sides. He could still play, even after a year away, even after almost losing function in his right hand from Zamora's bullet.

Even after losing everything he'd ever loved.

When he finally turned back, all of the Imperial's guests and staff were staring at him. Dalton stood up, walked back over to his barstool, and sat down, his gaze fixed on Randolph, whose eyes glimmered with recognition.

"Dalton?" Randolph's voice barely hovered above a whisper.

"Yeah." Dalton nodded, his teeth gritted behind his lips. "It's me."

Randolph shook his head. "But... how?"

"It's a long story." One that Dalton didn't want to tell.

"That thug—he hit you. You were out cold when his men dragged you outside. I heard them ride off, and I knew you were gone." Disbelief underpinned Randolph's voice. "You're supposed to be dead."

Dalton scanned the room. He recognized a few of the girls, but most were new. Their bored expressions had shifted to surprise, or at the very least, intrigue. Some new folks had even wandered in. Had they heard Dalton's music?

"They tried. Shot me three times. I took one in my right arm, one in my gut, and another—" He traced his finger over the scar that stretched from the left side of his forehead across his temple. "—grazed my head. You're absolutely right. I should be dead."

Randolph's eyes glanced over Dalton's shoulder.

Dalton leaned in. "But I'm not."

Randolph cleared his throat, looked past Dalton again, and barked, "Get back to work, all of you. Don't just stand around."

Dalton grabbed Randolph by the collar and pulled him halfway across the bar. "Why didn't you *help* me?"

Wide-eyed, Randolph stammered, "I—I, uh—"

"*Why?*"

"You know I don't get involved unless—"

"Unless it directly affects your revenue?" Dalton shook him. "Your nightly profits?"

"Unless it adversely affects my place of business, yes."

Dalton cursed. "Well, it's sure affected you since then, hasn't it? You left me for dead, and with no one playing music for you, now this dump's on its last legs, too. Maybe you should have *helped* me."

He shoved Randolph back, and Randolph's frightened visage darkened to anger.

"Always thinking about today's money, never tomorrow's. I almost got killed because of you." Dalton shook his head. "I might as well have."

"You acted on your own, of your own free will. You expected me to clean up after you?"

"I was trying to save Vanessa from that *murderer*. Trying to save *your* business. You didn't help me, didn't watch my back, didn't even warn me that Zamora was behind me, ready to take me out."

"You—you cost me one of my tables and three chairs, cost me seven broken glasses, two bottles of tequila, and—"

Dalton slammed his palm down on the bar and swore. "You cost me my *life*. I may not have died, but my life as I knew it has ended *twice* since that night, all because you were a *coward*."

Randolph recoiled a step and stared daggers at Dalton, who refused to look away or even blink. All the while, Dalton had his left hand on the pistol in his holster. If Randolph tried anything, he will have sealed his own fate once and for all.

Finally, Randolph broke the thick silence that had canvassed the Imperial, his voice uncharacteristically calm. "I'm sorry, Dalton. You're right. I was a coward. I still am. I didn't want them to gun me down, too. I couldn't bear to think of Max Warren coming in here after I died and taking over. You know he would, too."

Dalton just kept staring imaginary bullets into Randolph's eyes. His fingers flirted with his pistol and with the idea that maybe he ought to use real bullets instead.

"And you're right about business here, too. Warren opened the

Continental a few months after you were taken, hired some musician from New York, and now he's got all of my business." Randolph leaned forward and whispered to Dalton, "If things don't change soon, I can't stay here, and Warren will take over anyway."

"It's nothing less than you deserve," Dalton uttered.

Randolph nodded. "Yah, I know. I know. But now that you're back from the dead…"

Dalton scoffed. Was Randolph really trying to get him back? "You can't afford me anymore."

"Things are tight," Randolph said with a chuckle. "But I can still afford two dollars a night."

"I'm sure you can." Dalton considered his next words carefully. They would determine his future in this miserable little town. "But my rate has gone up since last year."

The smile on Randolph's face turned into a scowl. "What do you want?"

"Ten dollars every night."

Randolph gawked at him and folded his arms. "Two dollars an hour? *No* musician makes that kind of money."

"This one does." Dalton pointed to himself with his thumbs. "You cost me *everything*, Randolph, but I'm willing to let you make up for it with money. It's the only thing I have left to live for."

"No deal. I can't afford to pay you that kind of money." When Dalton raised an eyebrow, Randolph added, "And I wouldn't even if I could."

Dalton shrugged and reached for the two dollars he'd left on the bar. "Suit yourself. Maybe I can oust the musician at the Continental. Then he could come play for you for two dollars a night—if he doesn't go back to New York instead."

Randolph's hand clamped down on Dalton's hand and his money. "Wait. I'll give you three-fifty. It's the highest I can go. Three-fifty for five hours of music."

"Ten." Dalton yanked his cash away from Randolph and tucked it back into his billfold.

Randolph shook his head again. "No. Three-fifty. Best I can do." When Dalton started to stand up, Randolph added, "Plus you keep everything you make from gambling. I won't take twenty-five percent like I used to."

"I *gave* that to you to keep you from bothering me every night. It was to shut you up."

"Fine. Four dollars a night. That's double what you were making last year."

Dalton shook his head and put his hat back on. "I'm going over to the Continental. Maybe Mr. Warren will let me run this place for him after you're out of business."

"Warren won't give you anything." Randolph scoffed. The desperation in his voice diminished at Dalton's suggestion. "Not after your incident with his daughter."

"Either way, you're out of business if you don't pay me what I want."

Now Randolph cursed. "Five dollars per night. That's one dollar per hour."

Dalton shook his head again and started to walk away.

"And you keep all your tips, all your gambling money."

"No thank you." Dalton didn't look back.

"And you drink for free."

Dalton stopped and turned his head so he could see Randolph out of the corner of his eye.

"*Two* drinks," Randolph clarified. "Two drinks for free every night."

Dalton shook his head. "Still cheap as ever. Good night, Randolph."

"Okay, okay. All your drinks are free. Better?"

Dalton faced Randolph and stared into his eyes. "I gave up drinking."

Randolph didn't say a word. He just snatched a bottle of whiskey from behind the bar and poured it into a shot glass, then pushed the glass to the edge of the bar. "Consider this a down payment."

"I said I gave up drinking."

Randolph shook his head. "You gave it up for one year. You're back now. Besides, are you really going to turn down a free drink?"

"I'll drink it if he don't," a bearded, wobbly man said from across the room.

"Shut up, Foley," Randolph snapped.

"Awww, shucks." Foley's shoulders drooped.

"It's fine. He can have it," Dalton said.

"Woo-hoo!"

"No, he can't. Not until he pays for the two he's already had. And besides, it's for you."

"I don't want it."

"Dalton." Randolph tempered his voice. "It's free. It's my way of apologizing, of setting things straight. Are you going to refuse my apology?"

Dalton stared at the glass of bitter brown sulfur. The last time he'd had a drink was the night he'd fought Zamora. He hadn't had a drop of alcohol since then. What use did he have for it anymore?

Still, the prospect of free drinks wasn't the worst thing he could conceive of. He doubted he'd get any good sleep without some help along the way. Maybe booze could ease his passing into the world of dreams, and maybe it could keep him from having nightmares.

But Nizhoni wouldn't want him to drink it. If he did, would he dishonor her memory?

He sighed. What did it matter anyway? She was dead. She had told him not to waste his life.

Well, he wouldn't. He'd live it.

He'd *live* it.

Dalton reached for the glass.

♠ ♥ CHAPTER 20 ♦ ♣

A few hours, a few laughs, and more than a few drinks later, Dalton and Randolph locked up for the night. They'd finally settled on agreeable terms: Dalton would receive five dollars for five hours of playing, unlimited drinks, a line of credit worth five dollars per night at any of Randolph's gambling tables, and he'd keep one hundred percent of his winnings.

If Dalton won with the initial five, he paid it back to Randolph in full and kept the winnings. If he lost—which they both agreed wouldn't happen often—he'd only owe Randolph half the money.

"I think we need to do some advertising," Dalton slurred. "You know, put an ad in the newspaper, maybe put up a sign or two. Maybe we could find someone to make some for us."

"I'll make them myself. No need to spend money on something I can do on my own."

Dalton laughed, and his vision wobbled a bit. "Your handwriting is illegible. You spell half of the English words wrong, and you're the only one who can read it in the first place."

"I'm not paying for any signs," Randolph asserted. "You're already costing me too much money as it is."

"Fine. Have it your way. But you gotta do something."

"You're not kidding. Warren's been sucking me dry ever since the Continental opened. He's got cheaper drinks, more gambling, more girls—"

"More girls?" Dalton squinted. "He's a hypocrite. First time I met him, he wouldn't shut up about how *disgraceful* you were for having girls working here."

Randolph laughed. "He has *twice* as many girls as Madame DeBuire has here. I wonder if your uncle knows about that. Seems like appropriate grounds to dismiss him from his deaconship."

"Don't even talk about my uncle." Dalton rubbed his eyes. His head swam and encouraged him to sleep, but he resisted. Probably the alcohol.

No, *definitely* the alcohol.

"He doesn't know you're back?"

"No. I don't want him to know if I can help it."

"Dalton," Randolph said. "Spider's Rock may have grown since you left, but it hasn't grown that much. This is still a small town. He'll find out that you're back one way or another, probably by the end of the week. You might as well tell him yourself."

Dalton shook his head. "I have no desire to see him. He thinks I'm dead, just like everyone else. Let him keep thinking that."

"Whatever you say." Randolph held up his hands. "I don't want to get involved either way. Now about…"

Nizhoni walked into his memory, her bronze face illuminated by the setting sun on their wedding day. But she wasn't real—just a specter conjured from his broken heart to haunt him.

Then the memory flickered to her lying in his arms, covered in blood, dying. Dalton forced the image from his mind, but the sadness that had accompanied it still remained.

"Dalton? Are you listening to me?" Randolph snapped Dalton's trance.

Dalton shook his head. "She was beautiful, Randolph. The first time I saw her, I thought she was an angel. I really did."

"What? Who are you talking about?" Randolph asked. "Camille Warren?"

"No, not Camille. She doesn't even hold a candle to Nizhoni."

"I don't understand what you're saying. You slurred your last word."

Dalton frowned. "No, I didn't. That's how her name is pronounced. *Nizhoni.*"

"Who is Nizhoni?"

"Was. Who *was* Nizhoni."

"Fine. Who *was* Nizhoni?"

"She—" Dalton swallowed the lump in his throat and resisted the tears stinging his eyes. Was this real grief, or was the booze mixing with his emotions? "She was my—my—"

"You know what?" Randolph held up his hands again. "Forget I asked. I really have no interest in your personal troubles."

Dalton stared at Randolph and scrunched his eyebrows down. "What'd you just say?"

Randolph folded his arms. "I said I don't want to know what happened to you. I don't want you bogging me down with your worries, your problems. I have enough of my own."

Maybe it was the alcohol again, but Dalton wanted to slug him. He'd essentially left Dalton for dead a year ago, and now he had "no interest" in Dalton's "personal troubles?"

"Come on, Dalton. Don't glare at me," Randolph said. "When have I ever cared about your personal life, except when it interfered with my business?"

Never. Randolph had a point. At least he was consistent.

"Here, have another drink." Randolph poured Dalton another shot.

Dalton eyed him, then he eyed the shot. Randolph was consistent with the drinks too. That settled it. Randolph was forgiven. "Whatever you say, boss."

"Have you got somewhere to stay tonight? Room rate's gone up to an even three dollars per night now that the town's getting bigger. Warren can't build houses fast enough, so we get the Continental's over-flow, which still isn't much."

"Not gonna charge me five like you did a year ago?"

"Did I? If you want to pay five, I'm sure you could convince me to accept it." Randolph grinned.

Dalton waved his hand dismissively. "No, no. Three is good."

"You want a room, then?"

"I'll let you know." Dalton coughed, hacked. "Vanessa still work here?"

Randolph's eyebrow went up. "What about your long lost love, Niz—Nizh—"

"Nizhoni."

"Yah, her. And now you're asking about Vanessa Clark?"

Randolph's insinuation twisted Dalton's gut. through his stupor, Dalton fired back, "She's my *friend*. She might let me stay with her until I can find something else."

"Why don't you go back and stay with your uncle? I bet he'd love to have you back."

Dalton coughed again, this time for longer. His chest hurt—lungs burned. Too familiar. "I thought you didn't want to get involved in my personal life, Randolph."

Randolph smirked. "You're right. I'll mind my own business."

"Good. Is Vanessa here or not?"

"Yah, she's here."

Dalton coughed again. More fire in his lungs. "Didn't see her working."

"She's here. She might have someone with her tonight. I don't know for sure."

"What room?"

Randolph hesitated. "I don't want you interrupting anything."

"If she's busy, I won't bother her. If not, then I'll go from there. Which room?"

"Same room as always."

"I think I'll call it a night then." Dalton put his black hat on. "Looking forward to doing business with you."

"So am I."

From Randolph's tone, Dalton didn't know if he meant it or not. Then again, he'd been drinking, so he wasn't sure of much at the moment. "See you tomorrow."

"It *is* tomorrow. See you later today."

"Whatever. Good night."

Vanessa answered the second time Dalton knocked. She opened the door a crack and squinted at him.

"Can I help you?"

"Hi, Vanessa." Dalton leaned against her doorframe, mostly to keep from falling over.

"Do I know—" Her green eyes opened wide. "Dalton?"

"Yeah. It's me."

"I—I don't believe it." She opened the door wide and put her hand on his chest. "Is it really you?"

Dalton nodded, and it sent his head into a swirl. He gave a short groan and then asked, "Can I come in?"

"Of course you can," she said. "I must look somethin' terrible."

Dalton smirked. He'd always liked her Virginian accent, and the lace-edged satin nightgown she wore didn't hurt either. "You look fine, at least from what I can tell. Then again, I've had a few tonight, so what do I know?"

She held the door open and let him inside, shutting it behind her. She cupped his face with her hands. "I'm not dreamin', right? You're really here? Really alive?"

Dalton removed his hat and sat on her bed. "You're not dreaming. I'm really here."

Vanessa sat next to him and tucked a blonde curl behind her ear. "What happened that night?"

Dalton gave a slight chuckle. "After Zamora hit me, I woke up on my back in the desert. They'd surrounded me. I felt for my guns, but they'd already taken them. Then Zamora shot me three times—in the gut, in my arm, and in my head—and left me for dead. But I didn't die."

"He shot you in the head, and you didn't die?"

"The bullet just grazed me. See the scar?" Dalton pointed to the spot on his head. "The shot to my gut almost killed me, though."

She put her hand to her mouth. "Where have you been all this time?"

With a sigh, Dalton told her the entire tale. He'd managed to keep his emotions neutral this time. Maybe the alcohol in his body was finally dissipating. "And that's how I ended up back here."

"Oh, Dalton." She touched his hand. "I'm so sorry about your wife. That's so senseless."

Dalton just nodded. He felt nothing but emptiness.

"If there's ever anythin' I can do—"

"Actually, I was wondering if I could stay with you tonight." Dalton stared into her steamy green eyes.

Vanessa pulled away from him. "I didn't mean like *that*, Dalton."

Dalton shook his head. "That's not what I mean either. I just need a place to sleep for the night until I can make enough to afford my own room tomorrow night."

Vanessa bit her lip. "I—I don't think that's a good idea."

"It's fine. I'll sleep on the floor. You won't even know I'm here."

"No," Vanessa insisted. "I'm not comfortable with that. I'm sorry, but I think you should go."

Dalton tilted his head. He'd only been back for a few hours, and she was already tossing him out? "Did I... do something to offend you?"

"No, no. It's nothin' like that. I just—you've caught me at a strange time. I'm totally unprepared for you to be here."

"Like I said, you won't even know I'm around."

"Dalton, I can't." She shook her head. "You need to go."

"Why?" It didn't make any sense. She'd already said she was happy to see him, alive and all. So why was she behaving this way? "What did I do?"

"It's nothin' you did, Dalton. It's me. I—I can't. Please just trust me."

"What about your offer? What about 'if there's ever anything I can do?'"

"I meant someone to talk to, or if you needed some *money* or somethin'," she said. "I can give you enough to get you a room for tonight. How much do you need?"

"No, I'm not gonna take your money," Dalton said.

"It's okay, really. How much?"

"Vanessa, I'm not taking your money."

"You're not takin' it. It's a loan," she insisted. "You can pay me back after you start workin' again, okay?"

"What's wrong with you? All I'm asking is to sleep on your floor, maybe borrow one of your half-dozen pillows." Dalton motioned toward the mountain of pillows on the bed.

"And I'm sayin' I'm not ready for that. You *just* came back from the dead, Dalton Phillips. Feelin's, emotions I haven't felt for a year are swirlin' inside me—I just can't, alright?" Vanessa held out three dollars, each with the name of Max Warren's bank on them, for him to take. "Please trust me on this. Take the money."

"No." Dalton stared at her. "I'll leave, but I can't take your money."

"Alright." With a sigh, Vanessa lowered her hand. "I'm sorry, Dalton. I just can't handle this right now, not with what we've been through together. Especially not with you bein' a married man who just lost his wife."

Dalton snatched his hat into his hand. Hadn't she listened to him? He wasn't here for anything like that. "I'm fine, Vanessa."

She nodded. "Maybe you should go back to your uncle."

"Don't want to see him."

"He might let you stay with him."

Dalton shook his head. "I've got nothing to say to him."

Vanessa shrugged. "If you say so."

Dalton slipped his hat back on and headed for the door. He opened it, then he stopped and turned back to her. Even though she wasn't letting him stay, it *had* been good to see her.

"For whatever it's worth, I'm glad I stopped those bandits from getting to you. It almost cost me my life, but to see you now, safe and sound, knowing what I prevented by doing what I did—I can sleep well knowing I did the right thing, despite what happened to me afterward."

Vanessa looked at the floor and nodded again. "Yeah. Thanks."

"Don't feel bad about it. You were worth saving." Dalton swallowed hard. Was she worth him meeting Nizhoni, only to lose her the way he did? He bit his tongue to quell his rising emotions. Quickly, he said, "Good night, Vanessa. See you around."

"Good night, Dalton."

He shut the door just in time to conceal the first of the tears that streaked down his face.

The dark desert air clung to Dalton's skin, and he almost shivered. He'd gone out the door on the side opposite of the Imperial's saloon entrance so he wouldn't have to see Randolph again. He'd probably gone home by now anyway, but Dalton didn't want to take the chance.

The Continental finally slumbered for the evening, and the streets were mostly empty, save for the occasional vagrant more drunk than Dalton. He intentionally avoided everyone, and even resorted to hiding in the shadows of a building once.

The last thing he wanted tonight was trouble. Not while drunk, not as volatile as he felt. If someone crossed him, Dalton might—well, he didn't know *what* he might do. He might cry. He might kill. He might do both.

His feet found their way to Main Street, to the spot where he'd killed Tommy Roebuck. The bloodstained dirt had long since disappeared, replaced by cool, clean earth.

Forget Tommy. Forget Main Street. It was all in the past.

Dalton turned to his left, and his gaze panned up from street level to the six-foot cross mounted atop the church bell tower. His uncle's church. He swore. How had he managed to end up *here*, the last place on earth he wanted to be? His legs had taken him there, against his will.

Curse that cross. God had ruined Dalton's life, redeemed him, then ruined his life all over again. How could he serve a deity so diabolical? How could anyone?

Dalton soon found his hand on the wrought-iron handle attached to the massive church door. He pulled on it, and to his surprise, it opened. Had his uncle forgotten to lock it?

Now why was he going inside?

Because it was warmer in there, and because he could sleep on one of the pews. That's why.

Moonlight flowed through a large stained-glass window set into the back wall. Four shafts of colored light, separated by a giant opaque cross in the window's center, shone on the pulpit.

The church's grand piano sat on the right side, cloaked in shadows and covered with sheets. Warren had paid for it personally.

In a rare moment of cooperation, he had contracted a promising Prussian immigrant named Steinway to make it. Dalton had tickled those keys plenty of times. If Steinway kept making pianos as well as he'd made that one, he'd rule the industry in no time.

Forget the piano. That giant cross in the window commanded his attention. God's symbol, Jesus's symbol—whatever. God had never done anything for him but let him suffer.

"Can I help you?"

Dalton spun, skinned his revolver, and pointed it toward the voice.

A candle in the man's hand illuminated both his stern face and the shotgun hanging lazily at his side. His uncle, Reverend McCarroll.

"Dalton?" he asked in disbelief.

With a sigh, Dalton holstered his revolver and nodded. "Yeah. It's me."

Reverend McCarroll's shotgun barrel sank even lower. "Where in God's name have you been?"

Dalton shifted his shoulders. "I don't want to talk about it."

"I thought you were dead." Reverend McCarroll stepped forward. "Are you alright? Do you need a place to stay? Your old room's still open."

"I didn't come here for your charity, Uncle."

Reverend McCarroll cleared his throat, and his approach stalled. "Then why are you here?"

"I—I don't know. I had some drinks at Randolph's and then…" Dalton rubbed his face.

"What happened to you?" Reverend McCarroll's advance resumed, slow and steady.

"I said I don't want to talk about it. I just need sleep."

"Stay in your old room tonight. Please. Then, if you want, we can talk in the morning."

"You don't owe me anything."

"Never said I did. You're still my family, my blood. Please, stay here tonight."

Before Dalton realized what had happened, Reverend McCarroll had embraced him. Emotion flooded Dalton's body, and he heaved with each heavy sob, the wages of his broken heart.

♠ ♥ CHAPTER 21 ♦ ♣

" And that's how I ended up back here."

Dalton's tears had long since evaporated on the sanctuary's hardwood floors, and his rear-end hurt from sitting on one of the sturdy oak pews for the past hour, just like it had every Sunday morning during service.

He'd talked with his uncle well into the early morning. It had to be near sunrise by now.

"Guess I'm just unlucky," Dalton concluded.

"Luck has nothing to do with it Dalton," Reverend McCarroll said, his voice deep and gravelly as ever. "I don't believe luck exists."

Dalton cupped his face with his hands. "Then what is it? Why is all of this happening to me? First, the consumption, then getting sent down here. The gunfights, Zamora, Nizhoni… it's too much for one soul to bear."

Reverend McCarroll looked up at the cross set against the stained glass window. "There's no good answer to that, Dalton—at least no answer you want to hear from me."

"You think it's all my fault, don't you?" Dalton raised his hands and let them slap back down on his thighs. Now sober, his cognition had returned to full strength. "You think I brought this on myself."

Reverend McCarroll stared into his eyes. "What do you expect me to say? I can't lie to you Dalton. Yes, of course you brought a lot of this on yourself."

"Great." Dalton scoffed. Time for another lecture from his uncle the reverend. "You're a pastor. You're supposed to be encouraging me."

"If you'd *shut up* for a minute I could get to that part," Reverend McCarroll said. "You brought a lot of this on yourself—"

Dalton released a loud, unforgiving sigh.

"—but that doesn't mean it was *all* your fault. If you're honest with yourself, honest about the wrong you *know* you've done, then you can start over, live life the way you should."

Dalton stared at him. "You really presume to tell me how *I* should live *my* life after all that's happened to me?"

"Without a question, yes," Reverend McCarroll asserted. "You've obviously run your life poorly thus far, so if you actually want to move on and do right, then listen to me."

Dalton shook his head. "You don't know anything."

"This isn't about who knows more. It's cause-and-effect. Actions have consequences. The choices you made got you here, in church, broken. You're exactly where God wants you."

"Wow. If that's not love, I don't know what is." More sermonizing. Dalton rolled his eyes. "So God let all of this happen just to get me back in church? He let all of those Apaches—unarmed women and children —get murdered because it was part of His plan? Your God is a sick, sadistic—"

"We can talk all you want, but I won't tolerate you slandering the Lord's name, so watch your tongue." Reverend McCarroll pointed a thick finger at Dalton's nose. "And to answer your question, yes, God did allow all of that to happen, but I don't know why. Life isn't fair. We lose the ones we love, and yet we live on. It means you still have a purpose in this life."

"Yeah. To live my own life the way I want to live it," Dalton said, "not according to some worn-out book of myths."

"It's that same attitude that got you where you now sit," Reverend McCarroll said with a grunt. "I'm serious, Dalton. *Your* choices got you here, yet you have the audacity to blame God for all that's happened?"

Dalton was nearly shouting now. "So because the Apaches decided to fight the soldiers, their women and children got massacred, too? My unarmed, helpless wife got gunned down?"

Reverend McCarroll shook his head. "War is a curse, Dalton. A scourge upon our world. That had *nothing* to do with God, but He will hold those soldiers accountable for their sins when their day of judgment comes."

"That's *not* good enough." Dalton's heart raged in his chest. "They all deserve to die. And if I ever seen any of 'em again, so help me, I'll do it myself."

"Don't be a fool, Dalton," Reverend McCarroll chided him. "No one in this world can deliver God's justice or even speed up its arrival. Not you. Not me. Don't center your life on vengeance or retribution. It'll destroy you from the inside out."

Dalton sighed again and stood up. "All I ever get from you are lectures and sermons."

"Going to bed?" Reverend McCarroll rose to his feet as well. "Good idea. I'm beat."

"No. I'm leaving." If Dalton's uncle thought he was going to stick around after a conversation like that, he was delusional.

"What? Why?"

"We'll never agree. I don't want anything to do with your God. He's only ever let me down."

"You've never really given Him a chance to impress you."

"He's had the last twenty-four years of my life. If that's not enough time, I don't know what is."

"You don't have to leave, Dalton." His uncle approached him slowly, as if Dalton were a wild animal primed to flee. "We don't have to agree for you to stay. You're always welcome here."

"No I'm not. You don't approve of my lifestyle, of my choices," Dalton countered. "As long as I follow your rules and live your lifestyle, I can stay. And when I don't, you make sure I'm miserable. Maybe we're fine now, but when I come home drunk one too many times, or when I try to bring home another girl—"

"Okay, you're right." Reverend McCarroll held up his hand. "If you aren't willing to change, to abide by my rules—by God's rules—then you can't stay. But if you're willing to at least try to let Him fix you up, then I can be lenient—to a point. There are some lines I just can't allow you to cross if you're living here."

"Then we've got a problem. I have no desire to make peace with a God who's continually at war with me."

"Dalton." Reverend McCarroll held up both hands now. "That's all in your head. Your perception is wrong."

"No it isn't. I've got nothing to live for except me. And since I'm still here, I'm gonna live how I want until—"

A coughing fit interrupted Dalton's declaration. He covered his mouth with his hand as fire raked the inside of his lungs with each new hack.

When he finished, he noticed a few dark specks dotting his hand. Blood, burned black by the darkness of early morning. A familiar sight, but not one he'd seen for almost six months. Had he somehow aggravated his illness again?

"Until the consumption kills you?" Reverend McCarroll challenged. "Until you drown in alcohol or pick a fight with another mob of bandits who actually manage to finish the job this time? Until you get shot over a poker game?"

Dalton cleared his throat and inhaled a shaky breath. "We both know that last one would never happen."

"It might. Someone could come at you from behind, shoot you in the back of the head."

"Then I'll go out a little early." Dalton held out his arms. "Like I said, I've got nothing to live for anyway."

Now Reverend McCarroll sighed. "Look, son, I've said enough. You don't want to stay? Fine. I hate to see you continue to throw away your life, even when God has so obviously given you a second chance, but it seems that's your prerogative."

"No better options as far as I can see."

"Then I'm done arguing with you. I'm going back to bed. Good night, Dalton." Reverend McCarroll picked up his shotgun and headed for the doorway that led to the parsonage. "If you want to stay the night, stay."

"I won't."

Reverend McCarroll stopped. "Fine. You're welcome back if you ever change your mind. And if not—well, that's on you."

Dalton watched his uncle vanish into the darkness. Then he cast one last contemptuous glare at the huge cross in the stained-glass window and walked out the church door.

Inside his rented room at the Imperial, Dalton nursed his grief with a bottle of whiskey he'd procured from Randolph's stash. Dalton would pay for it tomorrow, of course, along with the extra dollar he owed Randolph for the room, but right now he needed the whiskey to wash away the sorrow and the remorse that plagued him.

Within fifteen minutes, his mind swirled with alcohol and emotion, everything from rage to shame to sadness. He had nothing left—nothing but an empty space next to him in his rented bed and a wedding ring on his finger. Nothing to live for.

Dalton glanced at the silver-plated revolvers hanging from the bedpost. He reached for one and slid it under his pillow. Easy access, should someone burst in on him. Who that might be, Dalton didn't know, but he took the precaution anyway.

The gun's handle just barely stuck out from under the pillow. He looked at it, his vision blurred, his mind hazy. Nothing to live for? Why not end it all right now?

He reached for it, but he hesitated.

One bullet. That's all it would take. Then he'd be out of his misery, just like a sick animal. That's what he was: a sick, wounded beast with no hope of recovery, with no purpose in life.

Instead of a bullet, Dalton opted for a shot. He grabbed the whiskey and swallowed a gulp. The bitter stuff burned his throat on the way down. He barely managed to set the bottle upright on the floor before everything went black.

Over the following days and weeks, Dalton wasted no time plunging back into his old lifestyle, his old routines.

At 5:30pm every evening, he played piano at the Imperial for his allotted five hours and then gambled after that, often long into the morning. At first, his take averaged around thirty dollars a night, but it gradually grew as new clients began to patronize the Imperial.

He enraptured the influx of beautiful young new women who worked at both the Imperial and the Continental with his Apache stories, his piano-playing, and perhaps with the raw, primal aura he exuded. Women loved him, but none of his relationships produced anything of substance.

That was fine with him—he preferred variety over validity, and it all helped him take his mind off of Nizhoni. The girls satisfied his need for attention and affection, and between the gambling, the piano playing, and the women, Dalton almost never lacked for company. When he did, the bottle filled the void.

During his waking hours, Dalton subsisted on alcohol—his nepenthe. He haunted the town in a state of semi-inebriation, a condition in which he couldn't feel the pain of his loss but didn't lack the reaction time or cognition to function in his often-hostile surroundings.

At night, before falling asleep, Dalton always drank more. That's when he needed it the most. That's when he thought of Nizhoni. That's when he couldn't think of anything else.

She visited him in the silence, when the music finally faded, when the ruckus of the patrons drifted away, when the creaking of the Imperial against the wind finally subsided. That's when he saw her in his mind's eye, always beautiful. Always bloody. Always dead.

He never went to bed sober.

Day and night he wore his silver pistols with pride. Before his disappearance, Dalton's quick-draw reputation had surpassed that of everyone else. Since his return he'd been elevated to the status of legend through whispered words that he couldn't be killed. Some even claimed he was a hellion in a man's body or that he was an ancient warrior reborn to immortality.

Thus far, he'd not tested his new set of smokes on any of the locals.

No one had dared to risk an encounter with Dalton Phillips, the man who'd dodged the grave, the man who'd stared Death in its ugly face and then doubled down on the pair of deuces in his hand.

Dalton basked in the reverence of those around him for a few months, but eventually he grew bored. The women no longer appeased him, the gambling became too easy. It seemed as if his opponents were letting him win, rather than risk angering the legend himself.

All the while, his left hand ached for action, for the chance to cut a man down in the blink of an eye, but no one dared oblige him.

Until tonight.

He'd finished his last piano set for the evening and played a half-dozen hands of five-card stud with some of the regulars and two or three new faces. Of that half-dozen hands, Dalton had won five. Now, with three queens and two eights in his hand, he not only knew he would win, but he'd take a lot of money with him, too.

The final bets came in, leaving Dalton to call or raise. The other players met the five-dollar wildcat he threw into the pot with groans and disdainful glares.

"Five or you're out, boys," he said, not even bothering to conceal his smile.

Half of them folded, but a few shelled out. A grubby blond-haired kid with blue eyes, probably no more than sixteen years old, sat two men over. He threw in the five then dropped another three dollars into the pot. "I'll raise ya."

"Cocky little bug, aren't you?" Dalton asked.

More players folded, but the kid just scowled at him.

"Only three dollars? You must not have a good hand." Dalton glanced at the kid's cards showing on the table—two kings, and a six, better than his two eights and a queen showing, for sure. They played with the first and last cards dealt facedown, so Dalton had to guess at his hand. "You probably have another six under there, huh? Gonna beat me with two pair?"

"Put up or shut up," the kid said, his face solid as stone.

No one said a word until Dalton broke the silence with a laugh. "I like this kid. Here's your three—" He dropped another five on the table. "—and here's another two."

"I'll see your two and raise you another three." The kid tossed the money in.

Dalton smiled. Maybe the kid had something, maybe not. Either way, Dalton couldn't give in now. He reached for his bottle of whiskey and sucked down a gulp, then set it back on the table.

"You've got a full house, then." Dalton shrugged. "You might want to stop putting money in the pot, though, kid. I'm gonna end up with all of it."

"You've got nothin'." The kid pointed at him. "I've been watchin' you. You bet more when you've got less to show for it. Now, are you in or not?"

By now a small crowd of patrons and their feminine consorts alike had formed around them. Their murmurs spurred Dalton to action.

He chuckled. "Alright, kid. How much you got?"

The kid dug into his pants pocket and pulled out a wad of bills, mostly ones. He counted it. "Thirty-four."

Dalton reached into his coat pocket and removed his leather billfold, the same one he'd taken from the dead soldier a few months earlier. Thoughts of Nizhoni resurfaced, but he washed them away with another swig of whiskey. After he won this hand, he'd buy a new billfold and use the old one for target practice.

He dropped some bills on the table. "Here's thirty-five. If you win, you get the extra dollar, but you gotta show first. Good?"

The kid's face lit up. He set the stack of bills on the pile. "I'm in."

"Let's have it."

The kid showed his cards: two kings, three sixes. A full house, just as Dalton had expected.

Dalton smiled. He flipped his other two ladies up. "Mine's bigger. You lose, kid."

The kid's eyes tripled in size. "You—you *cheated.*"

Dalton reached for the pile and pulled it over to his corner of the table. "Nope. Won it clean. If I were cheating, I'd have had aces instead of eights."

"No, you cheated. Ain't *no way* you had those from the beginning." The kid stood up.

"You must not understand how poker works, kid."

Dalton measured the situation. The kid wore a black revolver on his hip, but it was a big, clunky thing. Even with countless hours of practice, there was no way he was a quicker draw than Dalton.

"You see," Dalton continued, "I bet all of this money because I *did* have these cards from the beginning. Everybody loses big at some point. Hopefully you learned from it."

The kid swore and cussed. "This ain't over, bucko."

"*Bucko*, huh? Surely, your tongue doth drip with venom," Dalton mocked as he began to scrape the cash and chips into his shirt. He'd take the chips to the bar to cash out with Randolph, and then he'd probably just drink for the rest of the night. He'd earned it after winning that hand. "Anyway, seeing as you don't have any more money, the night *is* over for you."

Black steel flashed under the Imperial's lights, then silver, then fire.

A loud *bang* tore through Dalton's ears. Gray smoke hazed the air.

The kid dropped to his knees, then down onto his face, unmoving. His revolver lay next to him on the floor.

Gasps and even shouts sounded around Dalton, but they dissipated along with the smoke.

The kid shouldn't have pulled. Dalton had placed his hand on his revolver, ready from the moment the kid stood up. He'd been too hotheaded, and it had gotten him killed.

As Dalton stood and walked over to the kid, the crowd parted to give him space. He held up his revolver and blew the last of the smoke away from its barrel. "Guess you didn't learn anything after all."

"Nick? *Nick?*" called someone from over by the faro tables. A balding man with blonde hair and dirty laborer's clothes rushed over. He looked down at the kid, then at Dalton with familiar blue eyes. "You—you killed my son! You filthy—"

"He pulled first," Dalton said. "Everyone at this table saw it. He lost a big hand and then tried to shoot me."

"I don't care what happened. You *murdered* him." Dad reached for his own sidearm, but he froze when Dalton pointed his silver revolver in his face.

Dalton smirked. "Your son was *much* faster. I'm sorry for your loss, but he brought it on himself. Have a good night."

Before Dalton could lower his weapon, four men in soiled work attire similar to that of the kid's father surrounded him. Each of them pulled out revolvers of their own and took aim at his head.

♠ ♥ CHAPTER 22 ♦ ♣

"Easy, gentlemen," Randolph said from behind the bar. "We don't want any trouble."

"Only trouble's gonna be *his*," one of the workers said from behind. Dalton noted his position, more to the right, based on the direction his voice came from.

"Yeah, he's gonna pay fer killin' Nicky," said one off to Dalton's left.

"Please, *please* don't threaten him." Randolph extended his hand toward them. "You saw what happened to the boy. He'll do it to you too. I don't want any more blood spilled in my saloon."

The first worker, the one behind Dalton, laughed, but so did the other one behind Dalton, this one to the left. Meanwhile, patrons and the girls shuffled away from the site of the confrontation. Some even took cover behind the gambling tables while others fled the Imperial outright.

Without turning to look, Dalton visualized the men as the five points of a star with Dalton in the middle. The kid's father was at the front, two men stood on either side of him, and two more men stood behind him. This would be interesting at best, if not downright difficult.

"You think *he's* gonna kill *us*?" the first worker said. "Dunno if you can count, but there's four of us pointin' guns at him. Five if you count Nick's pa."

"Please, don't." Randolph's voice scraped with desperation. He knew as well as Dalton did what was about to happen. "I can't afford this kind of—"

"Just stay out of it, *Dutchie*," the first worker said—maybe he was their leader. "Now drop yer gun, mister, or we'll shoot ya down right here."

"Whatever you say."

Dalton slowly rotated his shoulder, pointing his gun away from the father and toward the man in front of him and to his left. He lined up the shot out of the corner of his eye, then he fired. The man went down.

Dalton was counting on shock and confusion to be on his side. At best, he'd get maybe an extra second or two before it wore off and the men decided to exact their vengeance like they'd warned. At worst, they'd shoot him right away.

But shock and confusion was what he got. In the stunned instant after shooting the first man, Dalton quickly rotated his shoulder again and shifted his body to shoot the man behind him on his left side.

With his arm already in motion, he twisted it behind his back, turned his head, and fired a round into the worker who stood in front of him and to his right, then he contorted his back to take aim at the first worker, the leader. He got a bullet from Dalton's gun, too, right as he got the hammer of his own revolver clicked back.

By the time Dalton returned his gun to its starting point, the boy's father had overcome his shock and drawn his revolver. But Dalton's last shot hit him in his chest and laid him out on Randolph's floor.

The whole exchange took less than three seconds, exactly five bullets, and now five more men lay dead at Dalton's feet in an ever-widening puddle of blood.

Despite everything that had just happened, only one thing entered Dalton's mind: Randolph was going to have a horrific time cleaning up his floors now.

Dalton wrote off the thought as a strange brew of alcohol and sudden stimulus and tension evaporating all at once. He scanned the crowd who still remained in the Imperial and absorbed the shock and the horror on their faces.

He smiled at them. "That's nothing. You should've seen me with my right hand."

"Dalton," a gruff voice growled behind him.

He holstered his empty pistol and turned. "Yeah?"

"You need to go," Randolph said.

"Yep. My evening's over now, isn't it?" He spotted his half-downed bottle of whiskey, his pile of cash on the table, and the various chips and banknotes that had fallen to the floor amid the commotion. "Can't forget those, can I?"

Randolph came out from behind the bar, something he almost never did, and walked over to Dalton as he collected his winnings and his whiskey. "Here, I'll help you up to your room."

"Easy, Randolph. I'm not drunk. I'm just—okay, maybe I'm a *little* drunk." Dalton shoved the bills into any and every pocket he could, from his pants to his coat. "Where's my hat?"

"Foley's got it."

Why did Foley have his hat? "Well, he'd better give it back, or I'll—"

"He's just holding it for you. See?" Randolph pointed.

With a quivering hand, Foley held it out for Dalton to take, and he did.

Then Randolph pushed him through the door that connected to the Imperial's boarding side.

With wide eyes, the girl running the innkeeper's desk asked, "Everythin' alright in there? I heard—"

"Make yourself scarce, will you?" Randolph cut her off.

Her mouth clamped shut, but she nodded and walked past them into the saloon.

Randolph shut the door behind her.

Dalton frowned at him and focused on staying upright. With slurred words, he asked, "What's going on? Why're you behaving so strangely?"

Randolph put his hands on Dalton's shoulders. "Dalton, listen to me. You just gunned down six people. *Six.* Do you understand that?"

"*Of course* I understand that. It was the most incredible thing I've ever done. Ever." He grinned. "They *were* trying to kill me, you know."

"But you did it in a public place—in *my* public place."

"So? They were asking for it."

Randolph shook his head. "Doesn't matter. That's bad for business. Very, very bad. I know the shots were all justified, but I have to let you go."

Dalton shrugged Randolph's hands off his shoulders, and immediately his ankles wobbled. "What do you mean?"

"I mean you're fired. You can't work for me anymore. People won't come around if they know you're here. You can't come around the saloon anymore either."

"*What?*" Dalton shook his head. "No. Uh-uh. You can't do this, Randolph. I *saved* you. I kept you from going out of business, and *this* is how you repay me?"

"You give me no choice. You're a liability now."

Dalton glared at him and swore. "That's what I think of you."

Randolph didn't say a word.

"You and the Imperial can burn in hellfire. I don't need you anymore, Randolph. I won more money tonight than I ever have before. I'll just play at the Continental from now on. We'll see how your business does then, won't we?"

"By all means, go to the Continental. Maybe you can scare some business my way."

"Big-talker," Dalton mocked. "I hope the Imperial burns down *tomorrow*."

"Good night, Dalton," was all Randolph said. "You can stay as long as you pay and don't cause any more trouble around here. If either of those things change, you're out."

"Then shut up and leave me alone."

Randolph nodded, then he headed back into the saloon.

Up in his room, a coughing fit and more whiskey concluded Dalton's night. Between hacks, he managed to suck the bottle dry, just enough to fling him into a total stupor. The last thing he remembered was wishing he'd snatched another bottle before Randolph had ushered him upstairs.

Oh, well. He'd buy more at the mercantile tomorrow. It wasn't free, but it would get him just as drunk. Good enough.

A combination of the clanging church bell and the hot coals inside Dalton's lungs woke him the next morning. When he finally managed to corral the coughing fit, he tasted copper. He dabbed his tongue with his forefinger and found blood.

A lot of blood. More than usual.

Dalton scowled. He reached for his bottle of whiskey from last night, and, finding it empty, tossed it aside. There was a bottle of gin stashed under his bed somewhere, but he didn't feel up to bending over to dig around for it, so he let it be for the time being.

He walked over to the porcelain water basin that sat on the dresser across the room. Dalton swished the tepid water around in his mouth and then spat it back out. The remaining water turned a pinkish color, much darker than Dalton had expected.

Not good.

He looked into the mirror above the basin. Aside from a spattering of red dots under his sharp blue eyes—probably broken blood vessels from coughing so hard—he didn't look too bad. He needed a shave, a bath, and maybe a haircut, but under that brute in the mirror, he saw a handsome, intelligent young man with money in his pocket.

A man who'd killed six people last night.

But those killings were justified. The kid had pulled first, and the other five had ambushed Dalton. It was either his life or theirs.

The last time five men had come for him, he'd barely survived. He wasn't going to make that mistake again. He'd done what he had to do to survive.

Then why did he feel so empty? So ashamed of himself? He'd killed men before and never felt this kind of remorse.

Maybe it had been too easy. After all, he'd gunned all six of them down without so much as a hint of resistance from any of them. Sure, he'd employed some fancy footwork and shooting—with his left hand, no less—but not one of them had even managed to get a shot off.

Had Dalton become an executioner? They might as well have lined up against a wall with their hands tied behind their backs so Dalton could dispatch them one by one at his leisure.

In the end, they'd all died because a kid had lost a hand of five-card stud. Dalton couldn't deny that it had been a waste. But, again, it wasn't his fault. He hadn't cheated; he'd played fair and won big.

He coughed again. Pain from his lungs seared his throat and tainted his tongue with the metallic tang of more blood. The man in the mirror looked back at him, his dazed blue eyes reflecting the guilt churning in his gut.

Even so, he'd killed those men. Ended their lives. It was easy.

Dalton shouldn't have done it. He shouldn't have killed the kid. He could've walked away from the table, or he could've let the kid win.

He shouldn't have even provoked the kid. But he had, and now six people were dead.

Dalton shook his head and rubbed his face. Nizhoni would be ashamed of him.

A familiar abyss of sorrow in his heart meshed with the guilt in his gut and the fire in his lungs.

Great. Why had he brought *her* into this? He swore.

God, he missed her so much. If only she'd survived, he could've avoided this... all of it.

Dalton hung his revolvers in their holsters and draped his belt over the bedpost again. All he had to do was take one in his hands, and then he could end it all. What did he really have to live for, anyway? He'd lost his love, his family, and now his job and means of income, leaving him with only physical, emotional, and mental grief.

And in the absence of that noise to occupy him, Nizhoni would certainly return. He would find no peace in busyness, no respite in work. He was all alone again with his thoughts.

But all he had to do was pull the trigger, and it would all go away. He could join Nizhoni in whatever afterlife she'd gone to, and then he'd no longer be a burden on the people around him. He could leave this wretched world behind, and he could begin again somewhere else.

The option seemed more appealing with each day that passed.

Dalton had a short discussion with Marshal Garmer about the previous night's excitement, followed by a long lecture about not killing any more townspeople.

In the end, Marshal Garmer didn't bother to even lock Dalton up this time. Too many witnesses had sided with Dalton, and no one had come forward with a complaint about the men who'd died.

That all suited Dalton just fine. He withstood the lecture, shook Marshal Garmer's hand, and headed out, determined to get his job back.

That afternoon, he hammered on the Imperial's front door eight times. He'd already tried to get in through the door that connected the boarding side to the saloon side, but it was locked.

Through the window, he could see Randolph standing behind the bar, wiping out shot glasses. Apparently that was the only thing he ever did to occupy his time.

After a few more moments of Dalton's pounding, Randolph relented and finally came over and unlocked the door. "Get out of here, Dalton."

Not a great start to the conversation.

"Come on, Randolph. Let's talk."

"No. You need to leave. Go now, or I'll get Marshal Garmer."

"What's he gonna do?"

"Arrest you."

"For what?"

"Loitering. Trespassing. Public Disturbance. *Murder*," Randolph said. "Pick one."

Dalton laughed. "He's got more important things to do than arresting me on a nothing charge, and we both know the shootings were justified. They drew first. Besides, I already talked to him, and the witnesses were all on my side. No crime committed."

Randolph arched his bushy eyebrows down. "I don't care what the marshal said. You need to get away from here. I don't want to see you anywhere near this place. You're lucky I don't throw you out of the boarding side as well."

Lucky. Yeah, that word described Dalton's life right about now.

Behind Randolph, Dalton could see a series of dark stains on the

Imperial floor. Randolph must've done his best to clean up the blood, but to no avail.

He had, however, rearranged some of the gaming tables and chairs to try to conceal the stains. Dalton supposed that at night, with low lighting, they might not be so noticeable.

Still, even the sight of the stains churned Dalton's stomach with regret. He pushed most of it out of his mind, but he held on to just enough to try to use it to his advantage.

He donned his sincerest expression and changed the timbre of his voice to a somber tone. "Look, I'm sorry for shooting those men last night. I shouldn't have done it."

"Sorry's not good enough." Randolph shook his head. "You can't come back."

"No, really. I'm sorry." Dalton held his hands out. "I can't get it out of my head. I feel terrible."

"I'm not a preacher, Dalton. You want forgiveness, talk to your uncle."

"That's not what I'm looking for. I want my job back."

"Not a chance." Randolph's stern brown eyes showed no sign of capitulation.

"I'll change. I'll stop drinking, stop gambling as much. I can control myself," Dalton was almost pleading. "I can prove it to you. Just give me another chance."

"No. Get out of here." Randolph tried to shut the door, but Dalton wedged his boot between the door and the frame to keep it open.

If Randolph was going to play this hard, Dalton could play even harder. His heart thrummed in his chest, and he injected anger into his voice.

"Look, you *need* me. Your business is booming, but do you really think people will keep coming if you don't have my music?"

"I already have someone else lined up to play. I don't need you anymore."

Dalton's heart banged a little faster, and his words stalled. "Who… who'd you get?"

"None of your business."

"Is it the fellow from the Continental?" If it was, then Dalton could just take his spot.

"No. It's someone new. Someone who won't *shoot* my patrons." Randolph added, "Cheaper too."

"Come on, Randolph." Now Dalton *was* pleading, but he no longer had any leverage. All he had was reason and logic, and if he couldn't get Randolph to see that... "You're being totally unreasonable. I had no choice. The kid pulled first, and then those goons surrounded me. You even warned 'em yourself, remember? They deserved what they got."

Randolph started shaking his head even before Dalton finished. "It doesn't matter. People won't come around if they know you'll be here. They don't want to get killed."

Dalton shrugged. "People have short memories. Enough time goes by, they'll forget what I did. They'll only remember it if they cross me."

"That's not good enough. You're done, Dalton. Go now, please."

Dalton sighed. "Fine. Have it your way. We'll see how well the Imperial does without me. The day will come when you'll want me back. And when it does, I might not *want* to work at your hellhole saloon, so you'd better think long and hard about what you're doing here."

Dalton pulled his foot from the door and stepped back.

Randolph didn't say a word. He just shut the door and locked it without giving Dalton so much as a second look.

Across the street, a man approached the Continental and went inside. Max Warren owned the place, but with everything else he owned, maybe he wouldn't be on the premises. But if he happened to show up while Dalton was there...

Warren or no Warren, the pile of cash Dalton had stashed in his room wouldn't last forever.

He crossed the street with money on his mind.

CHAPTER 23

D alton wore a smirk the whole night. By eleven that evening, he'd racked up over a hundred dollars in winnings—half from the Continental and half from the Continental's patrons.

The extra five hours of not playing the piano really accelerated his progress. If he could come in every night and replicate that kind of success, he'd never want for anything.

Within just a few hours of his arrival, Dalton decided that he actually preferred the Continental to the Imperial.

Warren had obviously spared no expense, but his taste differed from Randolph's on a foundational level: where the Imperial sought to give customers the feel of a luxury casino in Europe, the Continental targeted those rugged men who had traveled from the East to seek their fortunes in the western wilderness.

Antique weapons, Indian paraphernalia, the heads of bison, bear, deer, and other animals, and comparable rustic décor lined the interior walls, appropriately paneled with dark wood. Sweet cigar smoke seemed to cloak the entire place with a wispy haze.

Pioneers, prospectors, railroaders, trailblazers, and countless other adventurous upstarts clogged the space, each eager to engrave his name into the annals of history. Or, at the very least, each was anxious to claim a chunk of the Continental's money for himself.

What the Continental lacked in opulence it made up in whiskey and women. Voluptuous girls ran the bar, ran the tables, and ran up clients' tabs before convincing them to extend the night's revelry via overnight companionship.

Each and every one of those girls lived by the same desperate standards as Dalton: they had nothing to lose and little more to gain. They did what they had to do to survive. That desperation often polarized them—they either commanded the utmost of respect, like Vanessa, or they couldn't care less.

When it came to whiskey, clients drank for free while spending money at the gaming tables. But if they loafed about at the bar or chased skirts, they paid top dollar for their booze.

Dalton gawked at this bold strategy at first but then rationalized it as good business. *Great* business. When he'd first arrived in Spider's Rock, Dalton never thought he'd meet anyone as money-hungry as Randolph. After visiting the Continental, Dalton decided Max Warren was the new frontrunner.

But at a hundred dollars ahead at the tables, this was no time for analyzing business practices or admiring decorations. No, it was time to celebrate, to double his money—or even better, both.

Dalton motioned to one of the girls, a cute brunette with dark brown eyes. "Margie, more whiskey over here, please."

"You got it, handsome," she called over the ruckus.

Dalton won a hand against five other patrons seated with him at one of the Continental's many tables, among them, John Vernon, the shorter and chubbier Vernon brother whom Dalton had first met in the mercantile a year earlier. Margie returned and poured Dalton a drink right after.

"Thanks, hon'. Better make it a double, though, and make sure these fine gents get some too." Dalton looked into their eyes and smirked. "We need to keep things civil. Wouldn't want anyone to pull a gun, now would we?"

The rest of the table snickered—not out of nervousness, it seemed, but out of camaraderie. When one of them spoke up, he confirmed Dalton's thoughts.

"I agree with what you done, Dalton," said Hutch, a big ruddy trail-blazer with a thick brown beard. "Kid never shoulda pulled a gun on you. He was asking for it."

"Thanks, Hutch." The tale of Dalton's exploits at the Imperial had filled the ears of just about every townsperson in Spider's Rock by now, and his fearsome reputation had seemingly returned to its former glory overnight—almost as if he'd never been gone.

"And those other five? Hoo-wee! I'm still amazed you made it out of there alive." Hutch tossed in his cards, folding. "Much less completely unharmed."

"Wasn't as hard as you might think." Dalton tilted his head and looked at the ceiling. It was much easier to be cavalier about what he'd done when so many people seemed to admire him for it. "Well, I shouldn't say that. It wasn't hard for *me*, but I've had lots of practice."

"I know that's right," John Vernon said. "I still remember when you gunned down Tommy Roebuck. I couldn't believe how fast you were."

Dalton scrunched his eyebrows down and stared at John. "I thought you didn't see that."

"What do you mean?"

"You didn't know who I was when I met you in the mercantile last year," Dalton said. "Maybe my memory's just fuzzy from all the alcohol and smoke in here."

"No, I saw it happen, alright. Just didn't realize it was you until Gilbert said so," he replied.

Dalton shrugged. "Makes no difference, I suppose. You gonna bet or fold, John?"

"I'm out, too." John smacked his cards facedown on the table. "Can't afford to lose any more money on mismatched cards."

Margie had made her way around the table, ending back at Dalton. She filled his glass again, and again, and many more times after that as the night rolled on.

Within a few more hours, a cloud of haze descended over Dalton's world, and darkness encroached in his vision from the corners of his eyes. A few more drinks and he'd be out.

Maybe he should pull back, at least until he got back to his room at the Imperial for the night. If he passed out here, who knew what might happen to him, or to his money?

As Dalton fought to stay conscious, his gaze found familiarity across the room—soft facial features, flowing brown hair, and the same royal blue eyes as her mother. She was trouble incarnate, standing there on two long, perfect legs.

Camille Warren, dressed in a sea-green dress with purple trim and gold accents. A sweet piece of candy eager to be unwrapped and savored, the same as she'd been the first time he laid eyes on her.

Also as before, she couldn't take her eyes off him.

A haphazard cough seized Dalton's throat. He recoiled from the table and pointed his body away from the other players. Once the fit subsided, he could keep playing cards.

But this time, the fit didn't stop, didn't even calm down. Dalton continued to cough and hack, and each heave wracked his body with sharp convulsions.

The darkness around the edges of his eyes crept farther inward and blackened even more of his vision. Coppery blood coated his mouth, sputtered onto his hands, dribbled down his chin, and spattered onto the floor below him.

Would he die here? Now? In the Continental? He thought of nothing else as he slipped into the shadows of uncertainty.

CHAPTER 24

Yellow light seeped through two slits in Dalton's vision and banished the darkness away.

"Hold still, please," a man's voice said.

Dalton mumbled something not even he understood. His mind felt like a jumbled mess of thoughts and emotions, and he couldn't decipher any of them.

"Please, whatever you're trying to say, it can wait," the man said. "You could have died tonight. To tell you the truth, I don't know how you're even still alive."

Could have died?

Dalton's thoughts slowly crystallized, and he realized the other side of that statement. It mean he'd dodged the Gates of Hell for a little longer.

But when he tried to move, his throat, head, gut, and chest all rebelled against him.

"I said *hold still*," the man said.

Dalton didn't recognize the voice. Maybe he was in Hell after all—if the demons had Bostonian accents.

"I'm trying to help you, but I can't if you keep squirming."

Do they help people in Hell?

After his body's last painful rejection of movement, Dalton had no desire to try it again. Even so, he managed to mumble, "Whrrr emm I?"

"Don't talk. You're safe. I'm Dr. Richards, and you're in my home. I am examining you."

"Huh?" Dalton didn't know any doctors or Richards. Either the man had moved to Spider's Rock after Dalton left or—*Hell?*

"Keep quiet, please. I'm trying to listen for fluid in your lungs."

Fluid. Like blood? Mucus? Both?

Maybe whiskey was sloshing around in there. He'd certainly downed enough of it.

Cool metal pressed against Dalton's chest, which he now realized was bare, and he moaned. It went away just as quickly.

"There. I'm finished. You may move now."

Dalton wasn't sure he wanted to attempt it anymore, but he tried to sit up anyway.

"Easy. Let me help you," Dr. Richards said.

A hand under Dalton's back helped support him. His body protested again, but he somehow made it upright.

As soon as he opened his eyes, dizziness besieged him. He shut his eyes and held his head with his hands. His stomach lurched into his throat and he filled a basin between his bare feet with watery vomit that reeked of whiskey.

"I thought that might happen. That's why I put that basin there," Dr. Richards said.

Dalton clutched his stomach and crumpled to the floor over the basin from atop the doctor's examining table. He kept retching.

"By the amount of liquid in that basin, I'd say you probably drank enough to knock out a horse. Your body is rejecting the overwhelming amount of alcohol you consumed."

"Thanks, Doc," Dalton quipped between bouts of vomiting.

It wasn't the first time he'd been this drunk, but combined with the burning in his chest and throat, the vomiting hurt much worse. When he finally emptied his stomach, Dalton pushed himself up onto his knees, still a bit dizzy. Something moist and warm touched his hand, and it startled him at first.

"Here. Use this washrag to clean yourself up."

Dalton took it and wiped down his face and neck. The rag smelled of menthol and another equally strong, clean aroma, but he couldn't place it. He sniffed it again and felt it clearing his sinuses.

"That scent is eucalyptus oil. It normally comes from eucalyptus trees in Australia, but they've begun to grow them in California now."

"How…?"

"Well, the climate in parts of California is comparable to that of the Australian outback, where eucalyptus trees grow. Australian immigrants successfully transplanted—"

"No. How did I get here?" Dalton rubbed his eyes and looked up at Dr. Richards.

His thick silver hair and bushy beard would've made him look more like an old trailblazer than a doctor, were it not for his monocle and his slender figure. He wore a burgundy smoking jacket with a black shawl lapel, gray flannel trousers, and black slippers.

"Forgive my attire," he said. "But it is the middle of the night, after all."

Dalton just stared at him.

Dr. Richards flashed a sullen smile. "A trio of rough-looking fellows carried you in. One was as big as the other two combined. He had a curly brown beard and—"

"Hutch," Dalton said.

Dr. Richards raised an eyebrow. "I didn't catch any of their names."

Dalton patted his waist. "Where are my guns?"

"Mm. I've heard you had somewhat of an excitable trigger finger."

Dalton stared at him for a moment, but Dr. Richards didn't continue. "And…?"

"I removed them for my own safety."

"*And…?*"

"They're under your hat, hanging from that coat hook by the door."

Dalton grabbed the edge of the table with his left hand and slowly pulled himself up so as not to risk going dizzy again. He leaned against the table for a moment, then he headed over to his hat, coat, and guns. He patted his coat down and promptly asked, "Where's my money?"

"You'll find it."

171

Dalton pulled one of his revolvers out, but he didn't point it at Dr. Richards. "I don't want to ask you again, Doc."

"Mr. Phillips, threatening me is hardly a good use of your time or mine. I saved your life, yet here you are, wielding a gun? Perhaps I should have stayed in bed and allowed you to choke on your own vomit."

"Maybe you should have," Dalton said, his voice hard as steel.

"Surely you don't mean that."

Dalton pulled the hammer back on his revolver, but he still didn't point it at Dr. Richards. Why couldn't the man give him a straight answer? Slowly and deliberately, he asked, "Where is my money?"

"It's in your coat pocket."

"No it isn't. I checked."

"Check again."

Dalton eyed him.

"Check again," Dr. Richards insisted. He reached for a tobacco pipe on a small table next to an overstuffed chair made of burgundy leather and lit it with a match from his jacket pocket.

Dalton reached inside his coat again and surveyed the room. Dark wood. A stone fireplace. Bookshelves crammed with heavy reading, complete with titles from Aristotle, Plato, and the like.

What's more, Dr. Richards' examination table wasn't that at all—it was a polished hardwood dining table, and the yellow light that coated the room came from a modest crystal chandelier hanging over it, glowing with the warm light of about a dozen burning candles.

Dalton's fingers found paper. Lots of it. From his coat's left inside breast pocket, he pulled a thick bundle of banknotes, some federal, but mostly wildcats, and thumbed through them.

"I trust it's all there?" Dr. Richards puffed on his pipe.

"Looks that way." The truth was, Dalton couldn't remember exactly how much he'd won before he'd blacked out, so whatever he'd managed to keep with him would have to do for now. He slipped his coat on, then his belt, and holstered his gun.

"Your large friend was very clear: your money was not to be touched. I'm not the sort of man who would even think about stealing from you or any other patient, but you should know he made it especially clear that you simply would not tolerate anything of the sort."

Dalton's boots sat near the door. As he slid them on, he asked, "How much do I owe you?"

"It's not really a question of how much you—"

"Do you *ever* answer a question directly?" Dalton asked.

Dr. Richards's eyebrows went up. "I'm not sure what you mean."

"Forget it. I got my answer."

"You mentioned that you wished I'd let you die. Why did you say that?"

"That's not what I said," Dalton replied. "I said 'maybe you should have' let me die."

Dr. Richards frowned, but Dalton barely caught his expression because of his thick beard. "There's not much of a distinction between the two."

"I don't want to talk about this. How much do I owe you?"

"In addition to my medical degree, I am also well-educated in the field of psychology. Perhaps you'd like to discuss these negative feelings?" Dr. Richards stepped toward him.

Dalton scoffed. "No thanks. I'll be fine."

"I'm being quite serious, Mr. Phillips. I'm confident I could help you reach the root of your problem if you're willing to talk with me. Perhaps we could start with that overactive trigger finger?"

Dalton glanced at the door. "It's not overactive, Doc. I only use it when I have to."

"Is that so?" Dr. Richards took another step forward. "I wonder… what kind of situation necessitates that sort of reaction?"

Enough was enough. Dalton squared himself with Dr. Richards. "Look, you gonna tell me what I owe you or not?"

Dr. Richards smiled. "How much is your life worth to you?"

Dalton loosed a mirthless chuckle. "You don't want me to answer that."

"Why not?"

"Because you won't get paid anything."

"Why do you feel that way?"

Dalton shook his head and sighed. "Can't fool me, Doc. I know what you're trying to do, and I know why you're trying to do it. I'm not interested."

"Oh? And what am I trying to do?" Dr. Richards kept smiling.

"You're trying to get me talking. You think that if you can get me to betray something about why I don't care if I live or die, you'll be able to hook me, and get me to agree to a session, maybe several. You're trying to sell me on your services because you think I'll be a consistent source of revenue for you," Dalton said. "A cash cow of sorts, but with disposition issues."

Dr. Richards's eyes widened slightly, but he said nothing.

"What's more, I not only clearly have money to pay you for that time, but you actually find me interesting. You think I'd make a fantastic case study, one you could present to the medical community and universities back east, or even in Europe. Maybe you'd even write a book about me. You think I could bring you additional fortune and fame in the long run."

Now Dr. Richards's mouth hung open.

"Am I close?" Dalton asked.

"Remarkable. Have you ever had any psychological training, Mr. Phillips? Or in philosophy?"

Dalton just smirked. "How much do I owe you?"

"Remarkable. Simply remarkable." Dr. Richards smiled. "How about five dollars?"

Sort of a steep price, but if Dr. Richards had actually saved his life then Dalton might as well pay him for the extra time he'd snatched out of the Devil's grasp.

He pulled a duo of bills from his wad and slapped them into Dr. Richards's hand. "Here's ten. Thanks for everything."

"Mr. Phillips?"

Dalton stopped at the door. "Yes?"

"From a medical perspective, I'd suggest that you begin to live your life in a healthier way. With your consumption as advanced as it is, you're incredibly vulnerable. The coughing fits, the blood from your lungs—your pulmonary system is beginning to fail you," Dr. Richards said.

Dalton fought the urge to let out a harsh sigh. *Another lecture. Great.*

"If you don't already feel fatigued on a consistent basis, you will, and your excessive alcohol consumption will only accelerate and exacerbate your symptoms. I doubt you have long to live, unless you start living your life with less apathy and more care for your own well-being."

Dalton swallowed. "How long might I have left?"

Dr. Richards sighed. "A year, perhaps. Certainly longer if you restrain your raucous lifestyle and questionable choices."

"Thanks for the straight answer."

Dr. Richards nodded. "Where are you going?"

"Well, if I've only got a year left—" He looked back at Dr. Richards. "—I'd better make it one hell of a good year. Night, Doc."

"Good night. Oh, one last thing, Mr. Phillips," Dr. Richards called after him. "Make sure to at least get plenty of rest. It's key to your body's ability to fight off illness and heal from injuries. I'd recommend a period of extended bed rest—a break, if you will, from your lifestyle, before you resume your revelry. Then, at least, you can more fully enjoy the last of your days."

Dalton grinned. It made sense, what Dr. Richards had prescribed. "Thanks Doc. I'll take it under advisement."

He shut the door behind him and headed out into the street.

♠ ♥ CHAPTER 25 ♦ ♣

The early morning moonlight drenched the town's streets with silver. Dalton crossed Main Street over to the Imperial, now dark except for two solitary lights, one at ground level and another on the second floor.

He shivered in the cool night air. Had he lost a part of himself in Dr. Richards's house? The part that kept the rest of him warm at night?

Maybe he'd vomited it up along with all that whiskey.

One year left? That was it?

Then again, Dalton shouldn't have been surprised. He'd lost seven or eight of his nine lives in the last year alone. He should already be dead, but somehow he wasn't.

The consumption would do him in eventually—if the whiskey didn't get him first. Or maybe he'd get popped in the back of the head by some vengeful gambler hellbent on getting his money back, like his uncle had suggested.

He should be so lucky.

When Nizhoni was alive, he'd hoped for a family, for a future. Now, without her, all of that had vanished with the blowing wind, swept away like a tumbleweed in the desert.

As he turned the doorknob to the boarding half of the Imperial, the unmistakable rustle of clothing immediately crackled from the shadows to his left.

Dalton ripped his revolver from its holster and aimed into the darkness.

Was it that faceless gambler, come to claim his vengeance so soon? Sick or not, Dalton would gun him down just the same. He had no intention of going down without a fight.

"Dalton," a feminine voice said. "It's me."

He raised an eyebrow and let his gun barrel sink. "I can't see anything. Who are you?"

A feminine form stepped into the light. Long brown hair, soft facial features, royal blue eyes, and a fantastic shape in an elegant sea-green dress, all of which he recognized from earlier that night at the Continental.

"Camille Warren." He eyed her. "Just the kind of trouble I *don't* need right now."

"How are you feeling?" she asked.

"Never better. Why do you ask?" Dalton holstered his revolver.

"Come now, Dalton. You've no cause to be hostile. I'm not trying to get you in trouble."

"Last time I saw you, everything in my life changed. Got shot three times and left for dead in the desert before your father even had a chance to get to me. Lord knows what would've happened then." Dalton rubbed his shoulders.

"If you're cold, we can go inside," she offered.

"I'll go in, but you oughta stay out here. Better yet, go *home*." He reached for the door, but she grabbed him by the arm.

"I'm sorry about last year. I don't know how my father found out, but it was probably some indiscretion on my part. I never meant to hurt you or endanger you."

When Dalton looked into her eyes, his heart pumped faster. "That's kind of you to say, Miss Warren, but—"

"Camille, please," she said.

"If it's all the same to you, I've had quite a rough night, and I'd like to get to bed." Even in the moonlight, Dalton could see Camille blushing. "That's—that's not what I meant, Camille."

"I know. But a girl can dream, right?"

"Look, whatever we had last year—it's over now. I got married, my wife died, and—"

"Do forgive me for interrupting, but I know all of that. Let me plead my case. If you still aren't interested, then I'll leave posthaste."

The exasperated sigh that escaped Dalton's lips had to be offensive to her, but he didn't care. "Fine then. Let's hear it."

Instead of talking, she pulled him close and kissed him. Not just a peck, but a long exchange, full of passion and zeal. When they broke apart, she said, "That's the first part."

Dalton swallowed the lump in his throat. Though unexpected, her kiss sent lightning bolts crackling all the way down to his toes. *Incredible.*

"I'm listening," he admitted.

"The second is this: I adore you. I haven't gone a single day without thinking about you since you came back to Spider's Rock. I'm attracted to everything about you, and I want to get to know you better." She shrugged and added, "I'll admit, part of the reason I find you so attractive is that you're so dangerous, so complicated. And also because Daddy hates you."

Dalton scoffed. "Ain't *that* the truth."

"I may look like a well-mannered, soft-spoken priss, but I'm not. I want to see the world, discover new places, explore everything my father doesn't want me to see." She looked at Dalton. "I know you're concerned about Daddy, and rightfully so. He's very powerful, very rich. But I'm too wild to live in his house anymore. I'm moving out, first chance I get."

"That's great, but you're still his daughter. That won't keep him off my back."

"We can keep him off your back as long as he doesn't know about you."

Dalton laughed. "That's it? That's your plan? Hiding our tryst from him?"

A cunning smile parted Camille's lips. "So you *are* interested."

Dalton's expression hardened, but he knew he couldn't maintain his stoicism for long. "Don't change the subject. We both know he's the only man in this town who poses a real threat to me. If I get involved with you, I'll move to the top of his list."

"I'm my own woman now, Dalton. I was barely seventeen last year, but now I'm eighteen. Daddy doesn't control me anymore."

As if one year made that much of a difference. "That's easy for you to say, but we both know your father will do whatever he wants, whenever he wants to do it. If I cross him again—"

"You're not actually *afraid* of him, are you?" Camille asked.

Dalton glared at her. He didn't like this tactic, especially coming from a sheltered woman like Camille. "I'm concerned about what he might do to me—or to you—if he finds out."

Camille shook her head. "He won't hurt me. I'm his daughter. And as for you, well, you don't care if you live or die anyway, so what can he really do to you?"

"How do you know that?" Dalton asked.

"It's obvious. You live without any reservations, any cares. You drink yourself silly every night, you pick fights where the odds are overwhelmingly against you, and—"

"I didn't pick that fight." Dalton folded his arms. "I defended myself against six people when they pulled on me."

"Still, you enjoyed it, didn't you?"

Dalton didn't want to answer that. "I don't care if I live or die, but there are plenty of painful things your father can do to me while I'm still alive."

"Don't be a clod." Camille chuckled. "You think he's going to torture you or something?"

"Wouldn't put it past him." Dalton rubbed his hands together. The Southwest wasn't supposed to get this cold, even at night. He coveted Camille's gloves, feminine as they were.

"Don't worry about him. You only need to be concerned with *me.*" She stepped forward and touched his chest with her hand.

"What's the third?"

"I beg your pardon?"

"What's the third part of your case?"

Camille smiled. "I can't explain that one to you out here. Perhaps we could go up to your room and discuss it… in *private*?"

Dalton gazed into her royal blue eyes. He knew the variety of conse-quences he might incur from another Camille incident, but maybe she was worth the trouble. He really didn't know, seeing as her father had interrupted their first exchange.

Maybe it was time to find out.

"I can't commit to anything beyond tonight," Dalton said.

"Then I'll just have to do my best to change your mind by morning." Mischief flashed in her eyes, the same as when he'd first met her a year ago at Warren's house.

"I'm tired. I feel terrible. I smell like whiskey and vomit. You sure you want to do this tonight?"

"I didn't stay out this late and spill my heart to you to be turned away now," she said, her face now only inches from his. "You'll get cleaned up, and we'll move forward."

"But if your father—"

"Forget my father. You've got me to worry about instead." She leaned in and kissed him again, just a peck on his lips, then another.

He gently pushed her away and held her at arm's length. "Alright, but if we do this, we don't hold back."

Camille showed her perfect smile. "Oh, I'm counting on it."

Dalton sighed. For all the trouble she'd brought him in the past and probably would in the future, she sure was breathtaking.

Besides, Dr. Richards said he should take some time for bed rest anyway.

Warm sunshine poked through cracks in the curtains that hung over the window, casting long streaks of prospector's gold across Dalton's rented room. He shifted in his bed, and his leg touched Camille's. She was still asleep.

The alcohol must have finally worked its way through his system. He didn't have a headache, didn't feel nauseated. Perhaps his consumption had subsided as well, at least for the moment. The burning in his lungs and throat barely registered.

Overall, he felt pretty good—except for the hollowness in the pit of his stomach, a feeling derived from neither the drinking nor the consumption but from the sickness in his soul.

He'd betrayed Nizhoni. Again.

He'd been with other women since she'd died, of course, but the guilt that swelled in his chest this morning dwarfed everything he'd felt up until this point. Nizhoni may have died, but Dalton still considered her his wife. If that was true then he'd cheated on her with Camille Warren.

Camille stirred but still didn't wake.

Dalton sighed. He'd transgressed against her, too. He didn't love her. He'd just wanted what any man wanted when not thinking with his brain. And while she'd professed her strong attraction for him, she hadn't said anything about love.

They'd done things in the wrong order, and now confusion and shame gripped Dalton. For all he knew, she was just using him to cross her father, or maybe for her own personal gratification. Maybe both.

Aside from a fleeting, now distant moment of happiness, what had last night amounted to? What had either of them really accomplished? Even if Camille had happened to feel something real, he hadn't. He knew it all meant nothing.

When Dalton shut his eyes, the shame in his chest swarmed his entire body. He sighed, swung his feet over the side of the bed, and headed over to his clothes. While he buttoned up a clean shirt, he noticed two pools of royal blue staring at him from the bed.

Camille stretched her arms toward the ceiling and smiled. "Going somewhere?"

Dalton cringed and looked away. Hearing her pleasant voice deepened the emptiness inside of him. "Yeah. Out."

"Where to?"

"Just… out."

"For breakfast?" she asked. "I can come with you if you give me a few minutes to—"

"*No*," he snapped, his voice sharper than he'd anticipated. He recalibrated his tone. "No, not breakfast."

"Aw, too bad." She caressed the sheets with her fingers. "You sure you don't want to come back to bed for a bit?"

Dalton pulled on his trousers, then slipped on his boots. If there was one thing in this world that he had *no* intention of doing, joining her in bed again was it. "Yeah, I'm sure."

Camille folded her arms. "Why are you in such a rush? Did I do something wrong?"

Dalton shook his head and strapped on his belt. He checked the holsters to make sure he had his guns. He slid one arm into his jacket. "No, not you. Well—no. I just have to go."

"What's wrong?"

"Nothing." He put his hat on and checked his coat pockets for money. "I just need to get out of here. For now."

"Where are you going?"

"Don't know. I just have to leave. Goodbye."

"Dalton?"

He twisted the doorknob and stepped into the hallway.

Before Dalton could take a second step, something clamped onto his left wrist, then onto his right. A flurry of hands swarmed over him, and bodies pinned him to the wall as still more hands yanked his guns from his holsters.

He cursed and swore, trying to get a good look at his attackers.

A fist struck his cheek, then another hit his gut. The next thing Dalton knew, the men tossed him headfirst toward the staircase. His legs careened over his head and he banged his way down the stairs, bouncing between the parallel wooden railings that ran the length of the staircase.

His tumble ended when his chin smacked the dusty wood floor, followed by the rest of him. Fresh pain wracked his entire body.

When he opened his eyes, he saw a pair of black snakeskin boots which, aside from a thin coating of dust, had recently been shined to perfection.

He panned up over a pair of light gray slacks, a matching vest and suit coat, a crisp white shirt, and two hands with modest gold rings, one of them holding a thick cigar. The man wore something between a smirk and a scowl under his silver mustache, and his cold blue eyes bored into Dalton's very soul from under his gray, wide-brimmed hat.

Max Warren, III.

♠ ♥ CHAPTER 26 ♦ ♣

"Well, now, Mr. Phillips." Max Warren lit his cigar and took a few puffs. His thick, yet dignified Carolina drawl saturated his words. "What can I do for you?"

"Mr. Warren." Dalton chuckled and pushed himself up to his feet, but as soon as he stood, two sets of burly arms locked him in place. He didn't bother to resist. "I'd like you to go to Hell."

"Tsk, tsk. You always did have a whiplash tongue, Dalton. It's one of the things I most admired about you." Warren sucked on his cigar and pumped out a plume of smoke nearly the color of his suit. "And most hated."

"Spare me the small talk," Dalton said. "What do you want?"

"Oh, it's pretty obvious." He blew more smoke from his mouth. "I want my daughter back."

"Then take her."

"I will. I am. But I'm taking more than that."

A crash sounded behind him, probably from his room. Dalton couldn't see when he tried to turn his head. "What was that?"

Warren nodded. "Let him have a look, boys."

The twin gorillas holding him twisted him around. Up the stairs, one of the other men hauled Camille out over his shoulder, wrapped in Dalton's bed sheets and protesting the entire way down the stairs.

"Dalton, I'm sorry!" she said. "I never meant for this to—"

"You shut your mouth *right now*, young lady." Warren pointed a rigid finger at her. "I won't hear another word from you until we get home. Understand?"

Camille's mouth clamped shut. She looked at Dalton with despair in her eyes while the brute carried her out the front door then shut it behind him.

At this point, Dalton figured he'd already lost. Might as well lose as big as he could in the process. He quipped, "You sure talk down to your daughter."

"That's a groundless claim, no doubt substantiated by your lack of a father growing up." Warren puffed on his cigar again and shifted his weight. "But I guess I shouldn't expect anything else from the bastard child of a prostitute and a crooked, adulterous politician."

Dalton clenched his teeth and glared at Warren. He'd come ready for a fight, armed with ammunition that Dalton hadn't anticipated.

"Yes, that's right. I know about you, about where you came from. It's a shame you turned out the way you did. Your father, from what I could gather, knew he couldn't ever truly be your father. He disowned you before you were born but still saw fit to pay your tuition at some of New England's finest preparatory schools.

"Then you threw it all away, getting expelled from one school after another. Your mother eventually sent you out here to live with your uncle because she couldn't handle you anymore. The consumption was just a convenient excuse to get you on the train. The dryer climate's supposed to help, after all."

Dalton scowled at him. "How do you know all of this?"

Warren smirked, leaned in close. "I made it a priority to know. I have more connections in this country than you can possibly imagine." He leaned back. "Of course the disgrace didn't stop there. Not even close. Now, virtually on your own in a land where every man can become his own master until necessity forces him to accept a lesser degree of liberty, you decided to celebrate by taking the lives of four young men just like yourself.

"You shot Mark Fountaine over a pair of threes. Tommy Roebuck accused you of cheating, so you took your duel into the street again. David Burke, one of my workers, wanted to avenge your killing of his friend Mike O'Connor, who died because he added an extra ace to the deck, and you caught him."

"Every one of those showdowns was legal. If it weren't so, I'd be in jail right now." Dalton strained against the goons who held him in place. "There was a challenge, an agreement, and a duel. I *never* pulled first. Never needed to."

"Nonetheless, each incident boils down to killing a man over a *card game*. The same as the last six men at the Imperial." Warren squinted at him. "I just don't know how you live with yourself."

Dalton clenched his teeth. It was like Warren was in his mind, trying to dredge up every foul emotion that Dalton had hidden away.

But he could still fight back.

"Can we get this over with?" Dalton said, his voice casual. "I've got things to do."

Warren chuckled again. "No, not quite yet. I'm not done with you."

"Well, hurry up. If there's anything we can agree on, it's that I'm impatient."

"That's God's truth if I ever heard it," Warren said. "When you walked into my house that Sunday afternoon, trailing behind your uncle the Reverend, I knew you were trouble the moment I saw you. You had mischief in your eyes."

"Funny. I noticed the same mischief in your *daughter's* eyes that day too."

Warren pointed a long, thin finger at Dalton's face and his eyes narrowed. "Don't you dare even *mention* my daughter."

Dalton rolled his eyes. "Suit yourself."

"After the first incident, I wanted to kill you. I came up with, oh, about a half-dozen ways to do it without raising any suspicion or drawing any attention to myself."

What a load of manure.

"Come on, Max," Dalton challenged. "We both know you could shoot me dead in the street in front of the whole town and no one would so much as blink. You own Spider's Rock. You've got the marshal bought and paid for."

"Ah, but I knew I'd never get the opportunity to shoot you down in the street. You're far too quick, too nimble with those pistol-slinging hands of yours. You'd gun me down in a heartbeat, and where would that leave my assets? My family? No, Dalton, I couldn't let that happen."

Assets and family, in that order? "You're right. I would've shot you dead without a second thought and slept well that night. Probably better than most nights."

"Exactly. But then you got yourself shot up by that gang in the Imperial the very next night. How… *convenient.*"

Dalton's jaw hardened. "You sent 'em?"

Warren laughed. "No, no. I wish I could take credit for that, but I can't. I just happened to benefit from your misfortune. Justice doled out by someone else, and I didn't even have to pay anyone. The problem took care of itself, which never happens. *Never.*

"So when you showed up again a few months ago, I wasn't surprised. I'd always believed it had been too good to be true, and I was right. And when I'd learned about your escapades with the nearby Apaches, I knew your return would only mean more trouble."

"You got a point to any of this?"

Warren's eyes narrowed. "Just a question. What I don't understand is why you didn't pursue Camille right away once you came back."

"Sorry to have disappointed you," Dalton said.

Warren's voice hardened. "You know that's not what I meant. There's a reason you didn't take up with her right away."

Nizhoni. Warren must have known about her too, but Dalton didn't say anything.

"What happened to your wife, Dalton? Your Apache wife? Where is she?"

Dalton clenched his teeth and set his focus on Warren's boots. "She's dead."

"Speak up. I didn't hear you. What did you say?"

"I said she's *dead.*" Dalton stared bullets into Warren's eyes.

"Ah, yes. She's dead. Lots of folks you meet end up dead, don't they?" Warren said.

"That's not fair," Dalton growled. He hadn't expected this. Not only was Warren going to thrash Dalton for what he'd done, he was also trying to break Dalton's spirit. It made Dalton want to resist all the more. He refused to cave to this brigand.

"Fairness doesn't concern me. What does concern me is that you not only killed six of my men but then you also came to my saloon and walked away with over two hundred dollars *and* my daughter. Well, Dalton, I've taken my daughter back—"

"Just so you know, she came to me," Dalton cut in.

"That won't make a difference in what's about to happen to you, but I'll keep it in mind when her mother and I discuss this act of sedition this afternoon." Warren continued, "As I was saying, I've taken my daughter back, and my men have gone through your room and taken what money they could find to repay me for the two-hundred dollars you—"

"I *earned* that money on my own, from other men, not from your filthy saloon." Dalton lurched forward, but the goons held him back.

"Maybe so, but they earned it from me one way or another. The businesses, the land, the buildings, the workers' wages—as you said, I own it all. One way or another, it was either my money to begin with or it will end up in my pocket again at the end of the day. I'm just expediting the process."

Warren reached into Dalton's coat and felt around until he pulled the thick wad of bills out of Dalton's pocket.

"And now I've collected the interest due to me."

Dalton scoffed. Rebelling against Warren, even despite the remorse he'd felt over sleeping with Camille, was just too easy. "Do you realize that you just turned your daughter into a whore?"

Warren's eyes narrowed. He puffed on his cigar and asked, "I beg your pardon?"

Dalton shrugged, smirked. "I just paid you for my time with her last night."

Warren solidified into a statue of himself, so convincingly that Dalton wondered if he would ever move again.

Then he dropped the half-smoked cigar to the floor, ground out the embers with the heel of his boot, reeled back, and jammed his fist into Dalton's gut.

Dalton doubled over, but his captors wrenched his body upright again.

"That—" Warren adjusted the gold rings on his fingers. "—was for calling my daughter a whore."

Dalton coughed and hacked. Fortunately, Warren's blow hadn't triggered a full-on consumption fit. He said between wheezes, "I didn't call her a whore. I said you made her one by taking money from me after we—"

"I *know* what you said, Dalton." Warren cracked his knuckles. "And that brings me to my last order of business with you: revenge."

"Didn't you just take it?" Dalton coughed some more.

"Not even remotely." With an insidious grin, Warren handed his hat to one of his henchmen and began to roll up his sleeves. "Having been a successful, wealthy businessman for quite some time now, I usually don't like to dirty my hands with this sort of thing—"

Dalton smirked. "Your daughter had a *great* time last night."

"—but in this case, I'll gladly make an exception."

Warren delivered several stunning blows to Dalton's face and stomach. With every blow Warren's gold rings gouged marks on Dalton's cheeks and forehead. Just when Dalton didn't think he could take any more, Warren stopped.

"When next you want to have a 'great time' with a young lady, just remember that she's someone's little girl." Warren sneered at him between labored breaths. "And Daddy might just be vengeance incarnate."

Dalton couldn't respond, couldn't even move, but Warren continued to speak.

"Boys, take him out back. You know what to do."

The arms pulled Dalton toward the door.

From behind, Warren yelled, "And don't you *ever* come back to the Continental again, you hear?"

Funny. Warren had mentioned the Continental but said nothing about staying away from his daughter.

Before Dalton could enjoy the latest revelation of Warren's hypocrisy, someone hit him. Then someone else. Then someone else. Then someone else.

♠ ♥ CHAPTER 27 ♦ ♣

When Dalton awoke, someone was shaking him, saying his name just above a whisper. He clamped his eyelids shut to block out the hot white light that bored into his right eye—but not his left.

"Dalton, you need to get up," she said.

Who was she?

"Camille?" Dalton moaned. He tasted blood in his mouth, but not from his lungs. This stuff had the sharp tang of a fresh wound. His roving tongue found at least one sore in his mouth, and maybe a cut on his lip.

A sigh. "No, it's Vanessa. I need you to stand up, if you can."

He recognized her Virginian accent. "V—nssa?"

"Yes, it's me. Can you stand?"

Stand? It hurt to even breathe. *Everything* hurt.

"You've been layin' out here for almost twenty minutes. We need to get you back inside, get some water in you." Vanessa tugged on his arm. "If you can get up, I can help you upstairs."

Upstairs? Back to his room? Hadn't Warren's men trashed it?

She tugged on his arm again.

"Stop," Dalton said. "My arm hurts. Both arms."

"I'm sure they do, but you need to get up. You can't keep lyin' in the alley. Randolph will throw a fit."

Dalton moaned again.

"It ain't safe here. What if someone sees you and decides to put you out of your misery?"

Dalton gritted his teeth and scoffed. "Let 'em."

"You don't mean that, Dalton."

He looked up at her for the first time, but only his right eye opened. The left side must be swollen shut. "Like hell I don't."

She leaned down toward him and her head blocked out the sunlight. "You're comin' with me whether you want to or not. Now get up."

She yanked on his arm again, and pain streaked through it.

"Let go!" he yelped.

"Then *get up*."

Dalton slung a slew of curses at her, but herolled onto his stomach and tried to push himself up. His arms gave out after accomplishing only a few inches, and his tired, battered body flattened on the dirt. "I can't."

"I'll help you. Can you stand if we get your feet under you?"

"I don't know. My legs hurt."

"Roll over on your back again. I'm gonna try to lift under your shoulders, but then I need you to stand on your own. You're too heavy for me otherwise."

Dalton complied.

"Can you sit up at all?"

He tried, but his stomach rebuffed the effort. "No."

"Fine. I'll help you." Vanessa's arms curled under his shoulders.

Something pinched him. "Ow! Be careful.

"Then *help* me." She pulled.

Dalton maneuvered his wobbly legs to try to get traction with his boots. Together, they somehow managed to get him on his feet. Vanessa braced his body by standing under his right shoulder so he could lean on her. Then she wrapped her left arm around his waist and became a human crutch.

"Does that hurt?" she asked.

He ground his teeth and clenched his good eye shut. "Everything hurts."

Step by agonizing step, they plodded to the Imperial's boarding-side door then groped their way up the stairs, ending in his room. They might as well have climbed a mountain.

Vanessa helped Dalton into his rumpled bed, pulled off his boots and shirt, and then propped some pillows under his head.

"There." She tucked him in. "Now get some rest. I'll be back with hot soup and some water for you in a few minutes."

"What about my room?" he asked.

She looked around. "Don't worry about that. Warren's men messed it up real bad, but that's not your fault. You just focus on healing, okay?"

Dalton nodded slightly, then closed his right eye. He heard her leave the room before he slipped into a dark, painless sleep.

"Dalton."

His good eye opened, and the pain returned to his body. He moaned.

"I know. I shouldn't have woken you. But you really do need to eat somethin'." Vanessa held a tray with a steaming bowl of golden broth. "Chicken soup with wild rice. Made it myself. Will you have some for me?"

Dalton pushed himself up higher in the bed and winced at the throbbing in his limbs and head.

"Good. I'll get you some water too."

The soup smelled like freedom. He ate a few spoonfuls and gingerly chewed the thin slivers of chicken so as not to loosen any more of his teeth—at least he hadn't lost any during the beating. The broth soothed his aching stomach and warmed him from the inside out.

Vanessa returned and handed him a tankard of water. "I'm sorry it's not very cold."

He took the tankard and sipped the water. Pure, delicious, refreshing. He could have bathed in the stuff. "It's perfect. Thank you."

She smiled. "My pleasure. Are you feeling any better?"

"Can't see out of one eye. Feel terrible." Dalton gave her a weak smile. "But the soup is excellent."

"Your eye's swollen pretty bad. It'll go down eventually, but it might take some time." She looked him over. "I don't think they did any permanent damage. They must've wanted to send a message.

Dalton groaned. "Message definitely received."

"Anything feel broken?"

Dalton shook his head, which hurt. "No. Just really beat-up."

"Eat as much soup as you can. It's good for you. I'll be here if you need anything," Vanessa said.

"Why are you doing this?" Dalton asked.

Vanessa's smile shrunk in half. "Just eat the soup, get some rest. We'll talk later."

Dalton jerked awake, and it reignited the pain throughout his body. He moaned and stilled himself, and the pain dulled.

Subtle blue moonlight replaced the golden sunshine that was streaming through his window that morning. How long had he been asleep?

He fingered his left hand with his right to feel for his silver-and-turquoise wedding band. The metal ring felt warm to his touch, and he pulled his left hand from under the covers to see it.

A sigh slipped through his lips, laden with relief. At least they hadn't taken it from him along with everything else.

He scanned the room, now not nearly as disheveled as it had been earlier that day—if it was even the same day. Vanessa must've cleaned up a bit, but she was gone now. Probably at work. Would she come back to him after she'd concluded her duties for the evening?

Did it matter either way?

With his stillness, the pain prevading Dalton's body had deadened. Ferocious pricking sensations had faded to persistent aches, but only when he moved.

He also realized that he could now barely see from his left eye. The sore in his mouth and the cut on his lip had started to heal as well. Instead of blood, he tasted only the texture and the tart tang of the scab on his lip.

Not long after that, his door opened, and Vanessa walked in, clad in a familiar turquoise dress with silver trim. She looked at him and smiled. "Good, you're awake. How're you feelin'?"

He sat up and leaned against the pillows and the headboard. "Better. Still sore, but I don't feel as useless anymore."

"That's wonderful." She lit a nearby oil lamp which cast a bouncing yellow light into the room.

"Do you know if they took my guns?" Dalton asked.

"They did," she said. "But I went to the marshal. He said he'd take care of it for you, make sure you got 'em back."

"Marshal Garmer said that? I figured I was the last person he'd want to have access to a gun."

"He mentioned somethin' along those lines, but he was very clear that it's every citizen's right to bear arms, accordin' to the United States Constitution," Vanessa said.

"It's in the second amendment," Dalton said. "Written by James Madison, George Mason, and a few others."

Vanessa smiled. "Wow where'd you learn that?"

"Preparatory school. Back in New England, growing up."

Vanessa nodded, looking him over. "Well, anyway, he said he'd bring 'em over sometime tomorrow. I told him what happened to you, but he said there's not much he can do about it except make a record of it since 'Warren owns the town.' Those were his words."

"Warren *does* own the town." Dalton shifted in his bed. "Why are you doing this?"

She tucked a dangling blonde curl behind her ear. "Doin' what?"

"This. All of this. Helping me." Dalton thought he caught a hint of red on her cheeks.

"You needed help, so I helped you."

Dalton shook his head. She could play coy all she wanted, but it wouldn't help either of them in the long run. "No. It's more than that. Tell me why."

"Dalton, I—" She bit her lip. "You really don't know?"

"I have an idea, but I want to hear you say it."

She hesitated. "If you have an idea, then why do I need to say it?"

"I need to know what I'm dealing with here, Vanessa. I don't want either of us making assumptions that the other can't live up to."

"What makes you think I'm assuming something?" She put her hands on her hips.

Dalton's nerves spiked. She'd gotten defensive like this a year ago, too. "Don't get offended. I didn't say it was you."

"But you implied it was."

Dalton sighed. "I'm assuming you're in love with me. That's the assumption I made."

Vanessa didn't say anything at first. She just looked at him with sadness in her eyes. "You might be right."

Dalton took in a deep breath, and the burn reminded him of his deteriorating lungs.

"What? That doesn't make you happy?" she asked, her voice sharp.

"You're assuming that."

"Then what was that deep breath for?"

Was she really going to rake him over the coals for every little thing he did?

"Don't read into it," Dalton said. "My whole body hurts."

Her stare persisted. "You just said you were startin' to feel better."

"Yeah, *starting* to." Dalton closed his eyes. He might as well just say it. "Look... you have no reason to love me. I've been nothing but terrible to you ever since I first laid eyes on you."

"That's not true."

"Yes it is. For me, it's true," he insisted. "After we spent the night together, I ran away. I didn't want to get too involved with you or anyone else, but I could tell you wanted more, so I left. Started making excuses. You know it's true."

Vanessa pursed her lips. "I suppose it is."

"All you've ever done is care for me and treat me with love," Dalton continued, "but I've done nothing for you in return."

"That's not true," Vanessa said. "You fought those bandits who tried to—"

She stopped and looked down at the floor, her eyes vacant and sad. It must've really cut her up, knowing what he'd done to save her. Maybe that's why she was helping him now, even after their past disagreements.

"Yeah, I fought 'em, but that's the only thing," Dalton countered. "Not much good if I only step in to prevent something horrible from happening to you, and then I ignore you the rest of the time."

"Well, I'm not as kind as you think I am, either." She folded her arms.

Dalton raised an eyebrow at her. She'd practically nursed him back to health over the last day, and she clearly hadn't taken any suitors to her room that night, meaning she'd prioritized Dalton's wellbeing over her own gain. That was already a lot to give up just to help him.

"What do you mean?" he asked. "I got beat up in the street, and you're taking care of—"

"I told Mr. Warren about you and Camille last year," Vanessa blurted.

♠ ♥ CHAPTER 28 ♦ ♣

Dalton leaned back against his pillows, his mouth wide open. "You did *what?*"

Candlelight flickered in Vanessa's green eyes. "I said I told Mr. Warren what was goin' on between you two."

"I don't believe this." Dalton locked his gaze on Vanessa's. "Tell me you're lying."

"I'm sorry, Dalton. I was jealous. I—I made a mistake." She looked away.

"A *mistake?*" Dalton shook his head. "You made a *mistake?* How could you do such a thing?"

Her green eyes flitted back to his. Her voice slowed down and hardened some. "I told you. I was jealous."

Dalton cursed. "Did you tell him this time, too?"

Vanessa looked away and didn't say anything.

"You *did.*" Dalton wanted to thrust his arms up in protest, but they were still too sore. "Are you deranged?"

"I couldn't bear to see you with another woman, not when you belonged with me."

Dalton scoffed. "But I *don't* belong with you!"

"You think I wanted to do it? I *hated* doing it," she fired back. "I've watched you bring girls back here almost every night, always avoiding me. I could never do anything about it until you decided to bring Camille Warren."

"So you went and told her father? *Twice?*"

"I was hoping you'd come to your senses. That you'd finally notice me again."

"I sure as hell *noticed* you," Dalton said. "And after Warren's men beat me senseless, you swooped in like an angel and started trying to help me? Did you expect I'd come crawling back to you afterward? This is unforgivable!"

"I helped you because you need help and because I *love* you," Vanessa insisted. "Do you have any idea how many times I've turned down payin' customers with the hope that you might want to be with me again? How much money I could have made? How much time I've *wasted* on waiting for you?"

Dalton glared at her. What he'd mistaken for grace and generosity, she'd meant to use against him, to try to win him over in some twisted, backward way.

He leveled his voice. "You're a very manipulative person, Vanessa. Maybe you should consider a career in politics. I bet you could sleep and backstab your way to the top in no time."

Now Vanessa swore at him. "You think I *like* bein' a prostitute? I hate it. I *hate* it, Dalton. But I can't do anythin' else. Not out here. I don't have an education. I can't sew, can't cook, can't do much of anythin'. I don't have a *choice*."

"That's not my problem. You ruined my life twice, yet you say you did it because you *love* me. If that's your version of love then I want nothing to do with you." Dalton folded his arms. "You need to leave. Now."

"Fine!" Vanessa yelled. "Take care of yourself, you selfish, pompous idiot."

"Don't worry. I will," Dalton shouted back. "Just as long as you *stay out of my life*."

"I'm not comin' back. You had your chance. I'm done." Vanessa stormed toward the door and slammed it behind her.

"Good. Maybe I won't get beaten and left for dead as often," Dalton hollered after her.

She hollered a foul name at him from the hallway. A few seconds later, another door slammed down the hall.

Dalton winced, but not at the sound. Having her as a neighbor wouldn't be any fun.

Injured or not, Dalton didn't want her coming back under any circumstances. He forced himself out of bed, found a small reserve of strength that wasn't there earlier that day, and headed over to the door.

He locked it, then he headed back toward his bed. He stopped, bent down, stuck his sore left arm under the bed, and fished out the lone bottle of gin he'd stashed there just in case.

It wasn't whiskey, but it would do for the night.

THUD. THUD. THUD.

Dalton eased out of bed and over to the door. Whoever was pounding needed to *stop* before they made his headache any worse. A glimpse of his face in the mirror, complete with dark bruises and a nasty black eye on his left side, didn't surprise him.

Earlier that day, he'd managed to drag his aching body from bed to collect his revolvers from Marshal Garmer, who'd stopped by to drop them off. So now, revolver in hand, Dalton stood with his back to the doorframe and asked, "Who is it?"

"It's Randolph," said a gruff voice from the other side.

Dalton swore. This couldn't be good, whatever it was. "What do you want?"

"You owe me rent for the week. You're a day late."

"Kind of been indisposed over the last few days. Maybe you hadn't heard."

"I don't care," Randolph said. "Are you going to let me in?"

"Is it just you?"

"Yes, it's just me. Open the door, or I will open it myself."

Dalton swallowed but complied, his gun trained on Randolph the entire time.

At the sight of Dalton's revolver pointed at his face, Randolph scowled. "I said it's just me. Put the gun away."

"Sorry." Dalton glanced into the hallway and then holstered the pistol. "After what happened the other day—"

"Like I said, I don't care." Randolph held out his hand. "Money."

"Just need some time to get it for you."

Randolph grunted—or cleared his throat. Dalton couldn't tell which.

"You've got three hours to get your things out of here," Randolph said.

"What?" Dalton's brow furrowed. "No. I said I can get you the money."

"I don't play these games. Either give me the money now, or you're out in three hours." Randolph turned to leave, but Dalton grabbed him by the shoulder and turned him around.

"I said I can get you the money. After all we've been through, you don't believe me?"

"After all we've been through, I know that if you don't have any money now, you won't be able to come up with any three hours from now."

Dalton glowered at him. "You don't know that."

"Yes I do." Randolph put his hands on his hips. He wasn't as tall as Dalton, but his thick frame and broad chest made him seem almost as big. "You can't come back to the Imperial to gamble, and now that you've crossed Warren, you can't gamble at the Continental either."

"Look, I'd pay you now, but Warren took all of my money—"

"I don't want to hear it." Randolph held up his hand. "It's not my problem. My problem is collecting the rent owed to me by people staying in my building."

"Give me a break, Randolph," Dalton said. "Warren's goons beat me black and blue and left me—"

"The only colors I care about are *green* and *gold*. Unless you put either of those in my hand, you're out."

"Come on. I—"

"*No*," Randolph growled. "There is nothing you can say that will change my mind."

"I don't want to change your mind about that." Dalton's heart began to beat faster as desperation set in. "I want you to reconsider letting me work for you."

"Not a chance."

"I'll play piano for free."

"No."

"I won't drink at all. I'll cut you in twenty-five percent of my take on the tables."

Randolph shook his head. "No."

"Fifty percent. I'll give you half of what I make from—"

"*No*," Randolph said. "You can't come back into my saloon. *Ever*."

Dalton restrained himself from shouting back. "Then give me time to find another—"

"No." It was Randolph's new favorite word. "You can come back when you can pay for three days in advance."

"Where am I gonna go?"

"Again, not my problem. Go stay with your uncle."

Dalton's gut wrenched. "There's no way I'm going back there."

"Not. My. Problem," Randolph repeated.

Dalton grabbed him by his suspenders. "Randolph, I'm begging you. *Please*."

Randolph leaned forward, so close that Dalton could smell breakfast bacon on his breath. "I want you out of here in three hours, or I'll have Marshal Garmer escort you out."

"Fine." Dalton stared steel into Randolph's brown eyes. "I don't need three hours. I don't even need three minutes."

He put on his hat, slipped on his boots, grabbed his big coat, stuffed a few other personal items into a buckskin satchel, then walked over to Randolph. He fished a key out of his pocket and tossed it onto the bed.

Randolph didn't say anything.

"I'm disappointed in you," Dalton said. "If this is how you treat your friends, it's no wonder people like the Continental more than the Imperial."

"Say what you want." Randolph retorted, his voice calm. "You can't pay, so you're out. It's strictly business."

"Yeah?" Dalton said. "Well, your *business* can go to Hell for all I care."

Dalton stomped down the stairs and kicked the door open on his way out.

♠ ♥ CHAPTER 29 ♦ ♣

"What do you mean you've got nothing available?" Dalton accused more than asked. "I just heard you tell the last fellow how you needed to fill three more positions and that he should tell his friends to come in if they wanted jobs."

Behind a large wooden desk, a big bald man with a deep voice and bifocals over his hazel eyes arched his eyebrows at Dalton. The brass nameplate on his desk read R. W. Belvidere. "As I said, Mr. Phillips, I'm afraid we have no room for you in the mines."

"Then what happened to those three positions you just mentioned?"

"I promised them to that man's friends, not to you."

Dalton squinted at him. Was the man dense, or intentionally obstructing Dalton's efforts to work? "Mr. Belvidere, what if he doesn't bring anyone to you? Wouldn't you rather have someone young, strong, and willing to work *right now* instead of three friends that may not even exist?"

"If you did in fact overhear him, then you heard him assure me that he would bring his friends." Belvidere shrugged. "I'm sorry, but I have nothing for you."

Dalton swore and pointed his forefinger at Belvidere. "You're lying. I *know* you've got work that needs doing. Now cut the act and tell me why you won't hire me."

Belvidere's neutral expression crumpled into a frown. "Fine. I have several reasons. First of all, you're injured. You don't have full function in your right hand."

"What?" Dalton recoiled. "How do you know about that?"

"Please, Mr. Phillips. Everyone in this town knows by now. You haven't fired a gun with your right hand since you shot Tommy Roebuck last year, isn't that right?"

Dalton could only scowl in response.

"Anyway, I need men who are whole, and able to work. If you can't hold a gun, how can you grip a shovel or a pickax? That's more than enough to disqualify you right there."

"Hand me one, and I'll show you," Dalton challenged.

"There is no need."

"Alright, so even if I'm not the best choice for the mines, do you have any office jobs available, like the one you've got? I've got a preparatory school education from back east, which is more than almost anyone else in this town can say."

"That may be so, but we do not have any openings in our office at this time."

"Is that really true?" Dalton asked. "Or are you just saying that because this is Warren's mine, and he gave you orders not to hire me for any type of job?"

Belvidere pursed his lips. "You're very perceptive, Mr. Phillips, but I can neither confirm nor deny what orders, if any, I've received from Mr. Warren. But, truly, we do not have any office openings. That being said, do you require any additional reasons why I cannot hire you?"

Dalton scoffed. "You've got more?"

"Actually, I do. I assume you remember the six men you shot dead inside the Imperial a few days ago?" Belvidere asked.

Dalton frowned. *Not this again.*

"I suppose, even in spite of your inebriated condition, it would be hard to forget. While your shooting was remarkable, the six men you killed worked for the mine. *You* are the reason we have any positions open in the first place. It would be a great disservice, highly unethical—even disgraceful—if I were to offer you one of their jobs."

"*They* threatened *me*. It was *self-defense*. How many times do I have to tell you people that before you'll stop holding it over my head?" Dalton leaned forward and smacked the desk with his palms and glared at Belvidere. "I did *nothing* wrong."

"Whether your actions were right or wrong is of no consequence to me. However, I need to ensure that whatever action I might take to fill the vacancies left by our missing workers is ethical, honorable, and executed to the benefit of the mine as a whole. I must do what is right for the company."

"You mean you'll do what you must to cover your own rear end."

"Do you have additional questions, Mr. Phillips, or are we ready to stop wasting each other's time?" Belvidere's hazel eyes did not waver.

"No, I'm done." Dalton straightened up. "Thanks for nothing."

"My pleasure. Have a nice day."

Dalton slammed the door on his way out.

Dalton checked at the bank, the tailor shop, and the real estate office, all with no luck, so he headed for the town's stables. That ended in disappointment too.

Mr. Miller, the owner of the stables, wouldn't even hire him to shovel horse dung out of his stalls. He said he just didn't need the help.

So Dalton went over to the Marshal's office and tried to convince Marshal Garmer to take him on as a deputy. He started to cite his exquisite marksmanship and advanced education, but Marshal Garmer cut him off mid-pitch. Unlike Mr. Belvidere, the marshal gave it to Dalton straight right away.

"Mr. Warren wouldn't approve of that," Marshal Garmer said. "And frankly, while you probably could help me clean up the town, I can't help but wonder what kind of trouble you'd cause in the process."

No use fighting that logic.

He stopped at the mercantile next, but Gilbert couldn't help him either. Dalton considered trying to sneak into the Continental, but when he came near, he noticed two of the thugs who'd given him his last beating posted outside the entrance.

Not worth the risk. He didn't want to chance a second round with those ogres—at least not while he was still recovering.

The doors to his uncle's church hung open as he walked past, as if beckoning him to return. But Dalton couldn't go back.

He *wouldn't* go back.

Besides, he still had one place yet to try.

"Please, Doc," Dalton said. "I'd be a great assistant. I'm smart, I'm quick with my hands. I've survived more wounds than most folks, so you could call that hands-on training. You could use my help in a town like this."

Dr. Richards hesitated.

"Plus you'll get your chance to study me, to write that book you mentioned."

Dr. Richards smiled. "Actually, *you* mentioned the book."

"You know what I mean." Dalton swallowed. This was his last good shot at independence. "What do you think?"

"I have to ask," Dr. Richards began, "why aren't you out carousing and gambling instead? When last we spoke, you were pretty adamant that your plans weren't going to diverge from those two pursuits."

Dalton clenched his jaw tight. He considered formulating some story to tell Dr. Richards, but in the end, he opted for the truth.

"Randolph cut me off. I'm banned from the Imperial. Then I played at the Continental, but Mr. Warren found out and banned me from there. There's nowhere I can gamble anymore. I can't make any money that way, so I can't pay for a room. I need a job."

"Why here? Why with me?"

Dalton sighed. "I won't lie to you. I've tried everywhere else. It comes down to this: Mr. Warren owns the town, owns most of the land and the buildings, and owns most of the businesses too. No one on his leash will hire me because they're afraid of his wrath if they do. And without Warren's blessing, they won't get any business.

"I've been asking around, and aside from Randolph, you're the only man in Spider's Rock who owns his land and business outright. I don't think Mr. Warren's come knocking for a piece yet because he knows the town needs you, so he wants to keep you around. That means you're the only other person who could afford to give me a job, if you wanted to."

"Remarkable." Dr. Richards puffed on his pipe, and a plume of smoke hazed the air around his head. "As I noted the last time we met, you are very perceptive, Dalton."

"Thank you. So what do you think? Can I work for you?"

"Hm." Dr. Richards puffed on his pipe again. "From what you've just told me, and from what I've gathered about Max Warren since I arrived, he's got this town under his thumb. It's his legacy. When I paid cash for this house and this land, I got more than a few stares from the bankers.

"With that said, I know that Mr. Warren despises you. And while he hasn't encroached into my realm as of yet, hiring you would put me at considerable risk for such a thing to happen."

Dalton sighed again. He could tell where this was going.

"I'm sure you must be disappointed, but I simply must point to the lessons history teaches us. When Mr. Schultz set up the Imperial, he became an immediate threat to Mr. Warren, who eventually opened his own business to compete. If I hired you, I assume Mr. Warren would take notice and react accordingly.

"While he may not see me as a threat now, hiring you would certainly change his opinion of me." Dr. Richards chewed on his pipe and rubbed his hands together. "I have to wonder how long it would be until he found another doctor and established him as an opposing practice in order to run me out of town for hiring you."

"Yeah, I get it. I don't want to compromise your business." Dalton rubbed his forehead.

"I'm very sorry. Under other circumstances I'd probably take you up on the offer, but I'm afraid I can't justify the risk. The rate of return simply wouldn't be worthwhile."

Dalton nodded and headed toward the door. "Thanks for hearing me out, at least."

"Dalton?"

He turned back. "Yes?"

"If I may, I'd like to draw your attention to something I've noticed about you. Will you humor me for another minute or so?"

Dalton sighed. "I took up your time, Doc. If you want to spend any more on me, that's your choice."

Dr. Richards released another plume of smoke from his mouth. "Your life is a continuum. You've moved from bad to worse, then things got better. They peaked, and then they turned bad again. Now you're on the verge of plummeting down to a place much worse than your current state. What you may not realize is that you have a chance to stop the descent."

Dalton raised an eyebrow. How could his life possibly get any worse?

"You must make choices that set you on a path heading to a better place."

"That's why I'm trying to find a job."

"Even if you found a job, how would you change as a result? You would still spend most of your money on alcohol and on renting a place to stay instead of limiting your alcoholic consumption and thus saving money to purchase a home of your own."

Dalton shrugged. "Why does it matter if I've only got a year to live anyway?"

Dr. Richards stepped over to him and put his hand on Dalton's shoulder. "Even the smallest, shortest life can have a tremendous impact, one that transcends the confines of time and touches the future. If indeed you have only one year left to live, I encourage you to rethink, to reinterpret the words you said to me before you left my house the other night. Do you remember?"

"I said I'd make it a hell of a good year."

"Precisely. You're at a crossroads, Dalton. You can live one last year as a drunken, homeless vagrant with otherwise limitless potential, or you can harness your talents, your abilities, and your God-given gifts to live one last year in a far more exceptional way than most people will live in decades. Do you understand?"

"I hear you." Lectures, lectures. First his uncle, then Marshal Garmer, then Max Warren. Now Dr. Richards. "Thanks, Doc. Take it easy."

"I always do. You just make sure to take care of yourself."

Dalton nodded. He headed for the door and left the doctor to his pipe.

There was only one place left to go now, and his gut revolted at the thought.

But now he truly had no other choice.

♠ ♥ CHAPTER 30 ♦ ♣

The First Christian Church of Spider's Rock loomed overhead and cast long shadows in the evening sun. It still stood as the largest, tallest building in town, followed by the Imperial and the Continental, respectively.

Dalton stared at it and considered Dr. Richards's words to him about his choices, about his supposed impending decline. He'd implied that Dalton should make amends with his uncle, turn away from his drinking, and embrace a higher purpose.

But after everything that had happened, Dalton knew His uncle would never understand. He'd made that clear enough in their last conversation.

"Dalton?"

His gaze shifted from the cross down to Reverend McCarroll, who now stood in the open doorway. He sighed.

Reverend McCarroll walked toward him. "You know you can come back any time."

Dalton scowled at him. He could come back, but at what cost?

"I don't need any apologies, any promises of repentance," Reverend McCarroll said. "You can come home, and we'll work all of that out later. I'll take you as you are if you'll promise to take me as I am."

Dalton thought he heard a tinge of sadness in Reverend McCarroll's gravelly voice, but he wasn't sure. He stared into his uncle's cold blue eyes and noted the same sincerity he'd seen dozens of times, usually when Dalton had gotten himself in trouble. "Why should I?"

"There's nothing out there for you. We both know you wouldn't be here if you had a better option. Even so, I'm hoping you realize that *this* was always your best option all along. I'm offering you a chance to come home and start over, if you want." Reverend McCarroll held his hand, palm up, and motioned toward the church. "That door is always open to you."

Dalton looked past Reverend McCarroll into the church. While that building and his uncle's offer twisted him inside, he noticed a faint pull in his heart toward the church.

He pushed it away and looked back at Reverend McCarroll. "I'm not coming back."

His uncle nodded. "I'll be here when you change your mind."

"That's awful presumptuous of you."

"Is it?" Reverend McCarroll retorted with a fatigued sigh. "You have no money, no place to stay, and no job prospects. I'm the only person in this town with whom you can reside without Max Warren interfering. It's really only a matter of time."

Dalton gritted his teeth. If his uncle wanted him back, he sure had an asinine way of showing it. "You go ahead and keep believing that."

"You know it's true."

Dalton slung his coat over his shoulder and tipped his hat. "Time for me to move on. Have a good night, Uncle Bill."

"Can I convince you to come in for some food? Maybe give you some time to clean up before you head back out?"

"No thank you." Dalton started walking away.

"If you ever need anything, just stop by. I won't let you starve if I can help it, Dalton," Reverend McCarroll called after him.

Dalton wouldn't starve. He'd set out on his own, and he would make it on his own.

"Sorry, Dalton." Louise, a well-endowed redhead with big green eyes and a heavy southern accent frowned at him. "Can't letcha stay 'less you can pay me the rate."

"So after what we had, you won't even let me sleep on your floor?" Dalton asked. They stood together outside her door inside the boarding half of the Continental.

She sighed. "First of all, we ain't never had much to begin with. If I recall correctly, you paid me last time, even though I expressed interest in gettin' more serious. Second, I've since learned that you've spread your money all around town over the last few months. The other girls and I do talk, y'know. Seems to me you're just as much a whore as any of us."

Dalton raised an eyebrow, but she had a point. "So your answer's no?"

She shrugged. "Wouldn't exactly be good for tonight's prospects to have you sleepin' on my floor, now would it?"

Money. It always came down to money.

Dalton cursed under his breath. "No, it wouldn't."

"If you can scrounge up a few dollars for me, we can deal."

"Not likely."

"Then like I said, I'm sorry. Can't help you. Ms. Beatrice would have my hide," she said.

Ms. Beatrice was the Continental's version of Madame DeBuire—she ran the boarding side of the Continental and managed all of the prostitutes' transactions.

"Have you tried any of the other girls?" Louise asked.

Dalton nodded. "It's like you said. No one's willing to take me in without payment, not even just to sleep on the floor."

She shrugged again. "Well, hope you find somethin'."

"Me too. Thanks anyway." Dalton turned to leave.

"Dalton?"

He turned back. "Yes?"

"Make sure you take care of that handsome face of yours from now on. It's one of Spider's Rock's rarest treasures. I'd hate to see it ruined permanently."

Dalton smirked. At the moment, that might've been the only thing going for him, bruises and all. "Thanks."

"Hutch, I can't thank you enough," Dalton said as he followed Hutch into his rented room at the Continental. It was a risk to spend the night on Warren's property, but it was the only option Dalton managed to rustle up after leaving the church.

"Don't mention it." Hutch waved a humongous hand. "Plenty of room in here. But like I told you, I'm back on the road tomorrow at sunrise, so you're out, too, unless you can pay the Continental for an extension."

"I'll leave when you do," Dalton said. "Just really needed a place for tonight. I'll get back on my feet tomorrow."

"Sure thing. Glad I could help out. You can set up near the window, okay?"

"Fine with me. Don't have much to set up anyway." Dalton hung his black hat on the coat rack in the corner and tossed his buckskin satchel onto the floor. He'd use it as his pillow and his coat as his blanket.

"If you don't mind, I'm gonna go to sleep right away since I'm getting up early tomorrow morning." Hutch scratched his neck under his long, thick beard.

"It's your room. I'll abide by whatever you want."

"Great." Hutch kicked off his boots, peeled back the blankets, and crawled in bed, still clad in everything else he'd been wearing, including his revolver and its holster and his rugged attire.

"Sounds good." Dalton lay on the floor, covered himself with his coat, and rested his head on the lumpy satchel. He stared up at the pasty ceiling and watched the light from the room's last few candles flicker in silence until Hutch snuffed them out.

The combined sounds of the Continental's revelry and Hutch's sawblade snoring kept Dalton awake most of the night, but it gave him plenty of time to think.

The silver from his wedding ring glinted in the moonlight shining through the window, a reminder of his empty heart. He'd still be with

Nizhoni now had it not been for that silver-haired colonel and his soldiers.

Not even four months had passed, but now every waking moment—at least the ones he spent sober—dragged by. And they were always accompanied by pain.

With no alcohol, no gambling, no women, and no work to occupy Dalton's mind, Nizhoni crept back into his thoughts and resurrected the hurt in Dalton's soul—sorrow at her death, rage at God's injustice toward him, despair at the apparent hopelessness in his life, and an overwhelming desire for revenge.

Revenge. Distant, elusive, and yet utterly appealing. It churned the gears in Dalton's mind and heart.

But even if he had the means to exact his vengeance, with so many enemies, where would he begin? Zamora, the colonel, Max Warren…

Who was he kidding? Short of gunning Max Warren down in the street, Dalton would never find a way to get back at him. He was too powerful.

As for Zamora, how would Dalton ever find him again? He probably never stayed in one place more than a few days or so.

And the colonel? Whatever hope Dalton had for avenging Nizhoni relied on his ability to carve his way through dozens of soldiers—if not many more—before he could even catch a glimpse of the man, much less kill him. He didn't even know the colonel's name.

But he would never forget the man's stoic face. His silver hair and mustache.

Even so, revenge was a grand delusion, nothing more.

Like Nizhoni, like happiness itself, it would forever elude his grasp.

Unless he did something to change that.

Why couldn't he find Zamora? If he spent enough time looking, their paths would surely cross again, and then Dalton could avenge himself.

And why couldn't he get to the colonel? If he worked hard enough at it, Dalton could find a way to get close enough to him and kill him.

To not even try would mean he was giving up. Dr. Richards had given him one year to live. Dalton needed to do something with that time.

And he would do it starting tomorrow.

"Dalton. Wake up."

Someone shook him from his sleep. He opened his eyes and saw Hutch's bearded face, illuminated by the single candle glowing in his hand. Dalton moaned.

"I'm leaving. Time for you to head out as well." Hutch stood up straight and set the candle on a dresser.

Dalton rubbed his eyes. He didn't recall when he'd fallen asleep, but he knew he hadn't gotten much of it. And what little he had gotten lacked quality.

The first rays of sun were dawning on the distant horizon and creeping through the window. The sight reminded Dalton of the promise he'd made to himself—the promise that he wouldn't let his last year alive be a complete waste.

He'd find Zamora, and he'd find the colonel, and he'd take his revenge on them. And somewhere along the line, he'd find a way to get back at Warren, too.

First he had to get back on his feet. Maybe he could do that by traveling with Hutch for a bit.

"Hutch," Dalton said. "Any chance I can come with you?"

"Wish you could, my friend, but I'm not walking the trails this time. Got word yesterday that my daughter's come down with an illness back in Denver. The doctors don't know what she has, but my wife wants me back right away.

"I bought a horse from Mr. Miller at the stables, and I'm riding straight back to Colorado. If you've got money for a horse and supplies, I'd welcome you along, but…" Hutch shrugged.

"Yeah, I get it. I'm unlucky." Dalton sat up and stretched out his back. Sleeping on the floor hadn't done his aching body any favors. "I'm realizing it more and more these days."

"Wish I could help you more." Hutch reached his meaty hand down toward Dalton as if to help him up.

Dalton accepted it, and Hutch hauled him to his feet as if he weighed nothing. "I didn't even know you were married."

"Going on six years now." Hutch beamed, though Dalton could barely tell for all his facial hair. "I miss her something fierce, but soon I'll have enough money to bring her and my daughter out here so we can homestead a place of our own. Maybe even start a ranch. Once my daughter gets better, that is."

"Guess that explains why I've never seen you go after any of the working girls," Dalton collected his coat and his satchel from the floor.

"I may not be the smartest fella, but I'm faithful to my wife. Faithful to my friends too." Hutch squinted at Dalton, then he dug into his pocket and pulled out a few coins. He grabbed Dalton's hand and dropped them in. "Here. Take these. It's not much, but it'll buy you breakfast. Maybe lunch, too, if you stretch it far enough."

Dalton looked at the copper and silver in his hands. "Hutch, I can't—"

"I know you can't, but take 'em anyway. I just feel like I'm supposed to give 'em to you. Don't know why." Hutch's nearly hidden grin returned. "Maybe it's the good Lord looking out for you."

"Maybe," Dalton said. *Maybe not.* "Thank you. I'll pay you back someday."

"No need. They're mine to give, and I gave 'em to you." Hutch slung a large bag over his back and twisted the doorknob. "Well, I'm off. Been a pleasure, Dalton. If you can, please be alive when I finally make it back."

"No promises," Dalton quipped. "Any idea how long that'll be?"

"Not a clue. You'll see me when I get here. Take care, Dalton." Hutch gave him a wink and clomped through the door.

Fifty-eight cents.

That's what Hutch had dropped into Dalton's hand. Enough for breakfast, for sure, and perhaps a bottle of whiskey.

But should he spend Hutch's money on booze? That didn't seem right.

A few hours after Hutch left for Denver, Dalton stepped into the mercantile.

"Already said I can't help you, Dalton," Gilbert said from behind the counter.

"I'm not here for a job anymore," Dalton replied between yawns. "I'm here for breakfast."

"Oh, alright." Gilbert eyed him. "You got money?"

Dalton held out his handful of coins.

"Good enough for me. Those are federal coins, right?"

"Every one."

"Great. What would you like?"

Dalton selected a variety of canned and dried goods. When he finished, he counted his coins and laid them on the counter. "Will I have enough left for some whiskey?"

Gilbert counted it out. "You're short a dime. But it don't matter. We're out anyway."

"Really?" Dalton asked. "When do you expect to get more?"

"Give it a few days. I've got gin or rum if you'd like. Then you'd only be a half dime short."

"Fine. I'll take—" Dalton thought it over. "The rum. Haven't had rum in awhile."

Gilbert grabbed a bottle from under his counter. "This stuff comes straight from the East India Trading Company. They make it from molasses, then trade it to Africa for slaves, then the slaves end up in the south. Been doing it that way for years. Some of it ends up here, and I'm grateful for it. I prefer it to whiskey or gin. Tastes better."

Taste didn't matter much to Dalton. "Which one will get me drunk faster?"

Gilbert eyed Dalton at first, but Dalton remained unmoved, so Gilbert shifted his attention to the two bottles instead.

"Well—" Gilbert pursed his lips and squinted at the rum with one eye open. "—hard to say for sure. I'd guess the gin, but that's not based on any real knowledge or experience on the matter."

"That's fine. I'll just stick with the rum."

"Sounds good. Now, you're gonna have to put somethin' back if you want the rum. Maybe that can of yams?"

Not the sweet potatoes. "How about the corn instead?"

"You'd still be a little short…" Gilbert leaned in and lowered his voice. "But if you don't say nothin', I'll call us even. After all, since you got me those free drinks at the Imperial last year. I never did get to return the favor, y'know?"

"I won't say a word, but could you throw in a book of matches as well?" Dalton pressed.

"Shoot, I'll throw in a whole *box* for you. Good enough?"

"Even better. Thanks." He extended his hand, and Gilbert shook it.

"Great. You got enough room in that satchel for all of this?"

"Not yet. I'm gonna make myself breakfast first, then I'll have room." Dalton slid the coins over to Gilbert, who deposited them into his till. "Thanks for everything."

"My pleasure. Stop back in again when you have a chance, you hear?"

"Sure thing."

Dalton had a fire going within ten minutes of leaving town. He skewered the can of yams with a bullet, which punctured two nice holes on opposite sides. Then he threaded a thin rope he'd braided from strips of tall grass through the holes, then tied it to two saplings he'd cut down and braced between some rocks.

The whole setup enabled him to suspend the can over the flames, and in five minutes, his can of yams spouted sweet-smelling steam from both holes.

He removed the string, careful not to let the can drop into the fire, and set it on a nearby boulder, then he pulled out a knife and sawed through the top of the can. His first bite of yams tasted fantastic, but he almost burned his tongue in the process.

He groped for the rum he'd bought, but stopped. Should he start drinking so early?

Well, his tongue needed relief either way. One swig and the rum sluiced though his mouth, absorbed the heat, and actually complemented the flavor of the yams.

This wasn't so bad. He'd spent ample time in the desert before. He could live off the land if he had to, provided he could successfully hunt and kill some game. Maybe he could trade pelts at the mercantile like Victorio used to do.

Yeah, this could work out. He didn't need Spider's Rock, not when he could stay out here like the Apaches did. Dalton jabbed another yam with his knife and plopped it into his mouth.

In hindsight, Dalton should have made a wickiup before making breakfast, but he hadn't. Now he found himself running back into town through rare torrents of rain.

By the time he made it to the nearest building with an overhang—which happened to be the Imperial—he was soaked, along with everything he owned. He crept under the overhang on the boarding side and leaned against the wall.

He opened his buckskin satchel and swore. His burlap sacks of flour and sugar dripped with cloudy liquid. He took them out one at a time and squeezed them in his hands, and excess water dripped from them. Maybe he could still use *some* of it.

Thunder shook the sky. Was God mocking him? Laughing at him? Probably. Just when he thought he'd figured out a way to survive on his own, outdoors, it had started raining. Great.

Perhaps he shouldn't have spent Hutch's money on rum. Did that have something to do with it?

He wrung out his satchel, replaced the flour and sugar, his canned goods, and the bottle of rum inside it, and then slung it over his shoulder.

Millions of raindrops had turned the streets of Spider's Rock into shallow rivers of red-brown mud. They fell so thickly that he couldn't even see the Continental anymore.

Where would he stay tonight? With Hutch gone, no money, and no chance to stay with any of the ladies, where could he go?

To the church. He could always go to the church—but he didn't want to go there.

Maybe the Vernon brothers, John and George? Yeah, that might work. They'd let him stay the night, maybe even longer.

"Dalton," a man's voice said from behind.

He turned and found a set of hard brown eyes. Randolph.

"Get away from my property."

Dalton didn't say anything. Part of him wanted to draw his revolver and gun Randolph down.

Instead, he just glared at Randolph, shifted the satchel on his shoulder, and took off into the rain.

CHAPTER 31

Dalton pounded on the cabin door. John, the shorter, chubbier Vernon brother, finally opened the door. He wore only his long johns and a brown bowler hat.

"Dalton?" John looked him over. "You look like a drowned rat."

"Thanks. You mind if I come in?"

"Not at all. But stay on that mat inside the door until you dry off a little, okay?"

"Sure thing." John moved aside and Dalton stepped into the cabin. He noticed two wood frame beds stacked on each other nestled in the corner of the tiny room, a vanity with a white washbasin, and a small desk with a stubby pencil atop some paper.

For workers' quarters, the place wasn't all that bad. Dalton supposed that people could adapt to just about anything if they had to.

"Hey, George?"

"Yeah?" came a voice from the adjacent room.

"Dalton's here."

"Oh, okay."

Dalton set his satchel next to the doorframe. "How are you boys faring tonight?"

"Fine," John said. George walked in, wearing an undershirt with trousers and suspenders. "We just finished dinner. George was reading."

"Yeah?" Dalton nodded at George. "What book?"

"The best one." George stuck his thumbs under his suspenders. "The Bible."

Dalton wanted to sigh, but he restrained himself. "Would you boys mind if I stayed here tonight?"

The brothers exchanged glances. John spoke up. "We're not really supposed to let folks in unless they pay."

Now Dalton granted himself that sigh. "Any chance you'd at least let me stay until the rain clears up?"

"Well, I was gonna say you could stick around for the night if you needed to, but I don't think we can do any more than that for you," John said.

"That would be wonderful. Thank you." Dalton smiled.

"You can sleep in the parlor." John grinned and pointed to the doorframe where George had emerged. "This place used to be two separate rooms, but since we're brothers, we figured we'd merge them into a deeluxe suite. That way we can entertain guests in one room without them feeling congested. So we call that room our parlor."

"Good idea," Dalton said.

John shrugged. "I know it ain't much, but we made it our own. It's what we could afford together, renting from Mr. Warren and all. Most of the other miners don't have their own places, but since we're both foremen, we make enough to each have a room to ourselves."

George hiked his trousers higher up on his waist and adjusted his suspenders and nudged past Dalton back into the parlor. "Yep. Someday we'll get promoted again. Then we can afford a small house and a mortgage. That's the goal, anyway."

Dalton's mind jumped to criticizing the simplicity of the Vernons' aspirations, but he immediately realized his own hypocrisy. After all, with only one year left to live, he hadn't made any firm plans aside from vague wishes to strike back at Zamora and the colonel who'd killed Nizhoni. What was the point in planning for a future God had already denied him?

"That's great. I hope I'm around for the housewarming party."

John patted Dalton on the back. "When that happens, you can stay with us as long as you need to. Right, George?"

George had returned, now with a black book in his hands. His Bible, no doubt. His brow furrowed, but he smiled and nodded. "Right, brother-mine."

"If it wasn't for Mr. Warren, you'd be welcome any time, you see," John continued. "But he's really strict about visitors. Always wants more rent if more people are around."

"Right," George repeated.

Dalton smiled. "That's very kind of you boys."

"Well, make yourself at home. There's a loveseat in the parlor. If you don't want to sleep on the floor, it's all yours for tonight." John motioned toward the door.

"We've got to head to bed soon so we're ready for work in the morning, but you're welcome to stay up and read, if you like." George offered Dalton his copy of the Bible, but Dalton politely declined.

"Thanks John, George. Didn't get much sleep last night, so I'll turn in as well. And don't worry… I'll be out of here in the morning."

The next morning, a repetitive hammering on the door in the next room jolted Dalton from his sleep. Traces of sunrise crept through the crack in between the curtains and around the parlor window's perimeter—except when a shadow momentarily broke the light.

Dalton jumped to his feet and cursed, thankful he still had his boots on. He skinned his pistol and gripped it in his left hand, ready. Sounds of wood cracking, men's voices, and heavy footsteps sounded from the adjacent room where John and George had been sleeping.

They were gone now, which was good because they wouldn't be involved, but it was also worse because Dalton would have to face these men alone. And with someone lurking outside the other door, he couldn't risk going out that way.

"Stop where you are, or I'll burn you down," Dalton warned as he braced himself against the inside of the parlor doorframe.

The men's boots stopped moving inside the adjacent room.

223

"Dalton Phillips?" a twangy voice called.

Dalton muttered a few choice words. "Yeah?"

"You need to vacate the premises now."

Make me, was Dalton's first instinct. "Or what?"

"If you don't comply, the Vernons lose their jobs."

Still no faces—just noisy threats.

"Walk away, then," Dalton replied, "and I'll leave right now."

"No chance. We're comin' in there."

"If you want a mouthful of lead, by all means do." Dalton pulled the hammer back on his revolver.

A long pause lingered between them, and Dalton's pulse quickened. He didn't want to die in this crappy little dormitory, and they didn't want to die trying to come in and get him.

What's more, they had to be Warren's men, so they were not only tasked with protecting the integrity of the property but also its physical condition. They'd already broken the door open, but a shootout would also mean additional repairs and cleanup, and it would be on them to handle it.

It was a stalemate—albeit only a shaky one—at least for now.

Dalton called back, "I'll go out the opposite door, away from you. But I've got three conditions before I go."

Another pause, and then the voice said. "Let's hear 'em."

"One: I walk free. Anyone so much as *scowls* at me, I'll start shooting and won't stop 'til you're all dead. Don't test me, boys. You know I can deliver."

"What else?"

"The Vernons go free, too. They keep their jobs, their home, their property. You don't touch them. If I hear different a few days from now —hell, even a few *years* from now—I'll come for you. And it won't be pretty."

Another pause. "Understood."

"Last thing: I see your faces before I go. I'll let you come inside, but only because I need to know who I'm hunting if any of you breaks his oath today."

More silence. "Alright. We're comin' to the doorframe. Don't shoot."

"Nice and slow." Dalton abandoned his position at the doorframe and headed over to the other door, the one that led to the street. He kept his gun trained on the doorframe the whole time. "One at a time. Hands up when you come in, and don't do anything stupid when you see the business end of my gun barrel pointed at you."

As instructed, four men walked in with their hands up, one at a time.

"Really?" Dalton scoffed. "I heard at least *five* pairs of boots when you came in."

"Roscoe. Jenner. Come in here. No weapons," the leader, a big man with close-cropped blonde hair, said. The parlor door opened slowly, revealing two men, their hands at their sides.

"Hands up, but don't come in," Dalton ordered. "Just stand where I can see you."

"Do as he says," the leader said, and Roscoe and Jenner complied.

When Dalton scanned their faces, he recognized all six of them. "I still owe each of you for our last meeting in the alley behind the Imperial."

Some of the men shifted their weight, but the leader didn't move. He stared at Dalton with solid eyes and a stern expression.

Dalton pointed the revolver at him. "Especially you. What's your name?"

"Otis Redd."

"Good to know." Dalton studied them again. "I remember faces, boys. Don't cross me. Don't cross the Vernons. You know I put down six men at once a few days ago, right?"

A few of them nodded, but Otis stayed still, his expression as hard as his big arms and chest.

Dalton smirked. "I did that while I was drunk. Just imagine what I could do to you *sober*. Now clear the way, and stand against the nearest wall with your hands over your heads."

"We didn't agree to that," Otis said.

"I don't care," Dalton countered. "You'll do it, or you're the first one to go."

"You said you were going out the other door."

"You already had men hiding once, so I'm betting you've got a few more waiting for me when I go out that way. I'm not stupid enough to fall for that, so I'm going through you." Dalton motioned with his revolver again. "Against the wall. Hands flat against it. Now."

With a grunt, Otis complied, and the other men followed suit.

"I'm leaving now." Dalton gathered his coat, hat, and satchel. "Don't turn around or even move. Remember our deal? Nod if you remember."

He got five obvious nods and a subtle one from Otis, all of them still facing the wall. A brush with him minus a gun and with only one good hand wouldn't go well for Dalton.

"Good. Jenner and Roscoe, I'm heading your way. You stay well clear of me." Dalton slung his buckskin satchel over his shoulder, plopped on his hat, and headed out the parlor door.

Dalton headed through John and George's bedroom door and into the red-brown street.

The distant sun cast golden streaks of light onto Spider's Rock, but with it still being morning, so far it hadn't done much to warm up the town. Dalton could see his breath.

He kept his eyes on Warren's men as they exited John and George's room, and he kept his revolver out until they finally walked off in two groups.

Otis Redd came out last. He cast a long stare at Dalton, then he followed the others.

Dalton retreated to the shadows behind one of Warren's buildings for a few more minutes to make sure they weren't coming back. Satisfied, he turned and headed back into the desert.

Weeks passed, and the desert nights grew warmer as summer approached. Dalton weathered it all in his new wickiup.

He roasted small game when he could harvest it, and he occasionally ventured back into Spider's Rock from time to time to trade pelts for more groceries, alcohol, and other supplies, but in general he didn't need much else from the town.

Night after night he thought of Nizhoni, of the colonel who'd killed her, of Chief Beduiat's death. Dreams of war and violence spurred him to more drinking. Soon the only way he could fall asleep was to drink until he passed out. He woke up every morning with a headache.

His desire for revenge dwindled as more and more apathy set in. He had no purpose anymore, so why bother to make something of himself in his last days? In the end, he would return to the dirt, and no one would mourn his death. He ate to survive, and he drank to forget.

Over time, Dalton's coughing fits worsened. He found more blood in his mouth and more pain burned in his chest and stomach.

Each of his fits left him feeling as if he'd taken another beating from Warren's men. They got so bad that sometimes he grew dizzy and would even lose consciousness, only to wake up hours later, starving and parched, his lips encrusted with dried blood.

Every now and then he would stare at his revolvers, a pair of omnipresent reminders that he could escape from this life whenever he wanted to. But despite his sorrow and his sickness, Dalton lived on, persevered through the misery, soaked his troubles in rivers of whiskey, and slogged through the consumption ravaging his lungs.

Until, months later, he realized he only had twenty rimfire rounds left.

Only twenty rounds, twelve of which already filled the cylinders in his revolvers.

He'd shot through nearly the entire stock Chief Beduiat had given him on his wedding day, and with them being such a new invention, he doubted Gilbert would have any more at the mercantile. Even if he did, Dalton only had three rabbit pelts and a dead rattlesnake to trade.

Whether he had the resources or not, he had to check, had to get more ammunition, or he'd have to trade his rimfire revolvers for something older, something more mainstream.

No. He couldn't do that. Under no circumstances would he trade away the only things he had left to remind him of Chief Beduiat, Nizhoni, and his adopted Apache family.

That day, Dalton slung his faded buckskin satchel on his shoulder, tucked the revolvers in the holsters hanging from his belt, and headed for Spider's Rock.

"I'm sorry, Dalton," Gilbert said. "But ain't never even heard of 'rimfire' bullets. Where'd you get the ones you already got?"

"I already told you. They were a gift from a friend." Dalton swallowed. Chief Beduiat had been much more than a friend, but Dalton couldn't explain any of that to Gilbert. "He got them when he bought the guns. He had them brought in from out east. They're made by a gentleman named Wesson out of Massachusetts."

Gilbert shook his head. "Never heard of 'im. I can send an inquiry to our munitions supplier to see if he's got any, but this is the first I've ever heard of 'em."

"How long will that take?"

"Three to six weeks."

Dalton's eyebrows rose. In order to last three weeks, he'd have to take down at least one deer. Wasting ammunition on small game would deplete his supply too fast.

The problem was that deer weren't common in the desert and rarely came within view of humans. If he'd had a horse and a rifle instead, that would make hunting deer a lot easier. So getting a deer was a long shot, at best.

Dalton needed to keep enough rounds to fill both of his revolvers in case of trouble, like another encounter with Warren's men. Those rounds had to come within three weeks, or he'd run out too soon.

And if the munitions man didn't have any rimfire rounds available— well, he had to have them. That's all there was to it. Dalton had to get more, one way or another.

"Three weeks is too long, Gilbert."

"Sorry. Best I can do for you. Maybe someday we'll live in a world where you can get whatever you want sent to you overnight, but it ain't today." Gilbert shrugged. "Still want me to send the inquiry?"

Dalton sighed. "Yeah, send it. I guess you don't have any idea on pricing until you actually find out if they're available, right?"

"Right." Gilbert eyed the pelts and the snake. "But I can certainly take these as a down payment and give you a credit if they end up costin' less. 'Course that depends on how many bullets you want."

Dalton pushed the pelts and the rattler across the counter. "The last boxes I got came with sixty inside. I'd like at least two boxes, maybe more depending on the price."

Gilbert scribbled it down on a piece of paper. "You got it."

"Thanks. You'll let me know when you hear back, won't you?"

"Sure thing." Gilbert looked him over. "Say Dalton, you sure you don't want me to cash in one o' these hares now for you? Looks like you could use a good shave and maybe a haircut."

Dalton glanced into a mirror hanging from a wall to his left. Thick facial hair and scraggly brown locks covered the handsome young man he'd once known. He only recognized his sharp blue eyes, still keen as ever—although slightly bloodshot as well.

He turned back to Gilbert. "No, I'll be okay. How about some whiskey instead?"

♠ ♥ CHAPTER 32 ♦ ♣

Dalton didn't so much as see a deer, much less shoot one, over the following two weeks.

In that time he burned through the rest of his food supply, drained the last of his alcohol, and only bagged two more rabbits. It left him with enough rounds for each revolver plus a full reload for one gun.

In the distance, the church bell rang in Spider's Rock. That meant it was Sunday morning. Church service was about to begin.

It also meant he had to wait another day to trade the rabbit pelts because he hadn't made the trek into town earlier in the week. Nothing was open on Sundays except the Imperial and the Continental, and even then, not until that evening.

Dalton grunted. One more day without a meal wouldn't kill him. And if it did—well, maybe that was for the best.

At the beginning of his third week, sleep-deprived and sober, Dalton headed into town to trade the rabbit pelts for whatever he could get. He left with one more bottle of whiskey and three cans of food, enough to last him the week, he hoped. At least he'd get some decent sleep again.

When the third week ended, Dalton showed up at the mercantile, eager to collect his rimfire bullets. He headed straight to the counter. "Are they here?"

"Well, aren't you excited," Gilbert folded his arms and rested his elbows on the counter. "Just like my nephew on Christmas morning."

"Are they here?" Dalton repeated, slower and firmer this time.

Gilbert shook his head and straightened up. "Sorry to say they aren't."

"But you ordered 'em?" Dalton asked.

"I sent a request. Like I said, there's no guarantee that our supplier can even get 'em."

Desperation swirled in Dalton's gut. He shook his head. "That's not good enough. I was counting on these bullets, Gilbert."

"Look, what do you expect me to do?" Gilbert held his hands out to his sides. "I told you that it would take between three to six weeks. Maybe longer if—"

"*Longer?*" Dalton leaned closer. "What do you mean, *longer?* You said three to six weeks. That's what you said."

"Come on, Dalton." Gilbert's tone grew more defensive. "I really don't know when they're gonna arrive. No way to know. They'll get here when they get here."

This was bad. Without those bullets, he'd either have to trade in one of his guns for supplies, or he'd have to return to the church and deal with his uncle. The alternative was starving to death in the desert.

Dalton thrust his hands up into the air. "So what was all that 'three-to-six weeks' talk?"

"That's how long special-order products usually take to arrive, but since your request was so... *original,* I can't really say how long it might take. After all, someone has to *find* 'em before we can bring 'em in for you."

The desperation in Dalton's gut climbed up his throat from the inside. He lurched forward, grabbed Gilbert by his suspenders, and pulled him halfway over the counter. "So you *lied* to me?"

"What? No, I—"

"You said three to six weeks. Now it might be *longer?* I'd call that a lie." Dalton glared into Gilbert's wide green eyes.

"Easy, Dalton." Gilbert pulled on Dalton's wrists. "I don't want any trouble. It's me, your friend, remember?"

Dalton didn't care. He needed those bullets. "Friends don't *lie* to each other."

"Not usually," Gilbert conceded. "But they often perform small favors for each other, like getting each other free drinks at the Imperial or giving each other discounts on canned goods and a free box of matches. Sound familiar?"

Dalton blinked a few times, then let go of Gilbert's suspenders. He stepped back and shut his unhinged jaw.

What am I doing? Is this who I've become?

"I—I'm sorry," he said. "I didn't know what I was doing. I had no right to do that."

"Are you alright?" Gilbert brushed out his shirt and squinted at Dalton.

"No. I'm not." Dalton sucked in a shaky breath. "I haven't eaten for a day and a half, and I ran out of whiskey three days ago. I haven't slept well since."

"Can't you go shoot yourself another rabbit or somethin'?"

"I've only got eighteen rounds left. I can't afford to shoot any more."

"Why not? You only use one gun anyway."

"No. Well, yes, but if I get ambushed, I'll probably need more than twelve rounds," Dalton explained.

"Well, trade me one of the guns then. One of them will get you food for a month plus whiskey. Those are extra-nice shooters, even if I can't get ammo for 'em."

Dalton shook his head. "I can't do that."

"Why not?" Gilbert repeated.

"My friend—my closest friend gave them to me. I can't give 'em up. I won't."

"Then what about that ring on your hand?"

Dalton pulled his hand off the counter. "No. Absolutely not. This is my *wedding* ring. How would you like it if I asked you to trade your wedding ring in?"

"*Easy.*" Gilbert held up one of his hands. "I didn't know that's what it was. I knew you'd been married to some Apache girl, but that's it."

Dalton swore. "She wasn't just 'some Apache girl,' Gilbert. She was my wife. My love. She was the only reason I had for living."

"Okay, okay. Poor choice of words." Now Gilbert put both his hands up. "I'm sorry."

"Maybe you'd understand if you actually appreciated your wife." Dalton locked eyes with Gilbert, whose face contorted into a stern visage like the one Victorio used to wear. Dalton regretted his words immediately.

"We don't have your bullets, Mr. Phillips," Gilbert said, his voice flat. "I'm sorry, but I can't be of any additional service to you unless you got somethin' to trade. Now if you'll excuse me, I have to get back to work."

Stupid. Stupid, stupid, stupid. "Gilbert, I'm sorry. I didn't mean to—"

"Just go, Dalton. Please." He turned away and started scribbling on a piece of paper.

Dalton sighed and headed for the door. He'd check back in a few days—if he lasted that long.

Outside, morning sunlight warmed him and then promptly threatened to overheat him. The mercury might hit a hundred today. Dalton slipped on his hat and headed down Main Street.

He eyed the church on his way to nowhere and stopped once he reached the north edge of town. It didn't take long.

He turned back and ended up at John and George's house. He knocked several times before he remembered that, as miners, they were already at work in Warren's mine and wouldn't return home until five in the evening at the earliest.

After a few more stops, Dalton gave up and leaned against one of the stable walls facing the church, his hat tipped down. He lingered there, in the shade, for most of the day and just watched people go by until his uncle exited the church and headed straight for him.

Dalton stiffened and bristled as Reverend McCarroll approached.

"Dalton." Reverend McCarroll said.

Dalton expected spiritual wisdom, or an admonition to turn from his evil ways and come back home, or perhaps outright condemnation for his disheveled appearance.

Instead, his uncle asked, "Can I interest you in some lunch?"

Dalton eyed him. Was it some kind of trick? "What do you mean?"

Reverend McCarroll smirked. "I mean, do you want something to eat?"

Dalton's stomach growled so loud, he figured his uncle had actually heard it. "Yeah, I got that part. What's the catch?"

"You have to eat it with me. Inside the parsonage. That's all."

Dalton sighed. "Okay, but I'm not staying. Got it?"

Reverend McCarroll motioned toward the church with his head. "Come on."

Three slices of warm barley bread, two large bowls of beef stew, and several glasses of cool water rejuvenated Dalton. The food tasted so good that he didn't even mind Reverend McCarroll's near constant stare, at least not until he finished.

"Thank you for lunch." Dalton grabbed his hat and stood up.

"Leaving so soon?" Reverend McCarroll asked.

"Yes."

"Got somewhere to be?"

"Anywhere but here."

"Dalton."

He stopped. "What?"

"How are you doing?"

"I'm fine." It was true, now. After a hot, home-cooked meal, who wouldn't be?

"Are you?" Reverend McCarroll asked. "I'm concerned."

Dalton shook his head. "Don't be. I said I'm fine, and I am."

"Would you sit down for a few more minutes?"

"No, thank you."

"Fine. How about we go outside, then? Get some sun?"

"I'm leaving. You want to follow me, that's your business." With that, Dalton walked out the door and squinted in the early afternoon sunlight. As he scanned the dusty street, he heard a set of footsteps approaching him from behind.

Reverend McCarroll cleared his throat. "Why do you keep coming back into town?"

"The mercantile trades me for what I need."

"What do you have to trade?"

"I've been hunting. Shot several rabbits, a couple coyotes. Even got a rattlesnake once."

"Better you got him than the alternative, right?" Reverend McCarroll chuckled.

Dalton smirked. "Maybe not."

Reverend McCarroll stepped forward and faced Dalton. "Every time I talk to you, you make some reference to wanting to die. What's wrong with you? Why do you want to die?"

Dalton shook his head. "That's a stupid question."

"It's a *legitimate* question," Reverend McCarroll pressed. "Why do you want to die?"

"When have I ever said I wanted to die?" Dalton asked. "I never said that."

"You just implied that getting bitten by a rattlesnake would've been better than killing it," Reverend McCarroll said.

"No, you inferred that from what I said. You don't know what I meant."

"Stop playing games, Dalton. I heard it in your voice. I saw it on your face."

"I'm not doing this." Dalton diverted his gaze and started walking again. He needed to get out of there.

"Then again, you're so covered in hair and grime that I barely recognize you anymore," Reverend McCarroll said from behind.

He's trying to bait you into a lecture. Dalton knew it, but he couldn't resist fighting back. He stopped mid-stride and turned back to his uncle. "What's that supposed to mean?"

"Means you need a haircut and a shave. The 'wild man' look doesn't suit you." Reverend McCarroll approached and gave Dalton's beard a tug.

Dalton slapped his hand away. "Don't do that."

Reverend McCarroll chuckled. "Look at you. What happened to the handsome young man I used to know? Who is this overgrown rapscallion that took his place?"

"He died six months ago on a battlefield with his murdered wife,"

Dalton snapped. "What you see now is only a shell, a dead husk with no life inside. Only darkness. Only pain."

"You always had a knack for poetry. And for melodrama." Reverend McCarroll squinted at him, his face stoic again. "So you *do* want to die."

Dalton ignored his insult. "You're not listening to me. I'm *already* dead. My body just hasn't caught up yet."

As if on cue, Dalton coughed. It was only a short spell, but it hurt his chest all the same.

"I don't believe that," Reverend McCarroll said. "If your soul were truly dead, you wouldn't have any reason to keep eating, to preserve yourself. So why bother to keep prolonging your life?"

"I'm not gonna discuss mankind's instinct to survive with you. When I'm hungry, I eat. When I'm thirsty, I drink," Dalton said. "My consumption is worse then ever. Dr. Richards gave me a year to live, but I doubt I'll last three more months. I'll probably cough my way straight into Hell."

"Don't talk like that, Dalton," Reverend McCarroll chided. "You got time left. You're still here, and that tells me there's a reason you're still alive, even if it's not one of your own."

Dalton chuckled and shook his head. "All you ever do is talk about religion. I wish you'd give it a rest. I'm sick of hearing the same thing again and again."

"I bet you are. Lord knows I've said it enough times." Reverend McCarroll folded his arms. "But you gotta understand, from my vantage point, you keep putting yourself in the same type of situations again and again. You keep repeating the same idiotic actions. You've never once tried anything I've suggested, and you've always ended up in exactly the same place you started, only worse."

"You don't know anything," Dalton said. "You think the answer to everything is 'turn to God,' but that's a fallacy. A dream. You make it sound like a cure-all, like religion is a remedy for everything that's wrong with my life."

"Well, it's *not*," Reverend McCarroll countered.

Dalton stared at him, silent. That wasn't what he'd expected his uncle to say.

"I just want you to realize that there's a purpose for you, and that your life has meaning that transcends your own understanding. Can't we just start there?"

"God can keep His 'purpose,'" Dalton said. "I'd rather have Nizhoni back."

"Even if you got her back now, what would that change?"

"*Everything*." Dalton glared at his uncle. "*Everything* would change."

"Do you really believe that?" Reverend McCarroll asked. "How would you survive without any way to earn income? How would you provide for her?"

"I would find a way."

"Not with all the people you've aggravated. No one in this town will hire you."

"Then we'd go somewhere else."

"And then what? You have less than a year to live anyway. What would be the point?" Reverend McCarroll shifted his weight backward and let his hands drop to his sides. "And more importantly, how would you explain to her your string of infidelities since her death?"

Rage took over. Dalton swung his left fist at Reverend McCarroll, but he caught it with his right forearm then pinned Dalton against the parsonage wall with his left.

Dalton cursed and swore a genealogy of curses at him. "Let go of me."

"Not until you *calm down*," Reverend McCarroll growled. "Yelling at me is one thing. Taking a swing at me is—"

Dalton swung his other arm, unable to make a fist with his right hand.

Reverend McCarroll ducked the blow, spun Dalton around, and kicked his feet out from under him.

Dalton fell to the dirt, stunned but not surprised. When he recovered his footing, he snarled and reached for his revolver and—

It was gone.

He looked up at Reverend McCarroll, who held the gun by its barrel.

"I knew you'd go for it." He extended it back to Dalton, grip first.

"Do something, Dalton. Make a choice that will define your life once and for all."

Dalton glared at Reverend McCarroll, ready to blow him away.

He snatched the gun from his uncle's hand, pointed it at him, and pulled back the hammer.

♠ ♥ CHAPTER 33 ♦ ♣

"Go ahead. Kill me. You won't accomplish anything but wasting a bullet on an unarmed man, just like you're wasting your life." Reverend McCarroll spread his arms wide. "But if you really want your life to end, shoot me. Shoot me dead.

"If you do, I assure you this town will string you up faster than you can reload one of your shiny pistols." Reverend McCarroll lowered his voice. "And if you shoot me and I survive, so help me God, I'll thrash you worse than Warren's boys ever could. So if you're gonna do it, do it now, and *finish the job*."

Dalton swore again but didn't lower his revolver. He *wanted* to do it. His uncle had been a thorn in his side ever since he'd arrived in Spider's Rock. He'd sought to dictate every aspect of Dalton's life while disguising it as some sort of fatherly oversight or as some charitable act.

But it was all about manipulation and control. Nothing Dalton wanted ever mattered.

"You have nothing, Dalton," Reverend McCarroll said. "You have no hope. All I'm trying to do is give you some."

If that didn't sound like manipulation, Dalton didn't know what did. "All you're doing is judging me."

"I'm judging the condition of your life. It's time for you to wake up and realize you're running away from the truth: you've lost control."

"I still have control." Dalton glared at his uncle.

"Then why are you pointing a gun at me?"

"I haven't shot you yet, have I?" Dalton spat.

"Your finger's still on the trigger. Hammer's already pulled back. One twitch, and I'm a dead man."

"And now you're afraid I'll do it?"

"I knew the risk the moment I gave it back to you," Reverend McCarroll said.

Dalton applied pressure to the trigger but not enough to fire. Could he really kill his own uncle? He wanted to, but if he did, he'd be proving his uncle right. He didn't lower the gun. "I don't care what you say. I *am* in control of my life."

"Your problem—" Reverend McCarroll cleared his throat. "—is that you want to hang on to control, but look at where trying to control your life has gotten you. Your wife is dead. The consumption is killing you faster than ever. You're addicted to whiskey. You've got no purpose in life."

"Maybe my purpose is to *kill* you," Dalton uttered.

"No." Reverend McCarroll shook his head. "You need to give up control. That's the core of what I'm telling you. You've done a terrible job managing your own life. Why not let God have a try before it's too late?"

Perspiration beaded on Dalton's forehead. His finger flirted with the trigger.

He thought of Beduiat, Nizhoni, and Ahiga. They wouldn't want him to do it.

Even Victorio, despite his hate for Dalton, would tell him to save his bullets for an enemy.

Reverend McCarroll was *not* his enemy. Men like Max Warren, Zamora, and the silver-haired colonel were.

By now a small crowd had encircled them. Dalton diverted his eyes for a moment to scan their faces, many of which he recognized. If he killed his uncle now, everyone would see. What then? Would he run? Would they chase him? Would he shoot them, too, if they did?

What did he have to lose? His life was over. He'd said it and thought it many times. Maybe shooting his uncle would be a good thing. It would earn him a much-needed ticket out of this life. All he had to do was squeeze the trigger a little harder.

But he couldn't. He wouldn't.

Instead, Dalton pressed his thumb on the hammer and pulled the trigger, then he eased the hammer down to its position of rest on the block. He holstered the revolver and stepped toward Reverend McCarroll.

"I'm not gonna kill you. I've got nothing to prove to you, or to God, or to anyone else. I live for me, and that's that," Dalton said, his voice low and firm. "Stay away from me."

Reverend McCarroll shook his head. "I can't do that. I'm responsible for you. I'm only trying to help you, to put a roof over your head, to make sure you don't go hungry, to help ease your suffering. Don't push me away."

"I don't need you or your charity. I don't need anybody anymore. I release you from your responsibility. I've been on my own for months now, and I don't need you watching over me."

"You're fooling yourself."

"Believe what you want. I don't care." Dalton headed for the perimeter of the crowd, which parted to let him through.

"Dalton?" Reverend McCarroll called after him.

He stopped and turned back.

"I'm here if you need anything."

Dalton scowled at him. "Goodbye, Uncle Bill."

Over Reverend McCarroll's shoulder, from among the crowd, a pair of dismayed green eyes stared at Dalton.

Vanessa Clark.

He took a moment to give her a cutting glare, and then he headed down Main Street.

That evening, Dalton woke up under the overhang at the stables to the sound of metal clinking.

He opened his eyes in time to see a well-dressed couple walking away as if they hadn't noticed him, talking and laughing with each other. They made Dalton think of Nizhoni, a reminder that made his heart hurt.

When he noticed his hat sitting next to him, upside down with a few copper and silver coins inside, the heartache gave way to confusion. Had that couple just dropped the coins in his hat?

Another more pressing question pervaded his mind: how much whiskey could he get for them?

Only one way to find out. Dalton dropped the coins in his pocket, put his hat on, and headed for the mercantile.

By Dalton's analysis, Spider's Rock only lacked one thing necessary to truly establish it as a modern, cosmopolitan Gold Rush town: someone to occupy the coveted position of "town drunk."

Sure, the Imperial and the Continental turned out inebriated patrons on a nightly basis, but Spider's Rock had no one to roam the streets day-by-day in a semi-drunken state, begging for money. With no better options on the horizon, and with his death drawing ever nearer, Dalton decided he should be that person.

He subsisted on the generosity of others, slept under the stable over-hang half the day and half the night, and wandered through town to occupy the other twelve or so hours of his free time.

Rain in an Arizona summer almost never happened, and even if it did, so what? He'd get a much-needed bath.

Living a drunkard's life worked out well for Dalton at first. It seemed like everyone wanted to help him out, even if none of them would dare host him for an evening in their homes or rented rooms.

John and George scraped together almost a whole dollar in coins to give him. They said they felt bad that he couldn't stay with them anymore because of Warren and his men.

The news that Reverend McCarroll had recently preached a sermon on giving to the poor not only surprised Dalton but also accounted for the influx of coins flowing his direction. Dr. Richards routinely dropped whatever spare change he had in Dalton's hat, as did many others whose names he couldn't remember.

What he did remember, however, were the faces of those who neither gave him money nor even made eye contact. Even more memorable were those people whom he never saw, people who he'd once considered friends: Randolph, Vanessa, and Camille Warren.

He could forgive Camille; her father had no doubt barred her from having any contact with him whatsoever. But not seeing Randolph and Vanessa meant they were avoiding him on purpose.

Dalton supposed that was easy for Randolph. He almost never left the Imperial or its immediate vicinity.

As for Vanessa, Dalton hadn't seen her since the day he'd almost gunned down his uncle in the street, and he didn't expect to see much of her anymore. She'd probably moved on, plying her trade to the few Spider's Rock newcomers that showed up each week, the only men in town who weren't already sick of her.

Then again, should Dalton expect anything else from a whore and her pimp? They'd only ever cared about themselves, and their sentiments would probably never change.

Being a drunk, Dalton spent the bulk of his money on whiskey and used what little he had leftover to buy enough food to fill his stomach. He'd since mended his relationship with Gilbert to the point where they could share casual conversations while Dalton purchased his booze and food.

Dalton showed up at the mercantile every day for the subsequent two weeks to see if his rimfire bullets had arrived, but they hadn't.

Gilbert always gave the response: "Come back tomorrow."

To which Dalton always replied: "You know I will."

Even as a drunk, Dalton still served his own vanity. He stole lengthy glances at his image in the mercantile's mirror. His drunkard's beard had grown so long that it hung several inches down from his chin and jaw line.

What's more, now he could almost pull his long black hair into a ponytail. He considered braiding it like some of the Apaches had, but ultimately, he was too lazy to attempt it.

Dark circles tinted the areas under his eyes, and his cheeks seemed to have sunken into his face. When he looked at his body, he noticed that he'd gone from tall, thin, and strong to just tall and thin, like a lanky ghost of his old self.

One thing didn't change, but it had nothing to do with the way he looked: his quick draw. Drunkard or not, he practiced every day. He needed to be sure he could still outgun anyone in town.

As such, the dangerous aura surrounding him had remained intact, at least to the extent that no one bothered him, including Marshal Garmer. It was either that or his near-constant drinking that repelled people. Maybe both.

Or maybe it was his smell. He was probably due for a bath pretty soon.

"As often as you look at that mirror, you could have bought it by now if you'd just given me a dime every day," Gilbert said.

Dalton eyed him with blurry whiskey vision. "Why would I buy it if I'm homeless, don't have a place to hang it up, and can use it for free whenever I come in here?"

Gilbert nodded and set a paper sack on the counter. "Got me there. Here's your whiskey. I put some crackers in there too. Something for all that booze to soak into, y'know?"

"Thanks Gilbert. See you tomorrow."

"Don't trip on your way out."

Night approached, bringing with it a cold totally uncharacteristic for that time of year. Even under his big coat, Dalton shivered. The conditions resembled a winter night in a wickiup after rolling too far away from the fire. Tonight would be miserable if he had to stay outside.

He sucked down another gulp of whiskey. It warmed him on the inside, and he continued to hug himself.

Maybe he ought to take advantage of his uncle's offer for once. He could stay in the church—the nice warm church, away from the elements. Reverend McCarroll would have extra blankets for him on this cold night and probably a hot meal, too. Better than the crackers he'd been nibbling all day.

No, he couldn't go back. Not after their last exchange. It just wouldn't work.

What about John and George? Maybe they would take the risk just one more time. It was an exceptional circumstance, after all. A one-time thing.

But that's how he'd justified it last time, and then Warren's men had shown up. No, staying at their place would be asking too much of them. He couldn't jeopardize their futures with Warren's mining company for one night's sleep.

Dalton shook. He was drunk, but he still knew he had to do *something*, or he'd freeze to death. He got to his feet and staggered over to the boarding side of the Imperial. Once inside, he ignored the girl at the desk and headed straight upstairs to room 2C and knocked on the door.

Vanessa opened up, looked him over, then she shut the door just as fast.

"Come on, Vanessa." Dalton knocked a second time.

She opened up again. "Go away, Dalton."

"Can I stay here tonight? Just one night?"

"No."

"I'll sleep on the floor."

"No, Dalton."

He admired the purple, form-fitting nightgown she wore. Might've been silk. He gave her a wink. "Okay. I'll sleep in your bed."

"*No*," she said. "You need to leave, now."

When she tried to shut the door, Dalton held it open with his hand. "Please? It's freezing outside. I can't be outdoors tonight. No one else will have me."

"Your uncle will take you in. I heard him say it the other day in the street."

Dalton shook his head. "I'm not going back there."

"You're drunk, Dalton. You need to leave now."

He swore. "It's just one night, Vanessa."

Something stirred behind Vanessa. A man's voice asked, "What's the problem?"

A man with close-cropped blonde hair appeared in the doorway behind Vanessa, clad in only his trousers, a white undershirt, and suspenders.

Otis Redd.

♠ ♥ CHAPTER 34 ♦ ♣

"What's *he* doing here?" Dalton asked.

"You know what I'm doin' here." Otis's voice curled with a familiar southwestern twang, and his eyes widened with fresh anger. "What are *you* doin' here?"

Dalton glared at him. "Looks like nothing anymore."

"Yeah, I'm lookin' at nothin', alright."

"What did you say to me?" Dalton stepped forward.

"Hey, hey." Vanessa stepped between them. "Knock it off, both of you. Otis, get back inside. Dalton, leave."

"Oh, I'm leaving, alright. I've got no inclination to witness the atrocity that's about to take place in there."

"Yeah, 'cause you're so holy," Otis muttered

"You want holy? Come out here—" Dalton skinned his revolver quick as lightning. "—and I'll put six holes in you right now."

"Big man with a gun," Otis fired back. "Let's see how well you do without it."

Profanity ricocheted throughout the hall.

"I said that's enough!" Vanessa hollered above the ruckus. She turned to Otis. "Get back inside, or I'll throw you out, too."

"You can't talk to me like that." Otis tapped his chest with his fore-finger. "I'm a payin' customer, and the customer is always—"

"If you don't get back inside, I'll show you exactly how *wrong* a customer can be," she said. "Now get in there and get your shirt off. *Go.*"

"You heard her. Go." Dalton shooed him away.

Vanessa slapped his face. "Don't you say another word. Put that gun away, and get the hell out of here, now. I don't *ever* want to see you here again."

Dalton stared molten steel at her and holstered his pistol. "You won't. Have *fun*, Vanessa."

"Go to Hell, Dalton."

Dalton couldn't go back to his uncle. He'd only be proving the old buzzard right.

Frigid desert wind knifed through Dalton's coat as he stepped into the street. He gritted his teeth to stop them from clicking but found he couldn't help it anyway.

At least he hadn't lost feeling in any of his extremities yet. He'd seen the horrors of frostbite back in New England and did *not* want to experience anything of the sort.

Frostbite. In the desert. In the middle of summer. God must really have something against Dalton to turn nature itself against him.

At least it wasn't snowing. And even if it did, at least he'd have cover from the stable roof's slight overhang.

The stables. Why hadn't he thought of that before?

He could stay in there for the night, though he might have to contend with a horse for a good spot. Then again, when he'd asked old Chuck Miller for a job, he'd seen that the building had a loft above the horse stalls where he stored extra hay and oats. Maybe he could climb up there and stay the night.

Then, in the morning, he could sneak out before old Chuck Miller got back to feed the horses. Even if Dalton did oversleep, Mr. Miller probably wouldn't find him unless he needed more hay.

Only one obstacle kept him from his quarry: Mr. Miller had

wrapped a thick chain through the large steel door handles and locked it with a padlock. Unless Dalton shot it off or got ahold of a key, he'd be outside the rest of the night.

Or maybe he could get through one of the windows toward the upper half of the building? No, they were too high up, and he had nothing to stand on to reach them. It was through the doors or not at all.

But Dalton couldn't shoot the padlock off. The gunshot would be too loud, and it might wake someone up. He didn't need that kind of attention. And besides, Mr. Miller would notice any tampering in the morning.

Instead, Dalton examined the lock and tugged on each link of the chain. Nothing gave him any leeway.

Maybe one of the doors itself had enough give? He pulled on both handles. The chain hung loose enough that he could see a small crack of separation between the doors, but it was by no means large enough for him to slip through. Great. How was he going to get in?

He swore and kicked one of the doors. Some wood at the bottom of the door snapped off.

Dalton cocked his head and bent down for a look. It wasn't much, but he might be able to wiggle his way through the small opening if he widened it a bit.

He gave it another kick but didn't break much off. Dalton looked over his shoulder and scanned the streets for any onlookers, then he kicked it again. Still nothing.

Well, that wasn't working. Plus, for all the noise he'd made, he might as well just shoot the lock off.

He bent down and tried to get in. His arm fit through easily but only up to his shoulder. If he went headfirst, he might get stuck.

But the bottom of the wood looked pretty flimsy. Maybe if he just pulled on it—

Nails whined, then part of the door popped toward him. He'd loosened one of the long vertical panels that formed the door. Another two pulls on the panels adjacent to the first, and he had an opening big enough to squeeze through.

A few scrapes later, he was in. The stench of fresh horse hockey smothered Dalton's nostrils, but he'd rather suffer through that then stay out in the cold all night. Straight ahead of him, between the two columns of stalls that lined the building's inside perimeter, a ladder leaned against the edge of the hayloft.

He wasted no time getting up there. He found a cozy nook to tuck himself in for the night, laid down, and positioned his buckskin sack as a pillow under his head. The hayloft didn't seem much warmer at first, but eventually the lack of that cutting wind and the hay he'd pulled over his torso helped to warm him up.

Dalton sighed. He was in a hayloft, not a hotel. Was this what he'd reduced himself to? A vagabond with no other recourse than to break into a stable and sleep with horse food?

He coughed. No fit this time, no blood in his mouth. Just a few quick coughs, but they hurt enough to remind him of his fragile mortality. Death's train would soon pull into his station and carry him out of this life, probably straight down to Hell.

It was no less than he deserved.

He'd killed men—lots of them—and he'd enjoyed it every time. Sure, the men from the battle were soldiers—mindless nobodies he'd shot to save his Apache friends and family from death and humiliation. He could justify those, but deep down, he knew he'd never escape judgment for the men he'd gunned down in the street and inside the Imperial.

Worse yet, he knew the faces of the men he'd killed here in town. The last expressions on their faces haunted him. Looks of pain. Regret. Torment. Fear.

Just like what he'd seen on Ahiga's face as he died. Or Beduiat's. Or Nizhoni's.

Nizhoni. Dalton's heart broke all over again. Even the faintest memory, a familiar sight, a whisper of her voice carried by the wind would dredge up hurt he thought he'd buried deep inside himself.

Thus far, he'd done exactly the opposite of her last appeal to "not waste his life." Another failure. He couldn't save her from becoming a victim of a war that never should have happened, and now he couldn't honor her memory by being faithful to her dying request.

Dalton sniveled, but not from the cold. He took no joy in his life, no happiness. He had no reason for living, yet death still refused to come. Somehow his consumption and his drinking hadn't killed him yet.

Strangely, despite his body's weakness to the consumption, it showed extraordinary resilience to whiskey. No matter how much he drank, it never did him in.

He glanced down at his hip, at his revolvers.

There was still one way.

Dalton pulled one from its holster. Moonlight shone through a crack in the ceiling and washed out the gun's intricate engravings. Wind howled outside, threatening to sneak inside and claim Dalton, but it couldn't.

The gun reminded him of Chief Beduiat the most, the only man he'd ever wanted to call his father. The only man who'd deserved it.

But he was gone too, gunned down by the *real* savages: Dalton's own people.

He could join Chief Beduiat, though. Perhaps he could even be reunited with Nizhoni in death. He'd only need one shot, one bullet, just like all the other lives he'd taken. One bullet would do the job.

Suicide meant an instant trip to Hell. That's what he'd learned growing up.

Then again, what could be worse than the Hell he was already living in? And several biblical figures had even done it themselves. What did it matter if they were "villains?"

Dalton was a villain too, as far as the town was concerned. And now he needed a way out, just like those characters had. As he turned the gun on himself, his heart pounded in his chest. The cold circle of the gun's barrel pressed against the side of his head.

One bullet.

Perspiration dotted his forehead and his lungs pulled in sharp, heavy breaths. He'd come close before, but never this close.

He'd never needed it more than he did now.

Dalton cocked the hammer.

Only one thing left to do.

Pull the trigger.

His breath shook. Was he quivering?

His left hand felt like liquid, his forefinger like a feather on the trigger.

He couldn't do it.

Pull the trigger.

He heard Nizhoni repeat her challenge, "Don't waste your life."

Pull the trigger.

It repeated again and again in his head and in his heart, accompanied by an ominous reassurance that he'd be with her again soon.

Pull the trigger.

Dalton gritted his teeth and tension seized his neck. He drove the gun barrel into his temple. Nothing was easier.

Pull the trigger!

His left hand tightened. The barrel rotated. It was over.

♠ ♥ CHAPTER 35 ♦ ♣

*C*LICK.

Dalton's eyes opened. He looked at the gun. Why wasn't he dead? The hammer had gone down, but no shot had fired. Had he lost a bullet somehow? It didn't make sense.

He held the revolver in front of him, pulled the cylinder out and checked it. All six chambers contained unspent rimfire rounds. So why hadn't the gun discharged?

His heart thundered in his chest as he spun the cylinder and it snapped back into place. He put the gun to his head again, pulled back the hammer, and stopped.

Dalton inhaled quick, ragged breaths. What was he doing?

He threw the gun into the hay and lay back, his hands on his face. He should be dead, but the gun hadn't fired. He couldn't believe he'd tried it, but he had no intention of trying it again.

Dalton cursed himself to sleep that night.

Morning arrived quickly, and it sounded like Hell's chain gang coming for Dalton. He sat up and looked around. What was with all the hay?

When he noticed his revolver lying near his leg, last night came back to him: heading to Vanessa's room, finding her with Otis, leaving. Breaking into the stables, climbing up into the hay. That's where he'd tried—and failed—to kill himself.

His head throbbed, and grogginess dulled his senses like he hadn't slept more than a few hours. Daylight just now crept over the horizon and into the window. It was probably about 5am, which meant he'd only gotten about three and a half hours. No wonder he felt tired.

But he was alive. He'd survived the cold, miserable night.

The chains on the stable door continued to rattle, and that meant Chuck Miller, the stable owner, was on his way in.

Dalton snatched his revolver, then lay back in the hay, still as a desert rock. The stable doors opened with a creak.

"I know you're in here," Mr. Miller said. "I seen what you done to the bottom of my door, and I'm gonna fix you real good, Mr. Coyote."

Coyote? Did he think a real coyote had busted the bottom of his door? Or was it a derogatory term meant for Dalton?

He didn't know Mr. Miller very well, except that he talked too loud and had to be at least sixty years old, so all he could do was guess—and remain motionless in the hayloft.

Something cracked, like the sound of a break-action shotgun snapping shut. "Got somethin' for you, Mr. Coyote. You been terrorizin' my horses long enough. Now you come outta them stalls right now so I can blow you straight to Kingdom come."

Yep, he probably meant a real coyote. Whether Mr. Miller found his canine friend or not, Dalton refused to move. Unable to see Mr. Miller's actions from in the hayloft, Dalton imagined him checking all of the stalls and pulling the horses out one by one in search of Mr. Coyote.

After several minutes Mr. Miller said, "Well, I give up. You must not be in here after all. But if I ever see you again…" his voice trailed off in a series of mumbles.

Dalton heard oats and hay shuffling around below. Feeding time for the horses?

"Cold last night, ain't that right, boys?" Mr. Miller asked. "And lady. Can't forget Lula Belle in the corner. Now you boys behave. Lula Belle ain't your type."

After a few more minutes, Mr. Miller opened the stable door, then shut it and locked it once more. That was Dalton's chance. He emerged from the hay, snatched up his buckskin satchel, and clambered down the ladder. His boots hit the earth, and he scampered over to the doors. There, against one of the stable's support posts, leaned Mr. Miller's shotgun.

Good. At least Dalton wouldn't have to worry about that.

He pushed the door panels open, squeezed his way out. After a quick look around, he dashed around to the side of the stables and—

"Whoa!"

Dalton collided with a mass of man and oats, and all of them hit the ground. He sprung to his feet and staggered back, his eyes wide, chest pounding.

Mr. Miller squinted at him. "Dalton Phillips? Now don't you run away, boy. You help me pick this bag up, hear me? My back ain't what it used to be."

Dalton swallowed. He wanted to run, wanted to get away. If Mr. Miller found out about him staying in the hayloft overnight—

"Look, son, I ain't mad at you." Mr. Miller held up one of his hands. The other one rubbed the small of his back. "I'm just old and worn and need some help, see?"

He nodded. Mr. Miller clearly didn't know about last night, and he wouldn't find out either.

Dalton hunched down and hefted the bag of oats onto his shoulder then wobbled under its weight. If he'd been eating every day, maybe he would've fared better.

"Big, strong lad." Mr. Miller smiled. "Now would you carry it into the stable for me?"

"Sure." Dalton considered his stay in the hayloft last night. "Least I can do."

Mr. Miller led Dalton back into the stables from whence he'd fled and directed him to set the feedbag down near Lula Belle's stall. "That'll do, son. Here's somethin' for your troubles."

Dalton stared at the quarter Mr. Miller dropped into his hand. He could get breakfast and some more whiskey with that quarter. Perhaps today wouldn't be so bad after all.

But he couldn't take it. He'd stayed in Mr. Miller's hayloft overnight without telling him, broken the bottom of his door to get in, and on top of that, it was his fault Mr. Miller had dropped the feed in the first place. Now Mr. Miller was paying him for his help?

"Mr. Miller—I can't accept this."

"Of course you can," Mr. Miller said. "You helped me."

"But… I don't deserve it."

"Maybe you don't, but it's mine to give anyway. You did the right thing, helpin' me carry all that feed in after you knocked me on my rear end. Thought for sure you'd run off, but you didn't. That deserves a reward, if you ask me."

Dalton shook his head and held out the coin. "I'm sorry, but I can't take your money."

"You accept money from people in the street everyday for doing nothin' at all. Now, when you actually do somethin' worth gettin' paid for, you won't accept it? That makes no sense. No sense at all. You keep that, hear me?"

"I can't. I—I just can't."

"I'm not takin' it back, Dalton. You keep that quarter. Buy yourself some breakfast, and maybe a shave, too." Mr. Miller rubbed the stubble on his own neck.

Arguing wouldn't get Dalton anywhere. He smacked the quarter down on the corner of Lula Belle's stall and dashed out of the stable in spite of Mr. Miller calling after him.

A few days later, Dalton realized he should have accepted Mr. Miller's quarter when he'd had the chance. Since then, the town's contributions to his hat had dried up.

He'd managed to scrape together enough money for either a little whiskey or a little food, but not both. Dalton had chosen the whiskey, and now his stomach protested his choice with angry grumbles.

Not long after that, the whiskey ran out. By the next morning, Dalton had nothing to his name but his clothes, his empty buckskin satchel, and his guns.

Another day passed, increasing the total number of days since he'd eaten to four. In that time he'd fought off three coughing fits, two of them severe.

With no nutrients to replenish his strength, he walked the streets weak and woozy. Yet despite his gaunt, pale, and thoroughly desperate appearance, no one offered him anything.

He should have accepted Mr. Miller's quarter when he'd had the chance.

But today was Sunday. Perhaps he could catch some churchgoers feeling extra generous on their way out of the morning service. They had to. He *needed* to eat something.

While starvation might not kill him for a few more days, another coughing fit could do him in any time. If he could just get some food in his stomach…

Dalton planted himself at his usual spot outside the stables in plain site of the church folk as they left the church. A couple passed him by without making a contribution. Then an old man. Then a family with small children.

Still no money in his hat.

Had they not seen him? Dalton snatched up his hat and headed closer, and stood right in the middle of the street. Now they'd see him for sure.

But the patrons just kept passing him by. Were they blind? He stopped a man he didn't recognize, a short man with a brown bowler and a handlebar mustache a few shades lighter.

"Excuse me, sir. Could you possibly spare any change for me?"

The man shook his head, pulled his arm away, and eyed Dalton as he walked on.

Dalton approached two older ladies—a rare sight in a pioneer town like Spider's Rock. "Excuse me, ladies—"

"Excuse *me*, young man," said one of them, a pudgy lady with beady brown eyes and a scowl that reminded Dalton of his mother if she were older. "We are trying to pass, and here you've taken up residence in the middle of the thoroughfare. Do you *mind?*"

Dalton swallowed the bitter words in his throat. "I'm very sorry, but might you be able to spare some change for me?"

"Absolutely not." Pudgy turned to her friend. "Come, Gertrude. I shan't be bothered by this brigand any longer."

Gertrude squinted at Dalton and mimicked Pudgy's scowl. They walked away without saying so much as another word to him.

"How very *Christian* of you," Dalton muttered, then immediately wished he would have said it louder. Much louder.

He shifted his attention to another couple, this time a well-dressed man and a plain-faced woman, each in their forties.

"Excuse me, but I haven't had anything to eat for four days. Could you please spare some change for me? Anything would help."

"Four days?" The man rubbed his smooth chin and looked Dalton up and down. His dark eyes reminded Dalton of Beduiat's. Hopefully that was a good sign. "And when was your last drink?"

Dalton's eyes narrowed. Should he lie? He opted for the truth. "Two days."

The man grunted. "Perhaps you should have bought food instead of booze."

"You're right. Believe me, food's the first thing I'll buy when I can come up with—"

The man tugged his wife's hand. "Let's go, Lucille. I don't want to be late to the Warrens'."

At that name, Dalton's focus shifted from the man's kneejerk judgment to the man most responsible for his woes, to his primary adversary in this godforsaken little town.

Max Warren, III.

Warren attended church too. He'd not only paid for the building but now occupied one of the few deaconships his uncle had granted within the church, a position which he'd essentially bought for his lifetime.

A deacon not showing up on a Sunday morning would be unconscionable, unheard of. These days, despite all his greed and manipulation, Warren never missed a service.

So what would Dalton do? Beg from him?

Dalton had something far better in mind: vengeance.

He'd once mused about how he'd never get the chance to take revenge on Warren short of gunning him down in the street. He'd been absolutely right. So he'd have to settle for that instead.

Warren, his wife, and Camille exited the church behind some other parishioners. They closed on Dalton's position, still unaware of him, unaware of what he was planning to do.

Camille noticed him first. Fear widened her eyes, followed by curious, if not uncertain recognition.

How she could tell who he was—*if* she could tell at all—Dalton did not know. His dark beard now hung to his chest, and his long hair reached almost to his shoulders. The tall, strong build he'd once taken such pride in had withered to an emaciated frame, a scrawny white cloud compared to his previous life as a mighty thunderhead.

Mrs. Warren saw him next, then Max Warren himself. All of them stopped short, each of them staring at him with terrified expressions.

No, they weren't staring at him.

They were staring at the revolver in his hand.

♠ ♥ CHAPTER 36 ♦ ♣

No one spoke for an eternity. They all just stared at each other until Camille Warren finally broke the silence.

"Dalton?" she asked. "Is that you?"

"Be quiet, Camille." Warren yanked her behind him. "What do you want?"

Dalton said nothing at first. He just stared at them with fury raging in his heart. "I haven't eaten anything for four days."

Camille gasped from behind her father, who shushed her again.

"You've ruined my life, Mr. Warren. And now you're gonna make it right."

"I've done no such thing. You brought all of this on yourself, and you know it."

Dalton shook his head. "I tried to find honest work. Tried to work at the mines, tried to work for the bank, the marshal, the doctor, everyone. No one would hire me because they either work for you or they're afraid of you. It's *your* fault."

"Believe what you want, Dalton, but you're your own worst enemy, a parasite feeding on itself. You're a mess. That's why those people didn't hire you."

"You know I'm smart. I could learn *any* job in this town."

"You're also a drunk, a womanizer, a derelict, and a murderer," Warren fired back.

Dalton stepped forward and pointed the gun squarely at Warren's face. "You know that was self-defense. You *know* it."

Mrs. Warren and Camille gasped.

Warren glanced to his left and to his right. "How about we take this somewhere else? Somewhere less—*public?*"

"Like hell. We're staying here," Dalton said.

"Then how about you lower the gun and we talk like civilized people?"

"I'll say it again: like hell. You ruined my life. Now you're gonna make things right."

Warren shook his head. "Go ahead. Wave your gun around. You may scare my wife and daughter, but you don't scare me."

"You made sure no one would hire me." Aware of the audience gathering around them, Dalton raised his voice. "You know why he did it?"

"Dalton, there's no need to—"

"It's because I slept with his daughter. That's why he hates me."

Warren turned three shades redder. "You son of a—"

"*Twice.*" Dalton scanned the crowd for their reactions. "Don't act surprised. Almost the entire town knew about the first time, but we didn't get too far because *someone*—" He tried to pick out Vanessa, but this was a church crowd. She wouldn't be caught with folks like these unless her black heart had stopped beating. "—told him what we were up to."

"I'm going to have you killed," Warren uttered so only he could hear it.

"There's more," Dalton said. "After the second time, he covered it up. Not too many folks knew what had happened, except for a few of Mr. Warren's men. They came into our room at the Imperial, beat me to a pulp, and then left me for dead in the alley behind the building. Of course, he'd never tell you good *church people* that."

Warren turned around and put his arms up to the murmuring crowd. "The poor boy's drunk. You'll have to excuse—"

"There's *nothing* to excuse, Mr. Warren. Your men ransacked my room, took all of my money, left me for dead, and went on their way.

Then you prevented me from earning an honest living because you wanted to make my life as hard as possible. That's stealing. That's dishonesty and corruption. Now I know I've done wrong, but doesn't the Bible say we shouldn't repay evil with evil?"

"I already made clear that you brought your current predicament on yourself."

"Hey," Dalton called to his growing audience.

He caught sight of Reverend McCarroll's hard blue eyes and stern face among those in the crowd, but he continued nonetheless.

"What, exactly, does the Bible say about deacons? They're supposed to be holy. To keep the faith with a pure conscience. To be found blameless." Dalton scanned the crowd again, and his stomach twisted with voracious hunger. "There's more, but why bother? He's not even gonna come close. He bought his deaconship, pure and simple. Is this the kind of man you want guiding your church?"

Warren just stood there, stone solid, his jaw firm.

"No one is perfect, Mr. Phillips. You are a walking example of such a fact," Warren said.

"I know that all too well, Mr. Warren. All too well." Dalton stared into Warren's eyes. "Now you get to atone for your sins against me. You get to make up for the wrong you've done to me over the last year and a half."

"Are you going to murder me Dalton? Like the other ten people you murdered?"

"Oh, I'm *well* over ten now. And no, I'm not gonna kill you. I'm gonna take back what you took from me."

Warren eyed him. "And what is that?"

"Your men took almost five-hundred dollars from me, and I want it back. Now."

"*Five-hundred?* Please. That amount, and your entire story, is a fabrication."

"I'm accounting for interest. If your bank does it, so can I."

"My bank has authority—"

"I'm holding a gun to your face," Dalton snapped. "That's my authority."

Warren patted his pockets and smirked. "Wouldn't you know? Gave my last dime in the offering plate."

Dalton pulled back the hammer on his revolver. "You have three seconds. Three."

"And what happens when you count down to zero?"

"I'm gonna shoot you in your face."

Camille gasped again, as did several others in the crowd.

"Two."

"You might as well save your breath and do it now because I'm not giving you anything. You're not *worth* anything."

"One," Dalton said. "Last chance."

"You won't do it." Warren's smirk shrank and beads of perspiration dotted his forehead. "Like you said, you killed those ten men in *self-defense*."

Would Dalton do it? He didn't know, but Warren had to believe he would. "I've killed *more* than ten men. Quite a few more."

Warren swallowed hard. Perspiration dotted his forehead. "You can't."

"I can. I will."

"You won't. You're a coward."

"You really want to take that chance? Everything you love is in this life, Mr. Warren. You die, and it all goes away." Dalton forced his shaking hand to still. "And given your past transgressions, I'd wager you won't see St. Peter's pearly gates after I put a bullet in you. You're probably heading the opposite direction."

Warren shook his head. "You won't do it. They'll hang you."

"I don't care if I live or die. I've got nothing to lose. You've got *everything* to lose." Dalton pressed the revolver against Warren's forehead. "Zero. Give me my money."

Warren glared into Dalton's eyes. He leaned forward and whispered. "Go to Hell."

"I'm already there," Dalton whispered back.

"I'm not giving you anything."

Dalton pushed the gun barrel into Warren's forehead. "Give me my *money*."

Warren clenched his jaw even tighter. "No."

Dalton squeezed the trigger.

♠ ♥ CHAPTER 37 ♦ ♣

D alton didn't fire.

Nizhoni's voice repeated in his head. *Don't waste your life.*

He didn't have a life to waste anymore. It was over. He had no reason to live. If he could take Max Warren to Hell with him, he would.

But Nizhoni's words just wouldn't go away. *Don't waste your life.*

Why shouldn't he? He had no purpose. No joy or happiness. Only suffering, only strife. Death stalked him, always only a step behind, never more, never less. Eventually it would catch up. Why not stop running? Why not rid the world of a greedy, wretched man at the same time?

Don't waste your life.

Heat stung Dalton's eyes.

No, not now. Not when he was so close to—

He was crying. Why was he crying?

The revolver sank to his side, and the hammer slowly eased back to its cradle as he pulled the trigger and disengaged the mechanism.

Don't waste your life.

Dalton swore aloud and dropped his revolver into the dirt. His knees hit the earth next, and he wailed. He cupped his face with his palms, wept, and shouted intermittent profanity in between miserable moans.

After a few minutes, he felt a hand touch his back. He gazed up through his tears to see Camille Warren's pretty face, but she didn't compare to Nizhoni's beauty. Her concerned expression shifted to frustration when Warren pulled her away.

Then he delivered a brutal kick to Dalton's nose. It laid Dalton out flat on his back, and his vision swirled red with pain and numbness all at the same time. He clenched his eyes shut to try to quell the sensations.

"That'll teach you to cross me, you filthy piece of—"

"*Max*," a familiar gravelly voice yelled. "Get away from him *now*."

When Dalton finally opened his eyes, his face still throbbed. Was he bleeding? And who in this town would ever come to his aid?

Reverend McCarroll positioned his towering frame between him and Warren.

Of course.

"Back up," Reverend McCarroll barked. "*Now*."

Warren complied. He straightened his tie and shifted his focus to reprimanding Camille.

"Dalton." Reverend McCarroll looked down at him. "Can you stand?"

Before Dalton could answer, Warren cut in. "Don't waste your time, Reverend. Marshal Garmer's going to take the boy in."

"What?" Reverend McCarroll asked. "What for? He didn't go through with it."

"He tried to rob me. The only reason he didn't succeed is because I wouldn't give him the money." Warren faced a part of the crowd Dalton couldn't see. "Attempted robbery is still an arrestable offense, isn't it, Marshal?"

Dalton couldn't see him, but he heard Marshal Garmer reply, "Why, yes. I do believe it is."

"John, you'd agree to *anything* that man says because he pays your salary." Reverend McCarroll's tone softened. "Give Dalton a break, will you? He's clearly penitent. He's confused and hungry. A night in jail will do him more harm than good."

"I'm counting on it," Warren said. "Take him in, Marshal."

"Don't do it," Reverend McCarroll said.

Marshal Garmer must have hesitated, because Warren repeated, slower and more deliberate, "Take him in, Marshal."

"John, please. I'm asking you as a friend."

"*Marshal.*"

"I—I'm sorry Reverend. I gotta take him in."

"I'm afraid I can't let you do that, John."

"Oh really?" Warren asked. "Then perhaps you'd like to join him in the adjacent cell for obstructing the Marshal from doing his job. How about that?"

Reverend McCarroll stood there for a long moment, his face rigid and angry, then he stepped aside.

Warren nodded down at Dalton. "Take him in."

The cell door slammed shut, enclosing Dalton in a six-by-eight-foot cell in plain view of the rest of the marshal's single-story office. Marshal Garmer locked him in then put Dalton's guns in the bottom drawer of his desk. He disappeared from the room but returned a few minutes later with a tray.

"I don't care what Warren told me. I know you need some food, so here's some beef stew. It ain't very hot, but you'd better get somethin' in your stomach anyway."

Dalton took the bowl, the bread, the cup of water, and the spoon from the tray through a rectangular slot in the bars. "Thank you, Marshal."

Marshal Garmer nodded. "I got things to do. I know you're hungry, so I'll bring you another bowl and some more bread now, 'cause I might be gone for awhile."

Dalton nodded. "I'd appreciate that, thank you."

The first bite of stew tasted bland yet incredible at the same time. By the time Marshal Garmer returned, Dalton had finished almost the entire bowl.

"Good thing I brought two more bowls instead of one. Figured you'd need it. Here's some extra bread, too, and another cup of water."

Better than he deserved. Much better. "Thank you again, Marshal."

"You're welcome. I'm headin' out for awhile. Heard reports of some fellow who came into town and started to harass some of the workin' ladies. Gotta check that out. Be back before long, though, and if you're still hungry I can get you another round."

"Yes, please. Thank you."

Marshal Garmer nodded, then he headed for the door.

"Marshal?"

"Yes?" He turned his head.

Dalton swallowed the lump in his throat and stared down at his boots. "For whatever it's worth… I'm sorry for all the trouble I've caused you."

Marshal Garmer shifted his weight and squared his shoulders with Dalton. "I forgive you, Dalton. I'll be back later."

Again, better than he deserved.

Marshal Garmer walked out the door and shut it behind him, leaving Dalton alone in the office.

Dalton awakened to a clamoring outside his cell window. By the way the sun shone into the room, he gathered that he'd slept through the night and into the next morning.

A barrage of profanity and scuffling sounded on the other side of the wall. Perhaps the marshal had found his bounty.

It didn't matter to Dalton. He'd gone to sleep on a full belly for once, and he'd finally managed to get some good rest, despite the cell's rigid bed and the old, dirty mattress on top of it. His eyelids drooped shut again, and he tried to block out the noise.

A heavy slam jolted him back to cognition—the sound of the main door striking the wall as it opened. A slur of half-English, half-Spanish hisses and screeches filled the room, but Dalton didn't even roll over for a look. Marshal Garmer must've nabbed himself a Mexican.

"I said *calm down*." Marshal Garmer added his own profanity to the mix. "If I have to, I'll give you another whack upside your head."

More Spanish-English-gibberish. "Try it… and I'll kill you until you are dead."

"Mighty big words for a man in shackles." Marshal Garmer chuckled. "Now you sit down in that chair, and don't say a word 'less I ask you to."

A slew of Spanish followed, probably curses. Dalton hadn't picked much up during his time in the southwest, but by the tone of the Mexican's voice, he could tell they weren't nice words. He clenched his eyes shut and tried to fall back asleep.

"I told you to shut up and sit down," Marshal Garmer said, his voice flat but firm. "One more outburst like that and I swear to God Almighty that I'll gag you."

This time the expletives came in English.

"That's it. I'm gonna tie this bandana around your mouth. You try to bite me again, and I'll knock your face clean off with my bare hand. Got it?"

The prisoner protested, then coughing, gagging, choking, grumbling replaced his words. The Mexican's volume hadn't decreased, but his words became unintelligible. Easier for Dalton to drown out.

Eventually, the Mexican quieted down. Hopefully they wouldn't be cell neighbors for long.

Dalton slipped toward slumber once again, even as Marshal Garmer addressed his catch. "Now that's better. Behave and we can get this over with. Sooner I get this paperwork filled out, sooner you're outta here, assumin' the judge allows someone to post bail for you. But I have a feeling he'll set it pretty high, considerin' what you done to that poor girl."

More grumbles.

"Say what you want, but you're drunk, and she said she wanted nothing to do with you."

A long growl, then an even longer silence.

"There. Paperwork's set. Time to put you in your cell. Stand up," Marshal Garmer said.

The *clank* of the cell door opening and then clanging shut jarred Dalton from his snooze.

"Now turn around and put your hands against the bars so I can take those shackles off you." Chains clinked, and metal clacked against metal.

"There. Make yourself at home. I got a feelin' you're gonna be there for awhile."

The Mexican must have pulled the bandana from around his mouth, because he started spouting obscenities at Marshal Garmer again.

After a few moments of the Mexican's interminable shouting, Marshal Garmer finally interjected, "If you don't shut your dirty trap right now, I'm gonna thrash you again. Cut it out. You hear me, Zamora?"

Dalton's eyes snapped wide open.

CHAPTER 38

D alton's muscles tensed.

He couldn't go back to sleep now. He might never sleep again.

Zamora? Here, in the Spider's Rock jail? He shifted on his bed and rubbed his eyes.

The Mexican had his back to Dalton's cell, so Dalton couldn't tell if he was Zamora or not. Dalton stole a furtive glance at Marshal Garmer, who reclined at his desk, feet up, reading a newspaper.

His gaze shifted back to the Mexican again, who had turned enough so Dalton could see his full facial profile. Then he rotated his head ever farther and looked Dalton square in his eyes.

There, in the cell next to Dalton's, stood Alejandro "Diablo" Zamora, the man who'd beat him to a pulp, shot him three times, and left him for dead in the desert.

"What you lookin' at?" Zamora spat on the floor of Dalton's cell.

Dalton looked away. What would he do now? What if Zamora recognized him?

Revenge. That's what.

He'd exact vengeance on Zamora, whose actions had hurled Dalton into a new life of false hope and pain.

To this day he still couldn't grip anything with his right hand because of Zamora's first bullet. If he could've clawed his way through the bars separating them and torn Zamora apart, he would've done it.

"You deaf? I said 'what you lookin' at?'" Zamora staggered over to the bars that separated him from Dalton. "You got a problem, amigo?"

Dalton shook his head slightly and denied Zamora eye contact. "No. No problem."

Could I kill him through the bars? He's close enough to get a grip on him...

"Good. You don't want to mess with *el Diablo*, right?" Zamora spat on the floor a second time and backed away from Dalton's cell.

"Hey," Marshal Garmer said. "Don't spit on my floor. You do it again and you're moppin' the entire office with shackles on your wrists and ankles."

Zamora slung a slew of Spanish at him then sat down on the bed in his cell.

Marshal Garmer just shook his head and went back to reading his newspaper.

Did Marshal Garmer really not know about Dalton's last run-in with Zamora? Was he totally oblivious to the fact that Zamora had tried to murder Dalton? He must have been, or he'd forgotten. Otherwise he wouldn't have put Zamora in the adjacent cell.

A few minutes later, Marshal Garmer set his newspaper on the desk and stood up. "Well boys, I suppose I'd better go outside for awhile. No good to the public if I ain't *in* public. Ain't that right?"

Neither Dalton nor Zamora answered.

"Don't all sound off at once. Be back 'round lunch. Y'all stay out of trouble, hear me?"

Dalton nodded, and Zamora cursed at him.

Marshal Garmer approached Dalton's cell and muttered, "Keep a keen eye on this one, will you? He's drunk and even more of a handful than you are. You at least had common decency. This one's got no such thing. Probably never even heard the term before."

Dalton nodded again. "Okay."

"Good." Marshal Garmer tugged his pants higher up on his waist and sauntered out the door, which he let slam shut behind him.

"Hey, amigo," Zamora called.

Dalton hesitated, then he met Zamora's eyes. "What?"

"Come over here. I got a story to tell you."

This might be interesting. Maybe Dalton could choke him through the bars if he got close enough. "Yeah? What's your story?"

Zamora cackled, then belched. He pressed his face up against the bars. "It's how I ended up in here."

"How's that?" Dalton could smell the alcohol on Zamora's breath, and he wondered if his own breath had ever reeked as much. Dalton decided against trying to choke him. Too risky with only one functional hand.

Zamora laughed again, then he described a violent encounter with one of the girls from the Continental in such graphic detail that Dalton's stomach churned.

Zamora concluded, "Pretty good stuff, right?"

"That's why you're in here?"

"Yeah, she complained, went to the marshal. I almost got away before he could catch me, but he tricked me, and now I'm in jail. But it doesn't matter. I'll get out soon anyway, right?"

"Is that so?" Dalton ran his fingers through his long hair.

"Yeah. But I done much worse than that, man."

"Like what?"

"One time, in this town, I come in with my friends to one of these saloons. There's this beautiful girl—blonde hair, green eyes."

Dalton could see where this was going. He purposefully relaxed so he wouldn't give himself away by clenching his fists or his teeth.

"Anyway, so I'm talking to her, right? And she don't like what I say. She slaps me, so I slap her back, right? Like you do to any woman who disrespects you." Zamora's voice increased in volume and pitch as he spoke. "Next thing I know, I get hit in the face by some thug. He almost gets me and my amigos, but then *we get him* with a chair leg over his head."

Dalton scowled at him.

Zamora beamed a jagged yellow smile. "So we knock him out, drag him into the desert, shoot him, and leave him there. He's vulture food, or coyote food now, right?"

Dalton smirked. "Who was he?"

"Ah," Zamora waved his hand. "Just some nobody. The piano player. Doesn't matter anymore since he's dead, right?"

Dalton forced a chuckle along with Zamora. "Yeah, he's dead alright."

"You said it, amigo." Zamora dropped onto his bed. "Okay, amigo. Your turn. What are you in here for?"

"Attempted armed robbery."

Zamora sat up and cocked his head to the side. "Really?"

Dalton nodded.

"Not bad, amigo. You don't look like that type of man to me, though. More like homeless than an outlaw."

"Doesn't change the fact that I did it."

Zamora laughed again. "You sure did, didn't you? But looking at you, I figured—well, not that, anyway. So who'd you try to rob?"

"Probably no one you've heard of."

"Come on, man. I get around, right?" Zamora sprawled out on his back again. "Try me."

Dalton shrugged and shifted his weight to his back leg. "Max Warren, III."

"Really? You tried to rob *him*? He practically owns this little town."

"Yeah."

More laughter. "That's *loco*, man."

"What's so funny?"

"Because we're totally gonna rob him later today. We're gonna swoop into this town and rob him, man. Gonna wipe out this whole town, too." Zamora exhaled a sigh and rubbed his forehead with his hands.

Dalton raised an eyebrow. "When was your last drink?"

"No, man. It's not even like that. We're gonna take over the entire town today."

"Seriously, when was your last drink?"

"This morning. Maybe five minutes before the marshal brought me in." Zamora started laughing again. "Ohhh, I love tequila."

"No kidding," Dalton said.

The main door swung open and smacked against the inside wall, and Marshal Garmer stomped in. He twisted around and faced the door. "I said, 'not a chance.' He's stayin' here. I don't care who you are. You got no authority, no jurisdiction over me or this town."

A tall man in soldier blues clopped through the door. He removed his gray hat from his head, revealing silver hair that matched the thick mustache on his face. The rank of colonel adorned his shoulders. A military-issue cutlass sword hung from his left hip, and a holstered revolver hung from his right.

The sight of a familiar silver-and-turquoise ring on the man's left pinkie finger stopped Dalton's breath.

In the doorway, no more than fifteen feet from Dalton, stood the man who killed Nizhoni.

♠ ♥ CHAPTER 39 ♦ ♣

"Marshal," the colonel said, his voice deep and untainted by the southwestern region's customary drawl. He spoke more like an easterner. Probably graduated from West Point. "That man must be released into my custody immediately. He is a federal prisoner and—"

"Look, I don't mean to cut you off, Colonel… what'd you say your name was?"

"Judd. Colonel Morton Judd."

Dalton memorized that name and re-memorized Colonel Judd's face. The man had murdered Nizhoni.

Rage practically streamed from his fingertips. What he wouldn't give to have his revolver and just one single bullet. He only needed one shot. There was no way he'd miss—not at this range, not after being given a second chance.

But Dalton was locked in a cell. Even so, if he had even a whisper of a chance for revenge, he'd take it without hesitation.

"Colonel Judd," Marshal Garmer repeated. "I apologize, but you can't have him. He assaulted a young woman here in Spider's Rock last night, and he's due for a preliminary hearing with the judge tomorrow morning."

Dalton mused at his old thinking. A few minutes ago, he'd been thoroughly convinced that his life still had no meaning, and he'd resolved to die whatever miserable death came to him. A few days before that, he'd been ready and actually tried to end his own life.

But now, he'd happened upon a reason, a very poignant, potent reason to stay alive. Two of them, in fact.

In two separate, distinct instants, his apathy had blossomed into hatred, into an insatiable drive for vengeance. It flared inside of him and renewed his strength. He clenched his left fist to keep himself from exploding.

"I'm afraid you'll have to let him come with me, Marshal. I'm with the United States Army, and we have federal jurisdiction. Arizona isn't even a state. It's a territory. That means until Congress approves your statehood, I can come and go as I please, and I have supreme authority here." Colonel Judd adjusted the position of the cutlass sword hanging from his hip.

"Say whatever you like, Colonel, but Zamora's stayin' here. Can't let you take him. He's gotta answer for his crime against that young lady."

"He will. I assure you of that."

Marshal Garmer cackled. "Assurance from a federal employee. What a joke."

"I don't know who you may have dealt with in the past that inspired such an attitude, but I am a man of my word." Colonel Judd stepped toward him. "Alejandro Zamora will receive justice at the hands of the federal courts, not some hick-town judge."

"Well, *excuse* me." Marshal Garmer matched Colonel Judd's advance with a step of his own.

Dalton smirked. Marshal Garmer didn't scare easily. He'd never once backed down from Dalton. That alone said plenty about the man's constitution. Dalton just hoped the two wouldn't come to blows. He wanted Colonel Judd all for himself.

"You *can't* have him," Marshal Garmer continued. "How many times do I gotta say it? How many different ways?"

"My charge trumps yours."

"Yeah? What's that?"

"He's wanted for murder. He killed a federal official in Texas, and I'm here to bring him to justice. If you insist he gets what's coming to him, then hand him over to me. The federal government has no tolerance for criminals of his nature. He will be assured a swift trial and an even swifter execution," Colonel Judd said.

"You keep sayin' that word. 'Assure' this. 'Assure' that," Marshal Garmer said. "I got no assurances of anythin' except that if he stays, he'll stand before our court, be found guilty—there are several witnesses—and then he'll get locked up or maybe even hung if the judge feels spry that mornin'.

"And if by some miraculous miscarriage of justice he does happen to dodge the noose, he's all yours. But until then, he stays here and will be tried for the crime he committed last night in our 'hick town.' There's no negotiation to be had about this. I've said my piece."

Colonel Judd swallowed hard, then he cleared his throat. "Is it a matter of paperwork? I can have a federal warrant in here within a half an—"

"You just keep your paperwork. Got too much of that already. He's gotta stay. That's the bottom line. There's nothin' you can say or do that'll change my mind." Marshal Garmer sat in his desk chair and put his feet up on the desk.

Colonel Judd nodded. He turned away, his gaze fixed out the window, and sighed.

"Look, Colonel," Marshal Garmer said. "I'm really very sorry we couldn't work this out in your favor. But you see, I've got a job to do and—"

In one brutal motion, Colonel Judd spun around, drew his cutlass, and slashed Marshal Garmer's throat wide open.

♠ ♥ CHAPTER 40 ♦ ♣

D roplets of blood flung into the air and spattered against the wall. Marshal Garmer's eyes tripled in size. He clutched his gushing throat with both hands, and his chair toppled back. He spilled onto the floor, writhed for a moment in a pool of his own blood, and then stopped. His eyes fixed on Dalton, now just vacant orbs.

Dalton had recoiled into his cell and stood there gawking at the sight, but Colonel Judd paid him no mind. In the next cell over, Zamora whooped and hollered.

Colonel Judd stepped over Marshal Garmer's limp body, careful to avoid his blood, and grabbed a rag from the desk. He used it to wipe the tip of his sword clean, all the while wearing the same cold, stoic expression as when he'd shot Nizhoni in the desert.

Then he sheathed his sword and reached down for Marshal Garmer's keys. He walked over to Zamora's cell and dangled them just outside the bars. When Zamora reached for them, Colonel Judd pulled them away, which elicited a flurry of colorful language from Zamora.

"Not until you agree to behave," Colonel Judd said.

"Behave?" Zamora pointed at Marshal Garmer. "You just murdered the town marshal, but *I'm* the one who needs to behave?"

"He would have died soon enough anyway. Might as well be now."

Colonel Judd adjusted his hat and dabbed at his mustache again. "And this wouldn't have happened if you hadn't jeopardized our plan by getting thrown into jail."

Dalton eyed Colonel Judd. *Plan? What could these two possibly have in common?*

"Whatever, man," Zamora said. "I do what I do. I take what I want. It doesn't matter anyway. You're here now. You can let me out, and we'll get moving, right?"

"No."

Zamora's jaw hardened. "What do you mean, 'no?'"

"I mean *no*. I can't trust you. I may as well leave you in here to rot and do everything myself. You're too unpredictable, too dangerous to our plan."

Dalton blinked. Incredible. They were somehow in league with each other... but to what end?

Zamora put his hands up. "But it was *my* plan in the first place."

"Consider yourself plagiarized." Colonel Judd headed for the door.

"What? Wait—I don't even know what that *means*." Zamora rattled his bars.

Dalton frowned. *Drunken idiot.*

Colonel Judd turned back. "It means I don't need you anymore. I'll do the rest on my own, and you can watch from your cell."

"*No.*" Zamora rattled the cell bars again. "No, I'll behave. I promise I'll behave."

Colonel Judd raised an eyebrow.

"I swear. I won't mess up again. On my mother's grave, I *swear*."

"How do I know I can believe you?"

Zamora put his hands out to his sides. "Hey, it's me, right?"

"That's what I'm afraid of."

"Then what do you want from me, *ese?*"

"I want—" Colonel Judd glanced at Marshal Garmer's limp body. "—absolute *assurance* that you won't do anything but follow my orders from now on. Then, when we're finished, you can go your way, and I'll go mine."

Dalton squinted at them. What were they talking about? Why would Zamora ever follow Colonel Judd's orders? Zamora had rambled something about taking over the town… had he been serious, and not just drunk and delusional?

"Okay, amigo." Zamora nodded. "I'll do whatever you say. Just get me out of here, right?"

Colonel Judd's eyes narrowed, and he stared at Zamora for a long moment, as if considering, calculating. "Very well. But first we need to go over the plan once more. No more mistakes, no more distractions. Then I'll let you out."

"I'm all ears, amigo."

"You're drunk, so listen twice as carefully."

"Sure thing." Zamora belched again, then he snickered.

Colonel Judd's stoic visage didn't shift, even at Zamora's crudeness. "You will ride into town with your friends around two o'clock this afternoon."

Zamora waved his hand. "Yeah, yeah, I know that. Skip it."

"No. I'm not going to risk another mistake on your part."

"Hey, it's my plan." Zamora pointed his thumb at his chest. "*My* plan."

Colonel Judd exhaled a long breath through his nose, and his jaw tensed. "Will you let me finish?"

Zamora shrugged. "No one's stopping you but yourself, amigo."

"Once you come into town, you need to take an inventory for me."

"A what?"

"An inventory. Look around and figure out what kind of resistance we're going to run up against. If you think it's substantial, we'll just level the town with our artillery. Then we'll ride in and clean up whatever's left," Colonel Judd said. "But I'd like to avoid that if possible. I want to keep the town intact so we can use it once we clear out the inhabitants."

"*All* of the people?" Zamora asked.

"Yes, all of them."

"I can't even keep a girl or two for myself? Because I got my eyes on a few of 'em." Zamora winked. "It'd be a shame to let 'em go to waste, right?"

Colonel Judd sighed. "You may do as you please with the women as long as you finish them off when you're done. Anyone not directly in your care will be killed. We cannot allow any survivors. If word of this gets out we'll all be hunted down and hanged. The whole town must perish."

"Okay, okay. I got it."

"If the town is clear, then give the signal we discussed. Remember what it was?"

"Yeah, I remember."

"Very well. Once you give the signal, I will lead our soldiers into town from the southeast. We'll take our positions and begin the extermination."

"Then we get the money, right?" Zamora rubbed his hands together.

"Correct. Most of Max Warren's money is in his bank. His wildcat banknotes aren't worth anything without real currency backing them up, but he's got a huge vault loaded with gold, silver, and deeds to land, mines, and property. Once we finish sweeping the town, you and I will divide the spoils."

"I like that part." Zamora showed his jagged yellow smile.

"That is why I can't abide by destroying the town," Colonel Judd said. "The more we destroy, the less profit we gain from this endeavor. Do you understand?"

Zamora nodded. "I got it, amigo. I got it."

"Do you have any questions?"

"Only one. You gonna let me out, or what?"

Colonel Judd sighed again, then turned Marshal Garmer's key in the cell door's lock. The bars swung open, and Zamora stepped out with a crooked grin in his face.

Colonel Judd grabbed him by his arm. "I am neither a patient nor a forgiving man. Don't disappoint me again, Zamora."

Zamora wrenched his arm away and glared at him. "You just worry about yourself. I know what I'm supposed to do."

Colonel Judd returned his hard gaze for a moment, then glanced at a clock on Marshal Garmer's wall. "It's almost eight in the morning. I need to get back to my men. Make sure you're here on time. I'll be waiting for your signal at 2:30 this afternoon."

"Yeah, I got it." Zamora eyed Dalton. "What about him?"

Dalton swallowed and took a step back in his cell.

Colonel Judd surveyed him from top to bottom, then he looked at Zamora. "What about him?"

"He told me he already tried to rob Max Warren, but he couldn't pull it off. Maybe we could use him?" Zamora said. "Maybe he knows something we don't know?"

Dalton's eyes widened. What an opportunity. He could take his revenge on both of them on the same day if things worked out.

Colonel Judd locked eyes with Dalton, as if analyzing everything about him from the inside out. "No. Leave him here. We don't know him, so we can't trust him."

"You barely know *me*." Zamora pulled his guns and belt from Marshal Garmer's desk drawer.

Dalton recognized them immediately by their engraved ivory handles. They were the Colt sisters, the guns he'd had before Zamora had left him for dead. The sight of them and the thought of Zamora using them after all this time sickened Dalton.

Zamora extracted a flask next and shook it, then he opened the cap for a drink. He turned to Colonel Judd, whose gaze had remained fixed on Dalton the whole time. "Well?"

"No." Colonel Judd tossed the keys onto Marshal Garmer's desk, far out of Dalton's reach. "It's one more share we'd have to split."

Zamora shrugged at Dalton. "Sorry, amigo. Guess you're just unlucky."

Dalton couldn't help the smirk that curled his lips. "Story of my life."

"You go out the back door, I'll go out the front. I saw your horse near one of the saloons," Colonel Judd said.

"*Sí*, that's where I left him." Zamora winked at Dalton. "Take care, amigo. If you can get outta here before we come back, run to the hills. Run for your life."

Dalton watched his two nemeses walk out of the office, leaving him alone and once again consumed by thoughts of vengeance. He stared down at Marshal Garmer's exsanguinated body, then he looked at the keys on the desk.

If only he could escape from this cell.

♠ ♥ CHAPTER 41 ♦ ♣

Not long after Colonel Judd and Zamora left, Reverend McCarroll walked in. His mouth dropped open when he saw Marshal Garmer lying in a pool of his own blood, and then his gaze shifted to Dalton and hurled silent, furious accusations of murder at him.

"I didn't do it," Dalton said. "You may have noticed that I'm locked here in this cell, and I don't have any weapons. I didn't do it."

Reverend McCarroll clenched his fists. "Then who did?"

"No one you know. He's a colonel in the United States Army. And... you're not gonna believe this, but..." Dalton stared into his uncle's stark blue eyes. "He's also the man who killed my wife."

Reverend McCarroll blinked. "What?"

Dalton held his tongue and stared down at his boots.

"You're serious?"

"Yes. And when I get out of here, I'm gonna find him and kill him."

Reverend McCarroll set his jaw and glared at Dalton. "I understand how you're feeling, but you can't do this to yourself."

"Do what to myself?"

"You can't let revenge take hold inside your heart. It will destroy you." Reverend McCarroll held up a hand. "And don't give me any of that nonsense about you already being dead. I know you feel that way, but you're still here."

Dalton chuckled and shook his head. "Half an hour ago, I would've said that, but I feel more alive now than I have since the day Nizhoni died. I won't lie to you, Uncle Bill—I intend to kill that man with everything I am. And I *will*."

"Dalton—"

"You always talk about me needing to find my purpose. Well, I found one, and I've never wanted to stay alive so much in my life."

"That's not even close to what I meant, and you know it. You're twisting my words."

Dalton shrugged. "So?"

"God doesn't want you to kill out of vengeance. He said 'Vengeance is mine.' If you try to take something like that out of His hands, you'll end up like Samson. You may get your wish, but you'll die alone and with nothing."

"God wouldn't have put this murderer back in my path if He didn't want me to do something about it. And I'll die knowing I've avenged Nizhoni and avenged *myself*. That's far more than I have now."

Reverend McCarroll sighed. "Then I guess you'll have to stay in that cell after all."

Dalton huffed as his uncle headed for the door. "You're really leaving?"

"I need to get some help to deal with Marshal Garmer's body and to figure out what we're gonna do next," Reverend McCarrol said. "And you haven't given me a reason to stay."

"How about every living soul in this town?" Dalton moved to the bars and gripped them with both hands.

As he did, he felt something pop in his right hand, and fleeting pain stabbed at it. It faded just as quickly. He looked down at it and shook it out. What was that all about?

"What?"

"Huh?" Dalton looked up. "Oh. I said how about every—"

"I heard what you said." Reverend McCarroll waved his hand. "What did you *mean*?"

"I mean that the life of every person in this town is in danger. How's that for a reason?" Dalton folded his arms and leaned against the back wall of his cell. For once, he actually had leverage over his uncle—and it was really powerful leverage. Life-or-death leverage.

"How so?"

Dalton nodded to Marshal Garmer's body. "See him? Everyone else is next."

"What do you mean?"

"Colonel Judd and his men are coming back into town to wipe us out. They want Warren's money, his gold, and his land. They're gonna invade Spider's Rock, kill everyone so there are no witnesses, and then take it all."

Reverend McCarroll put his hands on his hips. "Is that right?"

His uncle's tone suggested that Dalton might be losing his audience. "There's a dead marshal on the floor not five feet from you, and you don't believe me?"

"I never said I didn't believe you."

"But you don't."

"I don't have any reason to trust you, Dalton."

"Here's one: have I ever lied to you? Ever?" Dalton flexed his right hand open and then tried to clench it shut.

To his surprise, it almost felt as if he had some grip strength in it. Then he tried to grab one of the cell bars again with it, and it didn't work. No matter—he had bigger issues to focus on.

"Come on," he said. "You can't think of even one situation where I lied to you."

"Maybe not, but you've certainly deceived me. Not much of a difference."

"It's enough of a difference. Sure, I went behind your back and did things my own way, and I ended up leaving, but I always told the truth. I'm not perfect by any stretch, but you *know* I don't lie."

Reverend McCarroll sucked a deep breath in through his nostrils. "I'm still not sure if I believe you."

"You ought to. They discussed their entire plan in this very room after the Colonel killed Marshal Garmer." Dalton folded his arms again.

"Who's 'they?'"

Dalton scoffed. "If you didn't believe me before, you really won't believe this part."

"Try me."

"Colonel Judd, the man who killed my wife, is working with Alejandro Zamora, the man who shot me three times and left me for dead in the desert."

Reverend McCarroll squinted at him. "You're right. I don't believe you."

"I know." Dalton nodded. "Sounds too good to be true, doesn't it?"

"Well beyond that. Are you sure no one slipped anything in your breakfast this morning? Perhaps some opium?"

"I'm sure. Couldn't believe it myself at first, but it's true. They stood face-to-face right over there—" Dalton pointed to a spot outside the adjacent cell. "—and went over the entire plan. Zamora was drunk, so Colonel Judd made him review it before he let him out of the cell."

"And why was Zamora in the cell?"

"Marshal brought him in this morning. He hurt some girl from the Continental pretty badly. Marshal Garmer got wind of it, picked him up, and dumped him in here."

Reverend McCarroll folded his arms. "And you're not making all of this up?"

"No, I'm not. What do I have to gain by lying?" Dalton pointed to Marshal Garmer's desk. "You need proof? Take a look at the marshal's paperwork. Zamora's name has got to be in there somewhere."

Reverend McCarroll glanced at the desk then back at Dalton. He stepped around the now-stagnant pool of Marshal Garmer's blood on his way to the desk and shuffled through some papers.

"Colonel Judd broke him out. He cut the marshal's throat and watched him die, stone-faced, just like when he shot Nizhoni." Dalton swallowed the lump in his throat. "Marshal Garmer was a good man. He didn't deserve to die."

"Neither did Nizhoni." Reverend McCarroll locked his gaze on Dalton.

For a moment, Dalton thought he saw the faintest glint of compassion, but then it disappeared, replaced by Reverend McCarroll's usual somber expression.

"But it happened, and there's nothing we can do about it except move on."

Dalton shook his head. "Your idea of what that means is different than mine."

"I know it is." Reverend McCarroll held a piece of paper at arm's length and squinted at it. "Don't ever get old, Dalton. Your eyes won't be the only thing to fail you."

Dalton scoffed. "I'm not planning on it. Believe me."

Reverend McCarroll shot him a glare. "Here. It says Alejandro Zamora."

"I told you I wasn't lying."

Reverend McCarroll set the paper down. "Alright, fine. You're right. But I still find it hard to believe that he and this Colonel Judd would partner to annihilate an entire town."

"Let me out of here, and I'll tell you everything."

Another sigh. "How about you tell me everything first, and then I decide if I want to let you out?"

"Don't you want to save the lives of the people in this town?"

"Don't you want to get out of there?"

"Touché." Dalton folded his arms. "I'll tell you if you promise to let me out afterward."

"Then I might as well let you out now." Reverend McCarroll stared at him. "But I'm not gonna do that."

"Well, what's your decision?"

After a long moment and a sharp sigh, Reverend McCarroll replied, "I will let you out, but I have a condition of my own for your release."

"What's that?"

"I'll tell you after you tell me the plan."

"No deal. Tell me now."

"Look, we can go back and forth with this all day. The fact remains that you can't get out of here unless I let you out." His voice sounded tired and thin. "Will you please just tell me?"

Dalton frowned. "Fine."

In less than a minute, he explained the entirety of Zamora and Colonel Judd's plan to his uncle.

"The only thing they didn't say is what the signal is. But if the soldiers don't get that signal, they'll flatten the town with their artillery first. Then they'll ride in and finish off whoever's left."

Reverend McCarroll pulled Marshal Garmer's chair away from the blood on the floor and sat in it with distant eyes and a hopeless frown on his face. "I don't know if we can stop them."

"I don't care either way, as long as I get my revenge." Dalton stuck his arm through the bars. "Hand me the keys, will you? They're on the desk behind you."

Reverend McCarroll looked up at him. "Not until you agree to my final condition."

Dalton sighed and rolled his eyes. "What do you want?"

A familiar smirk curled Reverend McCarroll's lips.

♠ ♥ CHAPTER 42 ♦ ♣

"Absolutely not. No way. Not a chance." Dalton faced the back wall of his cell.

"Then feel free to stay in here. If you'll excuse me, I've got plans to make with the rest of the townsfolk before two o'clock," Reverend McCarroll said.

Dalton swiveled on his heels. "Wait."

"Wait for what? You've made up your mind."

"Why do you need me? Why can't you just let me out so I can go my own way?"

"You're the key to this entire situation, Dalton." Reverend McCarroll stepped closer to the bars. "You've heard the plan. You've encountered both of these men before."

"I just told you the plan, and my experience with them is next to nothing."

"Those aren't the only reasons." Reverend McCarroll cleared his throat. "Dalton, you're unlike any other person in this town. You've survived more beatings, more bullets, and more booze than anyone I've ever heard of, much less met. And on top of all of that, you have consumption.

"How you aren't dead—I don't know, but there has to be a reason for it. I believe you're still alive because you're supposed to help us fight these brigands." Reverend McCarroll leveled his gaze at Dalton. "So I'll ask you again: will you help us?"

Dalton laughed and shook his head.

"What's so funny?"

"You are."

Reverend McCarroll scrunched his eyebrows. "How so?"

"You once told me that my mother sent me down here so you could keep me out of trouble. Now you're insisting that I dive into it headfirst. I find that beyond amusing."

"This from the man who landed in jail because he refused to *let* me keep him out of trouble." Reverend McCarroll motioned toward him.

"Easy to make claims like that as a reverend on the other side of the bars."

Reverend McCarroll shook his head. "I wasn't born a reverend. I'm not perfect."

"You sure act like it sometimes."

"Do I really?" Reverend McCarroll's hard blue eyes locked onto Dalton's.

Dalton glanced to the side, then he reconnected with his uncle's gaze. He sighed. "No. You don't. I shouldn't have said that."

Reverend McCarroll rubbed his forehead. "I've always tried to remain humble without compromising my beliefs, but also without staying silent in the face of sin or adversity. If I've ever seemed otherwise to you, please forgive me."

"No, Uncle Bill. You haven't. I was just saying it to get a response."

Reverend McCarroll cracked a smile. "You always were a little twit."

"Old buzzard," Dalton retorted. "I know you're not perfect, and you don't pretend to be."

"That's kind of you to say."

Dalton squinted at him, unable to read the expression on his weathered face.

"We need you," Reverend McCarroll finally said. "Even with only your left hand, you're still the best shot for miles. Maybe anywhere. God can use your talent to save the town."

"You seriously think God wants to use me for *that?*" Dalton smirked again.

"Laugh all you want, but I believe God gave you that gift and kept you alive through all of your trials so you could help stop them from wiping us out. Think about it. It makes sense."

"If I think about it, that makes *no* sense," Dalton said. "With very, very few exceptions, everyone in this town hates me. They'd never listen to me."

"Dalton, every society reaches a point of desperation," Reverend McCarroll said. "In that moment, when everything is at stake, one of two things happens: either they fail and are overcome, or a warrior arises and saves them.

"This warrior is a phenomenon, a master of extraordinary proportions, a god among men. Sometimes the people love him, and sometimes they hate him. But no matter what they think, he rises to the occasion and saves the day despite impossible odds and every conceivable disadvantage."

Dalton stared at him.

"I believe that warrior is you." Reverend McCarroll pointed at Dalton.

"I just want to kill Zamora and Colonel Judd. That's all I'm interested in."

"You may very well get your chance, but if that's your only motivation, I can't let you out of this cell. Do you really want to fester in here while people die?"

"Do *you* want that?" Dalton countered.

Reverend McCarroll folded his arms. "No. I don't want that. I want you to help us."

Dalton exhaled a breath and shook his head. "Look, I'll help you, but my motivation isn't to save the town. I just need to get close enough to Zamora and Colonel Judd so I can take my revenge. If you can live with that, then let me out. If not, then no deal."

Reverend McCarroll sighed. "'Be not overcome of evil, but overcome evil with good.'"

"'Let not then your good be evil spoken of,'" Dalton countered.

Reverend McCarroll smiled. "You could have been a pastor, you know."

"That idea's even worse than suggesting I help you save the town," Dalton said. "So what's it gonna be, Reverend?"

Silence lingered between them.

"You force me to walk a narrow path, Dalton. I can't justify letting you out because of the vengeance in your heart, but in order to do a greater good, I need you. I suppose, at some point, I've got to stop worrying about you and let God have a turn." Reverend McCarroll inserted the key into the lock on Dalton's cell door. "Where are your guns?"

"In the marshal's desk. I'll get 'em." Dalton walked out of the cell, stepped over Marshal Garmer and his blood, and pulled his revolvers and his belt from the desk drawer. He strapped them on and gave his uncle a nod. "Let's go."

CHAPTER 43

"There is no way we're staking the fate of this entire town on *him*." Max Warren, III pointed his finger at Dalton. A chorus of agreement sounded in the wake of his words.

"You're missing the point, Max," Reverend McCarroll said.

As soon as Reverend McCarroll showed Warren what had happened to Marshal Garmer, Warren had personally rallied the rest of the town and sent Mr. Belvidere to round up the miners, who still hadn't arrived yet.

While Reverend McCarroll tried to reason with the townspeople who had gathered inside the church, Dalton studied the faces of those in attendance.

Randolph was there. So were Madame DeBuire, Vanessa, and most of the ladies from both the Continental and the Imperial, Dr. Richards and his wife, Giselle, and Camille Warren—who wouldn't make eye contact with Dalton—and several of Warren's cranks.

After much talk regarding the validity of Dalton's claims, it seemed that Reverend McCarroll had finally won the crowd over on that issue. Now he needed to convince them that Dalton would do more good than harm.

"We need him. You're fooling yourselves if you think we don't need his help. Not only is he the best shot of anyone here, he's also faced these soldiers, this Colonel Judd before."

"I don't care if he's faced God Almighty and survived," Warren said. "He's a drunk, a brigand, a womanizer, and a murderer. Do we really want to entrust our lives to that kind of person? He's not good for anything except doing harm to himself and to others."

The crowd offered more affirmations.

Dalton flexed his right hand some more. Whatever had happened when he'd tried to grab the prison bars seemed to have dissipated, and his right hand was back to its non-functioning ways. It would've been great if he'd been able to use it for what was to come—shooting with two pistols might make some things easier for him in the long run.

But alas, it wasn't meant to be. His hand was still useless when it came to holding and firing guns. He'd have to do it all left-handed, just like he'd been doing it for the last year.

Reverend McCarroll held up his hands, and the crowd hushed. "That's exactly *why* we need him: he's dangerous. You're all afraid of him, and I understand why. That's just a part of who he is. Yes, he's offended most of you, even done some of you harm. But we are a people called to forgiveness, to justice and—"

"Skip the sermon, Reverend," Warren said. "I think I speak for everyone when I say that no words you conjure will convince us to trust your nephew. He ought to be locked back in that cell until this is all over, win, lose, or draw."

Reverend McCarroll opened his mouth to say something else, but Dalton spoke first.

"You're right, Mr. Warren." Dalton stood. If he wanted to get his revenge on Zamora and Colonel Judd, he had to humble himself before his other adversary, Max Warren. If he didn't, the town would perish, and he'd gain nothing. "He can't convince you, but he shouldn't have to try. It's my burden, not his.

"I wish I had something to say that might persuade you to let me help, but I know nothing I say or do will ever cover the wrong I've done to you and so many others in this room. Even so, I'm gonna try anyway."

Dalton fixed his attention on Max Warren and swallowed the pride that had coagulated in his throat. "I'm sorry, Mr. Warren. I'm sorry for all the wrong I've done to you, for all the hurt I've caused you and your family. I acted out of my own interests and never once considered yours. I'm sorry."

Warren didn't move, didn't show even the slightest sign of forgiveness or any emotion other than hatred. It didn't matter—Dalton had done what he needed to do.

He scanned the crowd and locked his gaze onto another set of eyes. "Dr. Richards, I owe you an apology also. You warned me twice about the way I was living, and I ignored your wisdom both times, even after you saved my life. I should have listened to you and spared myself the trouble. I'm sorry I didn't respect you enough to do as you suggested."

Dr. Richards gave him a slow nod.

Dalton found Randolph next, who folded his arms and looked away. "Randolph, I know how angry you are with me. I took advantage of our relationship and put the Imperial in serious jeopardy when I shot those men a few months back. I'm sorry. I drank, I gambled, I killed. I gave your business a bad name, and in doing so, I cast a bad light on you. I was selfish, and I'm sorry."

Randolph glanced at Dalton, then diverted his gaze again.

Maybe this apologizing thing wasn't going to work after all.

Dalton scanned the faces of the various girls he'd been with, most of whom sat only a few seats away from Randolph. "I owe almost all of the ladies who work at either the Imperial or the Continental an apology. I used you for my personal fulfillment and treated you like—well, like prostitutes instead of people. I'm sorry."

A few of them nodded. One girl even smiled. Most of them glared at him.

"I especially owe Vanessa Clark an apology." Dalton located her, seated between some of the other girls.

She was staring daggers at him, unhindered by anything he'd said thus far.

"You only ever wanted good things for me, but at the time, I couldn't see past my own inclinations, my selfishness. I betrayed a friend, and for that I'm deeply sorry."

Vanessa broke eye contact with him and looked down.

Great. Another failed apology. Regardless of how some of them received what he had to say, he had one more to go. He turned to Reverend McCarroll. "Uncle Bill, I've probably done you more harm than anyone else in this room."

Warren scoffed and folded his arms.

Dalton eyed him, then refocused on his uncle. "Like I said, *probably*. You've shown me nothing but love and compassion—sometimes very firm—but never too harsh or too severe.

"In return, I've done nothing but throw it back in your face. I always did what I wanted to do, when I wanted to do it, and I've only earned myself more trouble. Even worse, my deplorable behavior has cast a poor—" He glanced at the crowd. "—and *totally inaccurate* light on you.

"I've tarnished your reputation through my selfishness and my stubbornness. I only thought about myself, and never once cared how it might affect you or impact your role as the town's pastor. I owe you the biggest apology of all. I'm so sorry."

Reverend McCarroll squinted at Dalton for a moment. He rubbed his chin, then he nodded. "I forgive you, Dalton."

Dalton swallowed and faced the crowd again. "I know that saying 'I'm sorry' doesn't account for all the bad things I've done. It doesn't even come close."

They still showed him nothing but hard, angry faces. While some of those expressions could be blamed on the situation at hand, most of the town's anger burned for him.

"But I don't have anything else to give you. I'm broke. I have no money, no property, and even less pride. The only way I can think to repay you all for what I've done is to help you fend off this attack."

Warren stood and walked over to Dalton.

"You have been honest and forthright with us, Dalton, but as you correctly stated, apologizing doesn't go far to make amends for the wrong you've done. Given your record of infidelity on nearly every level, I am unwilling to let you play any substantial role in the forthcoming battle except that of a common soldier.

"You may serve as a faithful servant who will dutifully follow orders in a timely fashion. That is better than you deserve, and I think I speak for everyone when I say that your service to us in this manner would be an acceptable compromise."

Something clattered in the back of the church, followed by a large *thud*.

"You can speak for yourself, Mr. Warren," a voice rumbled. "And we'll speak for ourselves."

Dalton peered over the crowd and tried to make out the man who had just stormed inside the sanctuary. He knew that voice, that huge, distinct shape—

"I'd choose Dalton's leadership over yours any day of the week." The big, bearded man clomped up to the platform.

"Hutch?" Dalton gawked. "When did you get back?"

"Made it into town only a few minutes ago. One of the men outside the church explained the situation." Hutch faced the crowd. "Look, everyone, I know Dalton's been a burr in your boots for a long time, but there's no one better suited to save us than him. I know what he can do, and it's no joke."

"Mr. Hutch," Warren said. "It's very kind of you to stand up for your friend, but—"

"I'm not just standing up for him, Mr. Warren. I'm standing up for the entire town. If he doesn't lead us, if he doesn't play a critical role in this event, we're doomed. I'm sorry to be blunt, but Mr. Warren here is ill-suited to run a military operation."

Warren jabbed his hands into his hips. "I beg your pardon?"

"You're more concerned about money than survival. Sure, you own the town, but it's exactly that kind of bias that'll end up getting yourself —and maybe the rest of us—killed."

"Mr. Hutch—"

"Marshal Garmer's dead, so we need someone more objective. Someone who can keep a cool head on his shoulders. Someone who's got nothing left to live for." Hutch looked at Dalton and winked. "We need Dalton Phillips."

"I'm sorry, Mr. Hutch, but I'm going to have to ask you to sit down. I'm sure I speak for everyone when I say—"

"You do not speak for me, Max," growled Randolph. He stood to his feet. "I'm with Dalton."

Despite his shock, Dalton couldn't help but smile.

"You don't count." Warren waved his hand as if to dismiss Randolph. "Even if you did, the numbers are three—" He glanced at Reverend McCarroll. "—*four* against the rest of the town. Hardly even counts as a minority."

"Five." Dr. Richards stood up. "Six with Mrs. Richards, here. We trust Dalton."

Dalton smiled again. "That's all I'm asking for. Whether you forgive me or not, I'm asking you to trust me."

Warren started, "Still, it's not enough to justify—"

"Seven." "Eight." The numbers kept ascending. "Thirty-one." "Thirty two."

Warren's face reddened. He unclenched his fists and held up his hands. "Alright, alright. Quiet down. We have yet to hear from the miners. They're still not—"

The sanctuary doors opened, and a brigade of grubby, dirty miners poured in. Mr. Belvidere came in last and shut the doors behind them.

"Ah, my friends. Have a seat." Warren explained the situation to them in about a minute and then detailed the debate at hand. Hutch made his case as well, and then Warren said, "I take it you're all siding with me, are you not?"

A few of the miners grumbled a bit until George Vernon, John's taller, thinner brother, stood up. "I'm with Dalton."

John Vernon jumped up next to him. "Yeah, me too."

Warren shook his head. "Fine. You two are with Dalton. Even so, the majority is still mine. We're wasting time here. We should be planning for the attack—"

"Not so fast, Mr. Warren—" John's eyes grew wide and he added, "—*sir*. I think we'd like to hear what Dalton has to say on the matter."

Warren sighed and glared at Dalton again. "Very well."

Dalton swallowed. He owed them an apology too. He expressed his continued sorrow for gunning down the kid and the five other miners inside the Imperial, and how he regretted doing it, and then he pleaded that they give him a chance to make up for it now.

"Of course if you side with Mr. Phillips, you must consider the economical impact of your choice," Warren said. "In particular the *personal* economic ramifications it may have on each of you individually."

"Are you threatening their jobs, Mr. Warren?" When Hutch stepped toward him, Warren recoiled a half-step. Dalton couldn't blame him—Hutch was huge and reeked of nature.

The miners murmured in the background.

Warren shrugged. "I'm merely suggesting that this is an important choice that will affect all of our livelihoods."

"Then we'll put it to an anonymous ballot," Reverend McCarroll said. Warren whirled around to glare at him, but Reverend McCarroll just grinned in return. "To ensure a fair, unbiased vote, free of any 'personal economic ramifications.'"

"No. We don't need an anonymous vote. We don't have time for this nonsense. For heaven's sake, it's already nearly eleven o'clock. They're going to arrive in three hours."

"So quit stalling and get us some paper," Randolph bellowed from the crowd.

"You shut up, you Prussian son-of-a—"

"*Max.*" Reverend McCarroll shook his head. "Not in my church."

"I'll get some paper," Hutch said.

"There's plenty in my office, Hutch." Reverend McCarroll nodded toward one of the doors inside the sanctuary.

"Who's counting the votes?" Warren asked. "I don't trust most of the folks in this room."

"Have the Reverend count 'em," someone called.

"Yeah, if we can't trust him, we can't trust anyone," John Vernon hollered.

"*I* don't trust him." Warren turned to Reverend McCarroll. "No offense."

Reverend McCarroll smirked. "None taken. How about Mr. Belvidere, Dr. Richards, and I count? That seems like a balanced, unbiased panel. What do you say?"

The crowd rumbled in the affirmative, and someone let out a whoop.

"Well, Max, what do you say?" Reverend McCarroll asked.

Warren glared at him, then muttered, "Fine. Take your cursed vote."

Ten minutes later, Reverend McCarroll, Dr. Richards, and Mr. Belvidere finished counting the ballots. They tallied them up on a separate piece of paper and double-checked it before they presented the results.

Dr. Richards stood up from his chair. "The vote is ninety-eight for Dalton—"

That was it? Really? Only ninety eight votes?

"—and thirty-seven for Mr. Warren."

"What?" Warren thrust his hands above his head. "That can't be accurate. Count them again."

"I'm sorry, Mr. Warren," Dr. Richards said. "But we already counted them twice, in front of everyone, and you lost by a large margin."

"You're missing some ballots or something," Warren said. "There are well over two-hundred people in here. Where are the rest of the votes?"

"Maybe some of us didn't vote because we're afraid of you, Mr. Warren." George Vernon thumbed his suspenders. "Not me, though. I voted for Dalton."

"Me, too," John Vernon added.

"We don't have time for another vote, Mr. Warren," Hutch said. "You said it yourself. Not if we want to be prepared for these yahoos when they show up. Now are you gonna cooperate with us or not?"

"This is *my* town." Warren waved his hand over the crowd. "You all work for *me*. Even those of you who don't work for me, you really do, because one way or another I get a cut of every penny you spend in this town. *I* say what we will and won't do, and that's *final*."

"What about all that 'democracy' talk, Max?" Reverend McCarroll asked. "We voted. You lost. Dalton's gonna help us save your town."

"He's got no authority here. None."

"The people in this room just elected him to help us," Hutch said.

"It wasn't a fair vote," Warren said.

"Why wasn't it fair? Because you lost?" Hutch asked.

"You stay out of it, Hutch." Warren pointed his forefinger at him. "You're not even a part of this town. You're a transient *thug*. That's what you are."

"Transient thug or not, even without my vote Dalton still beat you like the dog you are."

Murmurs and ooohs emanated from the crowd.

"Either you join with the majority and help us, or you don't, and risk losing your town," Reverend McCarroll said. "But we need your help and your thirty-seven followers. We can't do this without you. We need everyone."

Warren dispersed hateful glares around the room with no reservation. Through clenched teeth, he said, "Fine. But since I have the most to lose, I want to be a part of the planning process."

"No one ever said you couldn't be," Randolph said.

Warren spun on his heels. "You *shut up*."

"Alright, enough." Dalton held up his hands. "The only way we survive this if we work together. From now on, that's what we're gonna do. Got it?"

The crowd murmured approval. Dalton caught Warren's steel gaze, but he didn't return it.

"Well, Dalton, you want us to work together. What exactly would you have us do?" Warren raised an eyebrow.

"Believe it or not," Dalton said. "I actually have a plan."

♠ ♥ CHAPTER 44 ♦ ♣

Everyone chipped in to prepare Spider's Rock for the impending attack while Dalton got cleaned up, courtesy of Gary Jenkins of Jenkins's Barbershop. By the time Gary finished, Dalton sported a short, well-manicured beard and mustache and a sensible, conservative haircut.

Next on the list: Dalton needed new rags. The Chinese couple who operated Song's Tailor Shop measured, chalked, and fitted him for a three-piece suit within fifteen minutes, but he'd have to come back in a couple of hours to pick up the finished product.

All the while, a small crowd of people followed him around, strategizing. Reverend McCarroll, Hutch, and Dr. Richards talked logistics with Dalton while Warren and Randolph mostly argued with each other. Yet despite the tension, they'd managed to come up with a solid plan to counter the impending attack.

"So where do we need the wagons?" Hutch asked, a pencil and paper in his hand.

"Behind the Imperial, and across the street in the alley behind the Continental," Dalton replied. "We'll post men on the surrounding rooftops with rifles."

"Those alleys don't line up very well," Randolph said.

"It'll work," Reverend McCarroll said. "If we time it right."

"We'd better time it right," Warren said. "I don't want them near the Continental."

"We're not putting them *closer* to the Imperial." Randolph glared at Warren. "I'm already shouldering most of the responsibility for the first part of—"

"They'll only be there to block the street." Dalton held up his hand. "Don't worry."

"What happens after we move the wagons into place?" Hutch continued to scribble notes onto his paper.

"Chaos will ensue," Reverend McCarroll said. "The soldiers won't be able to escape on either end of Main Street, so they'll look to the few side streets we have, maybe even the alleys."

Dr. Richards frowned. "There's no way we can cover them all. We don't have enough men."

"We can obstruct some of 'em," Dalton said. "We can stack crates, lumber, supplies, mining equipment, anything that will prevent 'em from moving forward."

"Belvidere can organize some of the miners to build the barricades," Warren said.

"I'll get 'em going." Reverend McCarroll walked toward Mr. Belvidere and a group of miners.

"Dalton?" Gilbert from the mercantile ran toward him. "Dalton! They're here!"

Dalton's heart jumped. "Already? We're not ready for—"

"No, not the soldiers. Your rimfire bullets." Gilbert held one up. "A Wells-Fargo courier dropped 'em off just a few minutes ago. As soon as I saw 'em, I came to find you."

Dalton wiped his brow and let out a relieved sigh. He eyed Gilbert. "You rascal."

"Well, are you comin' to get 'em?"

Dalton looked at Warren, then back at Gilbert. "I can't pay for 'em."

"Go get them, Dalton." Warren sighed. "Gilbert will open a line of credit for you, and once this is all over you can pay me back."

Dalton nodded. "I appreciate it Mr. Warren. Thank you."

"Don't mention it." Warren's face hardened to a stoic glare. "And I do mean that. Don't tell *anyone*. I don't like doing this."

"I understand. Thank you."

"Well, come on." Gilbert tapped Dalton on his shoulder.

"Gilbert?" Warren said.

"Huh?"

"Make sure every man in this town has a gun he can use. If he doesn't, you give him a rifle, a sidearm, and plenty of ammunition for both. Understand?"

"Yessir. I will, sir." Gilbert turned back to Dalton. "Wait 'til you see these."

At 1:20 in the afternoon, Mr. Song helped Dalton into his new suit. Fine black wool, pronounced chalk stripes spaced an inch apart, and deep pockets for extra bullets. Dalton had specifically requested that Song make the trousers and the armholes looser so he could better move around.

Under the suit, Dalton wore a stark white shirt with a red ascot, also applied by Mr. Song. The local cobbler, a Hungarian immigrant named Tibor, had polished the black rattlesnake boots on Dalton's feet so well that they almost looked like patent leather.

His new clothes, his new boots, and his new well-groomed look completed his new identity—perhaps the most important part of their plan.

The hot Arizona sun poured yellow light across the town. The sight reminded Dalton of lemonade. As he walked to the Imperial, he longed for some lemonade, preferably cold, definitely hard. Perhaps Randolph could come up with something if Dalton asked politely.

He stepped inside and headed for the poker table they'd set up for him. Vanessa stood in the center of the room, beautiful as ever but still unwilling to make eye contact with Dalton for any length of time, and Randolph occupied his usual spot behind the bar.

"I like the signs you put up. If they see 'Free Drinks' and don't come in here, then we're all doomed," Dalton said. When Randolph didn't say anything, Dalton asked, "That policy doesn't extend to me as well, does it? 'Cause I could sure use—"

"No," Randolph said. "It doesn't apply to you."

"Easy. I'm just joking." Dalton scrunched his eyebrows. "What's got you so uptight?"

"I would have preferred to enact this part of the plan in the Continental, not in here."

"I know, but Warren wouldn't abide it."

Randolph set his rag on the bar and looked at Dalton. "I don't care what he wants. I'm risking everything, my entire livelihood, for this plan."

"I'm not taking his side, but if you think about it, he's risking everything he owns too," Dalton said. "Sure, you might have action in here, maybe some bullet holes in the walls or in the ceiling, but this entire town could go up in flames if this doesn't work out. Really, you're both risking the same thing."

"I don't want to hear it. You just make sure you don't mess this up. Got it?" Randolph's glare reminded Dalton of a surly guard dog.

"Yeah, I got it." Dalton turned to Vanessa, who wore a pink dress trimmed with burgundy velvet. "I need you to do something for me."

Her green eyes, steamy as ever, finally locked on his, but Dalton saw no forgiveness in them. Her voice flat, she asked, "What is it?"

Dalton pulled out one of his silver revolvers and handed it to Vanessa. "I need you to hold on to this for me. Keep it within reach. If I need it, just toss it to me and I'll take care of the rest."

She took it. "Sure."

"Look, I'm sorry," Dalton whispered. "I hurt you. I shouldn't have. I'm sorry."

"You can be sorry all you want," she whispered back. "But don't worry 'bout me. I'm cooperatin', we're working together. I'll be fine, but I'm not ready to be your friend again just yet."

"Fair enough." Dalton smirked. "Nice and high when you toss me that gun. Crystal?"

Vanessa nodded. "Clear."

Reverend McCarroll clomped through the Imperial's door. "They're coming."

"You're sure?" Dalton asked.

"Spotter said he saw six men on horseback riding toward the town.

Dark clothes, mean expressions. At least one Mexican—so I figured it could be Zamora. I know it's early, but I think we need to assume it's them."

Dalton swore, then he caught his uncle's stern gaze. "Sorry."

"If there were ever a time for profanity, it's now," Reverend McCarroll said with a shrug. "They'll be here within five minutes."

"Where do we stand on the preparations we discussed?"

"We're close, but we still have work to do. Most of it is just getting the men into their positions, making sure they have extra ammunition— things like that, but we still need to set up a few of the barricades. It's nothing we can't handle while you do your part in here."

"Okay. Who's working with you?"

Reverend McCarroll counted them on his fingers. "Hutch, Belvidere, most of the miners."

"Try to keep 'em out of sight, will you?"

"Absolutely. We don't want to alarm our guests." Reverend McCarroll winked.

"I'm glad you're at ease." Dalton lowered his voice. "I'm nervous, to tell you the truth."

Reverend McCarroll laid his hand on Dalton's shoulder. "Then how about we say a quick prayer?"

Dalton eyed him.

"It won't hurt. I promise."

Dalton inhaled a deep breath and nodded.

"Would either of you like to join us?" Reverend McCarroll asked.

"I can hear you from here," Randolph said.

Dalton smirked.

"Sure." Vanessa came over and took Dalton's left hand in her right, forming a triangle with him and Reverend McCarroll, who led them in a short, encouraging prayer for strength, guidance, clarity of mind, and bravery.

"Amen," he said, and Dalton and Vanessa echoed him.

"How lovely." The voice came from the Imperial's door. Max Warren, dressed in his light-gray suit, sauntered in. Otis Redd and another man with an average build and thick worker's arms followed close behind him.

"What are you doing here?" Dalton asked. "I thought you were coordinating the—"

"Save your breath. Remember how we agreed I'd be a part of the planning process?" He puffed on the stumpy cigar that hung from his mouth. "Well, here I am."

Dalton blinked at him. "What do you mean?"

"You can't just sit here and play cards alone. You need opponents. Otis, Harry, and I will join you. It'll make this ruse look more realistic."

Dalton shook his head. "I don't think—"

"What you think is irrelevant," Warren said. "If the entirety of my wealth depends on your success, you'd better believe I'm going to play a role. If you don't like it, too bad."

"If I were you, I'd want to be involved too," Dalton said through clenched teeth. "I'll let you stick around, but when the shooting starts, don't get in my way. I'm not responsible for what happens to you."

"Rest assured, young Mr. Phillips," Warren pulled his jacket open, revealing a pair of revolvers holstered at his hips, "I am more than capable of handling myself. And if something were to go awry—well, that's why Otis and Harry are here."

Otis's smug expression reminded Dalton of their recent encounter at Vanessa's room the other night. Dalton hadn't forgotten about that, nor had he forgotten how Otis and his boys had nearly beat him to death at Max Warren's behest.

But ultimately, they were here to help, in their own way. Now wasn't the time to dwell on the past. He could deal with them when this was all over with.

"Fine. You can stay. But follow my lead, alright?"

"You needn't worry about us, Dalton." Warren cracked his knuckles. "Ain't that right, boys?"

"Yessir," Harry said.

Otis just stared bullets at Dalton.

"I'm gonna go finish up the preparations with the workers. You boys behave yourselves." Reverend McCarroll nodded to them, then he gave Dalton another wink.

Dalton gestured to the chairs. "Have a seat."

Otis took the chair across from Dalton. Warren sat next to him, and

Harry sat to Dalton's immediate right. Two open chairs beckoned, one on Dalton's left, the other on Harry's right.

"Who's dealing?" Harry asked.

"Before we get into it, there's one last thing I need to tell you," Dalton said. "When I say, 'today's my lucky day,' we jump into action. That's when the shooting starts. I won't say it until Zamora and his men give their signal to the soldiers." Dalton looked at Vanessa. "That's when I want you to toss me that pistol."

She nodded.

"But we don't know what their signal is," Warren said.

"Not yet, but we will. In the meantime, we just need to keep them occupied." Dalton fingered his wedding ring and looked at them. "I'll deal. What's your game?"

"They're here." Vanessa stared out one of the windows. "It's them. They're here."

♠ ♥ CHAPTER 45 ♦ ♣

As Dalton sat at the card table, he flexed his right hand again. He didn't know how it had happened, but that fleeting moment where his right-handed function had partially returned got him wondering. Maybe if he tried to work it a bit more, his hand could recover someday.

He pulled the revolver out of its holster on his left side and shifted it to his right hand. When he tried to grip it, his hand refused, as it always did. But this time, instead of just accepting it, he used his left hand to curl the fingers of his right hand around the grip.

Once they were in position, he paused. He was about to give everything he could into trying to grip the revolver, but he remembered the stabbing pain that had accompanied the action back in the jail. It had felt like the bullet had gone through his wrist all over again, albeit only for an instant.

Still, nothing ventured, nothing gained. He tensed his right shoulder and his right forearm and squeezed with all his might.

Another pop in his hand sparked fresh pain that ratcheted up his forearm and then raced back down again. It died quickly, as it had before, and Dalton gritted his teeth to resist its effects on him.

When he looked down at the revolver again, he saw his right hand lazily gripping it. He tried to depress the trigger with his forefinger and found that he could actually sense some tension there where none had been before. Then his strength faded again, and his right hand again refused to comply.

But he'd learned something valuable—he'd learned that there was definitely hope for his right hand to recover after all. After more than a year of no progress, he hadn't expected it would ever happen. Now Dalton wished he'd had these small breakthroughs earlier. It might've meant he'd be using his right hand to shoot today instead of his left.

He could hear Randolph beckon the approaching men from outside the Imperial. Had Dalton been in their place, he might have suspected Randolph's rants as disingenuous, but he probably would have come inside anyway for the free booze. Who wouldn't?

Apparently Zamora and his men couldn't resist either. As Dalton swiftly holstered his revolver again, the bandits followed Randolph inside, laughing and snickering with every step. Dalton's heart chugged in his chest when Zamora's eyes found his—then promptly shifted back to Randolph.

"What would you like to drink?" Randolph asked. "Bourbon? Whiskey?"

"Tequila," Zamora said. "So where's this person we're supposed to play cards with?"

Dalton shifted into action. "Table's full."

Zamora eyed him. "Is that right, amigo? Looks like you got two open chairs to me."

"They're reserved." Dalton shuffled the cards, not even bothering to look at Zamora. It was all part of the act.

"Look *ese*, the drinks are only free if we play."

Dalton scanned the Imperial as he shuffled the deck. "There are other tables open."

Zamora sauntered over to him, his head forward and cocked to the side. "You're the only ones in here, amigo. Playing against my friends won't do me any good, right?"

"Barkeep, how about some whiskey over here?" Dalton centered his gaze on Randolph, who scowled at him, but pulled a fresh bottle from behind the bar. When Zamora took another step forward,

Dalton finally looked at him with a hardened gaze. "Not my problem."

"It's about to be your problem," Zamora said, his voice low and threatening.

"I don't mean any disrespect." Dalton kept his voice flat on purpose. Cards flapped against each other when he bridged the deck. "It's just that I don't waste my time with *average* players."

"*Average* players? You think I'm average, amigo?"

"Of course you are. Look at you. Just rode into town, swindling free drinks from this establishment. Probably don't even have a dime to your name." Dalton looked Zamora up and down. "Why would I want to play against *you?*"

Zamora's eyes widened. He reached for his belt.

Dalton wanted to skin his revolver, but he froze when Zamora produced a thick wad of federal bills. A glint of silver caught Dalton's eyes from under Zamora's coat—one of the two Colt sisters.

If all went as planned, they'd be back in Dalton's possession soon enough.

"Does that look *average* to you?" Zamora tossed the wad of bills on the table where it landed with a *thump*.

Dalton smirked. He had Zamora right where he wanted him. "Have a seat."

Zamora sat between Otis and Harry, leaving an empty chair to Dalton's left. "So where's my tequila?"

"Right here." Randolph walked over with a glass of tequila and a glass of whiskey. In a disingenuous tone, he asked, "Anyone else want anything?"

"How about some tequila for my friends?" Zamora asked. "And how about it's free, right? After all, I'm playing."

"I'll have a gin," Warren said.

"Me too." Harry gave a slight wave.

"Whiskey and water," Otis said.

Randolph grumbled something as he headed back to the bar.

Dalton focused on Zamora. "What's your game?"

"Man, I can play anything. Stud. Draw. You name it."

"How about five-card draw?" Dalton asked.

"Doesn't matter what it is. I'm not gonna lose anyway, right?"

"Big talk for a vagabond."

Zamora squinted at him. "And what makes you so good?"

"He's a touring poker champion." Randolph brought over a tray full of drinks, all while wearing a frown. "He's from New England originally, but he's been all over Europe in tournaments."

"You got a name, poker champ?"

Dalton smirked. "Call me 'Lucky.'"

"Cute name for a poker player," Otis said.

Dalton eyed him but bit his tongue. "We don't have a sixth player. Are your friends as poor as they look, or does one of them want to lose a fortune to me as well?"

"You got quite a mouth on you, right?" Zamora grinned and then twisted around. "Jack, watch the door, will you? Murray, have a seat. Cortez, take Willy and Frank for a walk. Make sure you're back in time."

Back in time... for what? Dalton wondered. *The signal?*

"What's the ante?" Otis asked, still glowering at Dalton. Did he really not realize they needed to be on the same side today?

"Make it as high as you want to," Zamora said. "*Lucky.*"

"Let's make it a dollar." Warren pulled out his billfold.

"I thought this was a serious game." Zamora folded his arms.

Warren scrunched his eyebrows down. "Two, then."

"Why not five?" Zamora took out five one-dollar federal notes and laid them on the table. "If you're so sure you're gonna take our money, might as well do it fast, right?"

"I'm in." Dalton pushed a five-dollar wildcat note from Warren's bank into the middle of the table. "Who's dealing?"

"What is *that?*" Zamora pointed to the wildcat.

"It's a banknote from the First Bank of Spider's Rock." Dalton sipped his whiskey then shot a glare at Randolph. He'd watered the drink down so much that Dalton could barely taste the alcohol.

"How do I know it's worth anything? Just looks like colored paper to me."

"Because I own the bank." Warren fixed his focus on Zamora. "It's worth every penny of five federal dollars. Backed by real gold and silver bullion. Trust me."

Zamora smiled, rubbed his hands together. "So you're Max Warren? I've heard of you, *ese*. Yeah, I trust you alright. Okay. Your money's good with me, amigo."

Warren glanced at Dalton, who diverted his gaze. No need for Zamora to sense collusion between them. Perhaps their history of mutual animosity would actually come in handy.

"Deal the cards, will you?" Warren said to Dalton.

Zamora won the first hand. Then, in a surprising show of gambling dexterity, Warren took the second and third games by bluffing the cards from everyone's hands both times. Dalton could tell by the twitch in his left eyebrow.

The fourth hand and a pot worth almost fifty dollars went to Dalton by way of a flush topped by the king of spades. Upon collecting his winnings, he faced Randolph, who stood behind the bar.

"Barkeep, how about another whiskey?" Dalton held up his glass. "This one's really watery."

Randolph scrunched his eyebrows down. In a surprisingly even tone, he replied, "Be right over, Lucky."

Dalton glanced at Vanessa, who was wiping down a table in the corner. She met his eyes before walking to the bar and collecting the fresh glass of whiskey that Randolph had poured for Dalton.

"My deal." Warren reached for the cards and began to shuffle them.

"You handle those pretty well for a banker." Zamora leaned back in his chair so far that the front two legs came off the floor.

Dalton considered kicking his chair back and executing Zamora right then and there, but he refrained.

Warren kept his focus on the cards. "Everyone needs a hobby."

The poker play continued. Money changed hands, with Otis, Warren, Dalton, and Zamora staying pretty even. Zamora and Dalton matched each other drink for drink and hand for hand until Dalton pulled ahead by about a hundred dollars, and then he won the next hand, too.

Zamora slammed his palm on the table. "You're cheating."

"No, I'm not." Dalton sipped his un-watered-down whiskey. "You're drunk, and I'm better at poker."

313

"I may be drunk, but you're not better than me. Just a better cheater."

"Alright, so how am I cheating, smart guy?"

"I don't know *how*, but I know you *are*," Zamora insisted. "And I don't play with cheaters, right?"

Dalton laughed and folded his arms. "You really are as dumb as you look. You're accusing me of cheating, but you can't provide any evidence."

Zamora swore at him. "Keep talkin' like that, you might find yourself facedown in the desert with two bullets in you, *Lucky*."

Been there, done that. Dalton smirked. "So since you can't win at poker, you try to threaten me with physical violence? You're only proving my point."

"Why don't you both shut up so we can play the next hand?" Warren slid the cards to Otis, who started to shuffle them.

"You're next, Max Warren," Zamora growled. "We're coming for you next."

Warren glanced at Dalton, then fixed his gaze on Zamora. "We'll just see about that. You may be in for a surprise."

"Like you said, Max, let's just play *the next hand*." Dalton stared steel at Warren. Was he really that stupid? He was going to give everything away. "Enough talk."

Otis dealt the next hand, which Dalton also won. He lost the next two on purpose to give Zamora a chance to catch up. He stole a peek at the clock above Randolph's piano—2:20.

"One more game then I'm gone, right?" Zamora said. "This is boring. I got things to do."

"Sick of losing to me?" Dalton asked.

"Sick of *looking* at you," Zamora replied.

"Then why the rush?"

"I'm a busy man, amigo. I do good work for important people, right?"

"Can't be that important."

"Yeah? Why not?"

Dalton stared at him. He was going to relish this for as long as he could.

"When you first walked in, looking like a worn-out desert rat, I thought you'd make a good shoe-shine boy, but not much else," he said. "Now, having spoken to you and seeing you try—and fail—to play poker, I wouldn't even hire you to shovel horse dung."

"Say whatever you want, *Lucky*," Zamora said. "Because not long from now, I'm gonna have more money than you could ever imagine."

"How's that?" Warren asked.

"None of your business." Zamora snickered. "Literally."

"You're just shooting your mouth off," Dalton said. "Like everyone else who loses to me."

"Whatever, man. By tomorrow I'll be so rich, you won't even believe it."

Dalton muttered, "You're full of something, alright."

Zamora slammed the table with his fist. "You *shut up*, man. I don't gotta take this from you. I could kill you right here, right now, and no one could stop me."

Dalton smirked and feigned disappointment. "But then we wouldn't be able to play cards anymore."

"I could care less about cards. In fact, I'm done right now." Zamora threw his cards down and stood up. "Come on Murray, let's go."

"But Alejandro, I gotsa good hand," Murray said, his voice a whine.

"I don't care. We're leaving. You gringos are gonna regret your big mouths in a few hours."

THUNK.

Zamora turned back, and his eyes fixed on the solid gold brick in the center of the table.

"How about one more game?" Warren wiped a smudge off the gold brick. "Just happened to have this with me on my way to the bank. Nothing would give me more pleasure than to wager it against that wad of federal bills you have."

Even Dalton raised his eyebrows. He hadn't guessed Warren had a contingency plan, but perhaps he should've. He wanted to say, "Good move, Max," but he kept quiet.

Zamora looked at the gold, then at Warren. "I can't match that."

"You could if you and… what's his name? Murphy? Whatever his name is, if the two of you combined your winnings, you could match it."

Warren said. "Harry doesn't have enough either, but Otis does. And Lucky, too."

"I'm in." Otis's shifty gaze swapped between Dalton, Warren, and the gold all within one second. "We *are* playing for keeps, right?"

Warren glowered at him. "Did you really just ask that question? This is *poker*, numbskull. It's always played for keeps."

"Well, I know that, but—"

Warren cleared his throat.

"Yeah, I'm in," Otis said.

"Me too." Dalton caught Zamora's lusty stare. "One more game, for everything. What do you say, *amigo?*"

♠ ♥ CHAPTER 46 ♦ ♣

"There's only one rule," Dalton said. "No guns. I don't want to get shot over a hand of poker. It would be far too ironic."

Warren glowered at him, as did Randolph.

"Then no deal, amigo. I'm not givin' these babies up, not for no reason." Zamora patted the guns on his hips—the Colt sisters. "They never leave my side—unless I gotta do some business the hard way, right?"

"They won't have to." Warren removed his own pistol, a black revolver with a brown handle, and handed it to Harry. "Harry will set them on the bar, in plain sight."

"No offense, but I don't trust none of you." Zamora's eyes had barely left the gold brick since Warren had dropped it onto the table. "That isn't gonna work."

"Have Murray hold 'em for you, then." Dalton pulled out his other revolver—the one Vanessa wasn't holding for him—and handed it to Harry. "Look, we're all unarmed and ready to play an honest game of cards. Now hurry up and make a decision so I can win that brick."

Otis also handed his revolver to Harry, who set all of them on the bar in front of Randolph. Then Otis asked, "Is he just gonna stand there while we play?"

317

Warren replied, "No. Harry's going to shuffle and deal out the hand."

"Fine. I don't want him near the guns, and he's gotta leave his on the bar, too," Zamora said. "I'll leave mine with Murray."

"Fine, fine." Warren motioned toward Zamora's chair. "Have a seat. Let's get this moving."

"One other thing," Zamora said. "I want Jack to check you for hidden weapons."

"Are you serious?" Otis squinted at him. "How hard is it to just play a hand of cards?"

"Either that or no deal," Zamora replied. "I don't trust none of you."

Dalton gave an exaggerated sigh and rolled his eyes. He stood up and walked toward Jack, who came over from his post at the door. "If we must."

Warren, Harry, and Otis also acquiesced and were searched. Then Warren asked, "May we begin?"

Zamora nodded and took his seat.

Harry shuffled and dealt five cards to each player. Once they all had a chance to look at their cards, he turned to Otis. "How many cards you want?"

"Let me get one. No, two. Two cards." Otis tossed his unwanted cards on the table.

The saloon door opened. Cortez and Zamora's two other men walked in. When Zamora looked at him, Cortez nodded and said, "It looks clear."

"What looks clear?" Dalton asked.

"The weather." Zamora didn't even bother to look at Dalton. "Cortez, go take care of that errand we discussed on the way into town, right?"

Cortez nodded and walked out.

The signal—it had to be. Dalton hoped the network of men they'd posted inside buildings around the town would know to watch him, if they weren't already.

Uncle Bill will handle it, he reassured himself.

"How many cards, Mr. Warren?" Harry asked.

"Two please."

Harry doled them out, then he turned to Dalton. "How many?"

Dalton hadn't even looked at his cards yet. Ultimately, what did it matter? The hand, the game, the whole scenario was nothing but a ruse to distract Zamora and his men while the townspeople secretly continued making preparations for the real battle still to come.

Even worse, Dalton knew it was only a show for Zamora and his men too. They were here to crush the town, kill everyone in it, and reap outrageous rewards in the aftermath.

Zamora didn't need to play a silly card game for all the money on the table—he could just kill everyone when the soldiers arrived and then take it for himself. Perhaps he'd decided to play because then he wouldn't have to split these winnings with Colonel Judd and his men.

When Dalton finally did look, he found the ace of spades, the king of clubs, an eight, a six, and a three, a mix of red and black. A rubbish hand.

Maybe a straight draw? No, the probability was too low. He'd need to trade three cards, the maximum allowed, and all three would have to line up with the king and the ace. Not likely.

Then again, he might as well trade his three low cards anyway. He slid them to Harry, facedown. "Three, please."

Harry dealt him three replacements.

As he collected his new cards, Dalton's gaze centered on Vanessa, who stood near the bar and watched the game. She gave him a slight nod. She was ready.

He glanced at Randolph next. Dalton knew he'd stashed a double-barreled shotgun behind that bar. Hopefully he'd decide to use it this time instead of just sitting back and watching Dalton take on five men by himself like he had the last time Zamora came into the Imperial.

Dalton combined his three extra cards with his hand, but he didn't look at them yet.

"How many do you want?" Harry asked.

Zamora smirked. He set his cards facedown on the table. "None."

They all stared at him. Everyone knew what that meant. With nothing left to bet and with everything to lose, Zamora had been dealt a hand so good that it couldn't be improved upon, or at least that trying to do so wasn't worth the risk. He probably had a straight or a flush. Maybe even a full house.

Otis sighed.

"Alright, boys. Showdown," Harry said.

Dalton scanned his cards. He'd received another king, the diamond. A pair wouldn't defeat Zamora. Probably wouldn't even beat Otis.

But as he thumbed his cards, he noticed another spade and a heart. Each had a big K in the corner.

Dalton's heart pounded in his chest. Three more kings. If he combined that with the king of clubs and the ace of spades already in his hand, he'd have four of a kind—

But—how? The odds of getting the other three kings was miniscule —infinitesimal.

Dalton raised an eyebrow, then put it back down. If they hadn't figured out his tell by now, he'd just shown them one.

He glanced at Warren. His left eyebrow wasn't twitching this time. He must've had good cards, too. Otis wore a scowl, and Zamora—well, Dalton already knew he had a good hand.

But not good enough to beat Dalton. Only two types of hands could possibly beat Dalton: a straight flush or four aces. The latter couldn't happen since he had the fourth ace, and it wasn't likely that any of them had a straight flush.

Dalton looked at his cards again. He blinked a few times, still pondering them. His hand was a killer, the stuff of legends.

And it didn't matter at all.

In hundreds, maybe even thousands of card games, this was the best hand Dalton had ever landed. It figured that fate—or perhaps God— would deal him such a hand in the most important game of his life, a game that simultaneously meant nothing.

Dalton smirked at the irony.

"You look pretty confident, Lucky," Zamora said. "Maybe you should show first,"

Dalton swiveled his head toward Zamora. "You don't want me to do that. It's nothing special. We should've played a few more games."

"I'll go first," Otis said. "Don't have anything worthwhile."

He laid his five cards down: two jacks, two threes, and a ten.

"Two pair for Otis," Harry said. "Mr. Warren?"

Warren smiled. He spread his cards in front of him and flipped them over one at a time. Eight, nine, ten, jack, queen. A mixture of suits. "Straight."

"Great job, sir," Harry said.

Everyone eyed him.

"I mean, it *is* a great hand. And he does own most of the town. I'm just bein' respectful." Harry swallowed hard and perspiration dotted his forehead. To his credit, Harry shifted his focus to Zamora. "Whatcha got?"

Zamora's mouth stretched into a jagged yellow smile. He slapped the cards down on the table: three aces and two sevens.

Warren muttered a litany of profanity.

Zamora eyed Dalton. "Full house. Beat that, *Lucky*."

Dalton raised an eyebrow. What would happen if he showed his cards now? How much longer until Cortez gave the signal?

The four kings in his hand stared up at him. He had to show his cards. He couldn't pass up this kind of an opportunity—no one could.

"Well? You got anythin' or not?" Harry asked.

Dalton smirked. "You asked for it."

When Dalton laid his cards on the table, Zamora's eyes opened wide, and his mouth hung open. "I don't believe it… that's *impossible*."

Dalton glanced around in the Imperial. Each of the others wore an expression that conveyed just as much shock as Zamora's. Even Randolph, who never seemed to show any emotion other than annoyance and anger, looked like he'd just seen a bona fide miracle.

"It can't be." Zamora pointed at Dalton. "You *cheated*."

"No, I didn't," Dalton said. "Hand on the Bible. I was dealt the ace and the king of clubs and three low cards. I traded in the three and got three more kings. I'm not making it up."

"I don't care what you say." Zamora stood up so fast his chair toppled back and smacked the floor. "You cheated, and you been cheatin' the whole game. This *proves* it."

"This only proves that I'm lucky," Dalton said. "Hence my nickname."

Zamora glanced over Dalton's shoulder. "Grab him."

321

Two sets of arms pulled Dalton up to his feet.

"Search him again. He's gotta have cards hidden somewhere," Zamora said.

Warren stood up as well. "I really don't think that's necessary—"

"*Shut up*." Zamora pointed a dirty finger in his face.

"Easy," Dalton said. "It's fine. Let 'em search me. I've got nothing to hide."

As the bandits rolled up his sleeves, the sound of the town's church bell ringing filled the Imperial. Dalton glanced at Warren, who gave him a slight nod.

The church bell must be the signal.

It made sense—when Dalton had lived outside of town, he could've heard that bell from a mile away. Cortez was probably ringing it right now.

The bandits pulled Dalton's suit coat off, unbuttoned his vest, and then his shirt, exposing his bare chest. He smirked and looked around, making brief eye contact with all five of the townspeople in the Imperial.

When Zamora's goons let him go, Dalton held his arms out wide. "Not finding anything? I guess I was right after all: *today's my lucky day*."

No one moved.

Dalton swiveled his head and eyed Vanessa and Randolph, both still stationary, just watching him. He glanced at Warren, whose narrowed eyes told Dalton he'd understood the signal, but neither Otis nor Harry had reacted at all.

"Where'd you get that bullet scar, amigo?" Zamora squinted at Dalton's bare stomach.

Dalton met his eyes with a cold, angry glare and started to button up his shirt. "It's not important."

The church bell continued to ring.

Zamora met his eyes again, and he tilted his head and stepped forward. "You look familiar to me. Have we met before?"

"Not before today. I don't keep company with vagrants." Dalton finished buttoning his shirt and moved on to his vest. "Satisfied?"

They nodded, but Zamora said, "You sure about that, amigo? Because you remind me of a piano player I once knew who worked in this very place. People told me he used to be a good card player too—until I shot him in the desert."

"Never heard of him." Dalton diverted his gaze and buttoned up his sleeves next. As he shrugged back into his suit coat, "Well, I won that hand. I guess it's like I said, today's my—"

"I shot 'im three times. Once in his right arm, once in his stomach, once in his head." Zamora grabbed Dalton's chin and forced eye contact. "You got a nasty scar on your right forearm. Probably from a bullet, right?"

Dalton stared right at him and slowly pried Zamora's hand from his jaw, even as his heart pounded in his chest. "Old farming accident from when I was a kid growing up in New Hampshire."

"And what's that scar on the side of your head from? Another farming accident?"

Dalton's hand crept up to the scar on the side of his forehead. There was no point in lying. Zamora was on the cusp of figuring out the truth.

He stared straight at Zamora, unfazed. "No. That one came from a bullet. Just grazed me."

The church bell continued to ring. How much longer was Cortez going to keep up that racket? Hadn't he gotten his point across by now?

Zamora nodded slowly. "And how'd you get the one in your gut?"

"I said it doesn't matter."

"It matters to *me*, amigo."

"Look, I won the hand. I didn't cheat, so unless you've got more money to lose, I suggest you move along." Dalton did a quick scan of the room.

Everyone tensed, ready for him to give the signal again. He opened his mouth, but stopped when he noticed the church bell had stopped ringing.

They didn't have any more time.

"It's *you*, isn't it?" Revelation sparked in Zamora's eyes.

"No sir, it's not," Dalton said. "I'm Lucky, not some dead piano player."

"You're *lucky*, alright." Zamora's awe morphed into a crooked yellow smile.

"Indeed I am." Dalton glared at Zamora.

"I *know* it's you. I bet you're mad at me, right? Probably want some payback?"

Dalton's jaw tightened, but he didn't answer.

"I *knew* it." Zamora laughed. "Hey boys, this is that piano player I shot last year. He's still alive, and now he's taking his revenge on me in a card game, right?"

The bandits snickered and gawked.

"No, Zamora. I have not yet begun to take my revenge on you. But you're here now—" He glanced at Vanessa. "—and today's my lucky day."

Dalton rotated and stretched his left hand out to catch the silver revolver hurtling toward him through the air.

♠ ♥ CHAPTER 47 ♦ ♣

Z amora's bandits all reached for their guns.

Otis and Harry flipped the card table on its side, sending all the money, the cards, and the drinks crashing to the ground. Randolph tossed them their weapons while Warren, being nearer to the bar, lunged for his own.

Dalton caught his revolver first and whirled toward Zamora, who pulled a foot-long metal shaft from his boot—a hidden pistol. By the time Dalton got his revolver in hand, Zamora already had his gun pointed at Dalton.

No time for a shot. Dalton dove behind the poker table instead.

A gunshot cracked in the air, followed by the thud of a quarter-sized lead ball impacting the bar just behind Dalton's head. Zamora had missed, but not by much. *Lucky.*

Shouts, commotion.

Zamora yelled, "My guns, Murray!"

Dalton popped up over the table, took aim, and squeezed off three quick rounds, the first return fire of the skirmish. All three dug into Murray, who dropped dead at Zamora's feet with the Colt sisters still in his hands. The next three shots just missed Zamora as he scooped up the revolvers and rolled behind another upended table next to Jack.

Harry took a bullet to his shoulder, then another to his chest. He fell on Dalton and both of them landed on the floor outside of the table's perimeter, exposed.

Harry was heavy, too.

"Get him off me!" Dalton yelled.

Zamora peeked from behind his table and sneered at Dalton. He took aim, and Dalton couldn't move Harry off of himself in time.

Instead, he jerked Harry's body up to shield himself, and Zamora's bullets thumped into dead flesh instead.

Otis yanked Harry off of Dalton by his collar and then popped up to fire a few shots of his own, but he didn't hit anyone.

Dalton took cover behind the poker table again.

A shotgun blast split the air.

Dalton stole a look. Zamora's table splintered, and someone screamed. Jack dropped into view from behind the table, writhing, his shoulder and face shredded and bloody.

Only Randolph had a shotgun. He must have actually fired it for once.

"Randolph!" Dalton shouted over the gunfire as he holstered his empty pistol. "I need my other revolver!"

Randolph tossed it to him.

To Dalton's right, Warren squeezed off a few rounds with his black revolver.

Wood snapped. Cortez, Frank, and Willy burst through the front door. Cortez fired several haphazard shots with a pistol in each hand. Frank rolled behind a different table, and Cortez dove for cover toward Zamora along with Willy.

Dalton shot Cortez's left leg as he flew through the air and heard him yelp. Willy emerged from behind Zamora's decimated table and took aim, but two of Dalton's bullets put him down.

Zamora reached around the table and fired several rounds at Dalton's table, each of them burrowing through to the other side. One of them barely missed Dalton's gut.

The table wasn't safe. It wasn't thick enough. They had to move.

Dalton scrambled to his feet and vaulted over the bar as Randolph loosed another shotgun blast. There, behind the thick oak bar, they could return fire without their cover deteriorating.

"Otis, get behind the bar!" Dalton yelled.

In addition to Randolph and Warren, Vanessa now took cover behind the bar as well. She stayed low, not covering her head as Dalton thought she might.

Instead, she clutched a rifle in her hands. She didn't even look frightened—her hard green eyes and furrowed brow showed determination more than anything else.

"You know how to use that thing?" Dalton asked.

Vanessa spun around and straightened her spine. She fired a quick shot to cover Otis while he leaped over the bar as well, and then she took cover again. Without missing a beat, she met Dalton's eyes and then began working on reloading it. "What do you think?"

"Good enough for me." Dalton peered over the edge of the bar.

In the brief moment of calm, Zamora flung himself over to Frank's table, leaving an injured Cortez to fend for himself.

Dalton looked at Vanessa again. She already had her rifle almost fully reloaded. When she finished, Dalton told her, Warren, Otis, and Randolph, "Cover me."

They all stood together and fired a salvo of bullets at Zamora's table. Zamora returned fire blindly, and Dalton lined his shot up on Zamora.

Got you.

He squeezed the trigger.

At the last instant, Frank's shoulder moved into the bullet's path. Frank yelped and grabbed his wound.

Zamora met Dalton's eyes and smirked. He whirled around, leaped at the nearest window, and crashed through it.

Dalton popped up and fired his last bullet at Zamora, but the round hit the dirt behind him as he ran. Dalton swore. Zamora might get away if he didn't give chase.

While Otis, Vanessa, and Max Warren continued firing, Cortez and Frank, both injured, stumbled out the Imperial door and into the street.

"Come on," Dalton said. "We have to get in position for the soldiers' arrival."

"What about them?" Otis asked. "Zamora escaped."

Dalton wanted to chase him, wanted his revenge, but he needed to help organize the townspeople for the upcoming battle in the streets. That was more important. "We can't. He's not the problem anymore. If we're not in place when the soldiers get here, they'll gun us down in the street."

"He's right." Warren nodded. "Otis, come with me. Leave Harry there. We'll collect him later."

Dalton turned to Randolph, who was reloading his shotgun again. "Randolph, I'll send some men to shoot from your second floor windows."

Randolph grunted. "I suppose that's fine."

"Stay safe," Dalton said to Vanessa. He looked at Warren. "Let's go."

As Dalton had expected, Reverend McCarroll had already arranged the townspeople on rooftops, inside buildings, and in alleyways, all out of sight and ready. "I told them to wait until you fired first, and then they can open fire on the soldiers."

"Good," Dalton said. "Any sign of Zamora or his two men who escaped?"

Reverend McCarroll shook his head. "We saw 'em, but they slipped away. We don't know where they are now."

"It's fine. They're not the real threat anymore."

Dalton crouched low on the Continental's roof with Warren, Reverend McCarroll, Otis, Dr. Richards, Hutch, and three other men, all of whom worked for Warren. From their vantage point, they could see most of Spider's Rock, including the soldiers approaching from the southeast.

"For now, we just wait."

Minutes later, the soldiers finally reached the edge of town, led by Colonel Judd himself on horseback. Cortez and Frank hobbled out of a well-shaded alley and hurried toward them, their arms flailing as they cried for help.

Even from a distance, Dalton could read the anger on Colonel Judd's face. But when Colonel Judd reached for his sidearm and burned them both down in two quick shots, Dalton's eyes widened.

Then again, maybe he shouldn't have been surprised.

Dr. Richards gasped. "I can't believe he just did that."

"That's exactly what they intend to do to us." Dalton made eye contact with each of them. "So don't hold back. Kill or be killed."

"He's right," Reverend McCarroll said. "I normally don't advocate violence, but we have no choice. Either we fight or we die."

The men murmured in approval.

"Good. Stay as quiet, as still as you can," Dalton said. "We don't want to give anything away."

As Colonel Judd and his soldiers entered the town, Dalton's anxiousness peaked. He held an old single-shot carbine in his hands, one of his uncle's, and waited as the mass of navy blue uniforms moved closer to them.

When Colonel Judd came within range, Dalton centered the carbine's barrel on him and pulled back the barrel. He would die first, and Dalton would have his revenge.

Despite what his uncle had said, Dalton had to do it. For himself, for Beduiat, for Ahiga, for Nizhoni. Hell, even for the people in this town, too. Dalton lined up the shot as Colonel Judd approached the Continental and applied pressure to the carbine's trigger.

A gunshot split the hot summer air. A sergeant on horseback behind Colonel Judd yelped and toppled off of his horse, but Dalton hadn't fired the shot.

A chorus of gunfire reverberated throughout the town, and Dalton whirled around. There stood Max Warren, holding a smoking rifle in his hands and wearing a smug expression. Dalton glowered at him and then refocused on the soldiers.

The townsfolk fired a volley of bullets at the soldiers, dropping several of them, but still precious few compared to the remaining five hundred or so.

Colonel Judd hollered orders to return fire, and soon the soldiers began sending round after deadly round up at the townsfolk. "Spread out! Canvass the whole town! Eliminate everyone!"

Dalton fired his shot at him, but Colonel Judd rode through his mass of soldiers and out of range. Dalton fumed as he reloaded and shifted his aim back to the soldiers.

"Deploy the wagons!" Dalton shouted.

Two groups of townsmen pushed two large wagons full of hay into the middle of the street from the alleys behind the Imperial and the Continental, cutting off the flow of soldiers in that direction. On the opposite end of the street, two more wagons blocked that escape route as well.

Then the townspeople lit the wagons on fire.

Several townsfolk guarded the side streets and alleys, but some soldiers would still find paths to escape anyway. Dalton had accounted for that. But until the soldiers figured out that they didn't have to be trapped on Main Street, the townspeople on the roofs would have plenty of marks to shoot at.

"Hey, look over there!" one of Warren's men called. "Those soldiers are tryin' to break into your bank, boss!"

Sure enough, about a dozen soldiers hovered around the entrance of the First Bank of Spider's Rock. They pounded and fired at the bank's doors until they finally managed to get inside.

It meant the soldiers were divided, fractured. But it also meant—

"Otis, bring your men. We're going to stop them." Warren headed for the ladder they'd used to get up to the roof.

"No, you can't." Dalton abandoned his shooting and cut into Warren's path. "We need you here. You can't go."

Warren pushed him aside. "Get out of my way, Dalton."

Dalton stepped in front of him again. "I said we need you *here*. We can't win this battle without you, Mr. Warren."

"I'm not going to win *anything* if I don't protect what's mine. This is *my* town, and that's *my* bank," Warren said. "If they rob me, I'm broke. Now move."

Dalton didn't. "You can't—"

Otis and the other three men pointed their guns at Dalton, and Otis sneered at him. "Boss said move, so *move*."

Both Otis and Warren received equal portions of fire from Dalton's glare, but he stepped aside silently, then he headed back to the edge of the roof and kept shooting with Hutch, Dr. Richards, and Reverend McCarroll.

"They're gonna get themselves killed," Reverend McCarroll said.

"Not if we can cover them. Let's try to keep 'em safe if we can," Dalton said.

A few minutes later, Warren, Otis, and the other three men darted across the street to the bank, occasionally firing their weapons at soldiers. Dalton personally killed two soldiers who would have otherwise shot at the group, while Hutch, Reverend McCarroll, and Dr. Richards took out a handful of others.

Finally, the five men made it to the bank and went inside. Dalton kept one eye on the bank's entrance even as he kept reloading and shooting at various soldiers in the street. Minutes later, seven soldiers shuffled out of the bank, each of them hauling bulging white sacks.

"Oh, no," Dalton said.

"I see them too." Dr. Richards fired a few shots at them. "You think Warren and his men…?"

Dalton didn't want to venture a response, even though he knew the truth in his gut. As much as he'd hated Max Warren, it was a shame he'd died that way. Yet some part of Dalton also felt relief over it. One fewer dark cloud hovering over his head.

"It's his own fault." Hutch shot a soldier. "He couldn't control himself, couldn't control his greed, and it got him killed."

Dalton nodded. Nevertheless, he fired at the soldiers escaping the bank anyway. Together with the others on his roof, they took two of them out and wounded another. The bags they carried fell and burst open, spewing copper and silver coins and bars of gold into the street.

He kept shooting and reloading again and again, taking out at least a dozen soldiers on his own—until he saw Colonel Judd and some soldiers go inside the church.

Dalton caught Reverend McCarroll's glance and his subsequent nod. "Go after 'em. I'll handle things up here," Reverend McCarroll said.

"Are you sure?" Dalton asked.

"I've done well so far, haven't I?"

Dalton eyed his uncle. "Not bad for a preacher."

"Like I said, I wasn't always a preacher." Reverend McCarroll smirked. "Now go and get Colonel Judd. When you find him, listen to your conscience. God will show you what you're supposed to do."

"You're sure you don't need me?" Dalton asked. "I just tried to keep Warren and his men around, but now you're okay with me going?"

"If you can get Colonel Judd, you'll secure our victory. That's worth a try." Reverend McCarroll put a big hand on Dalton's shoulder and gave him a smile. "I know you can do it. We'll handle things here. Go do what you do best."

Dalton snuck into the church through the parsonage then made his way around to the back of the sanctuary where he ducked behind the last row of pews so the soldiers near the altar wouldn't see him.

His revolvers, both fully loaded, hung in their holsters from his belt, and he carried his uncle's carbine in his hands. A few dozen rimfire rounds sat in the pockets of his suit coat, ready for when he needed them.

He peeked at the soldiers. A quick count yielded eleven marks, including Colonel Judd, all in conference at the front of the sanctuary. Colonel Judd was giving orders and instructions to his subordinates about how to proceed with the battle.

It wouldn't be easy, but if Dalton could use the church's structure for cover, he might be able to hide long enough to take them all out. After all, he knew this church better than they did.

Or perhaps he could just shoot Colonel Judd and be done with it. A shot with one of his revolvers would be risky at this range, but the carbine was more than adequate.

Dalton raised the carbine and used the top of the pew as a brace to steady his shot. He centered Colonel Judd in the sights, ready to pull the trigger. He took in a deep, quiet breath, and—

A footfall sounded to his right. Dalton twisted his head to find himself staring down a black rifle barrel. His eyes panned up to a soldier's bearded face, contorted with a sadistic smile and arched eyebrows.

Dalton sighed. He closed his eyes and waited for the shot that would end his life.

CHAPTER 48

D alton twitched at the sound of a gunshot next to his face, but he felt no pain. He found that highly unusual because he'd been shot before, and it had definitely hurt.

He opened his eyes in time to see the soldier recoil. A buffalo jawbone club clattered to the floor in front of him, and a bronze-skinned blur leaped from behind a pew and thrust a scalping knife into the soldier's gut.

Dalton recognized the Apache immediately, but he couldn't believe his eyes.

"*Victorio?*" Dalton gawked at him. "What are you doing here?"

"Get down!" Victorio yanked Dalton to the floor behind the pew, and a bombardment of bullets smacked into the wall where their heads had just been. He spoke Apache over the ruckus. "I have been watching you for months. Your behavior has been worse than that of a small child."

"What do you mean, you've been 'watching' me?"

Victorio grabbed the soldier's rifle and started to reload it. "Just before he died, my father asked me to watch over you. That was his last wish."

Dalton tilted his head and shut his gaping mouth. "Why?"

"He said you would need me. I guess he was right." With the soldier's rifle reloaded, Victorio popped up, took aim, and fired at one of the soldiers standing near Colonel Judd. The round plunged into his chest, and he dropped to the floor.

Dalton snatched his own rifle and shot down another soldier trying to creep around the side to flank them. Dalton looked at Victorio. "But —you *hate* me."

"Aside from my little sister Lozen, you are the only family I have left." Victorio turned to him and began reloading the rifle again. "The bond of family is stronger than even the deepest hate. Besides, I would never disobey my father's final wish, no matter how much I hated you."

"So you're saying you *don't* hate me anymore?" Dalton asked.

Victorio smirked. In English, he replied, "Don't push your luck."

Together they fired almost two-dozen rounds at the soldiers, but whenever Dalton tried to shoot Colonel Judd, he either missed or Colonel Judd took cover. They developed a system for firing and reloading: Dalton covered with his revolvers while Victorio reloaded the rifles.

The firefight raged for almost ten minutes, with Dalton and Victorio gradually eliminating all of the soldiers except for Colonel Judd and three others.

Colonel Judd emerged from his spot, took aim with his pistol, and fired. He missed Dalton and Victorio, but as he fired a second shot, another soldier came at them from the side with his bayonet affixed to his rifle.

He jabbed it at Victorio, who deftly parried the strike with his rifle, but the soldier moved just a little quicker. He rammed the butt of his rifle into Victorio's head.

Then Victorio fell backward, and his head thudded on the floor.

"Victorio!" Dalton's revolver made quick work of the soldier, and then he rushed to examine Victorio.

His head was bleeding, but not a lot—he'd only sustained a small cut from the soldier's attack. Still, he wasn't waking back up. The blow had knocked him out cold. Dalton pulled the silk ascot from around his neck and pressed it against Victorio's head.

A fresh volley of gunshots pelted the pew and snapped Dalton back into action. Victorio would have to wait—they were both dead if he didn't finish the fight.

Dalton grabbed Victorio's jawbone club from the floor and hooked it to his belt, then he skinned the pistol from his left holster and popped fresh rounds into it. He did the same with the pistol in his right holster, then he put it back.

He abandoned Victorio and the two rifles and darted from one side of the center aisle to the other, miraculously dodging bullets the whole way. He figured that if he could get away from Victorio, then he could draw their fire away from him as well.

It worked.

A soldier emerged from behind a wooden pillar, but Dalton's pistol loaded him with three bullets to his chest.

Two more uniforms, then Colonel Judd.

The corner of Dalton's pew splintered and he dropped to his belly. From his vantage on the floor he saw a pair of soldier's boots under the pews. He took aim, fired, and the bullet plunged into the soldier's ankle.

The soldier dropped to the floor and clutched his foot, then Dalton put him out of his misery with a shot to his chest.

Dalton jumped to his feet and started toward the pillar where he'd just killed the other soldier. The large brass cross in front of him flickered with a sepia shadow. Without turning around, Dalton used the brass reflection to take aim, pointed his pistol over his right shoulder, and fired.

Behind him, the third soldier yelped, then hit the floor.

When he turned back, Dalton couldn't believe he'd actually pulled off the shot, but sure enough, the soldier was down, dead from a bullet hole in the left side of his forehead. The chances of that had to be—

Gunfire ricocheted off the walls near Dalton. He scurried behind the pillar and poked his head out for a quick peek. Only Colonel Judd remained. Soon Dalton would have his revenge.

He holstered his empty pistol and drew the loaded one, then he bolted to the side corridor in the sanctuary. He slid across the hardwood floor to a stop behind the base of a painted statue of post-resurrection Jesus, complete with nail holes in his outstretched hands.

Three of Colonel Judd's rounds tore into Jesus and his base. Dalton offered a silent prayer of thanks to Christ for his sacrifice, both then and now, and then he returned fire with three shots of his own. He only managed to hit the pew behind which Colonel Judd had taken cover.

They exchanged a few more shots before Dalton needed to reload. He emptied the spent cartridges from his revolver, then reached into his pockets to refill his gun.

"Don't move," said a deep voice next to him.

He looked up. Colonel Judd towered over him and pointed a black revolver at Dalton's face.

CLICK.

CHAPTER 49

C LICK. CLICK.
Colonel Judd was out of ammo, too.

Dalton sprung at a wide-eyed Colonel Judd and tackled him to the floor. Dalton straddled him and threw punch after furious left-handed punch to his face.

Colonel Judd blocked the next blow with his right forearm and clocked Dalton with a solid left hook to his jaw. Dalton toppled off of Colonel Judd's chest, his face stinging from the blow.

Colonel Judd got to his feet and delivered a quick kick to Dalton's gut, followed by another to his face, which left him dazed and hurting bad. Blood tainted Dalton's tongue with the tang of copper.

Shing. Dalton knew that sound: a sword drawn from its sheath.

Despite the fog in his mind, Dalton rolled just in time to avoid Colonel Judd's sword strike, which carved a deep gash in the wood floor.

Now on his feet, Dalton staggered away from Colonel Judd and tugged the jawbone club free from his belt. He'd learned a few basic strikes during his time with the Apaches, but he by no means considered himself competent with it, especially left-handed. Still, with no loaded gun, and no time to reload one, he'd have to make do.

But Colonel Judd didn't advance. He just stood there and squinted at Dalton. "Do I know you?"

A deep breath escaped Dalton's nostrils and he scowled. "We've only met once. That was this morning, in the jail, when you murdered Marshal Garmer to set Zamora free."

Recognition filled Colonel Judd's hard blue eyes. "You were the other prisoner?"

"Yes."

"You heard our entire plan—and you organized this resistance?"

"Yes."

Colonel Judd swore, mostly at Zamora. "I'm going to kill him."

"Not if I get him first."

"You won't." Colonel Judd's stare was as cold as the steel in his sword.

"No?" Dalton asked. "You think I'd let the man who killed my wife get the better of me?"

Colonel Judd eyed him, wary. "What are you talking about?"

Still holding the jawbone club, Dalton extended his left hand so Colonel Judd could see the silver-and-turquoise wedding band he wore on his ring finger. "A few months ago, you and your men slaughtered a group of Apaches. You personally shot an unarmed Apache girl from five feet away, then you took a ring like this off of her finger. You're still wearing it."

Colonel Judd looked down at his right hand. Light glinted off the silver-and-turquoise band on his little finger.

Upon seeing it, Dalton swallowed the lump in his throat and subdued the emotion rising in his chest. "She was my wife."

"Hm." Colonel Judd's stoicism did not waver. "She was just another savage to me."

Dalton's jaw tensed. He gripped the jawbone club so hard that his fingers hurt. He stepped forward, ready to bash the Colonel's head in.

Colonel Judd slashed his sword again, this time cutting through the front of Dalton's suit coat and leaving a small incision on his vest. Dalton backed up and gawked at the cut, amazed that his stomach hadn't split open.

"I won't miss again," Colonel Judd said.

Dalton glared at him. He was faster with his sword than Dalton was with his jawbone club.

Still, Dalton had to find a way to win. For Nizhoni, he had to.

Colonel Judd lashed at Dalton's left arm, but this time the jawbone club blocked the blow. In a quick counterattack, Dalton swung the club at Colonel Judd's head, but he parried the club away.

They exchanged attacks for almost three minutes. Colonel Judd lunged his sword at Dalton's gut, missed, then chopped at Dalton's head.

Dalton caught the attack with the jawbone club, then he gave his wrist a sharp twist—one of the few moves he'd learned from the Apaches. He batted the blade away then stepped in and delivered a hard right elbow to Colonel Judd's face.

Colonel Judd staggered back and tripped over the body of one of his soldiers. His sword clattered away, far out of reach. Dalton bounded over to him and pressed his right foot against Colonel Judd's chest.

"No, wait!" Colonel Judd finally displayed some emotion: fear.

Dalton reveled in it.

"Please—please don't!" Colonel Judd pleaded.

But Dalton could. He *should*. One vicious blow would satisfy the thirst in his pounding heart. One blow would fill the void in his soul. One blow would avenge Ahiga, Beduiat, and Nizhoni, as well as hundreds of other Apaches who died because of Colonel Judd.

"Please, I beg you." Colonel Judd raised his hands in surrender. "Please—"

No. No mercy. This man had murdered Dalton's wife and countless others. Dalton raised the jawbone club over his head, ready to strike. One savage blow. Only one.

But he hesitated. Was this the right thing to do? Was this vengeance truly his to take?

The sound of gunshots outside had faded and grown more and more intermittent with each passing minute. The townsfolk must have overcome the remainder of the soldiers—or the opposite had happened. Either way, with the soldiers' commanding officer at Dalton's mercy, it was over.

Then a gunshot resounded in the church and echoed off the walls a dozen times.

A sharp, fiery pain dug into Dalton's back like a hot poker, and he lurched forward and dropped the jawbone club. He whirled around, eyes frantic, and searched for the shooter.

Zamora stood on the far side of the altar, holding one of the Colt sisters, still smoking from the shot.

CHAPTER 50

Zamora fired three more shots at Dalton in rapid succession. Two rounds struck his chest, and one plunged into his left forearm.

Hot blood flowed from Dalton's new wounds and soiled his new suit and shirt. He dropped to his back and felt his life begin to drain from his body. He could barely breathe, and he could feel the bullets inside burning, scraping, killing him.

Zamora approached him with small, cautious steps, his pistol aimed at Dalton the whole time. "Tough dog, isn't he? Seven bullets—three last year, four today—and he's still breathing. But not for long, right?"

Dalton closed his eyes, and his nerves stabbed him all over. He ground his teeth, but the pain didn't diminish. At the thought of having failed, the pain grew even worse.

Why hadn't he killed Colonel Judd when he'd had the chance? He cursed his own foolishness.

A familiar, wicked voice above him cackled. "Guess you're not so *lucky* after all, are you?"

Dalton wheezed. Every breath felt like a herculean labor. He couldn't respond. Even if he could, he had nothing to say.

"This time I'm gonna *watch* you die, just to make sure you actually do," Zamora said. "By the way, Colonel, your soldiers are all either dead or run off. The townspeople turned the street into a meat grinder, right? Vicious, I tell you. We're not gonna win this one."

"None of this would have happened if you hadn't gotten yourself arrested," Colonel Judd said. He'd probably recovered to his feet by now, but Dalton couldn't tell with his eyes closed. "This man was the prisoner in the cell next to you. He heard the entire plan and told the town."

"And you're blaming *me* for that?" Zamora scoffed. "That's on you, *ese*. *You* insisted we go over the plan before you let me out."

"Which we never would have had to do if you hadn't landed in jail."

"Believe what you want, amigo. This is your fault. It's just easier to blame me."

"We could have been here this morning instead of this afternoon, but we weren't because I had to come get you out of jail," Colonel Judd said. "You're worthless. You and your whole crew of bandits."

Dalton opened his eyes in time to see Zamora point his revolver at Colonel Judd.

"Is that right?" Zamora asked. "Is that why you shot Cortez and Jack when they were coming to you as you entered the town? Planning on killing me off, too, were you?"

Colonel Judd recoiled a step. "No, that's not—"

"Because maybe I should just kill you instead."

"No, Zamora—Alejandro. You don't want to do that." Colonel Judd put his hands up. He held his sword in his right hand again, but he was too far from Zamora for it to be of any use. "I'm on your side."

"Look, amigo. I got two bullets left in this gun, right?" Zamora said. "One for you, and one more for our piano player friend here. I'll put one in each of your heads so there's no doubt you're both dead. What you think of that?"

Colonel Judd frowned. "No. That's a bad idea."

"Why? Sounds pretty good to me."

"Think it through," Colonel Judd replied. "The people in this town are out for blood. The only way we're getting out of here alive is if we work together."

Dalton could feel the life oozing out of him, pulsing from his chest and back and his arm.

After a silent moment, Zamora muttered something in Spanish and then said, "You got a point. But after what you did to Cortez and Frank, I got no reason to trust you."

"Yes, you do," Colonel Judd countered. "I let you out of that cell when I could have left you there to rot. Or I could have killed you myself, but I didn't. I trusted you when I shouldn't have. You owe me, Zamora."

Dalton coughed, and the taste of metallic blood tanged his tongue anew.

Zamora glanced down at him then refocused on Colonel Judd. "You're right. I do owe you. But once we get out of here, I never want to see you again, right?"

"Right," Colonel Judd said. "Come on. Let's go."

"Hold on." Zamora aimed his revolver at Dalton's face. "He's still alive. I'm gonna put a bullet in his head before we go."

"Don't waste the shot. You'll need all the ammo you can find to get out of here alive."

"No, amigo. Not risking anything this time." Zamora smiled his jagged yellow smile. "He came back from the dead once. I'm not gonna let him do it a second time."

He pulled back the hammer on his revolver.

Dalton clenched his eyes shut.

A gunshot rang out.

CHAPTER 51

Metal clattered on the floor near Dalton's right hand. He opened his eyes.

Zamora hunched over him, his eyes wide and his mouth hanging open. He clutched his right side, and dark blood seeped through his fingers.

Dalton scanned the sanctuary until his eyes landed on a luscious form with fair skin, blonde hair, and steamy green eyes. Vanessa Clark.

She was still wearing her pink dress with burgundy velvet trim, and she held a smoking black revolver in her hands.

Zamora staggered back and leaned against the nearest wall, his hand still pressed against his side. He stared at her with a face full of disbelief, as if she were a specter.

"You don't recognize me, do you Zamora?" Vanessa's gaze darted from Zamora to Colonel Judd, then back to Zamora.

His face contorted with pain. "You were at the Imperial today."

"That's right. I was," she said. "But that's not where you know me from."

Zamora winced, then he swallowed hard. "I dunno what you're talking about."

"Last year. You showed up in town one night. You came into the

Imperial and decided you liked me. When I resisted, you slapped me," Vanessa said.

Dalton shivered. Everything hurt so much—his lungs burned like never before. Had Zamora's bullets pierced them? Wherever they'd struck him, he was finally dying. It was inescapable now.

Vanessa stepped toward Zamora. "Then Dalton intervened. He tried to fight you off, and then you beat him up and left him for dead in the desert. But what Dalton doesn't know is that you came back for me later on. You came back and forced me to—to—" Tears streamed down her cheeks and she sniveled. "I would've been better off if you'd just *killed* me instead."

Dalton's eyes widened. Zamora had come back for her? Had Dalton's sacrifice been in vain? No wonder Vanessa had treated him so strangely when he'd shown up a year later.

"I'm sorry—" Zamora held his free hand up, then he doubled over with his teeth bared and his eyes clenched shut. "I was drunk. I'm so sorry—please!"

Vanessa whirled around and took aim at Colonel Judd. "And you're just as bad as he is. Marshal Garmer finally locked him up for doin' the same thing to another girl in town, and then *you* let him out. Just when I thought justice would finally be served, *you* interfered."

Colonel Judd swallowed hard and continued to hold his hands up, but he still held his sword as well.

"But now no one will deny me justice. I'll take it for myself." She pointed her revolver back at Zamora.

"No—*no!*"

Vanessa fired two more rounds into Zamora's chest. He slumped to the floor, motionless, but she shot his body once more anyway.

As she turned to fire on Colonel Judd, he sprang forward and struck her wrist with his sword. The revolver dropped from her hands and she screamed.

"You—you can't—" Vanessa's cold, confident gaze twisted into wide-eyed shock as she held her bleeding wrist with her other hand.

"Yes, I can," Colonel Judd said, his voice deep and menacing.

No...

Dalton had to do something, but what? He lay there, all but dead.

With his only functional arm now wounded from one of Zamora's bullets, he couldn't hold a gun with his left hand anymore.

But Zamora's pistol—one of Dalton's Colt sisters—lay next to his right hand, well within reach. Except his right hand still didn't function either. And even if he could manage to shoot, the gun had only two bullets left.

Didn't matter. He had to try. He'd almost gotten it to work earlier, back in the Imperial. Maybe now it finally would.

Dalton stretched out his right arm, and his fingers hooked the trigger guard. His wounds throbbed, searing him from the inside out, but he pulled the Colt closer. He tried to hold it in his hand, but the familiar weakness and pain prevented him from doing so.

If there was a God, Dalton needed Him now. He murmured a desperate prayer, a petition for strength just one last time so he could save Vanessa.

With everything he had left, he tried to squeeze the revolver again. As before, something in his hand popped. Sharp pain ratcheted all the way up to his shoulder and back down to the fingertips of his right hand, and then it was gone.

Slowly but surely, his fingers tightened around the handle. Then his forefinger caressed the trigger. An old, familiar strength saturated his grip —a power he hadn't felt since he'd gunned down Tommy Roebuck in the middle of Main Street more than a year earlier.

He rolled on his side as best as he could so he could get a clearer shot.

Vanessa now cowered beneath Colonel Judd, who'd raised his sword high above his head.

Dalton lifted his right arm, which wobbled. He winced and ground his teeth as he struggled to steady his aim, and he wedged his useless left wrist under his right hand for support. Then he pulled the hammer back with his thumb, exhaled a shallow breath, stilled his aim, and fired.

Colonel Judd lurched to the side and dropped his sword. Blood spurted out of his shoulder, and he stared at Dalton with eyes full of disbelief.

Dalton cocked the hammer back once more and stared at him down the barrel of his revolver. Despite everything, holding a gun had never felt so right.

Colonel Judd clutched at his shoulder, but otherwise he didn't move. "Unlucky."

Dalton smirked and rasped, "Story of my life."

The Colt's last bullet struck Colonel Judd right between the eyes.

CHAPTER 52

Dalton dropped the gun and sprawled out on his back. He stared at the sanctuary's lofted ceiling and at the stained glass window with the cross in the center. He didn't have long.

Vanessa dashed over to him, followed by Victorio, now conscious again.

"Stay with us, Dalton," she said. "I'm gonna get Dr. Richards. You'll be okay."

Before Dalton could call her a liar, she darted away, leaving him alone with Victorio.

"I saw the end," Victorio said. "You saved her."

Dalton nodded slightly and clenched his eyes shut.

"Nizhoni and my father would be proud of you." Victorio gripped Dalton's right hand in his own, and to Dalton's surprise, he could grip Victorio's hand back. "*I am* proud of you. I'm honored to have been your brother."

Dalton smirked, both at Victorio's admission and at how his right hand seemed to be the only part of his body that didn't hurt.

"I'll be right back." Victorio left, then he returned and gently lifted Dalton's left hand. He slipped something on Dalton's little finger. "My sister would want you to have this."

Through the tears that filled his eyes, Dalton saw Nizhoni's silver-and-turquoise wedding band on his little finger next to his own matching ring. He smiled and wheezed, "Thank you."

Multiple sets of footsteps clacked across the church's wooden floor. Several sad, dirty, concerned faces filled Dalton's vision as Dr. Richards crouched next to him.

Camille Warren and Vanessa wept, while tough men Reverend McCarroll and Hutch allowed a few tears to roll down their otherwise solemn faces. Even Randolph looked a bit misty, which made Dalton smirk again.

His voice weakened, Dalton asked, "You're not *crying* for me, are you Randolph?"

Instead of grunting or growling, Randolph chuckled. "Even now, your big mouth still wants to get you into trouble."

Dalton coughed. He waved his right hand, now red with blood. He took shallow, painful breaths between his words. "Forget it, Doc. You… you know I'm done."

Dr. Richards nodded. He straightened his back and wiped Dalton's blood from his hands on his own pant legs. "I'm truly sorry, Dalton."

"Don't be. You didn't shoot me." Dalton's gaze landed on Reverend McCarroll. "Don't have much time… but I have one last request… if you'll grant it."

Reverend McCarroll nodded. "Anything, Dalton."

Dalton coughed again. "I doubt God would want my… last act on this earth… to be killing a man, even if it was… to save Vanessa. Perhaps you and Hutch could… help me over to that piano?"

Reverend McCarroll smiled. Together with Hutch and Randolph, Reverend McCarroll carried Dalton over to the piano. It hurt to be lifted off the floor, but this was something Dalton needed to do.

It was the last thing Dalton needed to do.

"Help me… sit up?" Dalton asked.

Victorio and Dr. Richards sat beside him on the bench, each with their arms wrapped around his back to help keep him upright. They helped Dalton find the keys with his fingers.

"Thank you." Dalton didn't even know if he'd be able to press the keys, much less play anything cohesive, but he was going to try anyway.

He closed his eyes and positioned his fingers for the first chord of his favorite Beethoven, but he stopped. No, he couldn't play Beethoven. Not in the church as he breathed his last few breaths. Not in the face of mercy, of forgiveness.

He would atone for his sins. He would call out to God in the way he best knew how. And maybe God would hear him and show him grace.

Dalton shifted his fingers on the ivories and pressed down the first chord, G major. His fingers, caked with his own sticky, drying blood, tickled the keys in a soft, slow waltz of worship, a simple hymn overlaid with an elaborate melody.

Amazing grace, how sweet the sound.
That saved a wretch like me.
I once was lost, but now am found.
T'was blind but now I see.

With his eyes still closed, Dalton listened as the growing crowd of people in the church took up the song with their voices, singing slow and beautiful, just as he played it.

Somehow he made it through the first three verses, but upon hitting the final stanza, his strength faltered at an exponential rate. His fingers struggled, his melody ruptured, but he kept going. He had to finish it. The voices sang on, carrying his very soul with their worship.

As his end drew perilously near, Dalton's playing slowed down, and the voices followed his accompaniment.

We've no less days to sing God's praise,
than when…
we'd first…
be—

His bloody fingers slid off the keys before he could play the last chord, the last note. Dalton's breath left his body as the people sang the last note for him, a sound more majestic than any he'd ever heard before. They sounded like a choir of angels singing from the heavens above.

In his mind's eye, an olive-skinned man walked toward him. Dalton had never seen Him before, but somehow, he knew Him.

Then Dalton saw her. From behind the man, Nizhoni ran toward him in slow motion, more beautiful than ever, her arms outstretched.

Was he lucky?

No.
Luck had nothing to do with it.

THE END

♠ ♥ EPILOGUE ♦ ♣

Spider's Rock enjoyed steady growth into the early 1880s but by 1900 had fizzled to a ghost town. Sure as a bullet from an outlaw's gun, the depletion of local mines finally did the town in.

As with many other communities that existed in that time and geography, the town's inhabitants burned most of its buildings so they could sift through the ashes and salvage the nails and other metal for use when rebuilding somewhere else—somewhere they could have a future.

So perhaps a bit of Spider's Rock lived on, probably holding another town together—literally.

After her father's death, Camille Warren took over the family's business endeavors. Over time, she grew far wealthier through her generosity than her father ever did in his greed. She eventually fell in love with a handsome, intelligent young man, and they married. But whether right or wrong, she always harbored a special place in her heart for Dalton.

A few months after the Battle of Spider's Rock, Vanessa Clark went home to her parents in Virginia where she lived from that point on. Although her feelings for Dalton vacillated between extremes and often opposed her better judgment, she never found a man who measured up to the standard he'd set, despite his many imperfections.

Thanks to him and a long career in local politics pursuing women's suffrage, Vanessa never married and lived alone for the rest of her days.

Randolph Schultz married a wealthy Prussian immigrant three years his senior, and they had children late in life. Even though his wife ensured he never wanted for anything, Randolph ran the Imperial with the same frugality and shrewdness as he always had until the day he died.

Upon Randolph's death, his son Wolfgang assumed ownership of the Imperial and, having the foresight to recognize Spider's Rock's impending doom well in advance, promptly sold the establishment and headed to the east coast to begin anew.

After his daughter fully recovered from her illness, Hutch brought his family to Arizona in 1851. The ranch they started grew into a huge operation that made them very wealthy.

Despite his success, Hutch remained humble and often gave away huge sums of money to those in need. Today, his descendants carry on his legacy of generosity, and they still own that original ranch plus dozens of others across the southwest.

Victorio went on to become one of the greatest Apache leaders of all time, second only to Geronimo himself. He led many campaigns against Manifest Destiny with his sister Lozen at his side, whom he regarded as his greatest strength in battle.

In 1880, after many successful attacks on encroaching American forts, towns, and soldiers, Victorio and his band of followers died at the hands of the Mexican Army in Chihuahua, Mexico.

Reverend William McCarroll pastored his flock in Spider's Rock for the rest of his life. In cooperation with Dr. Richards, and using Victorio's connections, he provided aid to hundreds of Native Americans suffering oppression from the United States government and its citizens.

One day, about fifteen years after Dalton's death, Reverend McCarroll expressed to a parishioner that for the first time he actually felt at peace about his life because he had used it to do the Lord's work. He died that very night in his sleep.

The day after the Battle of Spider's Rock, Dalton Phillips received a hero's funeral at his uncle's church, attended by every surviving townsperson out of respect for his sacrifice on their behalf. With Victorio's help, Reverend McCarroll located Nizhoni's unmarked grave, and the townspeople buried Dalton next to her, his true love.

Their graves are still there to this day.

If you enjoyed *Unlucky*, PLEASE LEAVE A REVIEW on Amazon. Reviews are integral to the success of my books. Even a short review is helpful! If you leave a review, let me know so I can personally thank you.

I love talking with my readers about my stories, so send me your thoughts at ben@benwolf.com. I try to respond to every email I receive.

Lastly, join the Ben Wolf Pack on Facebook and hang out with fellow readers who have also enjoyed my books!

www.facebook.com/groups/benwolfpack/

ABOVE ALL ELSE, **THANK YOU** FOR READING *UNLUCKY!*

THIS BOOK IS OVER, BUT THE ACTION DOESN'T STOP HERE!

TURN THE PAGE TO DISCOVER YOUR NEXT GREAT ADVENTURE————>

WWW.BENWOLF.COM | @1BENWOLF | @WOLFNCROWE

FOUR LEGENDARY HEROES. FOUR THRILLING BOOKS.

460,000+ WORDS OF MAGIC, MAYHEM, AND MERCENARIES

JOIN THE BLOOD MERCENARIES IN THEIR QUEST TO SAVE THE
CONTINENT FROM ALL MANNER OF APOCALYPTIC THREATS!
FROM DARK LORDS TO DUNGEON-DIVING TO DRAGONS, THESE MERCS
WILL HAVE YOU TURNING PAGES UNTIL YOUR FINGERS BLEED.

GET THEM NOW AT AMAZON.COM/AUTHOR/BENWOLF

ACKNOWLEDGMENTS

First of all, thank YOU for reading this book. I had a blast putting it together, but it was by no means a solo effort.

Thank you to Jesus Christ for changing my life forever.

Second, thanks to my parents for believing in me from an early age and for helping to support my dreams and my growth. I love you both.

Thanks to my all-star beta readers, Daniel Kuhnley and Paige Guido, for your excellent feedback, encouragement, and for having my back.

Thanks also to my mastermind group. It's a secret group, but you all know who you are. (insert evil laugh)

Carla Hoch, thanks for your friendship and support. Keep beating me up as often as you like, and keep fighting!

Will Wight, you continue to bless me with your time and feedback, and you've been far better to me than I deserve. I really appreciate the time you've invested in me, and I'm honored to be your friend.

Dirty Mike Hueser and the BJJ boys, thanks for keeping me frosty.

Last of all, thank you especially to my intelligent, beautiful, thoughtful, and ultra-supportive wife, Charis Crowe. Your flexibility with my weird schedule for this book made it possible for me to get it done.

I love you.

FOLLOW US ON INSTAGRAM: @WOLFNCROWE

About Ben Wolf

In 7th grade, I saw the movie *Congo*. It was so bad, I wrote a parody set in Australia that featured killer kangaroos. So began my writing career.

I endeavor to produce stories that question the boundaries of morality, faith, justice, and interpersonal relationships. And I do it with action, explosions, gunshots, sword-fights, and battles.

I've spoken at 40+ writers conferences and comic cons nationwide. When not writing, I occasionally choke people in Brazilian jiujitsu. I live in the Midwest with my gorgeous wife, our kids, and our cat, Marco.

Check out my other books on amazon.com/author/benwolf:

Want a FREE book? Join my author email newsletter, and I'll send you Book Zero (the prequel stories) of my Blood Mercenaries fantasy series.

Sign up now: WWW.SUBSCRIBEPAGE.COM/FANTASY-READERS

WANT TO CONNECT DIRECTLY? FIND ME ON SOCIAL MEDIA!

facebook.com/1benwolf

instagram.com/1benwolf

amazon.com/author/benwolf

www.ingramcontent.com/pod-product-compliance
Lightning Source LLC
Chambersburg PA
CBHW060413030726
47495CB00003B/551